ROBERT GRAVES

Seven Days in New Crete

-◄◄◄◇►►►-

Introduced by

MARTIN SEYMOUR-SMITH

OXFORD UNIVERSITY PRESS

1983

Oxford University Press, Walton Street, Oxford OX2 6DP

London Glasgow New York Toronto
Delhi Bombay Calcutta Madras Karachi
Kuala Lumpur Singapore Hong Kong Tokyo
Nairobi Dar es Salaam Cape Town
Melbourne Auckland

and associated companies in
Beirut Berlin Ibadan Mexico City Nicosia

Oxford is a trade mark of Oxford University Press

Introduction © Martin Seymour-Smith 1983
First published 1949 by Cassell & Co. Ltd.
First issued, with a new Introduction, as an Oxford
University Press paperback 1983

British Library Cataloguing in Publication Data
Graves, Robert
Seven days in new Crete.—(Twentieth-century classics).
I. Title. II. Series.
823'.912[F]   PR6013.R35
ISBN 0-19-281385-4

Printed in Great Britain by
The Guernsey Press Co. Ltd.
Guernsey, Channel Islands

CONTENTS

Introduction by Martin Seymour-Smith . . . vii

   I   THE EVOCATION 1

  II   THE FIVE ESTATES 13

 III   LOVE IN NEW CRETE 24

 IV   THE ORIGIN OF NEW CRETE 37

  V   TAKE A LOOK AT OUR WORLD . . . 47

 VI   ERICA 65

 VII   THE RECORD HOUSE 74

VIII   THE BRUTCH 90

 IX   THE SANTREPOD 100

  X   MARKET DAY AT SANJON 110

 XI   WAR IS DECLARED 127

 XII   BATTLE IS JOINED 143

XIII   THE PEACE SUPPER 152

XIV   THE PATTERN 163

 XV   THE BREAK 177

XVI   QUANT 190

XVII   WHO IS EDWARD? 204

XVIII   THE NONSENSE HOUSE 214

XIX   THE RISING WIND 225

XX   THE SIGHTS OF DUNRENA . . . 239

XXI   THE WILD WOMEN 252

XXII   THE WHIRLWIND 267

INTRODUCTION

By Martin Seymour-Smith

IT is frequently assumed that Robert Graves wrote no autobiography after the justly famous *Goodbye to All That*. He said, in his revision of that book in the late 1950s, that the story of his life after April 1929 (where it stops) was not suitable for telling, being too scandalous. Nor, indeed, did he attempt a further autobiography—as such. But, although of course deficient in exact detail, his until now neglected novel *Seven Days in New Crete* does in fact tell the essential story of his life between 1929 and 1947 (when it was being written). It has two other remarkable features. First, it not only recalls his past, but it also anticipates his future in a manner of which he was certainly not aware when he wrote it. Second, it may now be seen as a book in every way as important as Huxley's *Brave New World* and Orwell's *Nineteen-Eighty-Four*. When it was first published in 1949 it was at least thirty years ahead of its time, for all that it is the idiosyncratic work of one of the century's most individualistic poets: in it ecology is seen as a clear-cut issue, if only by implication; and so is the question of what is to happen to the religious impulse in man in the face of barren scientism. Most important, it deals squarely with the theme of what has now come to be called Women's Liberation. Women who have appealed to Graves's work as a kind of bible in their cause invariably appeal first to *The White Goddess*, his 'grammar' of poetic myth—but this extraordinary novel, one of Graves's finest achievements in the field of fiction, would be much better grist to their mill. For in *The White Goddess* Graves fell victim to what is now recognized as a serious anthropological error: he assumed that in the remote past of the human species a condition of matriarchy, in which the women held the power, had existed. He did not make this assumption under Marxist influence (he never read Marx or Engels, and was never interested in them), and within the context of his poetry what he has to say about 'matriarchies' functions purely as a metaphor. But many women (and some men), impressed by his scholarship, took *The White Goddess* as further proof of what they wanted to believe—and some still wilfully ignore the work of Lowie, Malinowski and Lévi-Strauss, who, with others, demolished this legend.

In the novel such an assumption does exist, but it does not matter. Here we are much closer to the metaphorical force of his belief in the superiority of women (about which notion he is also more interestingly self-critical than he could be in *The White Goddess*); here we are dealing with a work of pure fiction. *Seven Days in New Crete* is Graves's most poetic and imaginative novel, unique in his fiction—which, with the exception of *Antigua, Penny, Puce*, a slight but impeccable comedy of manners, has been resolutely historical. It works at three levels: as one of the most original of all the many utopian (or dystopian) novels, which might be said to have started in modern times with the American Edward Bellamy's *Looking Backward: 2000–1887* (1888); as autobiography and critical self-description (which ought to be more easily discerned now that a detailed biography of him has been published); and, most remarkably in some ways, as self-fulfilling prophecy. Poets and novelists do not always know what they are doing—perhaps no writer sees the full significance of his work until long after he has published it—so that it is no surprise that the book came about almost accidentally, and that it would probably never have been written had not circumstances driven Graves to a place where he had no reference books. One of the keys to Graves's creative life—indeed, to his personal life as well—is his reluctance to do certain things which he none the less does. He never wanted to fall in love, because he found it painful. He did not want to write the Claudius books, because he was more interested in writing and reading poetry, and he hated Rome. When he sketched the outline for *I, Claudius* long before he wrote it, he commented that he would never undertake it. But he was obliged to do so because he found himself in a serious financial mess. He wondered if he ought to publish *The White Goddess*: 'Ought I to let all this be known?' he used to ask nervously. He was deeply anxious about his novel *King Jesus*. Equally, he did not want to write *Seven Days in New Crete*, and he hardly ever talked about it afterwards: 'Don't like it, really, it smells too much of the Barcelona clinic where I wrote it' was all he would ever say.

In the summer of 1947 Graves was writing *The Isles of Unwisdom*, a novel about a fierce she-admiral who discovered the Marquesas Islands. This, apart from the very early *My Head! My Head!* (1925), is probably the least well-known of his novels, and perhaps—though it sold over 100,000 copies and is an exciting tale—the least interesting. But although he began it as a chore, he was getting immersed in it (as he does in any job, however much he has disliked it initially), when he was interrupted.

In August Graves's seven-year-old son William had a serious bicycle accident; eventually it proved necessary for him to go to a Barcelona clinic, at which a complicated skin-graft operation could be carried out. There was nothing for it but for Graves to go with him, although it was highly inconvenient. Most men, even most writers, would have taken the time off. But Graves, until his old age, could never take time off. If he had to wait at the dentist's or the doctor's he would write a prose sketch or polish a poem: '*Work is far more interesting than play*' his mother had told him, and he never forgot it.

But in order to complete *The Isles of Unwisdom* he needed many books—too many to take to Barcelona. So he transported himself to the future as Edward Venn-Thomas (perhaps the name he chose was to appease his conscience about never having, as he was aware, properly appreciated the poetry of Edward Thomas, whom he knew to be excellent but whose work he could never, for some reason, take the trouble to read carefully) and began *Seven Days in New Crete*, the only novel he ever wrote for which he did not need a single work of reference (even *Antigua, Penny, Puce* had required much legal expertise and a knowledge of the postage-stamp industry).

Although *Seven Days in New Crete* must be classified as utopian fiction—the category might profitably be re-named as one of 'imagined' or 'speculative' worlds, since so much literature formally described as *u*topian is in fact *dys*topian, such as Zamyatin's *We*, Wells's totally neglected master-piece *Mr Blettsworthy on Rampole Island*, and of course Orwell's classic—it does not set out to present an ideal world. Graves's mind does not work like that: he is a relativist who does not believe in the doctrine of the perfectibility of man. The influences on him have been very few, but those few have been decisive. Nor are all of them well known. They include Samuel Butler, Einstein and, above all, the American poet Laura Riding—who looms large in this book. Shades of the Butler of *Erewhon* may be seen throughout. Graves's knowledge of Einstein explains the great ease with which he was able to move his characters about in space and time; such thinking about space–time, also influenced by J. W. Dunne, comes naturally to him, so that there is no obtrusively ingenious manipulation. No believer in reincarnation, Graves has none the less found it quite natural to see himself in different 'worlds', both historical and imaginary. He never found the apparently fantastic inferences that may be made from relativity and quantum physics in the least hard to understand, though he is not a mathematician. Thus the time-shifts and magical journeys in the novel read perfectly naturally and the book itself has much of the charm and, for all its occasional violence, serenity of fairy tale.

As for Laura Riding, here Erica Turner, he was influenced by his (literal) worship of her, while they were together in the years 1926–39; by her dedication to poetry as a means of salvation, by finding a form of words which would tell the 'magical' truth; and by what he saw as her apostasy from poetry. After she gave up writing poetry at the behest of her second husband, a failed writer, in 1940, Riding evolved a new religious philosophy. Graves was never interested in this, which he dismissed (probably rightly) as a bizarre and ill-written synthesis of undigested Platonism, Cabbalism, Hegelianism and Teilhard de Chardin. But he continued to regard her poetry as the most miraculous he had ever read, and puzzled endlessly over why she had rejected him—first as lover (1929) and then as intellectual companion (1939). In *The White Goddess* he resolved the problem in an intellectual manner: this book is chiefly important for the light it casts on all poetry of a certain romantic kind—all Dionysian poetry, one might say—and on his own poetry in particular. *Seven Days in New Crete*, a more relaxed book, the writing of which actually took him by surprise, does more than cast light, though it does that too: it has its own creative status. Here Graves is not justifying himself through scholarship (sometimes deficient), or doing what all poets who write criticism do: justify their own practice by generalization. Here, even if not always consciously, he looks at himself critically, describes himself as he is—and creates a world which he finds only half-acceptable, though his project as he began to write was to create one he could find ideal. 'The trouble is', he wrote to a friend when he was about a third of the way through (he finished the book back in his Mallorcan home in 1948), 'that there is always a nostalgia for evil.' He did not mean that he believed in evil. He meant that he was one of those who regarded life as being made interesting, tolerable, vital, by problem-solving, and that problem-solving involved, inescapably, evil—which might show itself in other people's unpleasant behaviour, the struggle against one's own baser impulses such as greed and lust, the immense difficulties involved in trying to be honest, in avoiding lies, or in the need both to know oneself and to avoid such painful knowledge.

He also meant something much more directly personal. While not regarding Laura Riding herself as 'evil', he did regard her apostasy from poetry as such—and he had considered some aspects of her behaviour evil, as had (not necessarily correctly) a large number of others. But, although happily married to his second wife, Beryl, he did sometimes miss the severe, occasionally cajoling, changeable, cruel, meticulous personality of Riding. This was because once, for two years (1927–9), he had loved her and she had returned his love—or so he thought. He conflated in his mind all his experiences of her: lover, bitch, genius and demon. During his first marriage he had worried that his nervous state, which he had endured and even wilfully prolonged because he found it conducive to poetry, was causing his wife (Nancy Nicholson) to suffer. When Riding came on the scene she had calmed him, and yet had given him something to write poetry about—at one time he even dismissed all the poetry he had written before he met her as worthless, though much of it turned out to be a foreshadowing of her. Then, in April 1929, when she tried to kill herself over a man he despised, he stuck by her—but discovered in her a new and worse terror than he had ever known, even in the trenches of the First World War. At the end of ten years of her capricious company he was reduced to a nervous wreck: in a far worse state than he had been in 1918. He could never reconcile her genius with her vulgarity. From that state his second wife, Beryl, had rescued him—and it was to her that he wrote his most serene and greatest love poems (in the 1940s).

He had previously written many disturbed and disturbing poems to or about Riding during his terrifying life with her. But now, eight years after he had last seen her, he realized—at first only dimly—that he had not written about her retrospectively, except in the non-fiction *The White Goddess*, and, to a certain extent, in his novel of the Argonauts, *The Golden Fleece*. And it was only here, in *Seven Days in New Crete*, that he did write directly about her in this retrospective sense, for—and he prophesies this in the course of the novel—all the poems he would write to the four young women who afterwards became (famously) his 'muses', were written indirectly to her, to a ghost of her, for he entirely forgot the woman herself. Those young women were non-intellectual surrogates for Laura Riding, and each of them he tried to remake into a Laura Riding who would treat him fairly, and without hatred. The first of these muses was to turn up very shortly after *Seven Days in New Crete* was published in 1949. But he had no idea of this. It was only at the end of this first serene period of his life (he would not find another until old age) that he could look at the problem of Laura Riding with balance and good humour.

All this would be peripheral, to say the least, if it had had no consequences. But it produced not just an erotic and spiritual autobiography of enormous value to readers of Graves's poetry, but a novel which has much that is universal to say about sexuality in general. In particular it deals in great depth with the puzzling but (at least in western society) inescapable phenomenon of romantic love. It is well known that Graves felt the need to suffer at the hands of women in order to write poetry and so discover truth. So too, of course, have many major love poets: Donne, Blok, Yeats, Rilke, Bacovia—to name only a few. One has only to read, for example, Mario Praz's *The Romantic Agony*, or Blok on the 'Lady Beautiful', or the love poems of Pedro Salinas, to recognize that Graves's tormented idealization of women is by no means an unusual phenomenon. In his case, however, it has become notorious, partly because of his 'living out his life in public' and partly because he has written so much and so emphatically on the subject: not only in *The White Goddess*, but in many other books and in his Oxford lectures as Professor of Poetry. However, *Seven Days in New Crete* contains his most balanced writing about relations between men and women—writing which is imaginative, good-humoured and gentle, and so unique in the work of a poet so neurasthenic. His only serene poems were to his second wife, in this novel called Antonia; and we may see her influence looming as large as Riding's in the book.

The background against which this sexual and ritualistic drama is played is viewed sceptically by Venn-Thomas-Graves. It is not altogether idiosyncratic—although it might have appeared more so to its original readers. Throughout, one of its targets is an early utopian work which Graves always loathed, both as totalitarian and over-solemn (Sir Karl Popper, amongst many others, has, incidentally, come to the same conclusion): Plato's *Republic*. Thus Graves eventually makes this Mallorca of the future, New Crete, into a place almost as imperfect as our present world: he rejects perfection as absurd and boring. He once wrote that 'heaven' (or 'hell') probably consists of a man's last thoughts . . . The New Cretan men, whom he likes, are nevertheless without character or humour. Human nature has not been changed. It is custom that has changed—apparently for the better—the daily practice of the New Cretan society. This is not surprising coming from a man of such a deeply ritualistic nature as Graves. This world is only better than our own, it turns out, in one respect: wars here are 'fun', no one dies in them except by accident—and if that happens then the war is stopped. This is Graves's reaction to his experiences in the trenches. It is remarkably shrewd, given the facts of human nature. One has to remember that horror at the idea of war—felt as intensely by Graves as by any of his contemporaries who fought in the trenches—prompted Henry Williamson into Nazism and even Edmund Blunden, Graves's close friend at one period, into a profound admiration of Hitler's Germany. Yet Graves always saw that some aggression was inevitable.

The rulers in New Crete are good, but they are also 'goody-goody, a word that conveys a reproach of complacency and indifference to the sufferings of the rest of the world'. This is a sideswipe at Plato's *Republic* (hated by Graves not the least because it expelled poets, a fact he mentions at the end), but it is also a demonstration of the apolitical Graves's humaneness. His New Crete is deliberately imperfect, as we have seen; but it is a country which suits the temperament of the poet better than the present world, or so he at first thinks—until the people want to tear him to pieces. Yet he is critical of his own preferences, and so draws attention to such imperfections. Ultimately his world is in his own mind: he avoids what he early called the 'godawfulness' of this one by withdrawing from its cities.

New Cretan society is hierarchic. Graves may have been wrong about matriarchic, but he knew enough anthropology to be aware of the fact that most 'primitive' societies (which he admires in the light of 'civilized' ones) are so constructed. Randall Jarrell, one of Graves's most acute critics, mistook his ritualism for 'Toryism'. But there is nothing Tory about Graves; indeed he has always regarded Tories as 'misguided'. Rather, as this book shows, he is a man who regrets the introduction of fuel-driven machinery (there are no machines in the novel) into civilization, and who cannot live happily in cities or even towns. He is a cyclical rather than a linear thinker—another attitude which might have seemed odd in 1949, but which now does not, at a time when a vast number of people are increasingly nervous about the consequences of scientistic, linear, atheistic thinking. There are five 'estates' in New Crete, an arrangement of which Graves approves. But he is no feudalist, for 'Birth is never a clear indication of capacity; parents of one estate may have children who properly belong to another . . . Attainments are the result of capacity . . .' We may infer that there is no struggle, as there was (and still is) in feudalism, to climb the ladder—indeed, there is no ladder, since there is no poverty. It is a note of realism, and not of ruthlessness, that is introduced when Graves says that those who violate custom, or their estate, are killed. As a realist, he maintains that people are killed more often under 'egalitarian' systems.

And here, if not always elsewhere, he is cautious about the status of women: they are 'superior . . . in the eyes of the men at least'; men 'never appraise women' (a reflection of his lifelong distaste for the habit of discussing women's physical qualities with other men, which he found intolerable in army life). There is no 'competition between the sexes'—poetry, too, is 'non-competitive'.

As for the custom of the New Cretans: this is based on the 'inspired utterances of poets; that is to say, it's dictated by the Muse, who is the Goddess'. But the Goddess is no deity in the sense that the God of Christianity is a deity; and there is no 'Other Life'. Rather, she exists as a centre of ritual. Graves's answer to the frequently expressed feeling of 'existential disappointment' (as Paul Tillich put it) in individuals of the twentieth century lies not in belief in an after-life but in ritual. Thus there is 'precedent of sorts' for dealing with every problem. This is Graves's way of being tidy. Once he vowed to lend no more money. But then he found he wanted to lend a trusted friend some money. So, characteristically, he found a 'precedent' in the Talmud by which one might break vows, and so lent the money. He has not always been as tidy as that in his own life; but it is his ideal. There must be order. But that order should not be an intellectualized one, imposed on people from above, by a tyrannical state. It must rather stem from custom. And the custom must stem from ritual. And the ritual must stem from the Goddess. And she is the fount of poetry. And poetry for Graves, as we know, is a distinct entity: not philosophical, not theological, but a means of getting to the truth of any situation by working relentlessly—by a purging of stupidity or self-love—at a rhythmic utterance first vouchsafed to the poet while he is in a trance-like state. The goddess is the feminine, the creative principle; but her vagaries must be endured—as ritually as possible.

As soon as he reaches New Crete, Venn-Thomas-Graves falls in love. It is with a teenage girl (Graves's final muse, twenty years later, was a teenage girl) called Sapphire, who tells him that he is the sort of man who holds back nothing when he is in love, and that this is 'right'. She tells him (she has telepathic powers—Graves has assumed the existence of these all his life, and has lived on that assumption, sometimes dangerously, since disagreements about trans-missions have occurred) that he has 'never been out of love for more than a few miserable days'; Graves is both shrewd and prophetic when he causes her to add: 'you look around [in New Crete, away from your wife who 'belongs to another age altogether'] for a fresh focus of your love'. Yet at that time there was in his own life no muse, no 'special focus'.

What Graves is dealing with here, apart from his own personality, is the perennial problem of the need in human beings for romantic novelty. He was hardly the first to be worried and dismayed by it. As Venn-Thomas he cannot make up his mind what his real feelings are, although he knows he is in love with Sapphire, though in 'no ordinary way'. She tells him: 'When you recover from the shock to your pride [at being told the truth] you'll realise that you're that sort of lover, and that many women would be pleased to return your love—for a time.' And Venn-Thomas answers: 'I can't love a woman unless I can convince myself, in spite of all my previous failures, that I'll love her for the rest of my life. So I try to see her always as I saw her first. A self-deception, perhaps, but that's my way.'

This self-dissection was never done so openly or thoroughly in his work—his conversation and correspondence are different matters—before or since. But to what degree, in the revelation of his own intensely romantic and idealistic desire-nature, does Graves manage to illuminate the nature of the 'rest of the world's' sexual psychology? The extent to which he is capable of so doing, and here does so, is disconcerting—otherwise his love poems would not be so highly prized.

At the subjective level *Seven Days in New Crete* is an attempt to work out just how Graves is going to manage in the future: to hold on securely and fastly to his relationship with his wife, and yet fall in love, and be in love 'always', with other women (who will be younger than he is). There is a discussion between Sapphire and Venn-Thomas about his real-life wife, Antonia (Beryl, Graves's second wife, and his saviour). Sapphire and she are 'almost the same person' Sapphire tells him when he objects that he can 'really love only one woman at a time'. Sapphire points out that her time and Antonia's are not the same: 'You can still love her faithfully all your life, and love me as long as you please.' Here already is an anticipation of the Gravesian 'fifth dimension', the 'impossible', which did not fully emerge in his writings until the Sixties, by which time he was in

trouble with real life muses. Then he denied the possibility
of a lasting 'absolute' love between man and woman except
by a miracle—but it was a miracle he persisted in trying to
discover until age overtook him.

We find here, too, another view put forward in the
Sixties. Marriage in New Crete is a bad institution: 'the
theory of marriage doesn't correspond in the least with the
facts, because it doesn't often happen that married couples
choose wisely'. The male magicians of New Crete, who are
the poets, 'avoid congress' unless they want children, in
which case they 'have it only with people [they] love and
trust so utterly that violence and cruelty become irrelevant'.
'We remove,' Venn-Thomas is told, 'and our bodies remain
locked in torment far below us.'

All rationalization and over-idealism! It would seem so.
But there are facts in Graves's life, as in this novel, which
make that interpretation flimsy and unsound. In the first
place, Graves did behave with his future muses very much
more in a 'platonic' way than many have supposed:
'consummation is achieved by a marriage of mind and
body, while the reproductive organs are quiescent but our
inner eyes are flooded with waves of light'. Graves did feel
that he sometimes experienced such consummation,
though whether he did so in fact is another matter.

But the novel itself—Graves's biography apart—contains
a refutation of the notion that Graves was simply a pious
rationalizer who needed to justify his adulterous require-
ments.

In the first place the poets of New Crete stay with any
woman to whom they have given a child (as Graves stayed
with Beryl). And the mass of people continue to believe in
romantic love, even in the face of the harsh proof that it does
not work out well in their own lives. They continue to look
out for it, and to dream of it. It persists. What Graves does in
Seven Days in New Crete is to create a terrible metaphor for
the price we pay for our persistence. He does this first by
describing his affair with Erica Turner (Laura Riding) in the
'real world' and in New Crete (she got there by clinging to

his hair), and second by telling of the consequences of romantic love if it is carried to its desperate conclusion (to which he has always insisted on trying to bring it). All he might be said to be doing is simply pressing home the facts of a phenomenon which almost all accept, and are moved to action by, but are afraid to question. Other love poets who have had less terrifying experiences than he actually had, have given different and equally valid answers; but few have pushed the lesson home so ferociously. Few or none of his stature have known and loved a woman such as Laura Riding.

Erica Turner, says Venn-Thomas, not only 'treated me foully but managed at the same time to put me in the wrong and make me feel a thorough heel, before suddenly going off with a man I detested and despised. She had also withdrawn all the money from our joint-account . . . and left me flat . . . Antonia caught me on the rebound, and I married her almost at once.'

We must not of course precisely equate the Laura Riding of real life with the Erica Turner of New Crete. But there are traces at least of Graves's experience of her. She now looks younger, not older—'and dangerously well and beautiful'. This new encounter is an almost exact replica of his first 'real' encounter with her in the 'real' world. She is very casual, and speaks of the cash of which she has relieved the hapless poet as her 'Benevolence' *to* him (i.e. forced loan). (That is more or less what Riding told Graves in 1939, in extant correspondence.) Venn-Thomas is furious at meeting this 'triple-faced, ash-blond bitch'; he is afraid of her power—and blushes to think of what she and he did together (here the reader might be referred to Graves's 1929 poem 'Sick Love').

Now we understand his phrase 'nostalgia for evil' even more clearly. For Erica seems to be using New Crete as a 'hideout': 'No more shameless gate-crasher than Erica had ever existed.'

What Graves is telling us is that however we politicize our world, however much we try to make it ideal, and just,

according to intellectual dogma, we shall still be haunted by
our romantic past, and by our romantic and irrational
longings: our particular pattern of erotic desire will follow
us, will attract us to the same kinds of situation as we have
always experienced. Thus there can be no utopias.
Romantic love cannot just be tucked away, unconsidered as
a factor in human behaviour. For even in New Crete there
are 'brutches': 'local emanations of bad luck'. And the
magicians, significantly, caused one when they called the
twentieth-century poet Venn-Thomas to New Crete. But
this one is made much more serious—by Erica Turner.
Could it be, Venn-Thomas asks himself, that 'all the misery
and shame' of the Erica episode—'I had managed that part
of my life very badly indeed'—is responsible for this
particularly nasty brutch?

Erica is now made to look like a vulgar sorceress, who
enjoys the 'deliciously appalling', the mercilessly vulgar;
she is possessed by an overwhelming spite, and is
simperingly obscene. Yet she has impersonated the Goddess in one of her (for Graves) most potent forms, that of a
crane.

Later Graves expatiates on a theme that is familiar to his
readers from the Sixties onwards (he never re-read this
book: he read his press-cuttings but had too little time for
even his own works). As he once put it to a visitor: 'The
political and social confusion of the past 3000 years has been
entirely due to man's revolt against woman as a priestess of
the natural magic, and his defeat of wisdom by the use of
intellect.' We learn more than that here. Venn-Thomas is
told that the Goddess put her power into the hands of Zeus
with two purposes in mind: so that man should discover
that a supreme deity in the shape of his own phallus was
doomed to failure; and to 'demonstrate the existence in
[man] of certain intellectual capacities hitherto unsuspected
by woman; woman was taking her sexual superiority too
much for granted and treating him as a plaything'.

That is his first and last swipe at Riding for her treatment
of him. When he is told that Erica *is* the Goddess, he

complains that it is hard for him to feel awe for a Goddess who can appear in such a likeness . . . And there follows a tender picture of Antonia, and one well deserved.

As to the price of love: this may be gathered from the latter part of the novel, when Venn-Thomas witnesses what he later discovers to have been the real killing of the 'Victim'—and has imagined himself in his place. As he does this, he splits into two: 'I'm my own worst enemy . . . I've always known that. But why? Because he [his double] and I are both in love with the same different woman.'

There is nowhere in Graves's work, aside from a score or so of scattered poems from his later years of over-prolificity, in which his sufferings in love are so concisely and so honestly explained. When he began to conduct his love affairs with muses he concentrated increasingly on the cruelty of the Goddess, until he came up with the unconvincing figure of the Black Goddess, a Sufi-influenced irrelevance which plays little part in the pattern of his work as a whole. Here, as in those extraordinary, if few, poems of his old age, he is able to summarize, for many people, the tormenting aspect of the experience of being in love. His metaphor for it is, even in this good-natured and, for him, genial novel, violent and sometimes obscene. But how far does it lie from common experience? Furthermore, his portrait of Antonia, the gentle woman, is here as moving and as convincing as he was ever able to make it.

A fascinating commentary, then, on sexual love—but no contribution to the literature of speculative worlds? Not political enough? Too personal?

We should not be so sure. Certainly this is the least schematic of all such books. Certainly it deliberately reflects Graves's scorn for theories and theorists. But it is a human work. His analysis of history and the future is shrewd and, as readers will discover, surprisingly relevant today. As so often, Graves, the traditionalist, was writing thirty years ahead of his time. There is our own age: the era of 'Logicalism, hinged on international science'. Soon, he predicts (though retrospectively in the book, as he is being

told of the 'past'), war will become 'impossible', owing to
the triumph of 'ice-cold logic'. He may not be quite right;
but the nuclear deterrent is certainly 'ice-cold' and 'logical'.
Then the lack of religion, poetry and feeling will lead to a
collective insanity. Is this not what so many are afraid of? A
lack of *feeling* of good will, an uneasy and loathsome 'peace'?

As to his path to the 'new sanity': this is based on the
precept that we must 'retrace our steps or perish'.
Essentially his message is that women must take back
power from men, to whom they delegate it. He might be
wrong about women alone running the world, since the
majority of them might not wish to do so without the
co-operation of reformed men; but he is assuredly right
about the results of the resolute trampling down of the
feminine by the masculine: the hydrogen bomb. War is
forbidden except as a game. Capacity is the sole criterion of
status. The profit motive must go: 'He said to the gold
wheels: "Out into the world, | Be the world's ruin" '—as
one of the poems in the book runs.

One is reminded of the theme of the play by a
deputy-mayor of Peking which unwittingly unleashed the
so-called cultural revolution, one of the most unfortunate
and horrible episodes in Chinese history: the past has value.
Graves (who admired most aspects of the Chinese Revolution) also believes this. He hates the banausic, and has been
in despair about how to halt its inexorable and suffocating
intrusion into life. He was consistently against all the
conventional wars fought after 1945. His programme in
Seven Days in New Crete is humbler and more tentative than
other blueprints for the future. It is also modified by a
knowledge of human limitations: the Greek scholar
understands very well what *hubris* meant, and means. But in
these days when everyone should be an ecologist—and
more—it gives food for thought. It is hard to remember that
it was written thirty-five years ago.

CHAPTER I

The Evocation

'I AM an authority on English,' the man in the white suit said in a curiously colourless accent and with a good deal of hesitation, like an authority on Sanscrit trying to talk conversational Sanscrit. 'I hope that you will pardon us for having brought you so far, i.e., so many generations ahead of your epoch. You are Mr. Edward Venn-Thomas, are you not?'

I nodded, still a little confused by the sudden change of scene but wide awake.

'Do I speak with correctitude?' he asked anxiously.

'With great correctitude,' I assured him, trying not to smile, 'but without the modulations of tone that we English use to express, or disguise, our feelings.'

'It is convenient to disregard such trivia; I understand that the scholars of your day similarly disregarded the modulations of ancient Greek. But I must not trouble you with fine points like these.'

'No trouble at all. The finer the point, the happier it makes me. I'm even ready to discuss ancient Greek modulations.'

'You are very kind, but I am not an authority on Greek, I regret. However, Sir, there is one question that my colleague Quant and I have been debating during the last few days—we are entrusted, you must know, with the revision of the English Dictionary. On the evidence of the Liverpool find of Christmas cards, in which occurred such couplets as:

> Just to hope the day keeps fine
> For you and yours this Christmas time,

and:

> I hope this stocking's in your line
> When stars shine bright at Christmas-time.

I hold that "Christmas-*time*" was often pronounced "Christmas-*tine*", and that this is a dialect variant of the older "Christmas-*tide*". Quant denies this, with a warmth that is unusual in him.'

'Quant is right.'

'Oh, that is very disappointing to me. I thought that I had made a discovery of value.'

'Who are you? Where am I?'

'Did I not make myself clear, viz. that I am a student of European languages of the Late Christian epoch and an authority on the English language? As for your whereabouts, if you look out of the window you will perhaps recognize this district.'

Yes, the district was familiar. That rocky headland, the low hill, with the church of Sainte Véronique on the top—except that it was not the same church, and perhaps not a church at all. But the Mediterranean had retreated a mile or more, a broad belt of farmland stretched nearly to the horizon, and the bare hills were now covered with trees. I thought they looked much better this way and told the man so.

'How did I come here?' I asked.

'You remember nothing?'

'Nothing at all.'

'Incantations were chanted over a fire from dawn until midday, and when you appeared you were nicely invited to visit us. You replied that you had no objection, though the future did not really interest you.'

'It doesn't. By the way, I'm not dead, am I?'

'No, we have summoned you from the living. The dead are, *nem. con.*, dead. You have still some years to live.'

'Then please tell me nothing about my immediate future. That would spoil the story as I have to live it day by day.'

'As you wish, Sir.'

'And I don't particularly want to know exactly how many hundreds of years I've been taken into the future. It might make me feel uncomfortably primitive.'

'As you wish, Sir.'

'Why have I been summoned?'

'The poets want to pose you a few questions about the Late Christian epoch, which has a certain melancholy fascination for us. Your answers, if you care to yield them, will be preserved in our records.'

'Do you make a habit of raising people from the past?'

'No, Sir. Our witches have not long perfected the technique and you are the first person raised from so early an epoch as the Late Christian, except for your uncle and namesake, who was raised one week ago in mistake for you. He was surprised and confused, because you had not been born at the time; but he answered us nicely enough.'

'I bet Uncle Edward gave nothing away; he was a diplomat of the old school. But why have you summoned me rather than anyone else?'

'Whom else in your epoch would you have had the witch summon?'

'Well, I don't know. . . . Someone with a greater knowledge of contemporary affairs than myself. I am neither a scientist, nor a statistician, nor the editor of an encyclopædia. Not even a trained historian.'

'We chose you because one of your poems, viz. *Recantation*, happens to have survived to our day and you are known to have dwelt hereabouts.'

'Are you a poet?'

He looked a little crestfallen at having to repeat himself again. 'No,' he said, 'I am an authority on the grammar and syntax of the English language in the Late Christian epoch.

The ladies and the poets await you in the next room. My task is to introduce you to them and act as your interpreter. How do you feel? Are you dizzy?'

'I'm very well, thank you. And I like this room: it reminds me of our Georgian style. Restful, solid, well-proportioned— though, of course, proportions don't change with the ages, so I'm not really surprised. But no pictures; why no pictures?'

'What sort of pictures would you desire?'

'Oh, I don't know. Family portraits, for example.'

'Isn't it stupid to record a face as it gazes today, when after a few seasons it will gaze differently?'

'Landscapes, then.'

'It's surely easier and preferable to admire a landscape in the original?'

I dropped the subject. 'I see that you still burn wood in your grates,' I said. 'Prophets of my epoch have promised a future in which atomic energy will supersede wood, coal and electricity in domestic heating.'

'That was a very temporary future, and, according to the *Brief History*, not at all a happy one. Would you care to drink?'

'What have you got? A glass of wine, and a biscuit?' It was a test question.

'I will consult the ladies of the house. Since you are a visitor from the past it would be inhospitable to deny you wine if you need it. But we should all feel more comfortable if you would consent to drink, e.g., a glass of lager instead. This is not the hour in which we drink wine. Wine, like meat, is reserved for festivals. But the lager is good.'

'Heavens,' I said, 'it's all the same to me! Lager, by all means.'

He smiled gratefully, went out and soon came back with a glass of lager and some salt-pretzels on a plate. 'This is the servants' holiday, otherwise they would have served you,' he explained. 'But this made it a convenient day for your evocation. Soon they will return.'

The lager was very good indeed. So were the pretzels.

'I wish I could take this plate back to my period,' I said, 'and this glass. Are they valuable?'

It took him some time to adjust his mind to this question. Finally he said: 'If you mean: "are they valued as worthy of daily use?" the answer is, that we use no objects that are not so valued; though the different estates, i.e., classes, of our society acknowledge and confess different sets of values. It is, indeed, the discrepancy in values that distinguishes the estates. This glass and plate are of the sort valued as worthy of daily use by what one might call the magician estate: I do not admire these objects at all.'

'Well, I do. But what I meant was: do they cost a lot of money?'

'Money?' he said. 'Ah, no! Money went out of use long, long ago. It misbehaved, you see.'

'Too true it did! What do you use instead—coupons?'

'Oh, no, no, no! Not *coupons*.'

'Cowrie-shells?'

He threw up his hands. 'Please, Sir, would you mind coming into the next chamber, where the ladies and the poets are waiting.'

We went into the room where two women and three men sat quietly around another fire. 'Introduce me, please,' I said to the Interpreter, with a slight bow to the company.

The men were already on their feet. They returned my bow. The women, who were almost embarrassingly good-looking, remained seated, smiling pleasantly. The Interpreter explained: 'We no longer name people publicly as in your epoch; we give only nicknames, or titles. This lady is a witch. No, please, we do not shake hands here.'

The witch, who reminded me strongly of Marlene Dietrich, seemed amused by my open-handed advance but said nothing.

'Her nickname is "Leaf-of-the-Sallow", or "Sally" for short.'

'Miss or Mrs.?'

'I beg pardon?'

I explained.

'Oh, no. Distinctions of that sort exist only among the commons, not here.'

'Not among the poets and other magicians, you mean?'

'Yes, that is right. Here, as we say, the house chooses the man, not the man the house; i.e., the women who rule a house do not derive a title from their congress with men.'

'Assure the witch that I intended no offence,' I told the Interpreter.

'This quite young lady is—well, she is a nymph—a nymph of the month. But perhaps you will not understand the meaning of nymph? We call her by her jewel title, viz: Sapphire.'

They were speaking a language based on Catalan—my mother came from Catalonia—but it had a good deal of English in it, with some Gaelic and a little Slav, and though they spoke with dignified slowness, I could not at first follow the conversation.

The three men had nicknames that reminded me of the Red Indians: 'See-a-Bird', 'Fig-bread', and 'Starfish'. They were poets, and also magicians. See-a-Bird was a tall, gentle, oldish man; Fig-bread and Starfish, who were in their late twenties, looked like brothers—both dark-eyed, broad-shouldered, slim and earnest.

'You have invited me to answer some questions. . . .' I said.

Sally caught Starfish's eye and he asked a question for her: 'Do you like us?'

'Very much.' I meant it.

There was a murmur of relief. The Interpreter explained: 'Our conversation can continue now. If you had hesitated, or if we had twigged a false note in your voice, we should have apologized and returned you to your epoch without a further question.'

'Why?'

'Conversations between persons who do not like one another's selves are always sterile,' he said with a consequential cough.

'Who would have recognized the false note?'

He seemed surprised. 'Everyone. This company are all magicians.'

Fig-bread looked about him for permission to speak next. 'How does it feel,' he asked, 'to be a poet of the Late Christian epoch?'

This was so wide a question that I was silent for half a minute. Then I answered guardedly: 'Do you wish me to compare it with the Early Christian or with the pre-Christian epochs? You can't expect a comparison with your own—by the way, what do you call it?'

'This is the New Cretan epoch.'

'—Well, you can't expect a comparison with your New Cretan epoch, of which as yet I know nothing.'

'It would be best to avoid comparisons. Nobody can speak for any age but his own.'

'Then may I say simply that I dislike mine? Or would you regard that as a confession of stupidity?'

'If you are happy in your personal friendships and still dislike your age, that is merely to indict it as one of violent change. Change must always be painful.'

'Thank you for putting it like that. By the way, how long is the Late Christian epoch to last?'

They consulted together, and the Interpreter reported: 'According to the *Brief History*, Sir, you still have several Popes to be elected. We date the end of the Christian Era from that of the Papacy, though Christianity itself persists in multifarious forms for many generations ahead of you.'

'Oh? And who suppressed the Papacy?' I asked with rising interest.

'Its seat was transferred from Rome to San Francisco at a

juncture of great wars, and it was suppressed a generation or two later by the Pantisocrats, or Levellers, of North America. Hadrian VIII and Pius XVI were the ultimate Popes. Then a World Council of Churches, convoked at Pittsburgh, agreed to distinguish the Israelite Jesus from Christ the God, whom they abolished by a majority vote, just as he had been established by a majority vote at the Council of Nicaea, and to regard him as the first Pantisocrat. This notwithstanding, the Christ was much longer retained by the heretical *Mystiques*, a French-speaking secret sect of Canada, as the Second Person of their Trinity; though they addressed him as "Peace", not "Christ", in part for security reasons, in part because they wished to dissociate themselves from concern with the Israelite Jesus, and because "Jesus" and "Christ" had become synonymous in popular usage. But I now hold my peace, since the future does not interest you, and since all that I was asked to provide was a temporal definition of the Late Christian epoch.'

'Perhaps that's just as well. But you mustn't think that what I said about the future implies that I don't enjoy this future. I meant that, in my age, to speculate on a futurity to which we don't belong and which we have no means of forecasting—we can't even forecast the prevailing winds for more than a day ahead—distracts attention from the present and often deranges people's minds. To have foreknowledge of even unimportant events, such as the results of horse-races not yet run, would put me at an embarrassing advantage over my contemporaries.'

'None of us will volunteer any unsettling information,' said Sally.

'You must understand,' I began a little nervously, 'that to be a poet is something of an anachronism in my age, when none of the people's main interests have anything even indirectly to do with poetry. I mean, for example, money and sport and religion and politics and science.'

'Are all these exclusive interests?' Fig-bread asked heavily, leaning forward in his leather armchair.

'Oh, no,' I said, 'not exclusive, certainly not exclusive.' Fig-bread's dark serious eyes made me feel rather a cheapjack as I rattled on. 'In theory, a business man puts money before everything in the world: in war-time he might even sell arms to an enemy power for use against his own country. An out-and-out communist, the most active type of politician, puts communism before everything: he is prepared even to denounce his own parents or children for "bourgeois activities". A religious fanatic will give all he has to the poor and die happily in a ditch. An out-and-out scientist would be pleased to blow up the earth on which he lives, merely to demonstrate a particular theory of atomic energy. But, in practice, the communist may also be a scientist, the businessman may teach in a Christian Sunday-school, the Christian may also be a communist, the scientist may be in trade. And all may be sportsmen. It is confusing, I admit. Well—poetry is not worth buying and selling on a large scale, so the businessman shows no interest in it. The communist condemns it as an individualistic divergence from marxist principles. The religious fanatic shuns it as frivolous. The scientist disregards it because it can't be reduced to mathematical equations and therefore seems to lack a principle. It bears no relation whatever to sport, being non-competitive.'

'Then how can anyone continue as a poet?'

'I often wonder about that myself; but at least the opposing interests are not united. It's the mechanization of life that makes our age what it is: science and money combine to turn the wheels round faster and faster. In communist theory the tractor is glorified as an emblem of prosperity; and no Pope has so far published an encyclical against the internal combustion engine or the electric turbine. But mechanization, and what is called standardization, are felt to have their disadvantages and dangers, and the poet is tolerated because he's known to be opposed to them. So the stream of true poetry has never dried up, though it's reduced to a very small . . . .'

Here I suddenly broke off. What I had been saying sounded too much like a contribution to a professional brains-trust to make proper sense. I always switch off the radio when it sputters words like 'standardization' and 'mechanization' at me.

Old See-a-Bird broke an uncomfortable silence: 'According to the Interpreter, you have lived through two World Wars. Did any poets take part in the fighting?'

'Most of the best ones. Does that shock you?'

'With us a poet may do whatever he pleases so long as he preserves his dignity. Both Fig-bread and myself have taken part in wars. But your sort of warfare appears to have involved loss of life and damage to property as well as other indignities.'

'Naturally. A commander-in-chief's task is to destroy the armies opposed to him and force the enemy's government to unconditional surrender.'

'Not at all a pleasant form of warfare. With us, a war is always great fun—apart from the defensive fighting in which our travellers sometimes get involved when they cross the frontier of New Crete—and if anyone were killed we should end it at once.'

'Our wars are altogether hateful.'

'Then is it really true that your armies show no respect for women and children? Surely no poet could kill a woman? That wouldn't make sense.'

'I never killed one,' I said lamely. 'At least, not so far as I know.'

Another silence followed, broken at last by Fig-bread, who said: 'Your voice carries unfamiliar undertones. I suppose that life with you is so complex that it's never easy to speak the truth. When you're discussing the institutions and events of your age the uncertainty in your voice contrasts strangely with the firm way in which you spoke first—when you said you liked us.'

'Well, we like you too,' said Sally. 'Would you care to stay with us a little longer, or do you feel uncomfortable, carried so far ahead of your age?'

'If I could be sure that my absence from home was causing no anxiety, I'd stay for as long as I was welcome.'

'You needn't worry about that. You're asleep in your epoch, and at liberty to spend months or years here in a dream lasting no longer than from one breath to the next.'

'Very well; but I shouldn't like to return and find my house in ruins and my two-year-old son with a long white beard being pushed in a bath-chair.'

I settled back comfortably and we talked until sunset, when a bell tolled in the distance and candles were lighted. They were made of bees' wax and set in heavy gold sconces. Somehow I had expected to find a more advanced form of lighting.

Most people from our epoch would have resented my new friends as altogether too good-looking—physically thorough-bred and with a disconcerting intellectual intensity. They seemed never to have had a day's illness; their faces were placid and unlined and they looked almost indecently happy. Yet they lacked the quality that we prize as character: the look of indomitability which comes from dire experiences nobly faced and overcome. I tried to picture them con-fronted with the problems of our age; no, I thought, they would all be haggard and sunken-eyed within a week. Not only did they lack character, which the conditions of their life had not allowed them to develop, they lacked humour—the pinch of snuff that routs the charging bull, the well-aimed custard pie that routs the charging police-constable. For this they had no need, and during the whole of my stay there I heard no joke that was in the least funny. People laughed, of course, but only at unexpectedly happy events, not at other people's misfortunes. The atmosphere, if it could be acclimatized in an evil epoch like ours, would be described as goody-goody, a word that conveys a reproach of complacency and indifference to the sufferings of the rest of the world. But this happened to be a good epoch with no scope for humour, satire or parody. I remember an occasion when See-a-Bird absent-mindedly hung up a mirror on what he thought was a nail but what was really a fly that had settled on the wall. Everyone laughed loudly, but not because of his mistake: it was a laugh of pure pleasure that he caught the mirror on his toe as it fell, and saved it from a crash.

CHAPTER II

The Five Estates

I AM no student of fashion, and careless, usually, about the way I dress. Since nobody on this occasion was either naked or wearing anything really eccentric, such as painted wooden armour, or a cloak made of old newspapers, I paid little attention to their clothes, except to Sally's. She was dressed in the witch costume in which she had officiated at my evocation ceremony: a conical moleskin cap, straw sandals, and a long-skirted, long-sleeved dark blue robe, embroidered in silver thread with an interlace of serpents and willow wreaths, and caught at the waist by a girdle of large lapis lazuli pentagons set in silver. For ritual reasons she had stained her feet dark blue. She sat opposite me and most of my talk was with her. But it was of Sapphire's presence—she sat between me and the fire, dark-haired, slim, grey-eyed, delicate-fingered—that I was most conscious.

'If my clothes embarrass you,' Sally said, 'I could change. It wouldn't be much trouble.'

'No, certainly not. They're very becoming. By the way, that isn't woad on your feet, is it? You don't mean to say that you New Cretans have gone back to woad?'

She nodded. 'It's a nasty-smelling stuff to make, but we witches have to use it every now and then.'

'May I ask what sort of a blue-stained witch you are? A black one? Or a white one?'

'We don't use those distinctions.'

'I mean: do you specialize in destruction or in healing?'

'There's no healing without destruction.'

'But do you sometimes kill people?'

She looked serious. 'Sometimes. That's the least pleasant part of our calling.'

'Whom do you kill? Personal enemies? Or public ones?'

'Bad people.'

'What do you mean by bad?'

'Bad is when, for example, a calf is born with two heads, or a hen crows and doesn't lay eggs. Or when a man behaves like a woman—'

'—What, you kill your poor homosexuals? That seems a bit hard.'

Sally went on unperturbed. 'Or when a man deliberately violates custom, and his estate, that is to say his class, repudiates him.'

'Oh yes, the Interpreter said something about estates. How many are there?'

'Five.'

'By the way, do you have kings? I've always had a weakness for kings.'

'Yes, indeed. Without kings there can be no true religion. The New Cretan world is divided into kingdoms.'

'Real kings, with gold crowns?'

Everyone laughed. 'Yes, kings with real gold crowns, entrusted to them by their queens.'

'What a stable world it must be! No classless state? No republic?'

'None.'

'How are the estates chosen?'

'I don't quite understand your question.'

'Is the classification, for example, by birth and property? Or by attainments?'

'By capacity, of course. Birth is never a clear indication of capacity; parents of one estate may have children who

properly belong to another. And property is an indication of
a man's estate, not his qualification for belonging to it. And
attainments are the result of capacity.'

'But who judges capacity? Local committees appointed by
your Royal Psychological Society? You don't still use the
Funck-Hulme intelligence test, do you—the one with jig-
saw puzzles and coloured electric light-bulbs and a trick slot-
machine?'

A gasp went up from the Interpreter. 'Please, Sir,' he protested, 'it would take me a sadly long time to translate the
second part of your question, the answer to which I can give
you myself. It is "no". May I be permitted to ask the witch
on your behalf merely: who judges capacity?'

'Very well, who does judge it?'

He translated this, and Sally answered: 'Parents and playmates and neighbours. The child remains in his mother's
estate until there's general agreement that he belongs somewhere else. A misfit is almost always recognized before his
education begins in earnest. Then representatives of the
estate to which he properly belongs come to claim him.'

'Don't the parents ever protest?'

'Why should they? It's painful to lose a child, but it's worse
to have one who doesn't belong in the house. The parents
are the first to reject him. Usually they get another of the
right kind in exchange—an orphan, or a misfit from some
other estate. I myself was hatched in the wrong nest, as we
say; my parents were recorders. On the whole the magicians
breed true; but then we have small families and about one in
every three of us was born in another estate.'

'There are five estates, you said? We English had five once:
nobles, clerics, yeomen, tradesmen and serfs. What are yours?'

'We reckon them on the hand, beginning with the thumb.
Look, *thumb*, the captains, who roughly correspond with
your nobles; *forefinger*, the recorders; *third finger*, the commons
—do you follow?'

'I understand why the thumb is the captain: it comes first and it's the strongest, and it combines easily with any of the other fingers. And the forefinger is the recorder because it directs the pen. But the third finger?'

'That's the middle one and the tallest; you see, the commons are the middle estate and the most numerous. Here it's called the fool's finger. The fourth finger stands for the servants, because of all the fingers it's the least capable of independent movement.'

'Palmists make it the Apollo finger.'

'I know, and Apollo, you remember, was once a servant. The poet Cleopatra says in her tercet, *Three Costly Errors*:

"The first, when Apollo forgot that he was a servant and played the master."

Servants, as you'll agree, make the worst masters. Well, that leaves the little finger, which stands for the magicians, and that's because——'

'Because in fairy stories it's always connected with magic?'

'If you like to put it that way. And because ours is the smallest of the five estates. They're all interdependent, like the five divisions of a plane-tree leaf. Each kingdom has its five estates, each kingdom is a leaf on the New Cretan plane-tree: that's about the first thing one learns at school.'

'Very neat; but I should like to hear how a child reveals his natural estate to his playmates. It sounds rather mysterious to me.'

'It's not at all mysterious. Take a ball-game, for example. Did boys play baseball in the Late Christian epoch? I forget. Or won't that happen until Pantisocratism comes in?'

'They play it quite a lot. Men too.'

'Well then, in a ball-game, if a boy's timorous, unenterprising and quiet, and if he prefers taking orders to making decisions, and doesn't care on which side he plays, and prefers fielding to hitting or pitching, then he's obviously a servant.

If he's more interested in discussing the fine points of the game, or keeping the score than in playing it, then he's a recorder. If he's more interested in organizing it than playing it, then he's a captain. If he prefers hitting and pitching to fielding and shows strong partisan feeling, then he's one of the commons. But if he plays without really taking part in the game, so that other players are made uncomfortable by his presence, even if he plays it well, then he's a magician.'

'What exactly do you mean by magician?'

'Magicians think in an active way; everyone else thinks passively.'

'I see. So mathematicians, philosophers and scientists are magicians?'

'No, people of that sort, if we had them (but we don't) would be recorders. One doesn't need an active mind to record.'

'But surely, you'd distinguish a man who adds up columns of figures from a man who invents a complex mathematical formula or generalizes about the nature of the universe?'

'There's no magic in a mathematical formula, however complex. It's only a recorder's convenience for his fellow-recorders: it's part of accountancy, or history. A philosophic concept about the nature of the universe is of the same order: it's part of history.'

'I don't follow you, Sally. What is active thought, as opposed to passive?'

'Active thought is to passive as rhythm is to metre; or as melody is to harmony. It's an event, not a condition. It's a proof of life, not a description of the limits within which life moves.'

I let this go by, and changed the subject: 'Do your kings actively govern their kingdoms?'

'No, do yours?'

'Only in name. Who does govern then? The captains? Or you magicians?'

'There isn't any governing estate. Custom is the governing principle, and each estate has its obligations to it.'

'In the short run that's all very well, but aren't you asking for trouble in the long run? Suppose some unforeseen natural disaster occurs? You still have droughts, floods and so on?'

Before she answered, Sally touched wood to avert ill-luck, but did this seriously and religiously, not with an apologetic smile. 'The recorders keep detailed accounts of past disasters and if a new one happens, the captains consult with them at once on the best way to meet it. There's always a precedent of sorts. Then they set the commons to work. They work until the danger has passed. The less responsible tasks are performed by the servants. The magicians stand by; they aren't consulted unless the disaster concerns public health or morals, when they're expected to intervene.'

'You're priests of a sort, then?'

'Oh, no, all the priests belong to the servants' estate. That seems to surprise you, but surely it's only commonsense. The priest's function is to give his deity faithful service. He doesn't need to improvise, or take decisions, or perform magic. He memorizes his ritual and loyally and unthinkingly carries out his duties. It was once proposed that our kings should belong to the servant estate, too, because the king is the supreme servant, capable of the most utter self-sacrifice; but that was a mistake. The commons were conceded the right, on the plea that "the fool's finger wears the crown" as the poet Vives had written, and that the priesthood and the kingship ought to be kept separate.'

'A sensible decision. You get a more interesting set of kings that way and it must give the commons a sense of pride.'

'It's a fine foolish thing to wear a crown; while it lasts.'

'Where do women come into this system?'

'We maintain it, because we act directly on behalf of the Goddess. We appraise men; we don't compete with them. Naturally, they treat us as the superior sex.'

'But more men than women are capable of active thought.'

'That's irrelevant. We don't regard magicians as more important than recorders because they think actively rather than passively; we regard them only as different.'

'Well, as the superior sex (in the eyes of the men at least) I suppose you do no work?'

'Of course we work. But in every estate women have different fields of action from men. There's no competition between the sexes.'

'Do men never appraise women?'

'That isn't the custom.'

'It seems a rather one-sided arrangement.'

'Yes, but the men are satisfied and we don't complain.'

Feeling a little crushed, I asked Sally to explain the difference between women magicians and men magicians. She said that evocatory magic was the women's field. 'That means removing spirits from where they have no right to be—'

'For example?' I asked.

'For example, in cases of demonic possession and haunting. Or summoning people from elsewhere in time or space for consultation. Invocatory magic is the men's field. That means calling the Goddess to witness and sponsor some magical action.'

'As a poet invokes the Muse?'

'Is your Muse a living woman?'

'I think of her as the woman with whom I'm in love as I write.'

'Is that usual in your epoch?'

'I don't think so. But it's my way, at any rate.'

'I'm glad; that will help you to understand us better. Custom here is based not on a code of laws, but for the most part on the inspired utterances of poets; that is to say, it's dictated by the Muse, who is the Goddess.'

At this point Starfish caught Sally's eye and began rolling

cigarettes. He rolled six neatly and rapidly, using some sort of leaf instead of paper. He handed one to each of us, except the Interpreter, and kept the last for himself.

'So you still smoke?' I said.

'Every evening at about this time,' said Fig-bread. Sapphire rose, lighted each cigarette with a wooden spill and spoke what seemed a traditional formula: 'Smoke, enjoy, be silent!' The Interpreter bowed slightly, took a meerschaum pipe from his pocket, and went out to smoke on the porch. Afterwards I found out that each estate used a different type of tobacco and kept strictly to itself while smoking or, in the servants' estate, chewing. 'Smokes do not mix,' was a proverb I was to hear many times in different contexts during my stay. There was no careless, nervous tobacco-taking at odd hours. Everyone smoked, or chewed, calmly and deliberately, once a day only. Before I had been there a day I got tobacco-hunger and used to long for the evening.

When we had finished, the cigarette ends were burned in the fire and Sapphire said: 'Now we may speak!'

See-a-Bird had apparently been considering what I had told him earlier in the evening about the population of London.

'How terrible it must be to live there,' he said, 'with some ten million people occupying territory that here would support only five or ten thousand! Whenever you leave your house to visit a friend in another part of the town, you must pass hundreds of new people.'

'What's so terrible about that?'

'Well, surely, whenever you see a new face in the street, even if no greeting is exchanged there is always a sort of contact, a recognition: you not only notice the face but you sum it up mentally and store it in your memory. Every personal contact is an expense of mental energy. Here we know practically everyone by sight, so our casual meetings make little demand on our energies, and on grand festival days we dull our sensibilities with drink. But we find visits to other regions exhausting; the brain dizzies after a time from the demands put upon it. That's why we travel little, and why, when we go abroad, our hosts take care to expose us to as few personal contacts as possible. When I try to imagine thousands and thousands of people all in different clothes and with thoroughly disorganized minds, threading in and out of one another's lives without knowing or greeting, each pursuing a private, competitive path—I think it would kill me.'

'Oh, no. One can get used to almost everything. The Eskimos who were brought to London in the eighteenth century didn't die of seeing too many faces. So far as I remember, they just caught bad colds and died that way.'

'Nobody dies of a cold,' Sally insisted. 'Seeing too many faces must have undermined their strength.'

'Have it your own way. At any rate, we treat people as if they were trees: when you're walking through a forest, you don't study every tree, but only the striking ones that will serve as landmarks to guide you back. In the same way we don't study people's faces as they go by. Old friends, relatives, even lovers may pass each other and not know it. We're conscious only of the policeman who regulates traffic, and of the ticket-collector in the bus or railway station. But unless the policeman pulls us up for breaking some traffic rule we don't study his face; and we know nothing of the ticket collector, unless he questions the validity of our ticket.' Here it took me a long time to explain policemen and ticket-collectors.

'But if a beautiful woman goes by?'

'The impression is as transitory as a picture in the fire. Women go by with their faces set in the same sightless mask as men: no true beauty is apparent.'

'This self-protective habit of not-seeing must blunt your poetic sensibilities and impair your memory.'

'Perhaps it does. Little poetry worth the name has been

written in London ever since it ceased to be a country town; but Londoners are in general long-lived, and they keep their memories in notebooks and ledgers. For me, the worst is the noise.'

'What sort of noise?'

'I don't mean the incidental noise of traffic—throbbing of motors, rumbling of buses and trains. One gets as inured to that as the Sudanese who live near the Cataracts get to the noise of falling water. It's the distractive ringing of the telephone, and the music blared out by a million radios from early morning till late at night. One can never escape that for long.'

'Do you mean to say that anyone can play what music he likes at any hour of the day he likes?'

'Anyone who has a gramophone or can strum on a musical instrument. Otherwise he has to rely on the radio pro-grammes. Most Londoners like to listen to music while they work, and don't much care what sort of music it is. When they have to live in a village for more than a week or two, they get desperately bored and lonely without the noise of traffic and the interminable stream of faces and the constant summons of the telephone. So they keep the radio going all the time.'

They all looked very grave and for a long time asked no more questions. Then Sapphire asked: 'Would you like to go to bed now?'

'Will it be safe for me to go to sleep? Shan't I slip back into my own age?'

'No. You'll be quite safe.'

Sally said: 'You've been looking at me most of the time, and making me do all the talking. But you're in love with Sapphire, whom you've hardly looked at.'

I blushed at the suddenness of her challenge, but made no denial.

'Then what are you waiting for?' she went on. 'You are

you, not a wraith. Sapphire is Sapphire, not a vision. What holds you back?'

'Compunctions of custom,' I mumbled with an appealing glance at Sapphire, and then felt cross and stood on my dignity: 'I don't think you have a right to talk to me like that, Sally!'

The effect of my words on everyone present was painful. A sort of spasm shook Sally, and her eyes filled with tears; I saw a couple of them trickle down her cheeks, though she neither sobbed nor cried. Starfish gave a little groan, and I think Fig-bread and See-a-Bird were almost equally affected. What a queer mixture of brutal frankness and sensitivity these people were!

I dared not look at Sapphire, but I heard her say in a fairly calm voice to the rest: 'Leave us two alone. We have a lot to say to each other.'

Love in New Crete

I FOUND it hard to face Sapphire when we were alone, but I made the effort at last. My heart was beating loudly and there was a wild singing in the air. Her eyes were grey and clear and steady. She did not seem to be embarrassed by the situation but studied me closely, her chin propped on both hands, her elbows on the table. I know women who affect this attitude when they want to appear profound and attentive and at the same time show off the manicured elegance of their hands; but Sapphire was no actress and after a time I felt like some low form of life under the microscope. She looked little more than half Sally's age, say seventeen, and her magical responsibilities seemed to weigh so heavily on her that she could not have been in practice for more than a short time.

'I'm ever so sorry,' I began, talking in Catalan, which was the nearest I could get to her language and which I found she understood fairly well if I talked slowly. 'I never expected anything like that to happen. Will Sally ever forgive me?'

'Forgive you for what?' Sapphire asked, in a rather absent voice.

'For getting cross. I didn't realize she'd take offence so easily.'

'You don't understand. She wasn't offended, only surprised; and sorry for you. No great harm has been done.' She continued to study me.

'Let me tell you about yourself,' she said after a while. 'I know now that you're the sort of man to hold nothing back when you fall in love; and that's right. But you're content to go on seeing what you first saw. Has it ever happened that the woman who was pleased by the first image of herself in your eyes grew dissatisfied when she found that it didn't change as she changed? And that she finally destroyed it by a violent act that you couldn't forestall?'

'Well—yes, that has happened,' I admitted. I was taken a little aback, because Madame Luna, a palmist on Brighton Pier, had told me much the same thing, in a pseudo-Oriental sing-song, some ten years before. 'Are you suggesting that it might happen again?'

'Now you're here, but your wife, from whose side we summoned you, isn't, because she belongs to another age altogether. So since you have never in all your life been out of love for more than a few miserable days, you look around for a fresh focus of your love. You focus on me, and I'm pleased by the bright way you see me. But for how long will my pleasure last? That's what I can't decide.'

'Is this how Sally summed me up?'

'Yes.'

'Did she tell you so?'

'No. I heard it in her voice.'

'Then she was teasing me when she asked what kept me back from you?'

'No—she was warning us both.'

'Well, are we to disregard the warning?'

'Why not say straight out that I offended you by telling you the truth about yourself?'

'I find it difficult to be as direct as you New Cretans; but yes, I do think your generalizations are rather sweeping.'

'In fact, you no longer love me?'

I didn't answer this. The truth was that I thought her the most beautiful creature I had ever seen, and felt as though I had always known her; but that I was not in love with her in any ordinary way—and could not yet make up my mind just what my feelings were.

'When you recover from the shock to your pride,' she said, 'you'll realize that you're that sort of a lover, and that many women would be pleased to return your love—for a time.'

'Even you?'

'Even I, until the image ceased to be a true one.'

'And in the end you'd hate me?'

'No, it wouldn't come to that.'

'I can't love a woman unless I can convince myself, in spite of all my previous failures, that I'll love her for the rest of my life. So I try to see her always as I saw her first. A self-deception, perhaps, but that's my way.'

'And when the separation comes, it's a sort of death for you. One woman kills; another reanimates the corpse.'

I disliked the way she was piloting the conversation and tried to seize the controls from her: 'We seem to have raced through several years of intimacy in the last minute or two. Shall we assume that we've had a passionate love-affair and that it's gradually worked out in the usual way, except that you haven't had to resort to violence. And that we're now "very good friends" as, in my age, ex-husband and ex-wife quite often are after a divorce. Love has ended, shall we say? But a warm after-glow remains.'

'Be very careful!'

'Why? Because a divorced couple may fall in love again? Of course, if you feel that it would be cheating to cut out the preliminaries. . . .'

'I mean: don't try to define your feelings. They're still unsettled. If you're not careful you may deceive yourself again.'

'But what happens now that we're alone together?' Her calmness disconcerted me; I couldn't make her out.

'We compose ourselves.'

As I sat on the edge of the bed, tense and undecided, Sapphire fetched a broad-toothed comb and combed my hair in a slow rhythm, her lips moving silently to the words of a song. My tension gradually relaxed and a feeling of extraordinary ease crept over me. If I had been a cat I should have purred loud and long.

She looked at me critically, her head tilted slightly, not saying a word. Then she seemed to come to a decision; she signed to me to lie across the bed, put her finger to her lips and massaged my left knee in silence for about twenty minutes. 'That's where the trouble was,' she muttered when she had done. 'Now sleep!' she laid my head in the crook of her arm and I fell asleep at once.

I awoke suddenly with the moonlight on my face. Forgetting all that happened and under the impression that I was at home, I whispered sleepily: 'Tonia, what's the time?'

'Was it unkind of us to fetch you here without your wife?' Sapphire asked. 'When you first saw me, you noticed how like I was to her, didn't you?' She added as a statement, not as a question: 'You have no secrets from her.'

'No. Does that make you jealous?'

'Tell me first whether she still loves you? Would she be jealous of me?'

'I think so. But you've frightened me. Now I don't know how long her love will last.' She had taken me off my guard; a warm bed at midnight makes a wonderful confession-box.

'Only so long as you see her as she is, not as she once was.'

'I'll remember,' I said. 'But it's only fair to tell you that. . . . I'm afraid I can really love only one woman at a time.'

'But her time and mine aren't the same. You can still love her faithfully all your life, and love me as long as you please.'

As I was sleepily puzzling out the logic of this, she pinched my ear affectionately. 'She and I are almost the same person,' she said. A little later I heard Antonia's laugh, which puzzled me still more, and Antonia's voice saying something which seemed very important at the time; but again sleep intervened officiously, and I lost its meaning.

It was morning and Sapphire was just getting out of bed.
'Who are you really?' I asked, sitting bolt upright.
'The woman you love,' she answered non-committally, over her shoulder, but in broad daylight I saw that she was no more than vaguely like Antonia. She must have laid a spell to make me hear her speak and laugh with Antonia's voice. 'No, perhaps not,' I thought, 'not necessarily. I was half-asleep, and now I'm awake. I'm not dead, and neither is Antonia; but I'm no longer my former self, or not altogether because Antonia isn't Antonia—she's Sapphire now. Is that it?' Yes, that seemed reasonable enough. I should explain that since I am fortunate enough to be able to work at home, my wife and I have become unusually close to each other and, after several years together, miss one another acutely if we are ever parted for more than a day. But now here I was, and here Antonia seemed to be too, though she talked a different language and was ten years younger and had a rounder chin and did her hair in a different way, and was a nymph of the month—whatever that might be.'
'What's a nymph of the month?' I asked. 'You never told me.'
'That's too complicated to explain now,' she said. 'It's against custom to discuss before coffee what can wait till after coffee. But my title has to do with the King and Queen and the twelve Court ladies.'
I accepted the situation provisionally. It was a comfort not to have to go through the usual awkward paces of courtship, for which I felt no inclination; and to show no more embarrassment when I met my new friends at breakfast than if Sapphire and I had been married for twenty years. All the same, I did feel rather like the engine-driver of the Royal

Scot express who had one wife in London and another in Edinburgh. 'And he never once called either of them by the other's name,' I remembered. 'Perhaps he loved them in entirely different ways?'

After a comfortingly civilized breakfast of coffee, rolls and butter, orange juice and a boiled egg, Sally asked me casually: 'With how many women have you slept in your life?'

'Are we playing the truth-game?' I asked defensively.

'What's the truth-game?'

This time I was careful not to hurt her feelings. 'I mean: must I answer? In my age no woman would ask a question like that except in the privacy of a bedroom, and even then she'd expect an evasive reply.'

'But why?' This surprised Sally a good deal.

'Because in theory a man's allowed only one woman at a time, the one he publicly undertakes to cherish and support until death. I admit that the theory of marriage doesn't correspond in the least with the facts, because it doesn't often happen that married couples choose wisely. Either they break their contract after a few years and get a divorce, or else they remain married "for the sake of the children", or for appearances' sake, and console themselves with illicit love-affairs—generally with other unhappily married people. Or else they stay married without such consolations and hate each other. But marriage still has force as a convention, which is what makes your question embarrassing. Illicit love-affairs are carried on in a hole-and-corner way, and if a man and a woman choose to live in open sin, as it's called, married people feel so uncomfortable that the guilty couple—they're assumed to feel guilty—aren't invited to public functions, and when they're travelling they find it difficult to get accommodation at respectable hotels.'

'And if their love-affairs are discovered?'

'There may be a divorce. But usually they're hushed up:

it's easier to overlook unfaithfulness than to separate.' I was determined not to give away any secrets of my past, to Sally at least; so I parried her original question by asking: 'What about marriage here?'

'Different estates have different customs,' she said. 'In ours women are promiscuous until they have children.'

'May I ask what anti-conceptual devices you use?'

This puzzled everyone a great deal, and I had the embarrassment of having to give an elementary lecture on birth-control. Sally bit her lip, but old See-a-Bird said gently: 'She didn't mean that magicians are promiscuous in the physical sense. In that respect we're peculiar. The other estates assume that the consummation of love can't be separated from the reproductive process; but we know that it can and that, as Cleopatra wrote:

> To couple as beasts couple,
> Is violence and shame.

Naturally, we avoid congress unless we want children, and then we have it only with the people we love and trust so utterly that violence and cruelty become irrelevant. We remove, and our bodies remain locked in torment far below us. At all other times, consummation is achieved by a marriage of mind and body, while the reproductive organs are quiescent but our inner eyes are flooded with waves of light. In cases of complete sympathy we lie side by side, or feet to feet, without bodily contact, and our spirits float upward and drift in a waving motion around the room. The greatest honour a woman can do a man is to allow him to father her child; but this she only grants after perfect proof of physical and spiritual sympathy. Once such a man is found he stays with her.'

'But if this sympathy dissolves before death—if either partner falls in love with someone else?'

'That doesn't happen. Once a woman has learned to know herself through friendships with a number of different men, a mistake is impossible.'

'And if one partner dies, does the other re-marry?'

'Not unless the survivor goes through a ritual death and is adopted into another estate after rebirth.'

'What reliable proofs of this lasting sympathy have you?' I asked incredulously.

'The simplest are best,' said Sapphire eagerly, before Sally had time to answer. 'When my mother was my age she went to the strangers' swimming-pool one day, feeling drawn that way, and sat down on the grass. She knew that someone was about whom she could love; but she felt the need of a love-token. So she said "Bearskin" in an unemphatic voice to no one in particular, not knowing why she said the word, and a young man on the other side of the pool swam across, and said: "You called me: I answer to that name." Then she recognized him as a magician who lived a long way across the mountains and hadn't visited our village since he had been a child. So she told him: "Think of a number, Bearskin." And he answered at once: "Thirty-two," which was the number she had in her mind. Then she asked quickly: "Thirty-two what?" And he answered: "Thirty-two white rabbits." "Where?" she asked. "Under an apricot-tree," he said. "What doing?" she asked. "Nibbling lettuces," he said. "Little lettuces?" "Lettuces with hearts," he said. "When?" she asked. "Tonight, tomorrow night and until the tree flowers again." So that night, you see, Bearskin came to stay with her and she conjured up an apricot-tree to grow over their bed. On the very first night they floated together among its boughs. He stayed for a month, then for two more; and at the end of the third month of quiet life together she put a bowl of primroses on a table in the room where they had breakfast, and of the whole large bunch only one had four petals. This flower was half-hidden by a leaf; but he noticed it. Not saying a word, he removed it while she was out of the room, and replaced it with a primrose of five petals. Do you follow?'

'I think so,' I said. 'Five is woman; four is less than woman; six is woman-monster. I learned that from a poet named Donne.'

'That's well put. When my mother saw what he'd done, she didn't say anything either, but replaced the flower with another five-petalled one, but red; and that night he composed a melody called "The Five Red Petals", which proved that he knew how deeply she loved him. (When he died, two days after my mother, the melody was recorded on gold, which happens very rarely indeed.) Then they parted for as long as they had been together, which is the custom: meanwhile they wrote to each other. The magicians' letter test is very severe. Each lover writes a message above a tablet, not touching it with the pen, so that it seems a mere blank: but the other can read it by pressing it against his or her breastbone.'

'If the letter were intercepted, could another magician read it?'

'No.'

'How very odd! But you haven't explained the white rabbits.'

'He meant that she had apricot-yellow hair and very white teeth—thirty-two is a full set of teeth, you know—and that he would love her until her hair turned white like apricot blossom.'

'I see. Well, what happened then?'

'Bearskin came to live with my mother for a year, and they began to share their dreams and go for long journeys together in them. And finally they dreamed of a daughter. So after the usual proclamation, she gave Bearskin the right of father-hood, and I was born the next year.'

'A very pretty story,' I said; adding under my breath, 'but a little too pretty to be true.' And indeed, I found out later that the New Cretans told many stories that, though not exactly lies, were true only in a manner of speaking. As for the 'floating', they certainly believed in it as a common sexual phenomenon, and pairs of lovers may well have created the joint illusion by the literalness of their belief; but I never had any subjective experience of it myself during my stay. They also seriously believed in the letter test, but the messages sent must have been very simple if they were really read: telepathy is an uncertain means of communication even in the most favourable circumstances.

'When I was born,' Sapphire went on, 'they gave me the name I had in their dream, and I'll always keep that name. A man, you see, is given a new name when he becomes a father, but a woman never changes hers, though she may change her nickname as often as she pleases.'

'Sapphire, what *is* your real name? You haven't yet told me.'

In her confusion she upset the coffee-cup.

The Interpreter, forgetting his part of studious impersonality, gave a shrill cry: 'Sir, pray remember yourself! You are no longer in your own age. You could not have asked a more offensive question.'

'I'm very, very sorry, though it's your fault for not warning me. But why? What's the reason?'

'All names are secret,' said Fig-bread earnestly. 'Until I die only my parents, the Goddess, and the mother of my children will know what name I bear.'

'In that case I can't see the point of having one. Surely, the whole object of a name is to identify a person?'

'We use a nickname for that purpose.'

'But the name?'

'That is the person himself, his private being which is publicly revealed only after death. We speak openly, for instance, of Cleopatra, but in her life time she had a nickname, or two or three even, now long forgotten. My name is kept secret so that no one can injure me by its use.'

'Nonsense! If I said: "Fig-bread is a—is a—" well, if I said something unpleasant about you, everyone would know that it was you I meant, not your brother Starfish.'

'If that were to happen, as I'm sure it won't, I could at once change my nickname, and your arrows, as we say, would be left sticking in my sloughed skin. But if you knew my real name they would enter my heart and I should die of shame.'

'How childish!' I thought. 'I might be back in the Bronze Age, or between the covers of Grimm's *Fairy Tales*. I wonder whether these magicians have a racket of guessing people's names and blackmailing them. Not Sapphire, of course, but I wouldn't put it past Sally.' I could not help laughing. Starfish asked me gravely what caused me so much pleasure.

'Nothing much,' I said, a little guiltily perhaps. 'I was only —er—thinking of a fairy-tale character named Rumpelstiltskin, who challenged a princess to guess his name and then gave it away by mistake and stamped his foot so hard in rage that he broke through the floor and fell down into the cellar and killed himself.' I added hastily: 'A mythical character, you know, and it's not really funny, of course, when a person falls through the floor into the cellar and breaks his neck, but you must excuse me: Rumpelstiltskin was a very unpleasant person in the story.'

Everyone was looking very glum indeed, except Sally. Did I detect a slight twitch of her lip, a momentary gleam in her eye, which distinguished her from her solemn friends? I could not be quite sure.

I saw I must skate rapidly over the broken ice. I turned to See-a-Bird, with whom I found it easiest to make conversation: 'May I ask how you came by your nickname?'

He was ready enough to tell me. 'It happened like this. A woman named Bee-flight once sat on a porch with several young men, myself among them, teaching us the principles of counterpoint, when a servant happened to pass by with a child in her arms. Bee-flight put up her finger for silence, and asked:

"Who sees a bird?" I waited, but when I found that no one else had understood, I answered quietly: "I see a bird." "Off with you at once," she said, "meanwhile we'll have a break; I'll finish when you return." So I hurried after the woman, took the child from her and prescribed a cure. Then I returned and she continued her lesson.'

'I don't follow.'

'Since no birds were to be seen from where we were sitting, she must have meant the death-scenting vultures that hover in the stratosphere out of sight. I looked at the child's face as it bobbed on its mother's shoulders and saw a premonitory cloud of sickness centred between nostril and ear. I turned to Bee-flight and met her eyes, and we wordlessly agreed on the treatment. The child recovered. That same night Bee-flight invited me to her house and a year later gave me the right of fatherhood. She had two sons by me, both of whom have remained in our estate; one's a physician, the other's a poet. But she's left the Magic House now and become an elder.'

Truth or half-truth? I could not be sure. So I asked Sapphire: 'Tell me, does it never happen among magicians that children are begotten as the result of a sudden impulse without the usual formal preliminaries?'

'Yes, occasionally children are conceived at their parents' first meeting. They're regarded as very lucky. They announce themselves by knocking three times on the bedroom door, which their parents must open at once and say "welcome!" and then come together. Door-knockers, as we call children that are unusually anxious to be born, always become famous for one thing or another.'

After this it seemed unnecessary to ask whether abortion was practised. But I asked: 'How do bad people get born, people of the sort that Sally has to destroy?'

'None is ever born to magicians; but other estates are less careful in their unions and if prospective parents disregard a failure of sympathy between themselves, the child may be born bad. The whole village is then disgraced, because it should have discountenanced the match. That happened two years ago a few miles away. The sequel was a war: the neighbouring village felt obliged to protest on moral grounds.'

'I should have liked to watch the fighting.'

'There's talk of another war being fought next week not far from here. If that happens, we'll take you to see it, if you like.'

'How kind you are! May the best village win!'

'Thank you. That's our formula too.'

Then the servants came in and with quick deft movements began clearing away the breakfast things. They pretended not to take any particular notice of me, but I could see that they were very much interested, though there was nothing notice-able about my clothes. I had been evoked naked, and im-mediately dressed in pyjamas and dressing-gown, but was now wearing an outfit that See-a-Bird had lent me: an open-necked shirt, baggy linen trousers, embroidered waistcoat and a short frieze jacket. He had also given me a black bear-skin cap. The effect was slightly Kurdish.

CHAPTER IV

The Origin of New Crete

IT was gradually borne in on me that I had been brought here for some special purpose. These New Cretans were not an inquisitive people and would hardly have risked shocking their finely-balanced sensibilities, by the evocation of such a barbarous monster as myself, merely to ask me routine questions about my epoch. And why should they take the trouble to show me around their country? Could this be mere hospitality? But what hospitality did they owe me? Why had they not dismissed me as soon as I told them what they wanted to know? Sapphire loved me, or so it seemed; but was it true love in the New Cretan style? I could not hope to live up to her exalted moral standards. Nor—if that was what she expected—could I make a nightly exchange of far-fetched poetic riddles with her. I am a poet only on occasion, as I think is the case with all poets, always; we are seldom on the crest of the wave and no amount of rhetoric or hard swimming can keep us there for more than a brief moment. But she had not only accepted me with all my shortcomings: if that laugh was hers that I had heard in the middle of the night, she had intuitively impersonated Antonia so as to gain my confidence. Why? Had she a secret motive—a public, rather than a private one?

Perhaps there was some information that my new friends wanted from me, not about my epoch, but about their own. I had only the vaguest idea what it could be, but I was pretty sure that they had a question to ask and that they would attach as much importance to my answer as when they had first asked me: 'Do you like us?' Well, I would not press them to frame the question prematurely: that would surely be the last thing they did before returning me to my own context in time. Meanwhile, I would look carefully about me. I was enjoying my holiday and, in a sense at least, I had Antonia with me: an improved model, a New Cretan Antonia, younger, brighter-eyed, less sharp-tongued, more energetic, more eloquent, more beautiful even, with a closer resemblance to the ideal Antonia of my love than Antonia herself. But . . . . And I knew that this 'but' was somehow closely related to the mystery of my poignant but unpractical affection for her.

What was wrong with me, anyway? Was I getting senile before my time? I remembered that ridiculous old M. Charretier, the retired silk-merchant, who had conceived a strange passion for one of our Sainte Véronique girls and wanted to adopt her. He explained to her mother, who kept the sweet shop, that he did not intend to make her his mistress: all he asked was the privilege of providing her with beautiful clothes, kissing her occasionally on the brow, and combing her long blonde tresses. 'Mais non, monsieur,' the indignant mother had told him. 'Ça ce n'est pas convenable du tout. Être maitresse attitrée, c'est toujours une chose certaine, mais être poupée platonique, qu'est que c'est que ça? J'en aurais grande honte, M. Charretier, je vous assure.'

Meanwhile the problem of why I had been evoked grew on me, and I decided to find out by what historical process the New Cretans had arrived at their present pseudo-archaic system of civilization. I told the magicians that I had changed my mind and would like to know, in the broadest terms, what had happened in the world since my epoch. And this is what I learned.

After a series of revolutions and minor wars, the close of the Late Christian epoch was marked by an unusually savage struggle between the so-called Roman Bloc, consisting of the communist and semi-communist states of Western Europe and North America, and the so-called Orthodox Bloc consisting of neo-communist Eastern Europe and the Far East, both Blocs being nominally Christians. This war which, as usual, lasted far longer than had been expected, laid most of Western Europe waste and was so tenaciously fought on the battlefields of China and Northern India, that the Romanist leaders became alarmed by the strong neo-communist trend among their own workers. At the crisis of the struggle, when Orthodox armies had overrun the whole of India and the Malay Peninsula, a meeting of Roman presidents and premiers was held in the Falkland Islands and, in the resulting "Falkland Declaration", a distinction was agreed upon between what they called Pantisocracy, or primitive Roman communism based on truth and love, and false Sino-Slav neo-communism, based on lies and hate. The Romanists won the war a few months later, and made a third of the world uninhabitable by the timely introduction of a new weapon referred to in the *Brief History* as 'bright AIRAR from Heaven'. (My guess is 'artificially induced radio-active rain', but I may be wrong.) They beggared themselves in the process, and as a result a thoroughly crooked form of Pantisocracy, hardly distinguishable from Orthodox neo-communism, held the field for a while. This was in turn succeeded by what was called Logicalism—pantisocratic economics divorced from any religious or nationalistic theory.

Logicalism, hinged on international science, ushered in a gloomy and anti-poetic age. It lasted only a generation or two and ended with a grand defeatism, a sense of perfect futility, that slowly crept over the directors and managers of the régime. The common man had triumphed over his spiritual betters at last, but what was to follow? To what could he look forward with either hope or fear? By the abolition of sovereign states and the disarming of even the police forces, war had become impossible. No one who cherished any religious beliefs whatever, or was interested in sport, poetry or the arts was allowed to hold a position of public responsibility: 'ice-cold logic' was the most valued civic quality, and those who could not pretend to it were held of no account. Science continued laboriously to expand its over-large corpus of information, and the subjects of research grew more and more beautifully remote and abstract; yet the scientific obsession, so strong at the beginning of the third millennium A.D., was on the wane. Logicalist officials who were neither defeatist nor secretly religious and who kept their noses to the grindstone from a sense of duty, fell a prey to colabromania, a mental disturbance which sent them dancing like dervishes down the corridors of their all-glass laboratories, foaming at the mouth and tearing in pieces any dog, cat or child that crossed their path. They all suffered from the same hallucination: of a white-faced, hawk-nosed, golden-haired woman who whipped them round and round as if they were tops and urged them to acts of insane violence. No cure could be found by the psychiatrists, who were themselves peculiarly subject to this new form of insanity: all who caught it had to be 'lethalized'.

Colabromania, sporadic at first, assumed the proportions of an epidemic that swept spirally over the world of Logicalism, and in six weeks had carried off all the sincerest and ice-coldest logicians. There remained only the defeatists and the luke-warm logicians, who carried on the system more than half-heartedly until the beginning of the Sophocratic epoch, in which Pantisocratic theory was abandoned and the responsibility for forming a new ideology was entrusted to the Anthropological Council. Its members were charged to decide under what social conditions mankind, viewed dispassionately as livestock, though with due allowance made for certain ineradicable artistic, literary and religious impulses, lived in the greatest concord and health; and, at the same time, how to clear away the detritus of the two previous epochs and safeguard the dwindling natural resources of the world. They decided that without a new religion nothing could be done on a large scale to alter the habits of humanity; but that a new religion could spring only from primitive soil—it could not be inculcated in the over-civilized. However, when they attempted to deduce practical remedies from these conclusions, they had to confess themselves baffled.

Then an Israeli Sophocrat named ben-Yeshu wrote a book, *A Critique of Utopias*, that greatly impressed his colleagues in Southern Europe, America and Africa. From a detailed and learned analysis of some seventy *Utopias*, including Plato's *Timaeus* and *Republic*, Bacon's *New Atlantis*, Campanella's *Civitas Solis*, Fénelon's *Voyage en Solente*, Cabot's *Voyage en Icarie*, Lytton's *Coming Race*, Morris's *News from Nowhere*, Butler's *Erewhon*, Huxley's *Brave New World*, and various works of the twenty-first to the twenty-fourth centuries, he traced the history of man's increasing discontent with civilization as it developed and came to a practical conclusion: that 'we must retrace our steps, or perish.'

He recommended 'anthropological enclaves', the setting aside of small territories in Lithuania, North Wales (which had escaped the devastation of South Wales and England), Anatolia, the Catalan Pyrenees, Finland and Libya, and the re-erection there, as far as possible, of social and physical conditions as they had existed in prehistoric and early historical times. These enclaves were to represent successive stages of the development of civilization, from a Palæolithic enclave in Libya to a Late Iron Age one in the Pyrenees; and were to be sealed off from the rest of the world for three generations, though kept under continuous observation by field-workers directly responsible to the Anthropological Council. Ben-Yeshu's theory was that 'these experiments will supply the necessary data as to when and why the freight train of civilization leapt the rails.'

His suggestion was officially adopted, but it was found impossible to recruit sufficient numbers of volunteers for the enclaves, and the Anthropological Council turned down a suggestion that these should become penal colonies for delinquents of both sexes: they pointed out that 'maladjustment to Sophocratic life was no guarantee of adjustability to less highly developed forms,' and that unless a better type of human being could be bred as a result of the experiments, these would be worthless. At that point a sudden epidemic of itching paralysis (deliberately, it seems, induced by the Council) made the Orkneys and Shetlands uninhabitable, and the survivors were persuaded to enter the Bronze and Early Iron Age enclaves and live the life prescribed by the anthropologists, with a guarantee of release after fifteen years if conditions should prove intolerable. The palæolithic and neolithic enclaves were never, in fact, occupied, but those of the Bronze and Early Iron Age proved so successful that it was found easy to recruit colonists, mostly from Catalonia, for the Middle and Late Iron Age enclaves; the Late Iron Age was held to end before the invention of gunpowder and the printing press and the discovery of America. No infiltration was allowed into these enclaves, but after three generations they became overcrowded and the occupants were invited to send colonists to a much larger region that had meanwhile been prepared for them, consisting of the entire island of Crete. Here they were introduced to such natural products as tomatoes, potatoes, tobacco, red peppers, soya and a rice-like grain called *dana*—all of which had hitherto been withheld from them as being anachronisms—and instructed in their cultivation and use.

Under their occupation the island became extraordinarily fertile, and presently the original enclaves were closed and the inhabitants taken to Crete. Together the five communities evolved a new religion, closely akin to the pre-Christian religion of Europe and linked with the festivals of their

agricultural year and the antique mysteries of their handicrafts
(imposed on their grand-parents by the Council, after long
and acrimonious argument in committee); but with the
Mother-goddess Mari as the Queen of Heaven. The New
Cretans, no longer the subject of anthropological research,
were now regarded as 'the seed-bed of a Golden Age', and
when their swan-necked wooden galleys put into the port of
Corinth, where they traded food and handicrafts for metal
ore, china clay and pedigree cattle, the sailors had great
trouble in keeping off would-be immigrants. Despite all
precautions, illegal landings on the island itself became frequent, and once there, the immigrant was either accepted or
destroyed; never sent back. The population increased rapidly,
and the spread of the New Cretan system was further stimu-
lated by apprenticeship: orphans of good physique and intelligence were sent there from all over the world, but the New
Cretans had the right of refusing any that they did not like.
A generation later, the islands of Rhodes and Cyprus were
set aside for colonization.

The limitations on the use of mechanical contrivances, which
had been imposed for historical reasons on the original
colonists, were jealously preserved by their descendants.
Never having had a chance to become used to explosives,
power-driven vehicles, the telephone, electric light, domestic
plumbing and the printing press, they had no need to legislate
about their destruction, as (speaking of Utopias) Samuel
Butler's Erewhonians did; and their view of the quays of
Corinth—where they were not permitted to land—did
nothing to recommend a more advanced form of living. In
fact, the sailors made the voyage with increasing distaste:
they called Corinth 'the terrible city', objecting to it on moral
and æsthetic grounds. Eventually it was arranged for all
trading to take place at Stalinopol, a small port some distance
from Corinth and at the quietest hour of the night, when they
would not be exposed to the whir of dock machinery, the

unceasing blare of amplified dance-music, the ugly outlines of waterside buildings, and the garish, raucous, three-dimensioned cartoon-comedies telecast every hour in mid-air over the harbour.

They elevated this regard for their sensibilities into the religious principle 'nothing without the hand of love'; meaning, that no product or process was acceptable unless love had a part in it. No product, for example, turned out by a machine, however harmless it might appear, whether a jam-pot, a screw-driver or a box of chocolates, had love in it, and neither had any hand-made goods produced for commercial ends only. An important incident in their new mythology was the Secession of the Drones, who left their hive, repudiated the Queen Bee—their Goddess—and went off to live in a privy where they contrived a mechanical Queen Bee and perpetuated un-love. In this myth, the Drones were led by Machna the god of Science, Dobeis the god of Money and Pill the god of Theft. Ben-Yeshu had stressed the need for the re-establishment of the long-defunct theory of sacred monarchy, and for separating the ecclesiastical side of religion from the magical; the latter should be fostered by every possible means. He pointed out that no writer of a *Utopia* had ever applied himself to make good the damage done by Plato, when he banished poets from his Republic and preached a scornful indifference to poetic myth. 'If we strengthen the poets and let them become the acknowledged legislators of the new world,' ben-Yeshu wrote confidently, 'magic will come into its own again, bringing peace and fertility in its train.'

An attempt was made to introduce 'a mitigated New Cretan system' into California and New Mexico, but since these mitigations included domestic plumbing, ice-cream machines, watches, rubber-goods and a long list of proprietary drugs, the New Cretans declined to have anything to do with it. Still later they were invited to colonize part of the State of New York on their own terms; but an advance party found it impossible to avoid contact with the press, sightseers and other incidentals of civilization. Nor had they been warned that they would be subject to the State and Federal Laws, as well as to the periodic visits of sanitary and agricultural inspectors, and that a public highway would run through the middle of their territory. They sailed back in their wooden galleys with a report that the climate of North America was too exhilarating, and the soil too denatured by artificial fertilizers, for the successful maintenance of the New Cretan system, even if political conditions were favourable, which they were not.

The *Brief History* was reticent about what happened in the Sophocratic world once the system was well under way in New Crete. There seems to have been a gradual realization that an age had ended and that thenceforth whatever might be done or thought outside New Crete would be anachronistic, since mankind had now been reborn, for better or worse; but with this realization went a good deal of envy, resentment, and even active hostility. However, no serious attempt to wreck the system was made until the Sophocrats lost control, and the people relapsed into savagery; by that time New Crete was strong enough to hold her own against aggressors, not by armed force but by magic—a combined exercise of moral power that debilitated the will of the enemy war-lords and made the soldiers drop their weapons. 'Three Invasions that Failed' are commemorated in the *Brief History*—two from America, one from North Africa.

Within five hundred years the system had spread over a great part of the still habitable world and absorbed many inventions of earlier ages which were held to agree with the principle 'nothing without love'. Some regions, such as Australia, Russia, Central America and Central Asia, were rejected as unsuitable for permanent occupation, cleared of inhabitants and written off as Lands of Mystery; others, such as Western China, Malaya, Central Africa, India and most of North America, were abandoned to degenerate forms of society and called Bad Lands. Eastern China, the East Indies and Japan had been devastated and their inhabitants massacred by AIRAR, but its deadly effects had not been permanent, and though uninhabited except for a New Cretan colony in the Pekin district and another in Southern Japan, they came within the boundaries of the new system, as also did the greater part of Africa.

CHAPTER V

Take a Look at Our World

'COME out and take a look at our world,' said See-a-Bird later that morning.

'With pleasure,' I answered. 'Who's coming with us?'

'Sally's coming, but not Sapphire or the brothers. Sapphire has business at Court and the three of them have ridden off together.'

'To the law court?'

'What's a law court?—No, the Royal Court at Dunrena, a morning's walk along the foot of the hill. Sapphire's saying good-bye to the King.'

'Is she giving up her duties as a nymph?'

'No, he's giving up his duties as a King.'

'Abdicating?'

'You may call it that if you like: next month he's due for death and despoilment.'

'How very sad,' I said politely.

'Not sad at all. Sapphire and the other nymphs are going to congratulate him.'

'Has he been ill for a long time?'

'Oh no. He's in perfect health, so far as I know. But all good things come to an end.'

I asked no more questions for fear of saying something that might hurt their feelings. 'Is the King going to commit suicide?' I wondered. 'Or are death and despoilment only a way of saying that his reign is ended?' Sometimes these New Cretans had a queer way of expressing themselves.

Sally opened the french windows, and the Interpreter, See-a-Bird and I followed her into the garden. The paths were paved with flags of moss-covered sandstone, and none of them ran quite straight through the smooth, green lawns. It was a very simple garden: a few gnarled apple-trees and leafy rose-bushes, two or three beds of brightly coloured flowers, like zinnias but shorter-stemmed and more profuse in bloom, a curving yew-hedge, an enormous oak, a mulberry-tree, three or four massive weather-worn stone benches, and a little brook running over slate pebbles. No rows of plants or bushes, no level surfaces whatever—the lawns were all slightly undulating—except the water of the fish-pool into which the brook emptied. Sally explained that straight lines, level surfaces and a large variety of flowers fatigued the eye, and that this garden was intended for relaxation. 'In our gardens we have only the thorned damask-rose and the white moss-rose, and all our cornflowers are blue; we grow no double dahlias and no giant-flowered sweet-peas nor anything of that sort.'

'Who does grow them, then?'

'You'll find thornless tea-roses and huge, pink cabbage-roses and different-coloured cornflowers, and so on, in the gardens of other estates,' said Sally. 'This is for magicians only. The orchard and vegetable plots are at the back of the house; the herbary, where we grow plants with magical virtues, is over there beyond the hedge.'

'I'd like to see it.'

I was taken through a tunnel in the yew-hedge, then down some steps and up again into a polygonal walled enclosure, each side built of a different sort of stone and lined with a different variety of tree; paths converged from the angles of the wall to a round central space and between them grew patches of disappointingly dull-looking shrubs and weeds.

'They're arranged in thirteen divisions according to their seasonal virtues,' explained Sally.

'Why thirteen?' I asked, trying to be interested.

'Because we observe the thirteen-month calendar and pick the herbs for use according to the age of the moon and the day of the week.'

'How charmingly old-fashioned! Do you whisper spells over your herbs and bruise them with a gold pestle in a silver mortar?'

'That depends on the herb. Quite often we use other metals.'

'I don't see any labels stuck in the ground to say which herbs are which.'

'No, and we don't write "apple" on the apples we eat; you must have noticed that at breakfast.'

See-a-Bird looked up sharply at Sally and his brow furrowed anxiously. Her answer had been very tart for a New Cretan.

'That's a pity,' I answered smoothly. 'I confess I can't distinguish sweet basil from devil's bit, or turk's nose from mandragora. They didn't teach botany at my public school—or very much else, if it comes to that—so without labels, please don't expect me to admire your lay-out. You'd better lead me out of here again, and show me the vegetables. I know my greens pretty well.'

'Tell me, what medicines do doctors use in your epoch?' See-a-Bird was tactfully changing the subject.

'Animal, vegetable or mineral extracts prepared in sterilized laboratories usually after experiments on rats, rabbits and monkeys, and packed in pill-boxes, or glass bottles, or little china pots.'

'No herbs?'

'A few herbalists do business in country towns, but they don't rank as real doctors. Public medicine is scientific and as most people trust science blindly, it works in most cases. A well as pre-scientific medicine used to work, if not better. When it doesn't have the right effect, the explanation given is that it isn't quite scientific enough: doesn't take into account all the relevant morbid factors. Ask an honest doctor whether such and such a drug is a reliable cure for sciatica, and he'll tell you: "Use it while it still cures." We pay no attention to the moon or the day of the week—that would be superstitious. And very little to the temperament, or moral peculiarities or spiritual condition of the patient: most doctors are too busy signing certificates and filling in forms and keeping their accounts to have any time for refinements of that sort.'

'How utterly loveless!' said Sally with a little shiver.

'Oh, we can't grumble. When the system was introduced into backward countries like India and Egypt it worked almost too well. The native systems discouraged the survival of weakly children or of people too old to do useful work. Now the population's increasing absurdly, and will go on increasing, I suppose, until war or famine reduces it to a sensible size.'

Beyond the herbary lay parkland with a few cows grazing over it. 'Magic houses are always surrounded by parkland,' See-a-Bird explained. 'We can't concentrate on our work if a highway runs close by or if a row of cottages is built at our gates. It's not merely the incidental noises that distract, but the agitation set up by alien rhythms of thought and feeling.'

'You're very particular.'

'What sort of a magician would an unparticular one be?' Sally asked.

'What indeed?' I wished that Sapphire had come with us. When Sally was about I felt the temptation to criticize all I saw, almost to the extent of feeling a loyalty to my own obviously inferior epoch. With Sapphire, it would have been different: I should have accepted everything without question for her sake, as I had once accepted Antonia's home and family at her own high valuation.

'I wonder that you allow cows in the parks,' I said, after a pause.

'Why not? They make no disturbance.'

'You misunderstand me. I wasn't thinking of their mental and emotional rhythms; I meant that their hooves and their droppings spoil the turf.'

'If you look closely you'll see that they're wearing wide leather shoes, and that there aren't any casual droppings. Cattle are trained to drop into pits—there's one over there by the wall—and the manure is returned to the land once a year, sprayed over the whole surface, so that the grass grows evenly.'

'How charmingly scientific!'

Sally pretended not to hear.

We were approaching a group of houses each with its garden and fence; a stream ran around the bottom of the gardens and dark-haired children were bathing and fishing in it. The houses were built of stone with tiled roofs and brightly-painted shutters. Most of the walls were white-washed, but some were colour-washed in yellow, smoke-grey or pink. A morose-looking man in leather shorts and sandals with criss-cross straps was setting out pea-sticks in a near-by garden. He looked up as we passed, greeting us with his fingers extended in the Latin blessing, and called something to his wife. She looked out of the window in obvious excite-ment, then disappeared and soon came hurrying to meet us with a basket of plums. She wore a short-sleeved white linen blouse with gold buttons, and a heavily embroidered skirt, and looked rather Moorish.

'In Mari's name, all's well?' This seemed to be the formal greeting.

'All's well,' Sally returned with a polite smile.

The woman looked inquiringly at me.

'A poet from the past, who has consented to visit us.'

'Offer him one of my plums and ask him to swallow the stone.' She spoke gravely but her mouth twitched.

'How's that?'

'To take the stone back to his own epoch so that it may in time become the ancestress of my plum-tree.'

It was a relief to know that the commons at least made their little jokes; but Sally, See-a-Bird and the Interpreter did not laugh. From the abstracted look on See-a-Bird's face I guessed that he was working out the logical possibility of the experiment.

'And your child?' asked Sally.

'Mari be praised! I did as you told me, Witch, and to-day he walks without a limp. He ran a race with the cat just now and beat her easily. She ran up a tree.'

'This is a village of the commons,' See-a-Bird explained, as we went on. 'It's called Horned Lamb. Each village is famous for something; this has a carp-pool and an unusual way of thatching barns with heather and rush. Over there on the green is the totem-pole, the centre of their worship.'

'What are the marriage customs here?' I asked. ('That's the first thing to find out,' as Knut Jensen the Danish anthropologist had once told me. 'There are some places, you know, where a man dies of shame if he accidentally catches sight of his sister-in-law's leaf-skirt hanging out on the line; and others where he's expected to lead her off into the bush three times a day. One can make dreadful mistakes if one doesn't discover which place is which.')

'Horned Lamb is strictly monogamous,' See-a-Bird told me. 'The girls and boys here have no sexual experience before marriage, unless they decide to migrate to another monogamous village where that's permitted—or to a polygamous one. They're free to go off if they like.'

'If they do go, are they estranged from their families?'

'Not at all. They visit them as often as they like and there's no ill-will between villages with different moralities. Only, every permanent resident of a village is expected to conform to local custom.'

'What's that large house beyond the bridge?' It was built in red brick with quadrangles, like a Cambridge college, and surrounded by a double-line of plane-trees.

'That's where the recorders live. The commons prefer to live in cottages with gardens and to have neighbours across the garden fence. The recorders prefer flats in a large building with communal dining-rooms, a communal nursery and an orderly routine. The north wing is the library and record-office. That field is their croquet-ground. It's a tradition with us that recorders play croquet, unlike any of the other estates: croquet and bowls.'

I saw a couple of elderly recorders coming down a path from the hill. They wore full-skirted coats, knee-breeches and buckled shoes, which gave them the look of eighteenth-century Quaker merchants.

'Is that the Recorders' garden?' I asked, '—there to the right of the plane-trees.'

See-a-Bird nodded. 'As you can see from here, it's very formal. Tulips massed in neat beds—one black, one white, one red—bushes clipped flat, lily-pools, delphiniums, espalier-pears, tea-roses—their rose-bushes and fruit trees are pruned pitilessly to get the best fruit and blooms, not left in peace like ours—sundials and a peacock. Peacocks are reserved for the Recorders' estate.'

'Indeed? Why?'

'A recorder is supposed to be all eyes like the peacock's tail, and without a peacock such a garden would be a little too severe. The severity of the tulip beds is mitigated by a custom that each bed must contain one flower of a different colour from the rest.'

'Suppose a recorder happened to dislike croquet, peacocks, delphiniums and tulips?'

'Then he wouldn't be a recorder,' Sally threw over her shoulder. She said 'good-bye' sulkily, and walked off. What was wrong with the woman?

I was beginning to feel less at home than before: this was something like a visit to the Ideal Homes Exhibition and something like a chapter left out from *Alice in Wonderland*. The Interpreter was the White Rabbit to the life. A few days before my evocation I had picked up a copy of *Alice in Wonderland* and read it for the first time for I don't know how many years. ('How good it is,' I thought, memories of a happy childhood surging back into my mind, 'how amusing, how exquisitely written'—until suddenly I came on the four pages at the end of the chapter about the Queen's croquet-ground, which I had always missed because my elder brother had torn them out of our nursery-copy to make paper-boats. 'How tedious,' I thought as I read them, 'how stupid, how out of key!') So I found myself asking the Interpreter what the Queen of Hearts had asked Alice: 'Can you play croquet?'

'I am passionately fond of it. I play game after game in my dreams.'

'With flamingoes for mallets, and hedgehogs for balls, and doubled-up soldiers for hoops?'

'Excuse me? I do not understand.'

'That's how Alice played it.'

'Ah, yes, of course.'

But I could not be sure whether he really understood the reference, or whether he was bluffing to show off his erudition. What a muff of a man he was! I pitied his colleague Quant.

'Where do the captains live?' I asked See-a-Bird.

'You see those cloisters leading from the Record House and ending in four or five cells? They live there. Look, one of them is coming out now.'

A tall, hatchet-faced hero in what looked like naval uniform had swung open a door and was striding masterfully down the cloisters. He might have stepped straight out of an American comic-strip. 'There goes Nervo the Fearless on the track of the Masked Girl!' I cried.

'Nervo?' echoed the Interpreter doubtfully.

'He looks as though he were syndicated in about five thousand provincial dailies.'

'Syndicated?'

'Oh, nothing! I was merely admiring his perfect he-manship. Does his wife have a lot to make her jealous?'

'He has no wife,' See-a-Bird said. 'Captains have no home-life, because they're so busy with other people's business; and though a few energetic young women belong to this estate they don't marry within it. As soon as they decide to have children and settle down they resign and become ordinary members of the commons.'

'Then why doesn't the estate die out?'

'The captains have a marriage agreement with villages of the commons where pre-marital promiscuity is practised. Since they're men of vigorous physique and compelling character—as you noticed at once—new recruits to the estate always get born. In fact, it was once a problem how to keep the estate from growing too large. The solution found was to forbid captains to mate with women either of whose parents had belonged to the estate, or who had themselves been captains.'

'And do the recorders breed satisfactorily in proportion to other estates?'

'They're so conscious of the need for proportional breeding that they regulate their birthrate with great exactitude.'

'And the commons? And the servants?'

'Those are the estates most susceptible to what in past epochs were called "the imponderable factors of genetics": but imponderable meant no more than that they couldn't be weighed in the scales of science. The birthrate can be accelerated or decelerated easily enough by simple means. The servants present less of a problem than the commons; they are always over-fertile, so we reduce their pulse-rate, and their sexual inclination, by giving them cola to chew. This has the additional advantage of making them content to perform monotonous tasks day after day without diversion. And we don't bother about slight variations in the birthrate of the commons: if one village has a few vacant houses or more land than it needs, it invites settlers from another village of the same marriage system as itself, and these "grafts", as we call them, make for movement and animation. But if a whole district becomes depopulated or over-populated, that's another matter. Since cola is reserved for the servants' estate, the usual remedy is a change in the regional costume, or music. Melancholy music stimulates breeding, serene music discourages it. As for costume, the more sombre and restrictive the clothes, the higher the birthrate.'

'Surely not?'

'But indeed! Melancholy music produces a vague anxiety in its hearers, vague anxiety carries with it a presentiment of death, presentiment of death suggests the need for breeding children. Sombre restrictive clothes have a similar effect on their wearers. The greater the sense of bodily freedom and exhilaration the lower the birthrate.'

'I shouldn't have expected that. Who prescribes these changes?'

'We magicians do. This is a matter that can't be left to custom. The recorders can be trusted to find the appropriate treatment for simple local mishaps, such as a plague of caterpillars or the burning down of a village or an outbreak of typhoid fever. But fluctuations in the birthrate may be due to so many causes that we're always consulted before any action is taken; we diagnose and prescribe. The prescriptions are announced by the priests, which gives them religious force. The commons aren't told why their customs are changed, but they accept the orders out of respect for their priests and the captains see that they're carried out.'

'Do the commons envy the captains their power and superior talents?'

'On the contrary, they pity a man like the one you saw just now for having to live without home or family; and they know that he's entered the estate only because of a talent or obsession for leadership—to which they feel the instinctive need for obedience. I imagine that the same sort of feeling must be aroused in your age by celibate priests?'

'Well, yes—I suppose so—by those who are serious in their profession and live free from scandal. Are your priests celibate too?'

'A few. A film of oil, as we say, separates the priest from his congregation, if only because he belongs to a different estate. You see, in the servant class the prevailing system is three-clan marriage: a woman sleeps with members of an associated clan, without having a constant mate. Her children remain in her own clan, but form alliances with a third clan, to avoid incestuous unions. Servants' children, once they're weaned, aren't left with their mothers, though the tie of affection remains fairly strong, and they don't know their fathers: they're communal property and begin their life of service at an early age. The most devoted, slow-pulsed, tractable and simple-minded of all are directed to the priesthood. In regions where the commons are unusually high-spirited and need a steadying influence we give them a celibate priest; they seem to have greater respect for a celibate priest than for a three-clan marriage one.'

'Are there any women priests?'

'No, only High Priestesses. All ordinary priests are men; but religious instruction, which consists in teaching children prayers and myths and other religious formulas, is given only by women, also of the servants' estate. All children without exception have to learn these rudiments by heart, and the teachers explain them in the same set words, revised every three generations or so to conform with changes of language.'

'I should like to see a school of that sort in action.'

'There's one behind those houses over the stream. The children have only just gone in.'

The school-room walls were white-washed and bare—no blackboard, no maps, no pictures—nothing to distract the children's attention from their lessons, which were given orally. They sat in a semi-circle around the schoolmistress—the boys in black overalls, the girls in white and blue ones—and behind them a window opened on a hill crowned with a circle of trees. The schoolmistress was installed in a high-backed chair; on one side of her was the fire-place, filled with the flowers of midsummer; on the other a carved and painted statue of the Goddess Mari, in white robe and blue mantle. The Goddess nursed a fair-haired, blue-eyed child in the crook of the right arm, a dark-haired, brown-eyed child in the crook of the left; the head and hands of a wrinkled hag appeared over her shoulder; a girl about twelve years old nestled against her skirt. Her breasts were bare: she held a snake in the left hand and a cross-cut apple in the right, and on her yellow hair was a coronet of stars. The hag wore a high, black conical cap like the one used by Sally at my evocation; the girl was garlanded with flowers and carried a bow and arrows.

The schoolmistress, a fat middle-aged woman with a deep emotionless voice, seemed not so much to be instructing as delegating for an unseen instructress—who, as I soon found out from her frequent sideway glances, was the Goddess Mari. The children, who were all between the ages of five and eight, addressed their replies to the statue rather than to her.

'Chant, children, after me, the story of Dobeis and Nimuë!' said the schoolmistress.

She struck the lowest bell of a chime fastened beside her chair, which acted as a tuning-fork for the chant. The story was in verse, of which this is a rough rendering. It is not my fault that it reads, in part, like a passage from one of Blake's *Prophetic Books*.

Dobeis was a young man, fat, bald and bad.
Dobeis did magic with wheels of gold,
Stamping them with pictures of creatures and men.
He lay on his bed at the open window,
He said to the gold wheels: 'Out into the world,
Be the world's ruin!'

Everywhere they rolled, into every house and farm,
Bewitching the people, rousing them to hate,
Death was in those wheels, plague and misery.
They rolled against custom, they rolled over love,
All the five estates into confusion fell.

The wheels assumed captainship,
The wheels recorded all,
The wheels clamped the commons in golden fetters,
The wheels forced the servants to serve without love,
The wheels annulled the magic of the magicians.

Dobeis, lying there by the open window,
Laughed as he saw the ruin of the land
Cut up and wasted by the golden wheels,
Laughed as he saw the ruin of the town
Crushed into rubble by the golden wheels,
Laughed as he heard the discordant cries
Of hate and despair that rose all about.

Nimuë awakened, Mari's daughter,
From her sleep in the branches of the catkin-willow,
Soon she was aware of what Dobeis had done.
Her beautiful face grew pallid and stern.
Slinging her bow across her slender back,
She strode along the path to the house of Dobeis,
The golden wheels circling giddily about her
And locking together, wheel with wheel,
As a shield to protect the house of Dobeis.

Nimuë leaped across the gold shield,
Her white foot alighting on the window sill.
She addressed fat Dobeis in reproachful words:

'Dobeis, Dobeis, what mischief is this?
What have you contrived against the five estates?
Call back your wheels while yet there is time,
Lest you forfeit the pardon of Mari and Ana.'

Dobeis laughed loudly from his silken bed,
Reclining at ease upon his left elbow:
'I am bad, I am bad, I am bad,' he said.
'I would have all the world resemble myself.
Away, little Nimuë, lest I do you harm.'

Nimuë called to the blackthorn-tree:
'Blackthorn, lend me a white-flowered branch
To humble the power of Dobeis the bad!'
The blackthorn lent her the white-flowered branch;
A magpie brought it to Nimuë.

Dobeis watched laughing as she trimmed the point
With a flint knife knapped in the crescent shape.
'Back to your dolls, little Nimuë.
Back to your dolls, before worse befalls.'
Suddenly she struck, weeping for sorrow.
Since never before had she taken life.
She struck at the hollow under his breastbone.
She did not pierce Dobeis, she drew no blood,
The magic lay in the wind of the blow.

Dobeis lay back upon the silken bed
His face was doleful, his frown was deep,
Dilated his nostrils, his dark eyes dull,
Profoundly sunk within their orbits;
Black shadows gathered all around.
His face and arms were white as marble,
His lips turned blue, his brow cold-sweated,
A chill spread over his trunk and limbs.

Then, in a voice, that was weak and hollow
'Alas,' he cried, 'Little Nimuë,

Who would have thought that the wind of the blow
Struck by a girl could have caused my death.'
Nimuë, weeping, addressed Dobeis:
'Let your vengeance fall on the blackthorn-tree,
On the magpie's claws, on the crescent knife;
But recall the course of your golden wheels,
I conjure you in my Mother's name.
Do so, and I will bury you.'

Dobeis called back the golden wheels,
And the ruin of man was thus arrested,
When the last bright wheel came rolling home
He died, and Nimuë buried him.

She brought the wheels to the witches' queen,
Who rid them, by long evocation,
Of the evil magic of Dobeis.
Then smiths with hammers beat them flat,
Into sheets of gold, into books of gold,
Of the sort that noble poets use
To make a record of Nimuë—
Of Ana, Mari and Nimuë.

How much of this piece of mythology—it was repeated
three times—the children were capable of understanding, I
could not judge. Certainly they seemed to be word-perfect
by the time that the lesson was over. I noticed a girl of the
magician estate weeping in sympathy with Nimuë each time
that the line recurred:

Never before had she taken life.

The estate of the children was shown by the number of
bands on the cuffs of their overalls. Estates sat together,
though I noticed that one or two girls were sitting out of place.
At a signal from the mistress all shouted a greeting to the statue
of the Goddess and ran into the playground, where they began

to play games in the same disorganized way that children do now. The mistress stayed behind, praying. She did not kneel, however, nor pray upright with palms spread out at the height of the thigh, as I later saw the priests pray, but stood with arms akimbo and a pleasant smile on her face as if respectfully chatting with the Goddess. She reminded me of fat Fanny, my grandmother's faithful cook, respectfully asking her permission to make the mushroom-sauce according to my great-grandmother's favourite recipe. I found that it was a general rule for men to address the Goddess with an adoration compounded of love and fear, whereas women addressed her familiarly as a friend, colleague or mistress, according to their estate.

See-a-Bird told me that education after the age of eight was the affair of the estates to which the children belonged. By then it was usually clear from the child's performance and preferences whether he was to continue in the estate into which he had been born; though some children developed unexpected powers or inclinations some years later when they had already been provisionally accepted as working members of a particular estate. It was a practical education outside the school-house, the children being free—within the limits of custom, which exacted a very high standard of good manners from them—to wander through the villages and observe all that was going on in field, workshop, office or kitchen, and acquaint themselves with their neighbours for miles around. This freedom was conceded only for a few hours a day; the rest of the time they picked up, orally, the traditions of their estates and ran errands, or helped their parents or guardians. At puberty they were apprenticed to a trade or, if they belonged to the magicians' or recorders' estates, taught to read or write. (The captains, the commons and the servants were forbidden by custom to do either and both the magicians and recorders were strictly limited in their use of writing.) At sixteen or so they were free to start their love life, and when fully grown to travel or engage in wars, becoming full citizens. When they had 'more white hairs than coloured' they could become elders if they pleased and were then treated with peculiar respect; they were emancipated from custom while in their club-houses but required to behave, elsewhere, with appropriate dignity and reserve.

As we walked home, I asked See-a-Bird: 'What year are we in?'

'The year before leap-year.'

'Yes, but what's the date?'

The Interpreter intervened. He explained to See-a-Bird that in my age we counted the years publicly and celebrated every first of January with a postmortem on the Old Year and speculations on the New.

'Here we have no public date,' See-a-Bird told me. 'The Chief Recorder keeps a count of years in the archives, but it isn't published and nobody but he and his assistants could calculate how many have elapsed since the foundation of New Crete. We also consider it highly improper to mention anyone's age or to count the number of years that he has held office or been married. In the same way we make no record of hours and minutes, as I believe you do with clocks and watches. We observe the phases of the moon; we distinguish morning from afternoon and afternoon from evening; we keep the days of the week; we mark the passage of the seasons; and the two parts of our double year end with the first full moon after the longest day and the first full moon after the shortest day. But time in an absolute sense was abolished on the same occasion on which it was agreed to abolish money; for the poet Vives pleaded passionately:

> Since Time is money,
> Time must be destroyed:
> His sickle and hour-glass
> Are in pawn to evil.
> Nimuë, save us with your bow again.'

'Then at what time do children go to school in the morning?'

'When the bell rings.'

'And when does it ring?'

'When the first three children have arrived.'

'And how long do you boil an egg?'

'Until the sand's run out of the egg-glass.'

CHAPTER VI

Erica

THAT same day, which was a Sunday, an alarming and quite inexplicable event happened, just before I had lunch with See-a-Bird and Sally.

It was a vegetarian meal, by the way: I found to my chagrin that custom forbade magicians to eat either meat or fish—only fresh cheese and an occasional egg, and no spices or pickles or even onions. No wonder they were so clear-headed, clear-skinned and humourless! Their irreproachable diet went far to explain their fanciful theories of love and amatory sympathy. Also the facility with which they shed tears: I once had an operation for a fistula, followed by a week of nothing but tap-water and barley sugar, and by the time the doctor consented to put me on milk and mush I was so unlike my usual self that one evening I shed tears at a waifs-and-strays appeal on the radio, and then lay in bed, still sobbing uncontrollably, and watched an imaginary but most realistic battle being fought on the window-curtain between stags and swans. Not that I was on an insufficient diet now: the food was plentiful and probably contained all the vitamins and calories needed for perfect health, and the glass of lager—though they didn't offer to fill my empty glass—was every bit as drinkable as the one I had been given before. But what my stomach expected was a real Sunday dinner with joint, Yorkshire pudding and roast potatoes, introduced by a couple of dry Martinis; it did not get any of this, and I felt like someone who has gone to the wrong restaurant, and finds himself confronted with nut-cutlets and hoax-in-the-hole.

What had happened was this. I told Sally that I proposed to stroll out by myself in the park for a few minutes, if that was allowed. She made no objection, so I took the other direction from the one we had taken that morning, crossed the orchard and made for a low ridge about a hundred yards from the house, where I stopped to take my bearings.

'Let me see,' I thought. 'That's where the *Coq d'Or* used to be, and there's the stream still running, and look, there's a new mill exactly where ours was; so I must be standing on the site of the *Mairie*, which was on the crest of this ridge; and my house must have been over there in the hollow where that cow's grazing.' It gave me a rather nightmarish feeling to look at the smooth green turf and realize that somewhere underneath the cow, if I dug, I might come across the foundations of my house, and very likely the concrete floor of the cellar, but absolutely no other trace of my life in these parts. Unless perhaps a fragment survived of my own gravestone; yes, I would probably have died here and been buried in the English Cemetery which my father, a retired clergyman, had bought and consecrated himself. Or would I have left the village and gone to live in Oxfordshire, as Antonia always wanted us to do, and died there?

Another large building not far from the mill caught my eye. The two elderly recorders whom I had seen that morning were coming out of a side door and making for the bridge. That was where the Doctor's house had stood and I sighed a little guiltily, remembering that Erica Turner used to stay there. Erica was a wild girl, the Doctor's half-American niece. She and I had had a passionate love-affair, which was in its final stage when Antonia came with her two brothers to stay at the *Coq d'Or*. Antonia caught me on the rebound, and I married her almost at once. She knew all about Erica, of course, from village gossip and what I told her myself—or

practically all, because there are certain things one does not
repeat and, anyhow, they were over and done with and
Antonia would not have enjoyed hearing about them. I had
made up my mind to forget Erica. She had not only treated
me foully but managed at the same time to put me in the
wrong and make me feel a thorough heel, before suddenly
breaking with me and going off with a man I detested and
despised. She had also withdrawn all the money from our
joint account at the *Crédit Lyonnais* and left me flat. No news
of her for many years and then I heard from a friend, some
months before the start of the Second World War, that she
had been seen in Florence going about with an Italian count
and looking a good deal older and thinner than when we had
known her. No news since. As I walked towards the Doctor's
house, or so I called it to myself, I was surprised to find that it
had been re-built on the original foundations. It stood in the
same position, though of stone this time, not brick, with
queerly curved gable windows and a very old vine trained up
the south wall. There was even a descendant of the Doctor's
walnut-tree at the back of the house, shading the stable-yard.
Just here, for the first time and quite unexpectedly, as I was
going to the Doctor with a poisoned finger, and rounding
the corner, I had run full tilt into—

'Erica, good God! It can't be true!'

'Oh, hallo, Teddy!' she said casually. 'I heard you were
about. I meant to come along yesterday.'

'But . . . . but . . . .'

'But what?'

I stood gasping.

'But what?' she repeated with her habitual Sphinx smile.
She looked much younger now, not older, and dangerously
well and beautiful.

'I thought I was the only person from our age whom they'd
evoked. Are you real?'

'Pinch me and see. Or pinch yourself. What's on your

mind, Teddy? You were looking as cross as hell when you came across the field.'

I automatically fumbled in my pocket for a cigarette.

'Oh, it's only that, is it? Have one of mine!' She produced a case full of very normal-looking French cigarettes. 'Contraband,' she explained. 'If you don't mind breaking the rules, you're perfectly safe. A light?'

She had a Ronson, too, in her handbag. 'You do the talking, Erica,' I said, 'while I get the most out of my *Gauloise Bleue*. This situation is beyond me.'

'Tell me first why you were feeling so cross, if it wasn't just the cigarette shortage. It can't have been that. You're still scowling.'

'I was thinking of you, of course.'

'I see. So you want me to talk about old times? You know, Teddy, if it wasn't so ridiculously long ago I don't believe I'd have forgiven you for the way you let me down. I didn't think you were that sort. The vulgar fuss you made about poor Emile, as though he meant anything to me.'

'He meant enough for you to sneak off to Cannes with him one week-end, when you were supposed to be visiting your mother in Geneva.'

'Your punishment for being so jealous.'

'I knew nothing about Emile at the time.'

'No, that's correct. You were jealous of that tall black Irishman with the yacht. Captain Thing—I forget his name. Dumb, but a heavenly dancer.'

'Henty was the name. And he wasn't a captain, only a dude yachtsman. And he wasn't in the least bit dumb; but a crook and personally disgusting and I told him so in a few well-chosen words.'

'Yes, that was where you slipped up! If you'd only told *me*, it wouldn't have been nearly so bad, but to make a scene in Harry's Bar as if you were my husband. . . .'

'I was drunk. So was he. So were you!'

'So what?'

'O Lord, Erica, let's forget it! Don't let's talk about Emile or Henty or the Cannes visit. . . .'

'I couldn't agree with you more. Or about my Benevolence.'

'I don't quite get you. What benevolence did you show me?'

'I thought you read History at Oxford? A Benevolence was how King Thing—how King Thing the What-th—used to describe a forced loan. Have you forgotten those hundred thousand francs I relieved you of? But I must say you never were mean about money. So don't let's talk about my Benevolence. And don't let's talk about Antonia either—you always were rather a bore about her—or about anything else except ourselves. All that happened ages ago: literally. You're staying with the Nymph Sapphire now, I hear?'

'I am.'

'And you've fallen for her already, haven't you? Cradle-snatching, I call it. She's got a good figure, of course, as most of these girls have, but I can't say I like her any better than I liked Antonia.'

'Now who's being a bore?'

'Oh, all right, have another cigarette.'

'I don't in the least mind if I do. But look here, darling, I must know what you're doing here.'

'Me? Nothing especially. I live in this village, that's all.'

'How long have you been here?'

'Oh, for years and years, off and on.'

'What's your name now?'

'Erica Yvonne Turner, of course; only I never use the Yvonne.'

'Except as an *alias* in divorce cases.'

'You beast! I didn't know you'd followed my career with such attention. But they don't have divorce courts here.'

'No. I suppose not. Lucky you! What estate do you belong to?'

She glared at me. 'Estate? Estate! Don't ever again use that word in my hearing or I'll scream.'

'Why shouldn't I? Surely, if you live here you're bound to belong to one estate or another!'

She stuck out her chin and let out a long, piercing scream, like an express train coming out of a tunnel. I might have known she would.

'Stop it, for God's sake, stop it at once, you little fool! You'll get us both into trouble.' I put my hand roughly over her mouth. She stopped at once and began to laugh.

'Teddy, do you remember that time at Ronda when I said I'd smash the gold wrist-watch you'd just given me if you ever laughed at another of your own jokes?'

'I do. And I did laugh at one, and you did smash it. And that annoyed me so much I threw you on the bed and wrestled with you and banged your head against the wall, time after time.' .

'And I cut your wrist with a piece of watch glass and you nearly bled to death.'

'I wouldn't have cared if I had bled to death. Or if I'd brained you, either. I've never felt more furiously miserable in my life. . . .'

'Stop pitying yourself, idiot. . . . Tell me, how do you like this place?'

'I was liking it very much, on the whole, until you turned up and complicated things. The life here's a little too good to be true, of course.'

'I'm glad to hear you say that. What do you think of the men?'

'They remind me vaguely of Jane Austen's heroes. Something cardboardy about them. Or—I know—the bigger boys in a co-educational school.'

'I don't know whether you remember that I went to a co-ed school in Switzerland. I was the head-girl—'

'Exactly, that's what made me mention your victims. Wherever women have perfect liberty to drink men's blood out of skull-goblets. . . .'

'As they do here, you mean?'

'That's right, isn't it?'

'Ah, of course. This is a women's world, and that's why I'm here.'

'Those poets—Starfish and Fig-bread—what sort of poems do they write?'

'Punk. Even your stuff's brilliant compared with theirs. But tell me, how do you get on with Sally?'

'Not too well. She's got something against me, I think.'

'Has she asked you any awkward questions yet?'

'Only one. She wanted to know with how many women I'd slept in my life.'

'Did you mention Erica Turner, by any chance?'

'No.'

'That was very gentlemanly of you. But why not?'

'I mentioned no names at all. I thought her question was in deplorable taste.'

'You mean: because Sally's in love with you and madly jealous of Sapphire?'

'You're talking nonsense, Erica, you know you are! Women here don't get jealous, or if they do they don't show it.'

'Did I ever lie to you, Teddy?'

'Often, but only by evasions and half-truths—I suppose you didn't need to waste your real lies on me. But you're not serious about Sally and Sapphire?'

'Certainly. It's a fact. Ask Sally if it isn't.'

'I shall do nothing of the sort. How do *you* know what her feelings are, anyway?'

'Oh, my spies are everywhere and I get about a good deal

myself. But look here, Teddy, there's no time for any more
talk now. You must go back at once—that's the bell ringing
for lunch. I'll be seeing you. No, I won't come over for a
day or two; it might cramp your style. But you know where
to find me.'

She pulled my head down, gave me a brief kiss, turned and
disappeared into the Doctor's house.

I stood looking after her until the bell stopped ringing.
Naturally, I said nothing to Sally or See-a-Bird when I got
back; and made up my mind to say nothing to Sapphire
either. But what a mess this was! Of all the people in the
world—my world—that triple-faced, ash-blonde bitch
Erica! It couldn't have been worse; in the old days her
savagery and recklessness had aroused a response in me of
which I couldn't have believed myself capable. I blushed to
think of the things we had done together; and might do again
if I wasn't careful. I shouldn't have called her 'darling' just
now, even though she had given me a couple of cigarettes; or
allowed her to kiss me; or discussed Sally and the brothers
with her. Perhaps I ought to apply for revocation—if that
was the word—and go home at once.

At table I was glad of the New Cretan custom that forbade
people to talk while they ate. It gave me a little time to sort
out my impressions. In a daze I swallowed a plateful of boiled
dana, served with French beans and tomato sauce. I couldn't
yet face the problem, or the set of connected problems: how
Erica had come here, what her status was, and why nobody
had mentioned her to me, what my attitude to her ought to
be, why she was so much younger now than before—she
didn't look a day over twenty-one, yet she was only two years
younger than I was, which made her thirty-four, no, thirty-
five. Instead, I set myself a minor task, which I somehow felt
was relevant to these problems; and that was, to remember the
right name of that long white-ribbed coat she was wearing.
Walnut . . . wainscote . . . dovecote . . . some word like that.

I'd think of it presently. It was a coarsely woven, yet oddly impressive garment mentioned in a Border ballad, or a Scottish folk tale, or something of that sort.

But, oh, for a plate of roast beef with horseradish sauce and a half-bottle of Pommard, with brandy and a long Havana cigar to follow!

CHAPTER VII

The Record House

THE Interpreter asked Sally to excuse him that afternoon: he had promised to report to his colleague Quant whatever discoveries about the English language he might have made in the course of the morning. 'My head is full to bursting,' he whimpered.

Sally gave him permission.

I was only too glad to see him go: I had begun to get the hang of the New Cretan language and hoped to talk it fairly fluently within two or three weeks, with Sapphire as my teacher. ('There's only one way to pick up a new dialect, old boy,' Knut Jensen had told me, affectionately prodding me in the ribs, 'and that's to share a mat with the woman who has the greatest number of plaited bangles—of telegraph wire, you know—wound around her neck and the largest wooden saucer fitted into her lower lip. First, you must count her fingers and toes: that will teach you the numerals as far as twenty. Next, you must learn the names for the parts of the body—you'll know from her giggles which are in polite use or not. Next, a few adjectives: hard, soft, warm, pleasant. Next. . . .' Knut was a coarse old man, and most of his advice could not apply to any lessons I was likely to get from Sapphire.)

'Hullo, there goes Nervo the Fearless on his mustang,' I said to See-a-Bird, looking out of the window. 'Do you mind if I follow him and watch him at his job? The man fascinates me.'

'By all means. We have a rule: "Never gossip with a captain," but so long as you follow him at a decent distance, say fifty paces or so. . . .'

'Is he sensitive too?'

'No, captains are the least sensitive of people both by nature and training. Still, it's considered very bad manners to distract one of them in the execution of his duties by catching his eye or carrying on any conversation that he may happen to overhear.'

'I shan't even cough. What's he doing to those little boys?'

'Let's go and see.' We went out into the park and towards the stream. Nervo had hitched his chestnut horse to a post and was haranguing four or five little black-overalled boys who had stopped by the bridge on their way home from school to take off their shoes and race bits of sticks in the stream.

'What's he saying to them?'

'He's telling them how to go about it. He says: "First be sure that all the boats are of equal size and weight, and that none has an unfair start; and, before you begin, agree on the winning-post, and put your shoes in a dry spot on the bank—"'

'Arranged neatly in pairs?'

'Yes, how did you guess that?'

'And what else?'

'And "hang your raincoats over the rail and never say '*my* boat', but only 'the black boat', or 'the brown boat', or 'the crooked boat'—so as to avoid quarrels."'

'Doesn't anyone ever tell Nervo to mind his own business and let the kids work things out in their own way?'

'Certainly not. Parents are only too pleased for their boys to be taught good manners and fair play and the right way of going about things, which it's the captains' business to teach.'

'Well, yes. . . . But the boys themselves? Do they like being ordered about, even in their private play?'

'He's a captain, remember, not a busybody from some other estate.'

'You haven't answered my question. Do they really like being ordered about?'

'What does it matter whether they like it or not? They're young and they must learn. Obedience is the mother of custom; custom of good manners; good manners of peace.'

'And peace?' I asked. 'Of what is peace the mother?'

'Peace is a virgin.'

'You're lucky then. With us she's got a long line of descendants: in fact, her genealogy turns round in an endless circle. Peace is the mother of prosperity, prosperity of idleness, idleness of boredom, boredom of mischief, mischief of slaughter, slaughter of terror, terror of obedience—and there you are back again at the beginning. One, two, three, four, five . . . yes, I make it ten generations.'

'Peace is a virgin!' he repeated in firmer tones than before.

Meanwhile Nervo had mounted Red Thunder and cantered off with a cheery farewell. I watched hopefully, waiting for the biggest boy to put out his tongue and for the smaller boys to snigger and shout something rude. But all that happened was that after waiting until he was out of sight, they stood about for a while in an undecided way. Then one of them took up the carefully graded and impersonal sticks that Nervo had cut for them, laid them out in a neat row on the bank beside the pairs of shoes and went off to make mud pies under the bridge. The others joined him. When they had made about a dozen, they recovered their spirits and were soon pelting the row of raincoats on the rail and shouting: 'Mine's the dirtiest now. No, mine is!'

'They'll learn good manners in a year or two,' See-a-Bird sighed. 'Theirs is the rebellious time of life.'

From two fields away, close to the Doctor's house, Nervo's fine baritone voice was raised in protest and exhortation.

'What's the matter now?' I asked.

'He says there's a swampy patch at the end of the meadow that badly needs ditching; he's urging the farmer to fetch two men with spades. No. . . . I don't think he'll get them. The farmer is shouting back that there's a *brutch* on that spot, and that it's against custom to meddle with brutches.'

'A brutch?'

'A local emanation of bad luck. Occasionally the result of a contemporary spell, but nearly always a relic of the distant past.'

'And is there really some brutch there?'

'None has been reported to us so far.'

'You mean that the farmer's been lazy and that he's trying to excuse himself for having neglected his field?'

'That would be dishonest—the behaviour of a five-year-old!'

'Perhaps. But if I were the farmer and Nervo talked to me in that tone of voice I'd consider it my duty to be dishonest.'

'Sir,' See-a-Bird asked simply, taking me by the hand, 'you can't possibly mean that you'd tell a lie to conceal your laziness?'

There were actually tears in his eyes. 'No,' I said, soothingly. 'Perhaps I didn't mean exactly that. What I meant was that, in my epoch, if a farmer got bawled at by a captain for not having ditched his field, he'd consider it his duty to lie to him. One of the reasons why we fought the Second World War was that Hitler had founded schools for captains of the Nervo sort—captains to order us about when he'd conquered us—and we valued our personal freedom.'

'Hitler? But surely Hitler didn't belong to the Second World War? I suppose you mean the one-armed Orthodox Commander-in-Chief who put the poet Horsch to death?'

'No, no. Adolf Hitler . . . . the paper-hanger with the silly moustache who made himself Führer of Germany.'

'Oh, him! Yes, I remember now. The *Brief History* says very little about that Hitler, except to describe the glass castle under the Kyffhäuser Mountains where he waited thirty years for revenge. His one-armed grandson of the same name is the better remembered of the two. And his great-grandson, nicknamed "The Pander". . . .'

'Please, please, I don't want to hear about any more Hitlers. I couldn't bear it. One's enough for a lifetime. So far we're labouring under the pleasant delusion that the original Adolf committed suicide in a dugout under the Chancellery at Berlin, and that his only virtue was that he died without issue. Let's go along to visit the Recorders' house and leave Nervo and Red Thunder to deal with the brutch.'

'Captains are not qualified to deal with brutches.'

'Even with imaginary ones, invented by lazy farmers?'

'Sir,' See-a-Bird said, 'do be serious. You must know by this time that it isn't the custom here for grown men to tell lies or make excuses.'

'Something put me in a bad humour,' I explained. 'I'm sorry.'

He made no comment, but I could see that he was feeling the strain of my company.

I pointed casually at the Doctor's house: 'Can you tell me who lives there?'

'No one lives there permanently. It's what we call a nonsense house: a club-house for elders.'

'Why the name?'

'I have just explained: it's the elders' club-house.'

'Do you mean to tell me that elders habitually talk nonsense, that one's brain softens here at the age of sixty or so?'

'No, it isn't that, but they have the privilege of saying and doing almost anything they please within the four walls o their nonsense house: they have ceased to be bound by custom. But the condition of this "inward freedom", as it's called, is not only that they must behave with exemplary gravity elsewhere but that none of their opinions or statements has any relevance in the younger world of custom.'

'May I visit the house some time?'

'I fear not. Nobody who's not an elder may enter a non-sense house; it's strictly forbidden.'

'But this very morning I saw a girl going into that house.'

'You're mistaken.'

'I tell you, I saw her go in, just before I came back from my stroll. She was young and beautiful and wore a white . . . . a white . . . .' I fought for the word.

'You're mistaken. You saw a nonsense. No one here pays any attention to the sights and sounds that reach him from a nonsense house.'

'But this girl was outside and went in. She stood for a time by that swampy patch where the brutch . . . .'

He took me by the arm and led me firmly away.

We dawdled along the lane towards the Record House, and See-a-Bird gave me an idea of what I should find there. No files, no blue-books, no forms, no blotting-pads, no waste-paper baskets; because Vives, a famous New Cretan poet who flourished towards the close of the Sophocratic Epoch, had written:

> Paper feeds on paper
> And on the blood of men.
> Engrave the durable
> On plates of gold and silver,
> Lest memory of it wavers.
>
> The rest, impress on clay,
> Or cut on tally-sticks—
> Though sparing even of these.
> Cretans, have done with paper
> And with parchment, its dour brother.

This poem, intended to warn the New Cretans against bureaucratic civilization, made so strong an impression on them that its exhortations acquired the force of custom. The manufacture of paper and parchment was discontinued almost at once—paper was no longer used even for wrapping or for toilet purposes—and all records of real importance were thereafter engraved on thin plates of gold or silver. For the rest they used slates, clay-boards, tally-sticks and their memories; but mainly their memories.

'Real importance!' I exclaimed. 'I've long thought what a blessing it would be to reduce the corpus of learning to manageable proportions. Four centuries before my time it was just possible for someone of unusual intelligence and industry to be well educated in all the subjects of knowledge then available. The Church had always limited and co-ordinated learning; but once Papal authority was defied in Germany and England these subjects grew in number and complexity until soon no one could hope for more than a smattering of some of them and perhaps a specialized knowledge of one. This, of course, led to intellectual disunity—I don't know whether you realize how much my age suffers from unrelated and often contradictory developments of such subjects as, for instance, biology, physics, æsthetics, philosophy, theology and economics. This led to moral disunity, social unrest, civil wars and commercial wars which gradually increased in bloodiness and horror. I've often thought that if the essentials of each subject of knowledge could be preserved and the rest jettisoned, it might once more be possible for people to be generally well educated, and for the contradiction between the subjects to disappear, and so for international peace to be restored. "And what's to prevent that happening?" I've asked myself.'

'Well, what did prevent it?'

'The cards were stacked and the dice loaded against any project of that sort.' (I was speaking more to myself than to See-a-Bird who, at the best of times, could only catch my general drift.) 'To begin with, every specialist would be loyal to his own branch of learning and insist that every least part of it was of the utmost importance and that practically nothing could be jettisoned. They'd quarrel as bitterly as assistant masters in a public school when the Headmaster tells them that he's decided to simplify the curriculum because of the parents' complaints about the boys' being overworked: "Head Master, if you ask me to give up my Special French Class, I shall resign!" "Head Master, if you think that I can get my boys up to Certificate standard on only three hours' Maths a week, you are sadly mistaken." So in their competitive efforts to cover each particular field decently they'd inflate, rather than deflate, the corpus. They'd also emphasize the contradictions between subjects. (Oh, what surly good-mornings used to pass between my Science master and my Classics master, and what spiteful remarks each used to make in class about the other!) But if the task of deflation were given to a committee of mere smatterers—men without a bias in favour of any one subject of knowledge—they'd not have the least idea where to stick in the pin, or how to gather up the slack afterwards. How did your people solve the problem?'

'It was easier for us. When we first came to Crete we carried no dead weight of learning with us; the Sophocrats had seen to that. And once our system was well established, without intellectual or moral disunity, because we were all bound together in religious awe of the Goddess, we began to import useful knowledge from the outside world. But we imported it in concentrated form, a little at a time. For example, the outside world boasted of their poet Shakespeare. On inquiry we found that two hundred and seventy-four thousand books had been written about him, two or three thousand of which were extant, besides I don't know how many articles and pamphlets. We asked for only three books. They were a complete original text of the *Plays and Poems*, with concordance, glossary and variorum readings; a well-documented *Life*; and a *Digest of Shakespearean Criticism*. Later, the *Life* and

Digest were reduced to three pages, and the *Plays and Poems* to thirty, apart from the New Cretan translation. We kept only what Shakespeare had written when inspired. Usually, as you know, he wrote as a talented theatrical hack.'

'Then no complete plays of his survive?'

'It would go against custom to stage them.'

'But you could read them. They read wonderfully.'

'A play, by its nature, has no existence except on the stage.'

'You don't seem to admire Shakespeare very much.'

'We admire no poets. We say: "The Goddess alone is worthy of admiration." But Shakespeare still figures at length in the *English Canon*. It is said of him there: "he climbed painfully by night up a broken stair lighted only by the Goddess's cruel smile; he loved her, though against his will." '

'How does the *English Canon* begin?'

'With Thomas the Rimer who wrote the early English Carols in the Goddess's honour, and Robin Hood the archer, who wrote ballads in the same style, some of them about his own exploits. Next comes the witty court-poet Henry Tudor, who defied the Pope and died in sanctuary. Next . . . .'

I did not bother to put him right. The post-Exilic Jews had shown an equal disregard for historical fact, in ascribing all ancient religious poetry to King David and all ancient amatory verse to King Solomon, and in rewriting their national annals for the purpose of moral edification. I found later that the New Cretans, who never gave dates for anything, telescoped history whenever they pleased. They had created such composite historical characters as the court-poet Henry Tudor, to whom they attributed, so far as I can remember, the best work of Wyatt, Skelton and Dunbar, as well as a couple of poems by Henry VIII, and for whom they wrote a plausibly dashing early-Tudor *Life*. Robin Hood was the English Homer—the Greeks had similarly fathered all early ballad-poetry on the semi-legendary Homer—and became the secret lover of Queen Berengaria, whose gallant husband, King Richard Lion-heart, was credited with the moralistic anecdotes of Alfred and the cakes, Bruce and the spider, Sidney and the drink of water, and with a great many more. Similar liberties were taken with the life of Shakespeare, which incorporated those of Sir Francis Drake, the Earl of Essex, Sir Walter Raleigh and Christopher Marlowe. I can't say that I approved of all this. As the son of a Shakespearean scholar who spent four years and a lot of money on a book called *Broken Letters as a Help to Establishing the Date of Certain Eighteenth-Century Shakespearean Forgeries*, I felt that this was carrying simplification a little too far.

'Tell me, what do your Golden Archives contain, more or less?'

'A hundred volumes exactly. *The Myths of Crete. The Myths of the Ancient World. The Brief History of the World* in nine volumes. *The Canon of Poetry* in fifteen. Four books of ancient melodies: two of recent ones. *The Book of Sums and Numbers.* Twenty-eight *Registers*—of plants, birds, fishes, stars and so on. Thirteen *Manuals*—of surgery, dyeing, metallurgy, navigation, meteorology, apiculture and so on. Twelve dictionaries. Three *Books of Maps.* Five volumes of *The Book of Precedents.* Five volumes of *The Book of Secrets. The Book of Death.* And that's all. It took a century or more for these records to be gathered, sorted, simplified and engraved on gold plates, but once this had been done the subsequent additions and emendations weren't very numerous. The editors spent as much thought on discussing what didn't need to be included, as on what did. They argued that it was better to record too little than too much.'

When I questioned See-a-Bird further, he told me that the archives gave no information whatever about philosophy, advanced mathematics, physics or chemistry, nor about the motivation of any machine more complicated than the waterwheel, pulley or carpenter's lathe. Silver plates, he said, were used for records which, though believed to be durable, were still on probation. For example, every poet on the occasion of his 'acceptance' was given twenty small silver plates on which to record his life's poems; it was assumed that no poet could write enough true poems in his lifetime to cover more than twenty. He was expected to keep a record on clay-boards of all he wrote and consult his friends, from time to time, as to which of them, if any, should be transferred to silver. He might take their advice or not, as he pleased, and everyone respected him if he 'kept his plates bright' until he was about to become an elder, when he could judge the value of his work more objectively. If he kept his plates bright to the end, this earned him posthumous praise, whether or not a poem worthy of engraving on either silver or gold was found among his clay-boards. See-a-Bird quoted the record of Solero: 'the Goddess tormented him greatly and when he was killed by the fall of a poplar at the shrine of Mari the Silent, a pile of clay-boards and slates were found on his cupboard-top. There now are forty plates in gold of Solero, who had kept his silver plates bright.'

'Never to commit one's poems to silver seems an easy way of getting a poetic reputation. In practice, does anyone ever use up his plates?'

'The poet Robnet had used all his twenty within a year of receiving them.'

'The Goddess must have tormented him pretty badly.'

'She did. She also put it into the minds of his poet-friends to present him with twenty-one more plates, three from each, so that she could torment him further.'

'He could surely have kept his poems on clay-boards like Solero?'

'The Nymph Fand, whom he loved, wouldn't let him do so.'

'What happened then?'

'He used all the new plates within six months; and then he took his life and became Fand's servant.'

'Say that again!'

'When the Goddess torments a man beyond his power to suffer further he goes to her principal shrine, removes his name from her register, and expires. He's re-born under a new name into the servants' estate; unless, of course, as sometimes happens, he has expired completely.'

'What did Fand do then?'

'She took another young poet as her lover; and presently disappeared.'

'You mean, that the jealous Robnet strangled her and disposed of her remains?'

But I had said the wrong thing again and had to make another apology. No: Fand, it seems, simply disappeared.

The New Cretans, I found, did not mine precious metals, but were still drawing on the huge hoard at Fort Worth in North America which had been discovered and excavated by the Sophocrats. Indeed, they had no need to mine for any metals. Their population was kept stable at a low figure, and large stocks of copper and malleable stainless steel were left over from the Pantisocratic, Logicalist and Sophocratic epochs, which served them for all domestic and agricultural uses.

Our lane passed over a railway bridge and we leaned on the coping as we talked. After a time, three four-wheeled trucks in close succession crawled slowly and soundlessly underneath. They were graceful boat-shaped structures, with painted timber and basket-work curving down within an inch or two of the track. A man of the servants' estate—one could tell them by their closely cropped heads—sat in the bows of each heavily-loaded truck, which was not power-propelled, but drawn by oxen. See-a-Bird told me that custom forbade passengers to ride in the trucks, except in special circumstances, and never for more than short distances. Travelling was done on foot or on asses, or by ass-cart in the case of elders. Horses were reserved for the magicians and captains.

'The railways,' he explained, 'are a legacy of the past. The trucks and rails were discussed at a Council of the Five Estates in the time of Cleopatra. It was clear that their construction was not according to the rule of love, yet the principle was a humane one. Cleopatra herself intervened in the debate: "If the principle, which is represented by the track and the flanged wheels, is judged to be humane, let that be preserved. It remains to exert love on the rest, namely the coachwork and the track, and incorporate it in our kingdom." The making of the new trucks was entrusted to the coach-builders, who copied the flanging of the original wheels.'

When I climbed down the embankment and poked about with a stick I found that the steel sleepers had not been removed, but covered with a few inches of soil which was then sown with a moss-like, drought-resisting grass. The trucks looked rather like gondolas and the drivers were, indeed, called gondoliers.

'Why the restriction on the use of horses?'

'People who walk feel an instinctive respect for those who are mounted, and this is why we give captains the privilege of riding horses—by custom theirs are any colour but white. Magicians ride on white horses, because magic is connected with the moon, to whom the white horse is sacred. White asses are reserved for high-priestesses, priests and school-mistresses.'

'But why the restrictions on passenger travel? And why not use fast-trotting horses and lighter trucks?'

'The poet Vives wrote:

> 'With wheels and wings and rockets
> The outlanders have shrunk their territory
> (Which is a thousand times more wide
> Than yours, noble New Cretans)
> To a mere village green and duckpond.

But ride no faster than a man may run,
And soar no higher than a man may leap,
Count distance by the day's march or day's sail:
Respect the fertile spaciousness of earth
As you respect Her who here reigns.

'Your policy seems to be to cut off your noses to spite your faces.'

'Do you really enjoy long, breathless journeys?'

'No, but I shouldn't like to feel that if I wanted to go, say, from New York to Hollywood, I'd have to do it in thirty-mile stages instead of flipping across the continent by plane in a few hours.'

'Why should you be in such a hurry to go to Hollywood?'

Antonia had asked me that very question only a week or so before and I couldn't think of any better answer than a weak: 'Oh, I don't know.'

'Oh, I don't know,' I told See-a-Bird.

To my surprise we found Sally already at the Record House. She was in the archive-room, reporting my evocation in matter-of-fact detail to the Chief Recorder. I caught: '. . . . white bull-hides stretched across hazel wattles; rowan-wood and vine-stocks kindled with need-fire in a gravel pit . . . . the siren call sounded, nine drops of blood drawn from the evoker's left breast and let fall on the instrument of induction. The charm: "Living, living, live and quick", five times repeated. . . . After the first appearance of his wraith, its embodiment with the sacred potion; also herb-Edward, sea-anemone and a net of white horse hair.'

Her voice dropped a little when she saw me come in and there was a line or two of the story she reported in finger language; the whole affair was more sinister than I had been allowed to realize. I hate being the subject of hypnotic experiments and fight the anæsthetic whenever I have an operation; but even ether or chloroform would have been less humiliating than this Druidical nonsense. I felt a sudden intense disgust; why did I ever consent to visit this place? Curiosity had borne down my commonsense. I didn't belong, and I dislike Utopias.

The Chief Recorder noted the report in shorthand on a clay-board and handed it to Sally for checking. She read it carefully, made a few alterations and said curtly: 'It must be engraved on silver by noon tomorrow.'

As she left us, the Chief Recorder turned to me with a grave bow: 'Sir,' he said, 'yesterday's events are, I believe, destined for gold.' Then he stroked his chin meditatively and looked me up and down. 'This is a day of change. Our engravers have been idle for nearly two years.'

'I'm glad that my arrival has done something to check unemployment.'

'You misunderstand me,' he answered rather stiffly. 'The less there is to record, the greater our honour.'

'Very well, then; in that case I'm sorry that my arrival has caused your engravers unnecessary labour.'

'You have no need to be sorry,' he said in the same stiff tones. 'The engravers love their work.'

'Indeed? They love their work, yet it dishonours you? Would you mind explaining the paradox?'

'With pleasure. The occurrence of recordable events does not cause positive dishonour, though bright plates are positively honourable. The engravers are pleased to perform a necessary task, as the undertakers of your age took pride in their profession, though they had no greater love for death than anyone else.'

'Thank you for the explanation, though I don't think your analogy is a very happy one—it makes me feel like an exquisitely groomed corpse in a quilted coffin.'

Five sleek-haired commoners in white smocks, with brightly polished copper basins slung around their necks, came

trooping up the stairs. 'You will excuse me,' the Chief
Recorder said, 'but here are the barbers. They come every
Sunday afternoon from their villages to repeat the gossip of
their shops. We collate these reports and each barber takes
back a summary, which we call the *pravda* (a word of obscure
origin, supposed to be a survival from the Pantisocratic
epoch), to his own village for public recitation. Once a month
the district pravdas are combined into a regional one; and this
is returned to the village in the same way. From the monthly
pravdas of our many regions an anecdotal history of the whole
kingdom is compiled at irregular intervals. Custom rules that
it must not take longer than three, or less than two, hours to
recite. It then becomes part of the oral stock-in-trade of the
district historian, who is a recorder. The histories of the
various kingdoms are reviewed and collated, at irregular intervals again, and their golden elements, if any, combined with
those of our magical, meteorological, agricultural and similar
records, are incorporated in the *Brief History*, or the *Registers*,
or the *Manuals*.'

'The rest is lost?'

'Unless it is preserved by local tradition. One of the duties
of the barbers is to memorize the more entertaining anecdotes
of their district. We have local records, in rough rhyme, going
back for many generations.'

'Do they recite these anecdotes while they're cutting hair?'

'Certainly not. Custom does not permit us to do two
things at a time. We recorders, for example, never discuss our
business or listen to music during meals, as I understand is
always done in your age.'

'Not quite always,' I said. 'But don't your ploughmen
whistle as they follow their team?'

This suggestion seemed to surprise and shock him. 'Here
only certain women whistle,' he answered, 'and then only on
solemn occasions.'

CHAPTER VIII

The Brutch

SHORTLY after the evening curfew, I heard the sound of horses' hooves on the road and leaned out of my bedroom window. Sapphire and the two brothers were returning from Court. She rode side-saddle and looked splendid: not in the least like one of those berry-faced women in long riding habits who used to ride side-saddle in the days of my childhood, but rather like 'the lady upon a white horse' in the Caldecott picture book. The childish simplicity of the New Cretan scene and the stern rules of propriety that guarded it invited constant quotation from the nursery classics. 'Rings on her fingers and bells at her toes!'

I waved to the party but nobody looked up; they were all too busy soothing their jittery horses.

'Strange,' I thought. 'After a longish trot to Dunrena in the morning and back again in the afternoon, those hacks ought to be manageable enough. They look as though they'd suddenly run into a steam-roller—how horses hate steam-rollers! —but there could hardly be one on the roads in this post-civilized age.'

They turned into the yard, dismounted, and handed the horses to the grooms. See-a-Bird and Sally had come out to greet them in the Goddess's name and Sally asked: 'Whatever's wrong with the beasts?'

'We ran into a brutch,' Fig-bread answered shortly.

'Where? Not near home, surely?'

'In the village itself, just outside the Nonsense House,' Sapphire answered. 'We cut across the corner of the mill-field and suddenly my mare reared as though a snake had bitten her. And then the other beasts plunged about like mad things. Starfish took a toss, and we had to chase his horse twice round the park before we caught him.'

Sally nodded. 'The farmer tells me that he's suspected a brutch at that spot for some time: he came to report it formally not long before you came back. He says it's suddenly flared up. I told him we'd inspect the place as soon as you returned.'

'Let's all go, as soon as we've had our smoke,' Sapphire said, frowning a little.

I spent the quiet quarter of an hour over my cigarette, thinking about the brutch. Was a brutch a malevolent spell deliberately cast—no, it could hardly be that, because Sally had made it clear that witches here were naturally benevolent —or could it be what, in our epoch, is called a ghost? Being a poet, not a scientist, I have a commonsense attitude to ghosts. I think that one should accept them very much as one accepts fire—a more common but equally mysterious phenomenon. After all, what is fire? It is not really an element, not a principle of motion, not a living creature—not even a disease, though a house may catch it from its neighbours. It is an event rather than a thing or a creature. Ghosts, similarly, seem to be events rather than things or creatures—and nearly always disagreeable events.

I reckon among ghosts the nameless and disembodied hauntings of particular stretches of road, clearings in forests, bare hill-tops. I have twice met with powerful examples of this phenomenon. The first occasion was on a North Welsh ridge crowned with an ancient earthwork; the second was in the Balearics on a lonely coast road, near a village where a temple of Diana had once stood. On each occasion it was dusk with a waxing moon, and I felt that sudden inexplicable dread that makes the hair of one's scalp rise like the fur of an angry cat and one's legs run with no sense of effort, as if they were skating. Previously I had thought that when Shakespeare wrote about the haunted ship in *The Tempest*:

> . . . not a soul
> But felt a fever of the mad and played
> Some trick of desperation. . . . Ferdinand
> With hair upstaring—then like reeds, not hair—
> Cried 'Hell is empty and all the devils are here!'

he was writing poetical nonsense. Since then, I know that he was giving a not exaggerated account of a disagreeable physical fact. The Greeks had a word for this sort of dread—'panic' —meaning the fear that suddenly struck them in the woods or on the hills when the God Pan was loose. In Ferdinand's case it was not Pan, of course, but St. Elmo; and the only way I can account for my two hauntings is that both places had once been the scene of horrific religious rites, and that the rocks and stones still periodically sweated out that horror.

Haunted houses, again. They seem either to enclose a sharp individual horror that centres in some particular room, or else a general feeling of misery, sorrow, boredom or vice pervading the whole building. Sensitive people can tell the difference between a happy house and an unhappy one as soon as they cross the threshold. But, in our epoch, most of them would be ashamed to tell the house-agent: 'I'd rather pay a thousand pounds than rent this place—it has an evil atmosphere.' Instead they would say: 'I'm afraid, you know, that my husband would find that dressing-room far too small, and there isn't enough space for his books in the sitting-room. Besides, the garden is much too large for just the two of us.' But perhaps haunting of the disembodied sort is a matter of degree. Every house that has had a previous occupant is, in a sense, haunted.

That horrible flat in Heliopolis, which Mr. Angelides the

house-agent found me when I went to Egypt to write a book. Antonia and I rented it for a month from an Assyrian widow, because it was the only vacant one to be had—the top flat of a modern block built by a Belgian firm. It was crammed with gaudy furniture in bamboo and red brocade; and I remember particularly a glass bookcase containing Hebrew books and a small French legal library. Hassan, our Sudanese servant, said at once that he didn't like the place and, later, complained that there were *afreets* about. I told him that it was only for a month, so he did not give notice; he slept out, of course. But the sense of evil grew thicker and thicker as the days passed. Soon the afreets were almost visible, as tall bright phantoms that appeared between sleeping and waking, or as little black creatures, seen only from the corner of my eye, that did nasty things at dusk in the shadow of the sofa or bookcase. The most alarming phenomenon was the sudden whiff of burning that constantly spread through the flat even when there was no fire in the kitchen. Hassan afterwards told me—I don't know how truly—that the Assyrian husband had been burned to death in the flat some months before, and that it had since been used as a brothel. But even this was not enough to account for the strength of our impressions. Perhaps someone had been monkeying with black magic there; black magic is a means of reviving and focusing ancient evil, and anyone sufficiently idle, cruel and curious can achieve horrible results with little effort. Since it was not worth while to attempt a reclamation of the flat, we cleared out after ten days and took a room in a hotel.

But that charming château which she and I and a couple of friends once rented near Rennes. Though five of the chimneys were full of bees, and there were crickets behind the library fire, bats in the attics and rats in the cellars, the atmosphere was excellent. One day I found an ancient sheet of cooking recipes in a box full of rubbish, which I began to decipher and translate. There was one for *Blanc-Manger*, which began: 'On the evening before, put two pieces of fish-glue as big as your thumb (or else gelatine) to melt on the embers. The next morning bring it to the boil. Take one and a half *quintons* of sweet almonds and half a *quinton* of bitter almonds. . . .' Late that night, when I was crouching over the kitchen fire, blowing up the embers with the bellows to heat a coffee-pot, I said to myself: ' "Melt the fish-glue on the embers . . . ." but gelatine, I think, would taste nicer . . . . and I wonder how much a *quinton* of almonds is. . . .' When suddenly a woman's voice behind me called out sharply: 'Marthe!' '*Oui, Madame,*' I answered automatically. But, of course, no one was there. And as I do not believe in the absolute reality of time this did not greatly surprise me. It may have been a cosmic coincidence. Somehow, by thinking about the fish-glue and the embers and the almonds, I had strayed into another level of time. Marthe's mistress, seeing me squatting over the fire in the half-light with my back turned, naturally thought I was Marthe. She must have got a shock when I stood up and she saw a tall, pale man in black corduroy trousers. In fact, I was probably her ghost, not she mine. . . .

On the whole, I decided, ghosts are an unimportant and far less mysterious phenomenon than many others—for example, poetry and love. People who manage their lives well leave only gracious emanations behind them. It is the wastrels, the bores and the deliberately evil who give a place a bad name: those and the self-tortured victims of their own folly. One should sternly disregard the ghosts that they leave behind, as one disregards drunks who stop one in the street and begin a rambling hard-luck tale mixed with threats and hiccoughs. In neither case should one show either sympathy, embarrassment or alarm.

Perhaps this brutch in the field by the Doctor's house was no more than a concise record of all the misery and shame and desperation of my affair with Erica—I had managed that part of my life very badly indeed—which had lain dormant for I don't know how many centuries until revived by our sudden meeting. No: wait a minute! Apparently the farmer had neglected the drainage of that field for some weeks before my evocation. But that still made sense—Erica's coming had revived the brutch strongly enough for him to avoid this corner, though he hadn't formulated his reasons for doing so until I'd come along and it had flared up. However, it was stupid to be speculating on the nature of this brutch until I could form some general theory about Erica. How did she get here, what was she doing here? She seemed real enough, or at least as real as I was: she had pulled my head down and kissed me with firm, warm lips. I could hardly dismiss her as a cosmic coincidence. Yet See-a-Bird evidently knew nothing about her, and had stubbornly refused to believe that I'd seen her enter the Nonsense House.

On the other hand, she might easily be using that place as her hide-out. Once she had bluffed her way in—and no more shameless gate-crasher than Erica had ever existed—who in the outside world would be any the wiser? Apparently what the elders did and said, and whom they entertained, was nobody's business but their own. I didn't suppose that it even figured in the barber-shop gossip. Perhaps, when the right moment came, I ought to tell Sapphire about the meeting, after all.

The last of the cigarette stubs had been burned in the fire and we could talk again. Sapphire turned to me, and said gently: 'I have been thinking about the brutch. Did you by any chance cross the park while I was away?'

'Yes,' I answered, 'just before lunch. Sally gave me permission.'

'What were your feelings at the time?'

'I felt rather lost without you: I was thinking about the old days, when my house still stood in the middle of what's now your park, and when I used to take the children down to the sea for a bathe, where there's now only cornland. And I also felt cross. . . .'

'And then you had a vision of a young woman going into the Nonsense House?' See-a-Bird prompted me.

'Not a vision. She was real enough.'

'What was she like?'

'She was wearing a sort of white .... wollacombe .... widdicombe .... I wish I could remember that word. And green slippers.'

'Green slippers? Are you sure?'

'Grass-green. I noticed them particularly. All right, then: here's a police description of the wanted woman. Fair, rather curly hair, pointed chin, long upper lip, sparrow's egg-blue eyes, good figure, medium height, ballet-dancer's legs, square hands—and she bites her nails when she's cross. . . .'

'Then she was cross too?'

'No, not when I saw her. On the contrary, she was feeling very gay. If you're interested, I can tell you more about her. She has a scar on her scalp where a man once tried to brain her with an ice-pick; and a bullet-graze low down on her ribs where a woman once tried to shoot her with a small automatic pistol. She was educated at Geneva; smokes *Gauloises* cigarettes for choice; is an expert fudge-maker and a champion figure-skater; has a code of morals peculiarly her own; and says she lives in that Nonsense House of yours by the mill. She knows all of you, claims to have read Fig-bread's and Starfish's poems, and plans to visit us soon. Her name's Erica Yvonne Turner, though she doesn't use the Yvonne, and I wonder you haven't told me before that she's been brought here. I used to know her well. Rather too well; but perhaps you're aware of that, which is why you're keeping me in the dark about her.'

They all looked puzzled and a little scared. Sapphire said to Sally: 'It's a brutch all right: something, I'm afraid, that he's brought with him accidentally. In a dream perhaps? No, I don't think so, do you? At his evocation another spirit, a woman's, must have clung to his hair and made the time journey in his company. A case of the sort is quoted in the third *Book of Magic*, in the Aldeboran chapter, you remember. But I don't at all like the sound of those green slippers and I'm surprised that we saw no trace of her when his wraith manifested itself. Perhaps she hid at the back of the pit?'

Then she said to me: 'I swear in the Mother's name that we know nothing about all this. Do *you* think this woman can have been bold enough to come with you?'

'Clinging to my hair? It's possible. She'd get into anyone's hair. Why, that girl once bluffed her way into the Royal Enclosure at Ascot, for a bet, by slipping her arm through the Archbishop of Canterbury's and pretending to be his daughter.'

That seemed to convince them all and they got up to go. As we went through the park to the Doctor's house they were discussing ways of catching and deporting Erica. When we reached the corner of the mill-field Starfish suddenly stopped and pointed. 'That's what your mare shied at, Sapphire,' he said gravely.

'What is it?'

'A cigarette stub, but it's wrapped in paper, not leaf.'

They all hesitated to touch the ill-omened thing, so I picked it up and said: 'Yes, didn't I tell you that Erica Turner smokes *Gauloises?*'

They shrank away. 'It must be burned quickly. And afterwards we'll have to purify your fingers.'

'But the brutch?'

'The field must first be fumigated with sulphur thrown on a bonfire of wild-olive and then swept in both directions with a birch-broom.'

'But suppose Erica goes on dropping stubs all over the village just to annoy you?'

'If, as you say, she's lodged in the Nonsense House,' Sally said, 'we'll have to wait until midnight, when the Elders will have gone home; I'll deal with her then.'

I dropped behind and furtively picked up the other stub where I'd thrown it down just outside the orchard; then I crushed them up together and burned them at the back of the dining-room grate. Sapphire purified my fingers with rose-water in a silver bowl and a short prayer.

We settled down for a pleasant evening around the fire. There seemed to be a general agreement to drop the subject of the brutch, and Sally asked no more leading questions and gave no more tart answers. From the friendly way she behaved towards me and Sapphire I decided that Erica had been making mischief as usual, and that there was no truth at all in that love-and-jealousy story.

I asked whether the leave-taking ceremony at Court had gone off well.

'Most propitiously,' Starfish replied. 'The King's dignity was superb; anyone would have thought that he was only going on a short holiday.'

'But what *is* going to happen to him?'

'He's going to die, of course.'

'And why?'

'Because his term ends this Friday when the moon is full.'

'Will he kill himself?'

'No. His other self will kill him.'

'Doesn't that come to much the same thing?'

'Not at all. As we say: "The right hand cannot be thrust into the left glove".'

When I'd worked that out, I asked: 'Tell me, who's the next king to be?'

'His other self, who reigns until midwinter; the left hand to his right hand.'

'Perhaps I'd understand that better if Sapphire would consent to explain what a nymph of the month is.'

'It's like this,' Sapphire said. 'The king's reign begins at mid-winter and he has thirteen consorts, who are called nymphs of the month. All are commoners but myself and one other, and we're all Queen in turn and share his bed during our respective months, and put him through his paces. The ritual is rather complicated and one can't afford to offend the Goddess by omitting any detail. In the seventh month he dies, and his other self reigns until the thirteenth month, when he dies too.'

'And your month is the sixth month?'

'It ended nine days ago. We're now in the seventh.'

'So last month you were the Queen?'

'Yes.'

'And the King was your lover?'

'Not in a carnal sense. The sixth month is the month of enforced chastity, so he and I lay in a bed with a labra—a double-bladed axe—between us. He's not allowed to have his hair or nails cut or to wear new clothes, and has to go about with a thorn-broom in his hand and keep to magicians' diet. But now he's having a glorious time again: the Queen gives him whatever he asks for—it's unlucky to refuse him anything, even if it's against custom.'

'No double-bladed axe in his bed now?'

'Of course not.'

'Wine, women and tobacco at his call day and night?'

'Yes.'

'In his last month, would a king be allowed to go for a long railway journey if he pleased, or learn his A.B.C., or talk during meals or whistle in his bath?'

'I suppose so.'

'And by the time he comes to the drop he's so pickled and gorged and fagged-out that he doesn't care very much whether he or his other self is to reign for the second half of the year? Is that the idea?'

'The Goddess is always merciful to fools.'

CHAPTER IX

The Santrepod

THEY told me that there would be music at sundown. I had already gathered that music was never used as a casual entertainment, but was reserved for special religious occasions. So I asked: 'In celebration of what?'

'Of the Goddess, Sir, always of the Goddess,' said Starfish. 'This will be a performance of the *Santrepod*.'

'And what, may I ask, is the Santrepod?'

'A group of three songs proving her triple power.'

'And why are they to be played this evening?'

'To introduce Monday, the Magicians' Day, the day of enchantment. Music is similarly used by the recorders to introduce Wednesday, the day of learning; by the captains to introduce Thursday, the day of authority; by the servants to introduce Saturday, the day of humility; and by the commons to introduce Sunday, the day of royalty. We begin our days at curfew of the previous evening.'

'What happens to Friday? And Tuesday?'

'They're not observed by any particular estate. Friday is the day of love and Tuesday is the day of war. In love, as in war, when a magician may belong to the same band as a commoner, differences of estate may occasionally be transcended.'

'Do you mean to say that on a Friday one is free to have a love-affair with a woman of a different estate?'

'Yes. Only we say it the other way about: a woman may choose a lover from a different estate.'

'And does she ever?'

'Very seldom, except for the customary union of captains and commons. "Smokes do not mix," as you know, and if for instance a woman magician falls in love with a recorder, or a recorder with a woman servant, and they form a Friday union, they're "without benefit of estate" while the union lasts. That's the subject of many of our stories, but a very awkward position to be in. When Saturday comes the lovers go to consult the Goddess, whom they must obey, whatever her orders. Sometimes she lets them off lightly; sometimes she torments them. Well, as I was saying, there'll be a Santrepod when the curfew sounds. By the way, See-a-Bird tells me that all isn't well between you and Sally. The Santrepod should remedy that.'

I stirred uneasily in my chair. 'There was a slight misunderstanding this morning,' I said. 'It was my fault, I expect. I like Sally very much,' and here I gave her what was intended for a friendly smile, but that was a mistake. Erica's arrows had penetrated deeper than I cared to admit to myself, and it must have been pretty obvious that my smile was forced. Sally may even have read my thoughts and felt that I was throwing her a bone. 'You're very generous,' she said, and stiffened noticeably.

Starfish bent down with a look of concern, removed one of her shoes and started gently kneading her foot. She sighed with satisfaction. I didn't inquire whether this was a common sedative practice among magicians, or in New Crete generally, or whether it was a peculiarity of Sally's that she liked having her feet kneaded. I never saw it done again.

With a grateful glance at Starfish I asked Sapphire whether there was any fundamental difference between the music of the various estates.

'Of course,' she said, and explained that the commons went in for part songs, military marches and dance tunes, played by fiddle, pipe and drum, and for other sorts of traditional popular music, none of it recorded in the archives: they played solely by ear and were given no formal musical education. But musical practice varied geographically, certain instruments in popular use being confined by custom to different kingdoms. I gathered that the flute belonged to what is now called France, the mandoline to Italy, the guitar and castanets to Spain, the accordion to Germany.

'Shades of Bach!' I exclaimed. 'The accordion!'

'The climate of Germany encourages spiritual pride and the accordion is the most homely of instruments.'

'And who gets the saxophone?'

But she hadn't heard of the saxophone.

The recorders, she told me, neither danced nor sang and limited themselves to piano recitals (but the New Cretan piano had a shortened keyboard) and the string quartette. Their music was intellectual and passionless in the manner of the eighteenth century; nothing happened in it—Sapphire meant that melody was jealously excluded—but they derived a great deal of satisfaction from an ingenious exploitation of musical theory. They had now taken theory far enough and acquired a sufficient body of music to satisfy their needs; their *Canon* was complete. The captains shared the music of the commons, though specializing in the trumpet. The servants chanted plain-song from a limited repertoire and played no instruments of any sort.

'What about the magicians?'

'You'll be able to judge for yourself in a moment. We don't dance and we don't have choirs and orchestras. We concentrate on pure melody and sing either to the harp or the lute; only one voice and one instrument, and never with more than four or five people present. Our musical education is rather austere; it's based on the songs in our three *Books of Music* and a close study of counterpoint.'

It was getting dark. The curtains were drawn and the candles lighted. Everyone stopped talking when Sapphire

opened a chest and took out her lute. She spoke a few words
of reverent dedication, paused for half a minute and then
began singing to it. The words were New Cretan, but, to my
surprise, the melody was Elizabethan: I recognized it at once
as 'Flow not so fast, ye Fountains' by John Dowland,

> .... whose heavenly tuch
> Upon the Lute, doeth ravish humaine sense

as Barnfield (or some say Shakespeare) wrote of him.

Sally sat completely motionless, but the men had risen and
were holding out their hands, palms outstretched, in the attitude of prayer. Knut Jensen's advice came grotesquely to my
mind. 'And remember, when they start hopping about and
wagging their genitals and rubbing mud in their hair and
rolling their eyes, you'll attract far less attention if you join in
the fun than if you just sit goggling at them and fiddling with
your note-book. Always join in the fun, old boy, always join
in the fun! It's the safest way.' I rose too, and held out my
hands. Indeed, I felt disposed to pray: Sapphire's voice and
her touch on the strings were so perfectly controlled that the
full sorrow of the music, the *lachrymae* as Dowland called
them, came welling out without distortion or loss. My eyes
soon began to smart, and I wept unashamedly, relieved that
there was no need to fight the impulse in the heroic English
manner.

She sang two more songs—the first by the celebrated
Cleopatra, very stately and scornful, but with funny little
grace-notes when least expected, called 'Heather's Mockery of
Holly' at which everyone was expected to laugh. Everyone
did laugh, including myself, because Sapphire again let the
song speak for itself. There was no need for any pantomime
business to point its dry humour.

The last song, called 'The Sleepy Lovers', was written by
Alysin, the most celebrated musician of recent times. Now, I
don't pretend to know much about music but, as Barnfield

pointed out in that very sonnet, music and poetry are 'the sister and the brother', and I find that if I apply poetic standards to music I am seldom far out in my judgements. Cleopatra's song, though of a different type from Dowland's, was of the same masterly order; but the 'Sleepy Lovers' left me unmoved. It was meant to make us feel drowsy, and Sapphire gave us the clue by smothering a yawn. Everyone but myself reacted as she intended. The three men swayed on their feet and at last sank gracefully to the floor, Sally's head dropped forward on her chest, and when finally Sapphire broke off in the middle of a bar they were all dutifully asleep.

I continued to stand with palms outstretched: an irreproachable attitude of respect to the Goddess, but a criticism of the music, which was not nearly good enough. Technically it may have been flawless, yet I felt that it was synthetic. Alysin, when he wrote the song, had not felt amorously drowsy as Dowland felt lachrymose, or Cleopatra drily humorous—he had been wide awake and industriously deducing from his memory of popular lullabies what combinations of mode, key, time and so on, have the most soporific effect. Doubtless he had invoked the Goddess in the approved style, but she was not present in the song, as she was in the other two—yes, Dowland, I remembered, had turned his back on Protestantism and returned to the Blessed Virgin for his inspiration—and I refused to be deceived. However, since everyone else, including Sapphire, had dozed off, by autosuggestion, nobody noticed my obstinate wakefulness. I decided that I could now, with propriety, return to my chair and sat there feeling rather at a loss. Instinctively, my hand went into my pocket for a cigarette.

A slight giggle aroused me. I turned round sharply and saw Erica tip toeing into the room. I waved her back wildly, but she took no notice.

'Why aren't you asleep?' she asked in a stage-whisper. 'They were playing Alysin, weren't they?'

I scowled at her. 'Yes, they were.'

'You think he's lousy?'

'I do. If I yawned at all it was from sheer boredom.'

'He's a bit of a come-down after Cleopatra, isn't he? She knew her stuff all right. Cigarette?'

'No thanks. The last two got me into plenty of trouble, so I blamed the stubs on you.'

'I ought to have warned you not to throw them all over the country-side. But why not take some of these and smoke them up the chimney when you're alone in your bedroom?'

'I don't want to risk offending my hosts; they're nice people.'

'Have it your own way; offer withdrawn. Do you mind if I smoke myself?'

'For God's sake leave me alone, woman! They'll wake up in a minute and throw five separate fits.'

'No, they won't. Not until I'm good and ready to go.'

She sat down in Fig-bread's chair and lit up. I glared at her, but she did not seem to be impressed, so I tried soft words.

'Darling,' I said, 'it's only fair to warn you that they've decided to deport you.'

'Yes, I heard about that. But why? Did you give them my dossier?'

'Only in bare outline, but even so it got them all worked up. They say you came with me when I was evoked, feloniously clinging to my hair. And for some reason or other my report on your green slippers caused quite a sensation.'

'The idiots! Now, I suppose, Sally will come along in the early morning to make a pattern around the Nonsense House and try to winkle me out.'

'What's a pattern?'

'Don't you know? She'll strip stark naked and go round the house widdershins, making funny noises. If I were you, I'd watch her at it; she's got lovely thighs and shoulders and she prowls like a tigress.'

'No, thank you. I'll be happy enough sharing a pillow with Sapphire—oh, thanks,' I added absently, accepting a cigarette and lighting it from hers. 'But I dare say you won't be at home tonight?'

'Why shouldn't I be? I've a sound-proof flat in the top storey of the house and Sally may growl and prowl all night so far as I'm concerned; *I* don't mind her trying to get rid of me. She can't be worse than a posse of Paris *flics*.'

'Why did you come to this place?' I asked.

She looked at me inscrutably and sang:

> 'There was a time when silly bees could speak
> And in that time I was a silly bee
> And fed on thyme until my heart 'gan break.'

'Another of Dowland's,' she explained, 'but the words are by the Earl of Essex. Do you think, if you stay here long enough feeding on thyme, your heart will break too? Essex went mad dog in the end and the Queen cut off his head.'

'When did you come? Will you tell me that, at least?'

'Ages ago. I told you so this morning.'

But I persisted: 'Your supply of cigarettes seems to have lasted remarkably well.'

'Do you want the address of my bootlegger?'

'No, thank you very much.' And then I realized that I was smoking, after all, and threw a perfectly good *Gauloise* into the fire.

'Have an Old Gold instead!' she said, opening her case. 'I got them specially for you. Have two, have three, have the lot!' In spite of my protests she emptied her case down the neck of my shirt.

I fished them all out and resolutely burned them. 'There's another thing I wanted to ask you, Erica,' I said. 'What's the proper name for this white coat of yours?'

'How should I know? All I can tell you is that I bought it off the peg in a shop in Princes Street, Edinburgh, years ago when I was living with Andrew—you remember Andrew? Andrew Mann, who used to write apocalyptic verse for *transition* and the *Little Magazine*. Work it out for yourself; I must be off. Good-bye, Teddy. I've got a date with a couple of elders down the lane. Now be a good boy, shut your eyes and pretend to be asleep, and I advise you not to mention my visit to a single soul. If you do, they'll think you're nuts and lock you up.'

'Good-bye, damn and blast you!'

She tiptoed out, just as Sapphire stirred in her sleep, stretched, rubbed her eyes and awoke the others.

They all seemed unaware of the interlude and I did not undeceive them nor even hint to Sally that she might catch a chill to no purpose if she made her pattern in the damp meadow. We wished one another a Happy Monday, and Sapphire and I went off to our bedroom.

We lay awake for a long time talking about the events of the day, but not touching on either Erica or the brutch. She allowed me to stroke her hair and shoulder, but went on talking meanwhile and did not betray by any change of tone that she was either satisfied or dissatisfied by my caresses. At last the conversation faded away, she laid my head in the crook of her arm again as before, and I fell asleep instantly.

The only event of the night was that just before dawn someone shook my arm and I heard Antonia say: 'Sally's just back from her pattern, Edward. She says that there's nobody at all at the Doctor's house. Isn't that good news?'

When I came to remember this the next morning, as soon as I awoke, I couldn't make sense of it. It wasn't a dream and I was sure that I had heard Antonia's voice. Yet how could Antonia have known about Sally and the pattern? Or if Antonia was now Sapphire, why should she have called it 'the Doctor's house'?

'Why did you call the Nonsense House "the Doctor's house" last night?' I asked Sapphire sharply, waking her.

She opened her eyes wide.

'But I didn't,' she said.

'Yes, you did. You said it in Antonia's voice, but you said it. You woke me up to tell me about Sally and her pattern.'

She sat up wild-eyed. 'I didn't wake you up. I said nothing at all to you after you'd gone to sleep.'

'Are you telling the truth?'

'Of course.'

'But the night before last, didn't you laugh and say something important—I can't remember what—in Antonia's voice?'

'No.'

'But *someone* did. It must have been you. It couldn't have been anyone else. You held out your arms to me.'

Sapphire turned pale. 'Someone has been playing tricks on us,' she said.

'Whom do you mean? Sally? Or is there another witch about?'

She stared at me in confusion and horror. 'Sally? But Sally is my dearest friend. Why should you think that it's Sally?'

'I'll tell you why, if you'll promise not to tell anyone else.'

She kept silent, but continued to look horrified, her mouth wide open like a child's. So I asked: 'Isn't it true that she's fallen in love with me and is madly jealous of you? It's not a nice question for a man to ask, but we must get things straight before we see her again.'

As she still kept silent, I continued: 'I'm a stranger here and don't understand your ways and couldn't say how powerful your magic is. But if someone has been playing tricks on us— and it's a woman, we know that—then everything points to Sally. She seems to have a motive, at any rate, and I don't see who else it could have been.'

I didn't suggest Erica. After all, Erica was no witch and it was absurd to suppose that she could have impersonated Antonia.

At last Sapphire said: 'We're breaking custom. We shouldn't be talking like this before breakfast. But one thing: there's been a spell around this house since dusk and it should have prevented anyone from coming in without the password which only Sally and I know. We laid the spell together on purpose to keep the brutch out.'

Should I tell her that it had been a remarkably ineffectual spell? No: I needed more time yet to get things straight in my mind.

'I must have been mistaken,' I lied soothingly. 'I must have had a particularly vivid dream. Forget all I've said.'

But I could see that this did not altogether convince Sapphire, and her manner towards Sally at breakfast and after was noticeably reserved.

CHAPTER X

Market Day at Sanjon

THIS was a Monday and my friends were bound to spend the working day in private study of poetry, music or magic. That was fortunate, I thought: it would give Sapphire a chance to commune with the Goddess before she said anything to Sally, and perhaps solve the Antonia mystery that way. After breakfast Sally told me that since we should not meet until the evening smoke, I was free to go out with the Interpreter and visit other estates, unless I wished to observe custom by remaining at home and studying.

I pointed out that I should be only wasting my time if I stayed, not being able to read the shorthand in which their books were written. Besides, I wanted to see more of the commons. So she recommended a visit to Sanjon, a few miles' walk along the coast—or what had once been the coast—where there was a market. I guessed that Sanjon must be the small town of St. Jean-des-Porcs where Antonia and I used to go by bus every Saturday to shop: it would be fun to see what the New Cretans had made of the place.

I was once again baulked by custom. The Interpreter had to go on foot because he belonged to a dismounted estate, and if I had to keep with him all the way I could not very well borrow a horse, as I had intended to do. 'No,' said Sally. 'You couldn't do that in any case. If the commons saw you on a white horse on Monday, they'd be shocked to the marrow. They'd force you to dismount and walk home.'

We started off together along the railway line. It was a very close day, but turf makes easy going and I had nothing to carry. The Interpreter wore a milkmaid's yoke on his shoulder with a capacious wicker basket hanging from each end. This had at least the advantage of preventing him from taking my arm, as politeness to a fellow-traveller would otherwise have obliged him to do. I rather like walking arm in arm with a woman, though it makes me shorten my pace uncomfortably, but to have a man linked to me in tender-hearted brotherhood embarrasses me.

'What's the yoke for?' I asked.

'I am going to buy at the market,' he said. 'I hope to find certain vegetable produce of sorts that are not raised in our own village, i.e., alligator-pears and red potatoes.'

'Buy? But I thought you used no money here?'

'That is so. But I use the word advisedly. Villagers do not go empty-fisted to Sanjon market.'

'Do you mean that they swap peas for alligator-pears, say, and baskets of strawberries for bottled beer?'

'I will explain the system. Yesterday and this morning the gondoliers have conveyed truck-loads of produce from the outlying villages to Sanjon. It is whatever the villagers find superfluous to their needs: for custom rules how much food shall be withheld for consumption in the home. At Sanjon the trucks are unloaded and their contents conveyed to the market, where all is displayed, and anyone is allowed to carry off whatever produce he happens to require. That which remains when the market closes at midday is collected and sorted by the recorders of Sanjon; and all that can be stored for future distribution, or pickled, or conserved, is handed over to the people whose obligation it is to keep the store-houses replenished; the rest goes to the pigs or poultry. Most villages are self-supporting in food, and those that are not so have some other product to offer, e.g. wool, or linen, or charcoal, or baskets, or shoes, or soap, which they send to the same market.

But no record is kept of the amount of goods that are delivered or consumed, since custom ensures that everyone shall farm according to the most enlightened principles and that no one shall lack the necessaries of life. The commons supply the other estates with the aforesaid necessaries; but these must make some token-payment, consisting of a present to the Goddess, to show that they are not "eating idle bread". In my left-hand basket I carry a gift, viz., a peacock's feather: in the right-hand, another, viz., a bunch of delphiniums. The rule is: "A gift for a gift". For this reason I use your word "buy".'

'Shall I be able to shop too? I haven't anything to give.'

'You may pay, if you please, with a poem or a prayer.'

'And in exchange for my prayer, I may help myself to whatever happens to be on sale?'

'To as much as you please. What you do not wish to carry in your arms you may leave with the gondolier to drop at our village on his return journey.'

'That's extremely generous. But don't some people get more than their fair share under this system?'

'Why should they do so? It is part of our religion never to waste food or any other product of the soil; and since there is enough to go round no one carries off more produce of a perishable sort than he needs for himself and his family until the next market day.'

'That's all very well, but it's hard to believe that religious scruple, or even commonsense, can keep a family from behaving selfishly: from grabbing more than their fair share, for example, of sugar and fruit and making a larger quantity of jam than they can eat. Jam keeps for years.'

'But why should they make more jam than they can eat?'

'To exchange for something of lasting value that can't be bought in the market—jewellery, perhaps, or silver spoons, or a china dinner-service.'

'You are right in thinking that jewellery and silver-spoons

and china are not offered for sale in the market; they are to be
had in the shopping-streets of the town from jeweller or silversmith or dishmonger.'

'But surely not free?'

'As free as fruit and sugar. If a woman needs half a dozen
silver spoons and forks when she marries, or a gold scarf-pin
if she has lost one, she needs only to define her wants and they
are satisfied. She has no hesitation in doing so. "A gift for a
gift", she will say, confident that neither the silversmith nor
the jeweller eats idle bread.'

'But if she were to ask for three dozen silver spoons and
forks?'

'Why should she want so many unless, e.g., there had been
a flood or a fire and a great number of homeless people had
come to live in her house.'

'She might merely want to be better off than her neighbours.'

'How would she be better off with three dozen silver spoons
and forks when all she needs is half a dozen? Silver must be
cleaned. It is against custom to let it tarnish.'

'Well, say half a dozen gold scarf-pins. They wouldn't
tarnish.'

'But she has need for only one.'

'Surely some women would like to wear a different scarf-
pin every day of the week?'

'Not in our midst. The scarf-pin has a design that incor-
porates the owner's nickname. She always wears the same pin
unless, perchance, she changes her name.'

'Well, then, clothes? Can a woman buy as many dresses as
she pleases?'

'She may buy the material, but she must labour at it herself,
or with the help of her neighbours. Custom rules that what
she needs and can be troubled to make for herself she may
wear, after asking the Goddess's permission at gown ceremonies held in the sixth and tenth months. But a woman of

the commons is limited to the possession of two thin Sunday gowns, two thick Sunday gowns and a gala gown, five in all, besides plain working frocks, the number of which is not limited by custom.'

'Who makes *your* clothes, by the way?'

'I make them myself.'

'I thought so.'

He took this for a compliment and looked at his oddly cut white linen suit with satisfaction. 'I have worn this and its fellow for seven years. But you should see my gala suit! It is in rain-grey linen, covered with little pearl-buttons. To-day I go to buy half a dozen more, to replace ones that have fallen away from the hinderpart.'

'What else are you buying?'

'For myself, nothing more. But I am instructed to order a pair of wrought-iron gates for our new garden; I have the measurements on a tally-stick in my pocket. The master-smith of Sanjon will wright them for me.'

'Excuse a criticism of your otherwise faultless English, but there is no such verb as "wright".'

'Indeed? But surely "wrought" is formed from "wright" as, e.g. "fought" from "fight". And, surely, one can wright many things, inclusive of plays and wheels and wains and carts?'

'Did you get this misinformation from your colleague Quant?'

'Regrettably no! Quant holds that "wrought" is formed from "wreak", so I suppose that I should have said: "The smith will wreak them for me".'

'No, Quant himself has slipped up, for once. One can't wreak gates; about the only things one can wreak are vengeance and havoc—as, by the way, one can't monger dishes, but only iron, cheese, scandal, fish and whores, but don't ask me why. "Wrought" is a very irregular past participle of "work".'

'Oh, how glad Quant will be to hear that he is proved wrong!'

'Glad?'

'Yes, overjoyed! It so seldom happens that he is wrong. As it so seldom happens that he wins a game of croquet. When he does win, we all garland him with daisies from the grass-borders.'

'Let's get back to your economic system. You say that everyone here works hard without hope of reward?'

'Sir: what greater reward could there be than the know-ledge that the Goddess approves and that one's neighbours will benefit?'

'That's all very well. What about oneself?'

'Every man is his own neighbour, *verb sap.* as Cleopatra has shrewdly said.'

'Exactly my point. Charity begins at home. What's to keep people from getting lazy and not sending enough to market?'

'It is the captains' duty to see that all goes well in that respect.'

'By waving the big stick?'

'They carry no sticks; they merely exhort to virtue and the good life.'

'I may be perverse, but at school I always preferred the master who threw the book at my head to the one who exhorted me to virtue. I think the captains are about the worst feature of your society.'

'Come! Come! As yet you know very little of our society. Captains are the friendliest and most devoted of people.'

'In a way, that makes it worse.'

But, of course, he refused to see my point. 'You cannot prefer tyrants to friends?' he asked, wide-eyed.

'No, but I prefer potshots to pijaws.' While he was trying to work this out, I asked him: 'But what would happen if the captains were to fail in keeping the commons up to scratch?'

'The magicians would then be consulted. They would diagnose the malady and prescribe a cure.'

'And if that failed, too? If there were a general malaise? If even the magicians lost their interest in maintaining the good life?'

He stopped, took off his yoke, and sat down under a service-tree. 'Excuse me, Sir,' he said, 'but I find this last question difficult to answer while walking.'

'Take your time.'

He opened and shut his mouth two or three times, as if afraid of divulging a secret, yet at the same time anxious to tell me the truth. Suddenly his eye caught something in the distance and his face lighted up. 'Look!' he said excitedly. 'Look yonder!'

'I don't see what you're pointing at.'

'Flapping through the air across the hill, with her legs stuck out behind her!' He bowed his head nine times.

'Oh, that heron. What of it?'

'It is no heron. It is a crane.'

'Well then, that crane.'

'She brings the answer to your question.'

'I'm very dense. Explain.'

'It is the Goddess.'

'The crane is your Goddess?'

'No, but evidence of her presence. When four estates fall spiritually sick and the fifth cannot heal them, the Goddess must intervene in person.'

'How? With a thunderstorm, or a flood, or an earthquake, as the gods used to do in the old days?'

'No, I tell you that she appears in person, taking whatever form she pleases. She alone is free of custom. At her first theophany she declared from an acacia-tree: "I am whatever I choose to be."'

'You mean that we might meet the Goddess walking in disguise along this railway track?'

'If we were so honoured.'

'Let's hope we recognize her at once. But I want to get this straight: briefly, what keeps your system going is the force of custom, based for the most part on inspired pronouncements of poets and reinforced by fear of the Goddess's sudden, capricious appearance?'

'Not fear alone, but love answering her love. As Cleopatra wrote, speaking in the Goddess's name:

> When water stinks I break the dam,
> In love I break it.

which is entirely different behaviour from that of the Thunder-god to whom for a while she delegated her authority. According to our *Myths of the Ancient World* he used to cause natural catastrophes in sheer ill-temper, whether the people were living virtuously or not.'

'Yes, he was a terror, wasn't he? I always think of him as M. le Générale le Vicomte de Martinbault, my former landlord, a bearded monster with the rosette of the Legion of Honour in his button-hole, who used to fling his valets downstairs when he was drunk and crunch brandy glasses until the blood from his mouth stained his dress shirt and white waistcoat: M. le Vicomte seated on a cloud, drunkenly wagging his thunderbolt, with a terrified Ganymede in white velvet plying him with more Hennessey. I'm all for Goddesses; they do at least keep the peace.'

He went on to explain that trade between kingdoms was arranged on much the same principle as trade between villages: each kingdom exported its superfluous products by sea and sent buyers to bring back in exchange whatever goods would be welcome at home. There was no bargaining; only a grateful exchange of gifts. It was a New Cretan principle that one's debt of hospitality to a stranger increased with the distance that he had travelled, so only the choicest products of a kingdom were considered good enough for export. Apparently the system worked well enough, I suppose because the world population had been stabilized at a sensible figure and there were no shortages of food or metals or textiles or labour—and, of course, no bills or receipts or ledgers or customs or tariffs or taxes or trade balances or any other technical obstacles to free exchange of superfluities. Economically speaking, it was the unsoundest system ever invented: it did not even provide for the study of economics, being wholly without statistics.

As we rested, a party of five villagers, two women and three men, overtook us. They were in holiday dress; the women walking ahead, the men, with yokes on their shoulders, following in single file. They were singing a melancholy catch about the sorrows of love, but broke off when they saw us and called out a greeting. Evidently they knew who I was, because one of the men said: 'I deny that he's a phantom, sister—I can't see through him!' and the leading woman reproached him: 'Silence! He's said to understand our language.' They would have stopped, but the Interpreter signed to them that we were engaged in an important conversation, so they passed on, but turned about and walked backwards, still watching us, until they passed out of sight around a curve. Their baskets were full of small scarlet radishes.

'They are from Rabnon,' said the Interpreter. 'Good people, but very hot-blooded and so amorous that their football team spend the half-time interval in bed with their sweethearts, when the match is an important one.'

'Do you mean: "even when the match is an important one"?'

But he shook his head blankly. 'No, I do not.' Then he said: 'When we reach the town I fear you will be the cynosure of every eye unless you protect yourself by disappearance.'

'That sounds a useful trick. How is it done?'

He took a small stick of grease-paint from one of his many pockets and drew something on my forehead.

'What's this?' I asked.

'It is a mouth with a protruding tongue, the sign that we use for "Look away!" If a man is in grief, or in deep thought, or does not feel well enough to converse with those whom he may meet, he puts this sign on his forehead and disappears, for nobody dares pay attention to him while he is so marked.'

'Excellent! I must try to introduce that custom into my age when I get back.'

He rose, resumed his yoke, and we went on. I commented on the kitchen-garden richness of the fields. 'Nothing is ever taken from the soil without subsequent restoration,' the Interpreter said. 'What all but destroyed the human race in your epoch was the sewage system. Half the population of the world lived in big towns; the other half provided them with food in exchange for manufactured goods. The food, in the form of excrement, flowed down the sewers to the sea, and was lost. The fields were given artificial fertilizers in exchange and in process of time became denatured. There followed a shortage of food, which made for wars; and the wars did further damage to the soil. It was the Sophocrats who first realized that the greatest enemies of the human race were three: viz. the water-closet and incinerator which robbed the earth of its richness, and the tractor which enabled farmers to plough up and turn into desert a vast acreage of inferior land that should have been relinquished to grass or forest in the Goddess's honour. But they left it to us to embody the principle of soil-worship in our religion. We boast that with every new generation the top-soil grows blacker and deeper.' His lecture on agricultural customs continued until we reached the end of the line. Apparently the New Cretan farmers had much in common with the Moors of Granada, the most enlightened husbandmen of the middle ages, whose work the Spanish Christians wrecked with such fanatic zeal; and New Crete had also been fortunate enough to inherit the best strains of fruits, fodder and vegetables from the intervening scientific age. But some of their methods seemed to me perversely old-fashioned. I challenged the Interpreter's praise of the ox as a draught-beast, though as usual he quoted an ungainsayable authority, this time a fairly modern poet called Dodet:

> The ox though slow
> Is willing and unwearied.
> His pace keeps time
> With the Earth's breathing.
> Strong are his shoulders,
> Sweet his breath,
> Richly he dungs the fields.

'But the horse is a much better farm-animal in every way,' I said.

'Horses are reserved for captains and magicians to ride upon,' he said stiffly. 'Would you dare put a horse between the shafts of a hay-wain? A horse, indeed! The idea!'

He went on muttering indignantly to himself: 'The very idea! Horse—hay-wain!'

The town of Sanjon—when we came to it—was smaller, neater, and built higher up the hill than in the old days. It was also a great deal cleaner, and the Alys, the stream that ran through it, looked surprisingly drinkable. The filthy French habit of throwing every sort of rubbish and refuse into streams had been given up for religious reasons. Running water was particularly sacred to the Goddess. But when we climbed the hill I missed the yellow brick railway station, the police-barracks, the Cinéma Moderne, the cement works, the soda-water factory, the church of St. Nicholas with its over-crowded cemetery, the fourteenth-century Château, and the Departement Lunatic Asylum, which had all contributed to the rich, muddled charm of St. Jean-des-Porcs. However, we passed a magnificent football field and the Interpreter told me that since games had been brought within the framework of religion, Rugby football had become an obsession of the commons. 'There can't be much wrong with a place where Rugger's played serious-ly,' I reassured myself. Nor could I quarrel with the archi-tecture of the houses in the streets and squares. They were solid and well-proportioned, built in the local stone without meaningless excrescences or *petit bourgeois fantaisie*. No two of them were alike and, since the commons could not read, every front door had its painted sign-board, or carved figurehead, or group of statuary.

The symbol on my forehead was so effective that on my way to market I had to be continually dodging stupid people who would otherwise have tried to walk through me. The market itself suggested a flower show held in a church. All sorts of wonderful fruit and vegetables were artisti-cally heaped in painted stalls; but since there were no prizes, no prices, no bargaining and no competition, and since the people in charge of the stalls were public servants, not the owners, and had nothing to do but to replenish stocks as they were exhausted, the dramatic element was lacking. We buyers went in at one door, leaving our gifts at a con-venient shrine near the vaulted entrance, drifted round with our baskets, silently helping ourselves to whatever we wanted, not even taking the trouble to weigh our purchases; and when we had completed the circuit, came out again. The procedure recalled that of an American super-market, except that when we left no watchful accountant stopped us at the gate to add up our purchases and collect our cash. Personally, I disliked haggling over *centimes* with vegetable sellers. I had always left that to Antonia, who was good at it, while I bought at the *prix-fixe* stalls. But I disliked still more the feeling of getting things free; it made me feel as though my personal liberty were threatened.

No, the market was not nearly as lively as it had once

been. Where was the Veuve Koko, the pox-scarred old woman who used to bring a pet monkey and a Bombay duck with her, to help sell her late husband's patent medicines? Where was the lame boy, Le Petit Vulcain, who sold fireworks and mechanical toys? Where was Old Monsieur Démosthène with his boxes of second-hand books, and his pretty grand-daughter selling papers at the kiosque? New Cretan custom had done away with them all. On the other hand, it had done away with congenital idiots, drunkards, stray dogs, policemen, dirt, smells, fist-fights and knee-length *pissoirs* plastered with advertisements for anti-syphilitic compounds. Still. . . .

Silently I helped the Interpreter fill his baskets, and silently followed him out of the market to the Refectory Square, set with a couple of hundred tables, where visitors from the villages were provided by public servants with free lager and pretzels. We sat down at a table and listened to the extraordinarily polite and musical conversation around us; but the only subject that had ever really interested the people of St. Jean in the old bad days, money and prices, did not come up now, and though farmers exchanged information about the weather, the hay harvest, and pigs, their remarks had little edge to them. Not even when yesterday's hard-fought Rugger match and the captains' horse-race came up for discussion; because in a moneyless world there is, of course, no betting.

I had never before realized how much I enjoyed spending money; I always prided myself on having a soul above it. Though intellectually I agreed with the New Cretans that the supersession of the religious motive by the profit motive in human dealings had been a disaster of the first magnitude, emotionally I agreed with the Fool in the Old English Christmas Play who cried to his sons Pickle-herring, Pepper-breeches and Ginger-breeches: 'Boys, times are hard! I love to have money in both pockets!'

Yet what dignified old men and women, what serene girls, what handsome, courteous young men were seated all around me at their lager and pretzels. My great-great-etc.-etc.-grandchildren, bless their hearts. Human equivalents of the prize exhibits artistically grouped on the market stalls. I remembered Coleridge's lines:

> And though inveterate rogues we be,
> We'll have a virtuous progeny
> And on the dung-hill of our vices
> Raise human pineapples and spices.

'Let's be going home,' I said to the Interpreter. 'I feel unworthy to drink in company like this.'

He went off to buy his pearlies and order his wrought-iron gates, while I looked in at the windows of a china-shop and a jeweller's. It was a relief to see new things for sale not mass-produced to a mean and conscienceless design; in my age anyone with sensibility had been forced to shop in the past. If only I could buy that little dove-in-bush pendant, or that oval gold brooch with the red and green enamel inlay, and take it back with me as a present to Antonia. Red and green, should never be seen, except upon an Irish Queen. Antonia, who is Irish, though not particularly queenly, has a sincere passion for red and green in which I always humour her. Or that splendid Spanish-looking plate striped in yellow, blue and chocolate with the sailing ship in the middle and the three tunny-fish sporting around it! She'd simply love that. But when the Interpreter appeared, he told me that they were designed for the commons. I gathered that, as a poet, I was not supposed to admire them.

As we passed the football field on our way home, taking turns to carry the yoke, a match was about to start. The players were naked except for coloured shorts and wore no

5

boots. The visiting team, in daffodil yellow, were singing a familiar hymn in honour of the Goddess as they tossed the ball from one to the other.

'Why do you laugh?' asked the Interpreter.

'For pleasure,' I answered. 'The best match I ever watched was at Murrayfield, near Edinburgh, when Wales beat Scotland by a dropped goal to a try on the stickiest ground you ever saw. The visitors sang "O Land of our Fathers" too.'

'"O Land of our Mother, the footballers' Queen",' he corrected me. 'But do not dally here unless you wish to see the match out. It is not respectful to stay only for a short time. . . .'

On we went.

'What's the population of Sanjon now?' I asked after a while.

'That is a question which you should not ask, even if I could answer it.'

'Why?'

'It is most unlucky to make a count of heads, or even an approximation to a count. E.g., we never say "a crowd of about a thousand people." We say: "about as many people as would fill Sanjon church". What the poet Vives wrote long ago has acquired legislative force. His *Satire on Numbers* begins:

> To count heads was a felony.
> It was to give each man a number
> And rob him of his name,
> The name that was his soul.
> When all were known by numbers,
> Behold a featureless mass,
> Each face a hapless zero,
> Filled with the blind emotion
> Of collectivity!

Vives had come to a sensible solution, viz., that the most destructive social force of past epochs had been a mass emotion that exhibited itself in nationalism, fascism, communism, neo-communism, pantisocratism, logicalism and so on, and which was derived from thinking in terms of collective interests rather than of individual ones. In periods when the rich man oppressed his poor neighbours, who cried out in vain for justice, these collective interests had seemed more virtuous than individual ones, and it had also seemed necessary to count heads to demonstrate that these poor people greatly outnumbered the rich and were therefore deserving of consideration. But once people accepted the principle, viz. that the individual, whether rich or poor, must subordinate himself to the million-fold State, regarded as the repository of collective interests, then, Sir, everything went awry. Since this State was a social not a religious concept, and based upon law not upon love, it had no natural cohesion. It was too unwieldy an aggregate of diverse and unrelated elements for any single person to comprehend it; and therefore only charlatans came forward to govern it:

> Charlatans came forward,
> Boldly adopting titles
> Of mathematic virtue.
> Square Root of Minus One
> Proclaimed himself Dictator
> And swelled a private grudge
> By arithmetical progression
> Into a mad crusade.

Thus through Vives's influence our world has been kept as a network of small communities where everyone is known to his neighbour by nickname and face, and no count of heads is ever taken. States exist only in so far as these communities are bound to one another by common ties of custom and acknowledge the same king.'

'But you count the number of districts and regions and kingdoms?'

'As we count the days of a month or the stitches in a row of knitting. But people must not be counted, except as one is aware, without enumeration, of how many people are present in a room. Thus, not being headless millions but known individuals with names, we are swayed by no passionate political or economic theory, as in your epoch. Only local events stir our emotions.'

'There goes that crane again,' I said. 'Look, it's flying up the mill stream and, wait!—yes—it's perched on the roof of the Nonsense House. What does that mean?'

The Interpreter's face was grey with alarm. 'Oh dear, oh dear, oh dear!' he said, bowing like a marionette. 'Oh my good Sir, I hope that the Goddess's heart shall prove to be merciful!'

I tried to find out what all the fuss was about, but he grew incoherent in his distress, and when we reached the bridge he sat on the parapet with his head buried in his hands.

'Can I help you up the hill with the yoke?' I asked. He only stared back at me miserably, as though he had never seen me before in his life, so I said goodbye and returned to the Magic House, where the servants brought me a solitary lunch of bread, cheese and salad.

Afterwards I tried to write a poem in my head, but found that without pen and paper I couldn't get past the first three lines.

CHAPTER XI

War is Declared

My friends seemed subdued and pale when they came in for the evening-smoke, especially Sapphire, but I put that down to their exhausting studies. I was greeted as warmly as usual.

'How did you like Sanjon?' asked See-a-Bird, when the cigarette stubs had been burned.

'It's perfect in its way,' I said, without much enthusiasm. 'If I were an elderly ex-army officer with an inadequate pension, who never read nor smoked, and avoided the company of other elderly ex-army officers, and set great store on good manners and cheerfulness, and liked his pint of beer in the sun, and made a hobby of studying native customs, I suppose Sanjon would suit me down to the ground. . . . How did your studies go?'

See-a-Bird shook his head resignedly. 'A small cloud obscured the sun in the middle of the morning and pursued it across the sky all day.'

'That's why I failed to compose the last line of my poem,' added Fig-bread sadly. 'I'd hoped to be favoured today; it has eluded me Monday after Monday ever since mid-winter.'

'How long is your poem?'

'The customary five lines. In these days of peace, we never attempt poems of greater length. It's about stars seen through the branches of an olive-tree.'

'None of us made any headway,' said Starfish. 'My strings were out of tune; the Goddess withheld her presence.'

Sally frowned. 'It would have been stupid to expect any-thing else, with this trouble in the house,' she said.

'Is anyone ill?' I asked.

'No one is ill, Nimuë be praised!'

'Servant trouble?'

'The servants never give trouble: they alleviate it.'

I looked searchingly at their faces. Sally's was indignant, See-a-Bird's worried but kindly, Fig-bread's plainly scared, Starfish's excited, and Sapphire's utterly miserable.

I thought it was my duty as a guest to put them at their ease. 'Well, you *are* a glum-looking lot,' I said teasingly. 'You look like relatives at a French funeral when the lawyer has just broken the news to them that the old girl has left all her money to the young curé with the lisp.'

Nobody so much as smiled politely.

I turned to Sapphire: 'I suppose, darling, I ought to have brought you a present from Sanjon,' I said nervously. 'Some sort of a jewel. There were some really lovely things in the shops. But the Interpreter told me that I'd have to pay with a prayer or a poem and, though I suppose the Goddess would have accepted one in English, I didn't want to risk offending the priest on duty, so I kept quiet. In any case, I had no idea what you'd like: I might have brought you something alto-gether unsuitable. You're all so conventional here in matters of taste.'

'Not all of us,' said Sally, carefully not looking at Sapphire.

'Do, for Heaven's sake, tell me what's wrong with every-one this evening,' I said in exasperation. 'Has the brutch returned?'

Sally signed to the others that she wanted to make the dis-closure herself without interruption; but she had hardly said three words when a servant came in with a verbal message, which he repeated a second time to make sure that he had delivered it correctly. It was a request for them all to ride out at once to the village green at Rabnon and assist at a Council of Five Estates.

'Whatever's happening there?' I asked.

See-a-Bird said: 'Probably the war about which we were telling you will now break out. Between Rabnon, the next village but one up the railway line, and Zapmor, which lies half-way between us and the sea. I'm afraid we can't very well refuse to go, though the request comes at a most inconvenient moment. Would you care to come with us?'

So the disclosure was postponed.

They lent me a horse and we set off at once. As we trotted along the tree-shaded bridle path to Rabnon, Starfish cleared his throat and began: 'Part the First—Rabnon is a gay, red-tiled, green-shuttered, polyandrous village—'

'Famed for its radishes and its hot blood?' I put in.

'Yes, that's well said—and Zapmor is a dour, slate-roofed, brown-shuttered, monogamous village, famed for its manufacture of square-toed shoes.'

This was his story. Three little boys had run away from their homes at Zapmor one evening about a fortnight before and were found wandering in a wood near Rabnon long after supper-time. When questioned, they said that they did not want to go home for supper.

'But why not?' asked the Rabnon woodman who had found them. 'Are your parents not kind to you?'

They shrugged their shoulders politely.

What was it then?

It appeared that they were always given the same supper of bread and milk and damson jam, and that they were sick to death of it.

Rabnon sent a runner to Zapmor at once with a message that the boys were safe, and would be brought back after they had been fed. They were given tea, cheese-straws, lettuce and radishes, and taken home happy and overfed just before midnight. End of Part the First.

Part the Second. A week later at supper-time the boys turned up again in Rabnon village at the house where they had been fed before. 'What, damson jam for supper again?'

'Yes, always the same damson jam.'

'Do you like it any better now?'

'It comes out of our ears when we eat.'

Then their parents had not taken the hint! They must now be made to realize the seriousness of the situation. Rabnon brooded over the affair for a week and then called the Council of Five Estates to which, as the nearest neutral magicians, we were now invited.

'End of Part the Second,' said Starfish, and fell silent again.

'If I may be allowed to make a comment,' I said, 'without prejudice to the deliberations of the Council, the story sounds a bit fishy to me.'

'What do you mean by that?'

'Little boys are conservative about food; if it were a case of a single problem child with a grudge, that would make sense, but three is too many.'

'As a visitor you won't be able to bring this up at the Council, I fear.'

'Perhaps someone else will.'

Part the Third. We found all Rabnon assembled on the green, squatting in a semi-circle in front of the totem-pole, and talking in low voices, the elders seated on rush-bottomed chairs at the back. An austere-looking priest in a white robe, golden sash and scarlet cloak, broke a branch from a tree and walked round the inside of the semi-circle sprinkling everyone with water from a green-glazed pot. When a part-song in honour of the Goddess had been sung, business was opened by the local captain, who pointed with his thumb at a man called Hammer-toes. 'Speak!' he said, curtly.

Hammer-toes was the woodman. He sprang to his feet and gave an impassioned account of how he had found the boys

wandering in his wood, eating dewberries. He reported the
ensuing dialogue dramatically, using deep solemn tones for
his own questions and a squeaky little voice for the boys'
guarded answers. His main refrain was 'damson jam', more
and more passionately repeated.

Other witnesses were called in turn, until the whole story
had been told. A long silence that followed was broken at
last by Open-please, the tall, loose-jointed Rabnon goal-
keeper, who said in a ruminative voice: 'Damson jam is good
when you eat it two or three evenings of the week. En-
thusiasts may even say "four evenings".'

When this remark had been well pondered, a fat, jolly
woman in a partridge-feather hat slapped her thighs decisively
and said: 'It's a shame when boys have to leave their homes at
supper-time to go berrying in the woods; a shame on the
whole neighbourhood! Has anything like this ever happened
here in Rabnon?'

No answer. Obviously nothing quite like this had ever
happened in Rabnon.

Presently an old man called Randy, who looked venerable
enough to be an elder but was still the most incorrigible play-
boy of the village, introduced the topic that nobody had yet
ventured to discuss. 'At Green Hill, in my grandmother's day,
a war was fought for less provocation than this.'

The captain pointed to the Chief Recorder, who rose to
give a rapid, passionless summary of the Green Hill War
which had been fought because of a howling dog. Randy
supplemented this with salacious by-play, greeted by ripples
of laughter. The captain then called for order, and pointed to
a pretty, pig-tailed girl called Peaches, who rose and said
sadly: 'There's much danger in war, both for those who
declare it and for those on whom it is declared.'

The fat woman with the partridge-feather hat took her up:
'It's a worse danger, by far, to let still waters rot.'

'Personally, rather than cause my parents trouble,' Peaches
5*

continued, 'I should have been content merely with bread and milk on evenings when I grew tired of damson jam.'

Here Peaches' mother broke in: 'You forget, my dear, how difficult it was to feed you as a child. You wouldn't eat vegetables or fruit or even sweets unless I sat over you with a spoon for hours. You even disliked radishes and cheese-straws.' There was general laughter, in which Peaches joined. The tension relaxed, the captain sat down and meditatively polished his finger-nails; presently people began to chat about football and skittles. The elders hobbled home.

'Is that all?' I asked in disappointment.

'What more do you want?' Sally snapped.

'I expected them to decide whether to declare war or not.'

'But they did decide.'

'When?'

'When Peaches' mother had spoken.'

'But there was no show of hands or anything of the sort.'

'And why should anyone show his hands?'

I explained the system of majority voting in English parish councils.

'Didn't you tell us yesterday that in your country hardly one person in five is well enough educated to think sensibly on a political problem? This means that, whenever you take a show of hands, the minority is more likely to be right than the majority? And in any case, I don't see how a parish council can hope to get any decision properly carried out when the voting shows that it's not wholeheartedly reached. Just now, if even a single person, for whatever reason, had stood out against Randy's proposal it would have been dropped at once. We all know that unless a village is unanimous in its declaration of war, it's beaten before the fighting begins.'

'But how was the decision taken?'

'Didn't you feel it? As soon as they laughed, discussion

naturally ended. There was no more to be said. Unless Zapmor owns itself in the wrong the war will start at dawn. We
always fight our wars on Tuesdays.'

'Does it ever happen that one kingdom declares war on
another?' I asked.

'Certainly not. Only neighbours know each other well
enough to go to war. The inhabitants of one kingdom are
complete strangers to those of another, and even within a
kingdom the neighbourly ties between district and district
are not strong enough to allow for warfare on a large scale.
It is a pity, because war on a large scale would be great
fun.'

Then the captain announced that the formal declaration was
to be made the same night. I asked Sapphire whether I might
attend the ceremony. I wanted to get away from the tense
and uncomfortable atmosphere of the sitting-room, and pretended not to notice the obvious reluctance with which she
gave me leave.

'You'll get very little sleep if you go, unless you're prepared to miss the opening stage of the war,' she said.

'If you don't mind, I'd like to see it through from beginning
to end.'

When Starfish volunteered to come with me, the others
rode home. I sounded him about the trouble, but he said that
his lips were sealed. All I gathered was that it concerned
Sapphire. Well, if so, I preferred to hear her account before
Sally said her piece.

After about half an hour's preparation, the fighting men of
Rabnon, headed by the captain, the football team, the barber,
and various other people of importance in the village, marched
off in single file towards Zapmor, with banners and pennants
flying. Every fifth man carried a lighted torch and all wore
their gala-clothes of slashed silk. A bugle band played a
familiar march; I forget its name, but the words that go with
it in our epoch are:

Here comes the Boys' Brigade,
All smothered in marmalade,
With a tuppenny-ha'penny pill-box
And a yard-and-a-half of braid.
Pum! Pum! Pum!
Pum! Pum! Pum!

There was a great deal of shouting, cheering and good-natured banter, at which the village priest who brought up the rear of the procession smiled absently, crossing himself every now and then. Starfish and I walked our horses behind at a discreet distance.

When, half an hour later, we halted at the Zapmor border, Rabnon began to bang drums and blow conches, until the fighting men of Zapmor, who had been warned what to expect, came marching up to meet them, in gala-clothes of black velvet. The rival priests advanced towards each other, kissed and exchanged gifts—a statuette of the Goddess with a radish clasped in both hands against one of the Goddess bending down to admire her square-toed black shoes—while a hymn of universal friendship was sung in unison by both villages.

The Zapmor barber—the barbers were also the village spokesmen—then inquired politely: 'Why have you brought drums and conches to this border, dear radish-growing friends?'

'Kind shoemakers,' the Rabnon barber answered, 'the conches are blown to ask a question to which, of course, you need not reply: "Is damson jam still pleasant to eat on the seventh evening of seven?" '

'This is a question that we are proud to answer. Its taste grows upon the eater: damson jam is better even on the forty-ninth evening of forty-nine.'

'But three little boys of your village do not seem to be of that opinion.'

'They were attracted by the reputation of your radishes and

cheese-straws. When they returned, we feared that they might leave us altogether, seduced from our austere village custom by your delicate living. We tried to persuade them that damson jam is the best of all, and that the more one eats it, the sharper grows one's appetite for it.'

'But did you succeed in this?'

'We have not yet given up hope. A custom of ancient standing cannot be lightly broken.'

'But is it not a somewhat loveless custom?'

'We cannot possibly accept that view. Zapmor is a nest of constant and enduring love.'

There was no more to be said. As soon as it was clear that Zapmor stood firm, the Rabnon priest returned the gift of friendship with the formula: 'Brother, at daybreak there will be war between your village and ours. Guard your bridges and your cross-roads, and keep your children safely at the upper windows of your houses.'

The rival captains now discussed the limits of the fighting, what orchards and fields were out of bounds for agricultural reasons and how long a truce was to be observed at midday and at the hour of afternoon prayer. They also decided at what commanding points the district recorders should be stationed, and how many magicians would be needed to part combatants who were carried away by the excitement of the battle.

As soon as all this had been amicably settled, the Rabnon conches blared again, but no answering blare came from Zapmor; the Rabnon men performed a wild war dance, brandishing imaginary weapons and making hideous grimaces at their opponents, who saluted nonchalantly, turned their backs and stalked away.

When I got home at about half-past-eleven there was nobody in the sitting-room. I found Sapphire in the bedroom, seated swollen-eyed and miserable in an arm-chair.

'Sapphire! My poor darling!'

'It's a blessing to have you back,' she said. 'I did so badly want to talk to you, but you wouldn't take my hint. This has been a horrible day for me—the worst of my whole life.'

'What on earth happened?' I asked. 'You haven't quarrelled with Sally?'

'Of course not. We never quarrel here. But just after you went off to Sanjon I asked her if she could explain the midnight haunting in our bedroom, and she said that she knew nothing about your Antonia but that she wasn't surprised if queer things were happening; and she asked me whether I hadn't been rather rash to admit so crude a person as yourself to my bed. "Wouldn't you have done the same if he had said he loved you?" I asked her. She flushed, but I didn't mean to hurt her feelings any more than she meant to hurt mine.'

'I'm sure of it, beautiful. I can't imagine you being catty— only as saying things in perfect innocence that would raise blisters on the most leathery face. What happened then?'

'She asked whether she might divine for trouble before we went off to our studies; and of course, I said yes, though really I should have done the divining myself, since it was in my own bedroom. So she put on her witch robe and fetched a blackthorn trouble-diviner from the herbary and peeled it. Then she came in and balanced it on her forefinger and said the necessary prayers. Presently it began to revolve. It revolved three times and when it came to rest the thin end pointed at that cupboard in the wall, just above your head. That's where I lock up my most private possessions: my crystal ball, my silver plates, my jewel of the month and the nine secret objects given me at my initiation. I said: "Sally, quick, give the thing to me!" not believing my eyes. She gave it to me with a curious look on her face. I repeated the prayers and when I put the diviner on my forefinger it revolved at once and pointed at the cupboard again. She asked: "What's in there, Sapphire? Do you know?" And I told her: "Oh, only my silver plates and my sacred things." "Well," she said, "if there's trouble in that cupboard, it's there with your connivance. There's only one key and you wear it around your neck." '

'I said: "Yes, of course, Sally, it's my cupboard. Leave this to me, please." She went out, and when I unlocked the cupboard and found what was in it, I felt quite sick: it was so horrible. I gave a shriek and Sally came in at once—she must have been waiting outside—and saw what it was. I'll never forget how she looked at me.'

'Now, before you go any further, Sapphire,' I said, 'you must understand that I've not been at your cupboard and know absolutely nothing about the whole business.'

'Of course you don't, my love. Whatever anyone may say, this has nothing whatever to do with you.'

'But what exactly was this horrible find?'

'It's there,' she said, pointing with a gesture of loathing to a sort of china dish-cover with three ugly faces painted on it, lying on a table in a far corner of the room.

'What, that cover?'

'No: the thing underneath it. I put the Three Ugly Faces over it as a prophylactic, until I could speak to you about it. Lift the cover, have a look, then put it back at once, please.'

I went over to the table, and gingerly lifted the cover by its snake handle. Then I burst out laughing. 'Well, I'll be damned!' I said. 'What an anti-climax! How on earth did Erica manage to plant this on you?'

'Erica? The brutch woman?'

'Erica Yvonne Turner, about whom I've told you quite enough already. It's her nasty little cigarette case.'

I picked it up carelessly and opened it. It was the one she had been using the night before: dingy white metal with a very stiff clasp and an appliqué design in stamped brass of a leering nude squeezing milk from one of her breasts into an outsize champagne glass. Inside were twelve cigarettes.

'She must have meant these for me,' I said. 'She knows I like Old Golds. Yes, isn't it an evil-looking object? It made me feel queer too when I saw it first. I can tell you all about it. There was a time when I thought Erica wonderful and used to give her the most expensive presents I could afford: one of them was a chaste gold cigarette case from a London jeweller's called Cartier's. I gave it to her at Marseilles, when we were just going off to Algiers. "Thank you, Teddy," she said. "I can always raise two or three hundred dollars on this heirloom. But it's not like me, really. You've got me all wrong; I'm not an English gentlewoman." That afternoon she went down to the Basin and bought that horror at a shop in the negro quarter. "Yes, isn't it deliciously appalling?" she said. "But exactly like me, the real me. The merciless vulgarity is American; the simpering obscenity is French." She always carried it about after that, just for spite. I never saw the gold case again; she probably gave it to a dead-beat called Emile.'

'But how and when can she have come into my bedroom and put the case in my cupboard?'

'I don't know for sure. My best guess is that she did it when you'd sent yourself to sleep at the end of the Santrepod. Anyhow, don't take it so personally. The joke's on me. She offered me a caseful of cigarettes when we last met, and I refused them.'

'But, my love, you don't seem to realize what this means!'

'If you want me to get rid of the case, that's simple. It doesn't horrify me in the least; I've known it too long for that. Tomorrow I'll ride down to the sea—no, tomorrow's the war—very well, early the day after tomorrow, and drop it in. "The sea cleanses all"—didn't I hear one of you quote that from some poet or other? I don't suppose the horse will buck, and anyhow you'll probably give me a charm against that. When I get home you can pour rose-water over my hands, and that will be that.'

'But you don't realize in the least what it means. It means that I'm disgraced for ever. By having had that horrible thing locked in my cupboard I forfeit the respect of the entire estate; my only course now is to go off and die.'

'Nonsense, you didn't put it there yourself and you dislike it as much as anyone.'

'No, but my magic failed me. It failed me completely.'

'If it comes to that, so did Sally's. She needn't behave so virtuously. It was her job as much as yours to keep this house free of brutches. Look here, darling, take things easy. It's absurd to talk about dying, just because a devious-minded slut with whom I used to be in love ages ago has decided to play a schoolgirl trick on you. I'll break her neck if I see her again, you see if I don't. She's the sort that hates to see a discarded lover of hers happily paired with someone else; especially with someone obviously better-looking than herself. Blow your nose, bathe your eyes and promise me that you'll not talk about going away until I've had a chance to settle things with her myself!'

'Very well, I promise,' she said meekly. 'I'm sorry I look so awful. I was past caring. But who *is* she?'

'I've told you.'

'You can't have told me everything, because if she's just an evil woman of your epoch, how did she get here and how does she perform her magic?'

'Not being in the know, I can't explain technicalities of this sort. And if you can't either—well, then, I suppose all that you can do is to consult your Goddess. She was visiting the village in person just as the Interpreter and I came back from Sanjon.'

'Edward, don't blaspheme!'

'Darling, I'm doing nothing of the sort. She flew up the mill-stream in the form of a crane with her grey legs sticking out behind her, and perched on the Nonsense House roof. Unfortunately a tree was in the way, so I couldn't see what she did there; but I don't think she flew off and when we came up she'd gone. The Interpreter got all worked up and . . . .'

But Sapphire had fallen back in a faint. I put her to bed and then knocked up Sally, who came out of her room wide awake and fully dressed.

'What's wrong?' she asked coldly.

'Sapphire's fainted.'

'That's no affair of mine. You brought this trouble on her. It's your duty to remove it.'

Then I lost my temper. 'No, Sally, you won't evade your responsibilities so easily as that. It was you who brought me here, and it was you who threw me into Sapphire's arms, and it was your job to lay the brutch. She's your best friend, and this world of yours is supposed to be ruled by principles of perfect love. If you don't come along at once and put things straight, I'll compose such a biting satire on you—in English, but none the less effective for that—that your nose will peel and your hair fall out in handfuls. Sapphire's good—'

She interrupted me: 'No good woman keeps obscenities in her cupboard.'

'But she's the victim of a bad joke.'

'No good woman is ever victimized.'

'We'll soon see about that. And if you don't go along at once and fetch Sapphire out of her faint I'll tell everyone that you planted that cigarette case on her yourself.'

She smiled contemptuously, rang for a woman servant and when she appeared gave her brief instructions for treating Sapphire. Then she said 'Good night', and strolled back to her room.

I could have strangled her. But instead I quickly wrapped the cigarette case in my handkerchief, and handed it to the servant, not letting her see what it was. 'When you make Sally's bed tomorrow morning, please put this under her pillow,' I said casually. 'It's a poetic gift.'

She pocketed it without comment, nodded, fetched restoratives from somewhere downstairs, and then signed to me that I should leave her alone with Sapphire.

When I was admitted again, Sapphire had regained her colour and something of her serene beauty. She was fast asleep and breathing normally.

'The Nymph will not wake until midday tomorrow,' said the servant, 'unless she's disturbed.'

I thanked her, and she went away with a respectful 'good night'.

Then I undressed, lay down beside Sapphire and studied her lovely childish face by candlelight. Somehow I felt that she was miscast as a magician; obviously, she had talent and intuition and was absolutely sincere, and had studied hard, but was that enough? Magic demanded duplicity, not simplicity. Sally now. . . . But was I being honest with myself? Was Sapphire's attraction for me merely physical, despite the mysterious inner compunction that prevented me from wanting her in the ordinary way? We had no jokes, no 'little language', no small talk and no experiences or old friends in common, yet when I had come upon her crying in the arm-chair I had felt absurdly touched. . . . What was that version of the *Song of Solomon* that the B.N.C. rowing men used to bawl at bump-suppers to the tune of *Come, All Ye Little Children*?

> Why were you born so beautiful?
>   Where did you get those eyes?
> Your nose is straight, your lips are full,
>   Your teeth would win a prize.
> Your belly's like a heap of wheat,
>   Your breasts like two young roes.
> O come to bed with me, my sweet,
>   And take off all your clo'es!

How simple love was for Solomon or a rowing blue! But I did not feel like that about Sapphire, and she would not have accepted me if I had: on the contrary, she counted on me as a poet to take wing and soar with her in spirit to a psycho-erotic seventh heaven far above my reach. I was in a thoroughly false position. Now, to make things worse, she was in trouble, in very bad trouble; and, indirectly, on my account. She groaned and muttered something in her sleep, and another rush of tenderness overcame me.

'Don't you worry, darling,' I whispered, 'I may not be a magician, but I'm damned if I'll allow anyone to ill-treat you while I'm still about.'

CHAPTER XII

Battle is Joined

SEE-A-BIRD, Fig-bread, Starfish and I, all mounted, reached the boundary between the two villages as dawn was breaking. I had felt little compunction about leaving Sapphire; apparently all was well until noon, when I would ride home to see how she was.

We found the rival armies marshalled in irregular ranks, already confronting each other. 'A very fine body of men,' I found myself saying to Starfish, professionally, 'and under a good sergeant-major they should make an even better show. Don't you go in for drill here?' But that was another of my stupid questions. Village warfare, it turned out, had more in common with the Old English game of Shrove-tide football than with war as I knew it. The fighting men, whose ages ranged from sixteen to sixty, were all well greased and naked except for leather breeches, gauntlets, mocassins and round leather helmets, and armed only with a light quarter-staff padded at one end. Rabnon, who outnumbered Zapmor by about three to two, were stained all over with a crimson and white criss-cross; Zapmor were patched irregularly with red ochre and had blackened their faces with burnt cork.

The sun rose above the eastern hills, a trumpet blew, and the priests approached each other solemnly, as at the previous ceremony. Rabnon's priest, holding up a painted bunch of wooden damsons, declaimed: 'Brother, this is our war-token. With the Goddess's aid, we shall carry it over your village green.'

The Zapmor priest replied in antiphony: 'With the Goddess's aid, we shall send it back whence it came.'

'The war-token is a symbol of the conflict,' Fig-bread explained. 'Rabnon intends to carry it by force or subterfuge across the boundary into Zapmor territory. You remember our own totem-pole with the wide-mouthed godling at its base, and the similar one on the Rabnon green? Every village has its godling, and reveres him as the personal genius of the place. The war will end when the godling of one side or the other has been compelled to swallow the war-token. It's one of the many rules in our code of war that the token must always be kept uncovered and above ground; then there's another which obliges a man, once his quarter-staff is wrested from him, to stay out of action until his comrades succeed in recapturing, or permanently if it's broken; and another is that a captain may fight only a captain. You'll soon get the hang of it.'

Besides ourselves, ten other magicians had turned up from near-by houses: six men and four women. When Fig-bread introduced me to them, they asked with a show of interest: 'How do you like New Crete?'

'It defies criticism,' I answered politely; this had also been my stock answer to the question 'How do you like our New Germany?' when in 1937 Antonia and I stayed with friends at Freiburg.

Then followed anxious enquiries about Sapphire and Sally: why had they not turned up? 'Oh, Sapphire? She's asleep and Sally's at her bedside,' said Fig-bread, who was doing all the talking. 'It's nothing of consequence—nothing at all. If the Goddess pleases, they'll both be here this afternoon.'

But I could see by their manner that rumours of the trouble at home had already reached them.

There was something rather queer about Fig-bread this morning. I looked at him more closely and noticed an unusual lightness of gesture, a quickening of speech, a flashing of his usually sombre eyes. Was he drugged, I wondered. He had been chattering without pause all the way, mostly about the speed and beauty of famous horses of the past, with an honourable mention of his own glossy steed. Something must have happened to him, or perhaps was about to happen. . . . Was he going to volunteer for the fighting, as two other young magicians had already decided to do, one on each side? Or did his behaviour merely reflect his nervous solicitude for Sally? He reminded me strongly of someone—but who was it? Not a physical resemblance, but the identical manner. . . . 'Legs' Doughty-Wyllie, of course, on the night before our attack on Monte Cassino—'Legs', a regular soldier, the driest and most taciturn of our company-commanders, talking breezy nonsense about the superiority of the Large Black pig to all other breeds in the English countryside. Queer, that nobody else seemed to be aware of the change in Fig-bread.

The bugles sounded the Advance and battle was joined. Zapmor made a determined rush to secure the token but Rabnon kept tossing it from hand to hand until Goose-flesh, their fastest runner, caught hold of it and raced for a wood just inside the Zapmor border. A Zapmor outpost was on guard there but Gooseflesh swerved, slipped past and was soon lost among the trees.

The Zapmor captain sent fast runners to the wood. They fanned out and surrounded it, but could not be certain whether Gooseflesh was still inside or whether the distant shouts from a look-out on a tree meant that he had gone away and was making for a wood deeper in Zapmor territory. Scouts streamed in pursuit and Gooseflesh was eventually caught and disarmed as he emerged from the second wood. However, they did not find the war-token in his possession and were forbidden by the code to question him about it.

A game of bluff and counter-bluff now ensued. Zapmor, pretending to have found the token, raised an excited halloo. Rabnon, who had it all the time—because what Gooseflesh had taken into the wood was not the token, but a bunch of roses—pretended to be deceived and crowded after the shouting enemy. A Zapmor patrol then made a detour and carefully searched the first wood until they found the decoy roses. Mocking laughter greeted them from the top of a tree where a Rabnon scout was posted.

A heavy quarter-staff fight was in progress inside the second wood. Starfish and I galloped over and it was a sight worth watching: the fighters used their staffs as blunt spears for thrusting, as clubs for striking, as poles for jumping or for tripping up their opponents. They were incredibly dexterous in its use; the clash of staff against staff was incessant, varied by shouts, laughter, war cries and the occasional dull boom of a well-aimed blow on a leather helmet. Rabnon were outnumbered in this skirmish and soon had to withdraw, leaving ten men disarmed. When reinforcements came up, the fight developed into an attempt to rescue the captured staffs before they were taken off to Zapmor, but several more were lost in the attempt.

Zapmor were the stronger and better-disciplined fighters, but Rabnon still kept possession of the token. They now made several feints at carrying it across the border and Zapmor did not catch sight of it until about eight o'clock, when it had become the centre of a brisk battle fought up and down a stream, only half a mile from Zapmor village. Rabnon decided to fight it out; but by a clever concentration of his reserves on a hill dominating the stream on the Rabnon side, the Zapmor captain succeeded shortly afterwards in launching a heavy attack on the enemy centre, which he broke. Zapmor seized the token and carried it a mile or so over the border, where they ran up against Rabnon's general reserve and were fought to a standstill. At this point Starfish was hastily summoned to separate two fighters, both disarmed, who seemed intent on strangling each other. The way he went about this was simple and effective: he seized the lobes of their ears and said: 'In Nimuë's Name, break away!' They disengaged at once, choking and laughing.

By ten o'clock bitter fighting had brought Zapmor within half a mile of Rabnon village. Nearly fifty of the enemy had been disarmed and their staffs taken back to the shrine for safe-keeping; this brought the rival sides to something like equal strength.

From now on Zapmor showed little tactical finesse. They formed a sort of Macedonian phalanx, with the token dangling from a quarter-staff in the middle, and forced their way forward yard by yard across a broad meadow. But the ground was soggy and Rabnon put up a furious resistance. By eleven o'clock they had gained only a quarter of a mile; but soon after Rabnon broke once more and by noon the war-token had been carried within sight of their own totem-pole. Then a trumpet blew the Cease Fire and both armies lay down panting, while their women folk hurried up dispensing kisses, advice, massage, plasters, food and drink. A Zapmor man had broken his collar-bone and another had twisted his ankle; See-a-Bird and Fig-bread took charge of them. These, apart from minor cuts and bruises and one case of slight concussion, were the only casualties so far reported.

I had eaten my lunch of bread and cheese in the saddle; now I tried to find my way home by a short cut through an oak wood and across some water-meadows. Presently my horse sank up to its fetlocks in mud and I found myself entering a grove of alders planted in a wide spiral. A crane, standing pensively on one leg not far off, observed my approach. It tilted its head, but did not appear alarmed.

There were no buildings about, nor any votive offerings on the trees, but it was clear that I had blundered into a sacred grove; I must get out at once and take the proper road. As I turned my horse round I thought I heard the crane squeak shrilly in English: 'Wait a moment, you!'

My hair stood on end. I had never been addressed by a bird before, except parrots, budgerigars and one monosyllabic tame raven.

However, when I looked back it turned out not to be the crane after all; the crane had disappeared. In its place stood a tall old woman, the oldest and dirtiest hag I had ever seen; Gran'mère Michel, the pipe-smoking centenarian of St. Jean-des-Porcs, would have looked middle-aged and well-groomed beside her. She must have been crouching in the mud behind one of the trees.

My dappled rocking-horse began to snort and shiver. 'Quiet, old boy, quiet!' I said, but that was no use. The devil had entered into him. He went completely daft and played me all the maddest bronco tricks ever seen in a Wild West rodeo—bucking, plunging, shimmying, barking my legs against trees, jumping sideways like a kitten, trying to bite my feet. The hag stood cackling at us.

'God damn you, you witch!' I shouted. 'Calm this beast for me, won't you?'

She cackled louder than ever. 'God! That's rich! That's very rich! "God damn you!" he says.'

In the late Twenties after I had been sent down from Oxford I spent a couple of years on a ranch in Arizona. Since I was the only Britisher within two hundred miles, quite a few rogue horses had from time to time been humorously incited to murder me. So this was nothing new; but the mud was greasy black and I was determined not to be thrown. Somehow I managed to keep my seat until the hag hobbled up, laid a skinny hand on the horse's withers, and mumbled something to him in New Cretan. Instantly he behaved himself, let out a friendly whinny and started to crop the rank grass at his feet.

'Where the Devil did you spring from?' I asked, panting and furious.

'First God and now the Devil!' she squeaked. 'My dear Teddy, you forget yourself.'

'Please forgive my rudeness, but you scared me. How do you know my name?'

'It's my business to know names,' she said. 'I know every-one's name hereabouts. What made you ride through my cranery? It's strictly against rules.'

'I'm a stranger here. I was taking a short cut. . . .'

'You needn't worry about Sapphire. She's all right. In fact, you'll only make things worse if you go back now. There'll be hell to pay about that cigarette case under Sally's pillow; not that I think the girl didn't ask for trouble. You'd better stick around here and watch the fun.'

'What do you know about the cigarette case?'

'I know all I want to know.'

'Isn't that rather a large claim? Do you by any chance know all I want to know, too?'

'Yes.'

'I don't believe that!'

'Look in my eyes!'

I looked steadily into them. They were as blue as mandarin beads and as sharp as sacking-needles.

'Now, do you believe me?'

'I can't very well help believing. But when I return to my own sceptical age, how shall I know that—?'

'Would you like to ask a test question?'

'If you won't be offended.'

'Nothing ever offends me.'

Before I could speak she took the question out of my mouth. 'What you're going to ask me is: "Who killed M. le Vicomte de Chose et Chose et Martinbault?" '

I gasped. 'Well, who did?' I faltered, after a pause.

'I did myself. I cut his throat with his own hunting-knife. Then I castrated him. I threw the knife into the Alys.'

'Oh!'

'Oh, what?'

'Who . . . . who are you?'

'I am whatever I choose to be.'

I seemed to hear Knut Jensen's voice whispering in my ear: 'Quick, old boy, remember your manners, or it'll be the worse for you!' I leaped off the horse, uncovered, spread out my hands and bowed deeply.

She grinned at me mischievously. 'Wasn't there one more question you wanted to ask me, something about Erica and the coat she was wearing?'

'Th . . . . th . . . . that's right,' I answered, lapsing into my childhood stammer. 'Wh . . . . wh . . . . what was it called?'

'If I tell you, you won't try to break her neck?'

'I promise.'

'It was a white walicot.'

Then it all came back. The witch trial at Aberdeen in 1597, that I had been reading about somewhere, when Andro Man confessed to carnal dealing with the Queen of Elphame who 'had a grip of all her craft' and who attended a witches' sabbath riding a white hackney. 'She is very pleasant and will be auld and young whenas she pleases,' Andro Man had testified. 'She makes any King whom she pleases and she lies with any she pleases.' The witches called her Our Lady, and she wore a white walicot, which must have been a coat woven with wales or stripes. 'Then who *is* Erica?' I asked in confusion.

'Last night you claimed to know all about her. There's no more to know than all about her. How do you like New Crete?'

I blushed, and said slowly: 'Why ask me, Mother?'

'Mothers often ask their children questions to which they already know the answers.'

'Oh, well—it isn't really beyond criticism. Though the bread's good and the butter's good, there doesn't seem to be any salt in either.'

'That's why I sent for you.'

'*You* sent for me?'

'Of course. Surely, you don't imagine that the magicians would have done anything so dangerous without my orders?'

'And what are your orders to me?'

'None at the moment. You're doing nicely, so far. If you get into trouble, consult me.'

'Here?'

'Anywhere. Or, wait, I'll give you my pass. You may want to visit a shrine, or a nonsense house, or even a bagnio.' She fumbled in her dirty rags for some time and at last produced an egg-shaped locket made of crystal. Then she stooped painfully, picked up a crane's neck-feather that was clinging to a tussock of grass, shut it in the locket and handed it to me.

I accepted the pass gratefully and kissed her filthy claw of a hand. 'You're a good boy,' she said. 'I shall be seeing you again one of these days.'

I bowed deeply, turned, caught my horse by the bridle, but was hardly back in the saddle when she gave him a sudden vicious kick in the rump. He reared, plunged and bounded off at full gallop; I was too busy keeping my seat even to wave a hand in goodbye.

CHAPTER XIII

The Peace Supper

A FEW minutes later I was back in Rabnon; Starfish came hurrying up to meet me.

'Where have you been?' he asked anxiously.

'I tried a short cut home but got held up.'

'You shouldn't have done that; you might have trespassed into the alder grove. Are you all right? And have you had anything to eat?'

'I'm all right, thank you. Yes, I've finished my lunch. I hope you didn't wait for me?'

'No, no! We dispense with such formalities in war-time. What do you think of the fighting?'

'I prefer the open Rabnon style, of course; it's more fun to watch. But I'd probably have said the same about the Highlanders who took such a beating at the battle of Killiecrankie. Who's going to win?'

'Only the Goddess knows.'

'You've got something there,' I said decisively.

The trumpet blew the Rally and both armies raced to take up their previous positions. After a second blast the fighting broke out again. Zapmor had closed their ranks and, with the war-token as their standard, made a rush forward.

Rabnon met them courageously, but despite all efforts they were forced farther and farther back. Screams of alarm and exhortation rose from the Rabnon girls as the enemy rolled forward to the fringe of the green. From the back of the scrimmage rose the voice of the barber of Zapmor in an improvised song of triumph:

> It's up with the damsons of Zapmor,
> We'll carry them over the green!
> And it's down with the cheese-straw and radish—
> That's food not fit to be seen!

Open-please who, as Rabnon's goal-keeper, had been posted all day at the totem-pole to guard against one-man rushes, suddenly began to dance about excitedly and fling his hands up to heaven as if in supplication. Then he kissed his quarter-staff and bounded into the scrimmage with hair bristling and eye-balls protruding. He had clearly gone berserk, drunk with the Goddess whom he invoked roaringly as he ran.

> And it's up with the cobblers of Zapmor,
> And up with the ochre and black!

sang the barber. With a prodigious jump Open-please sprang on the shoulders of the tightly packed Zapmor phalanx, seized the war-token, leaped forward again, then sideways, and was off like a hare zig-zagging across the slope below the village. The barber's song tailed away, but Open-please was out of sight before most of the other Zapmor men realized what had happened. He ran four miles, meeting no opposition, and was in sight of the outlying houses of Zapmor before their general reserve closed with him. Even then he showed no signs of tiring: he knocked two Zapmor men down with his charge, felled two more with heavy blows on their helmets, and broke through. At last, in a narrow lane only fifty yards away from his objective, three men ambushed and held him; but they had to call their goal-keeper and his assistant from the green before he could be overpowered and disarmed. His last frenzied action was to toss the token over a low hedge into a paddock where a few sheep were grazing unattended.

The Zapmor men did not go after the token at once: they were too busy with Open-please, who had to be drenched with cold water—scooped in their helmets from a near-by pond—before he came out of his berserk trance. When they went, they could not find it anywhere. They searched in the hedge, they searched in the grass, they looked up into the branches of an apple-tree in the paddock. It could not be very far away, but where was it?

Nobody else was about. They searched methodically for half an hour, until the Zapmor scouts came streaming back, to find them still at a loss. The captain arrived on horseback and urged them to continue their search, while he kept his men well forward, playing the same game of bluff that Rabnon had played earlier in the day. In a few hours the war would be over, and even if the token was not found by then, Zapmor at least would have preserved its honour and could claim the greater number of prisoners.

About five o'clock the trumpets blew for afternoon prayer, in which everyone joined; after that, for tactical reasons, the Zapmor Captain let his phalanx be forced back for half a mile. The Rabnor men were mystified by the absence of the war-token and suspected a stratagem; but none developed. The day wore on, the battle swayed pointlessly to and fro. In a growing spirit of petulance harder and angrier blows were exchanged and a few men were disarmed on both sides, but it was soon realized by everybody that since Open-please's heroic performance the war had passed out of human control.

The only event of interest during this incoherent fighting was a challenge to a duel from the Zapmor captain to his opposite number, who accepted it gratefully. The captains fought on horseback, first tilting at each other with quarter-staffs for lances, then grappling in the saddle. Both were soon unhorsed and continued their struggle in a rough-and-tumble on the turf. They wrestled in the North of England style, with 'nowt barred', but with the added complication of their quarter-staffs, which both had managed to keep and which were unhandy weapons for in-fighting. During the duel the magician on duty had ordered a general truce, and now the captains struggled in the centre of a dense ring, with the Rabnon women in the front rank almost beside themselves with excitement. The issue remained in doubt until Peaches, unable to control herself any longer, ran forward and shouted to the Rabnon captain: 'If you beat him, I'll give in to you. Tonight, if you want me. Do you hear? I promise!'

His strength was failing, but he made one supreme effort. Abandoning his own quarter-staff he snatched at the top of his opponent's, which lay underneath them, locked his feet and knees around the butt and heaved until the veins stood out on his forehead. A sharp crack, the wood splintered and the duel was won. Peaches darted from the ring to hide her emotion, pursued by her girl-friends who smothered her with kisses. This was a victory to be set off against Zapmor's successful haul of prisoners but it did not end the war, which dragged on for another half-hour.

The Cease Fire was blown at dusk and the rival armies lined up facing each other. The priests kissed again, once more exchanged statuettes in token of friendship and began chanting the hymn of peace, in which everyone joined.

'Is this where we go home?' I asked See-a-Bird.

'That would be very impolite. There's still the survey of the war to be made and judgement pronounced, after the big peace-supper. That will be held at Zapmor. The village against which war has been declared always provides the feast, whatever the result. We are of course expected to attend.'

'But I feel that I ought to get back to Sapphire.'

'There's no hurry. She's in good hands. By the way, Starfish, what's become of Fig-bread?'

'I haven't seen him since he took charge of the second concussion case about an hour ago.'

6

'It wasn't serious, was it?'

'I hardly think so. He ought to be back by now.'

'There was something on my brother's mind,' Starfish said, frowning. 'Perhaps he grew worried about Sally and rode back. In that case, he should have told us. He hasn't seemed quite himself all day.'

'What do you expect?' See-a-Bird sighed. 'Perhaps we'd better make no inquiries about him. His absence may pass unnoticed.'

I did not tell them about my presentiment, not wishing to spoil the party for them, but I could not help casting an anxious glance in the direction of the cranery.

'Have you any idea where he is?' Starfish asked me.

'Only the Goddess knows!' I answered thoughtfully.

We watched Zapmor march home to wash and change into their gala-clothes. Rabnon dispersed to do the same. Then we rode ahead and brought the Zapmor villagers the news of the later stages of the fighting. They were already making preparations for the feast, which I watched with a greedy enough interest. Hundreds of little, low, heart-shaped tables, each laid with the implements of a four-course dinner and provided with a small olive-oil lamp, had been carried out to the green, and arranged in circles of varying size. Children were now lugging out hassocks, some black, some red, for the diners to sit on, with their legs outstretched and the tables between their knees, in the style of the country. Women servants busied themselves at a long line of earthenware pots that bubbled cheerfully on charcoal fires; men servants, chanting lugubriously, were jointing meat for the roasting-jacks, or beating steaks for the grills. Mountains of French loaves, heaps of Mahon and Brie cheeses, serried rows of pickle-jars, trays loaded with cold meats ready sliced, huge piles of white-fleshed lettuces, baskets brimful of cherries, strawberries, greengages and nectarines, stacked crates of bottled beer. Pies and pastries, cooked in private houses during the day, were now being carried out by the housewives to be kept warm in the communal bread-oven close by. The totem-pole was garlanded with flowers, and illuminated kites in the shape of animals, birds and fishes flew fantastically overhead.

Presently Rabnon arrived in force, but waited politely just inside a wood near the green until they were summoned to supper by a gong. The women came first, then the men, then the children, and lastly the elders, all in single file, dressed in their gala clothes. They sat down at the little tables wherever they saw red hassocks; the black ones alternating with them were reserved for Zapmor. The servants were too busy cooking, carving and helping out to act as waiters, but Rabnon kept Zapmor's plates and cups well filled—not, as I had expected, the other way about—and from the start there were no feelings of reserve or animosity between the red and black hassocks, though neither was there any conversation. Among the commons, as among the magicians, talking at meals was prohibited.

I had resigned myself regretfully to a magician's vegetarian diet, when I noticed that Starfish and See-a-Bird were both tucking into what looked remarkably like steak-and-kidney pie. Wonderful! So when magicians sat down to eat with people of other estates the taboo on meat was lifted, was it? I quickly secured a large cut off the joint, garnished with roast potatoes, brussels sprouts and horseradish sauce—the boiled dana I dispensed with—and followed this with three or four generous slabs of ham flavoured with cloves, mayonnaise and prawns in aspic. I washed it all down with a quart bottle of strong black beer. Zapmor was a fine place, I decided. Then followed plum-cake, trifle, fruit and black coffee. Zapmor was the finest place in the world, I decided; no wonder its men fought so well!

At last there came a stir and a subdued rattle, as everyone laid down his dessert spoon or knife; then a dead silence. At the Zapmor captain's invitation, Starfish rose to survey and judge the day's fighting: 'Women and men, children and elders of the Five Estates, please listen! At first this was a pleasant war, fought lovingly throughout the morning and for the earlier part of the afternoon. Afterwards it became loveless and spiritless, except for the noble interlude of the captains' duel. The issue is still obscure and without precedent: the war-token has vanished without trace.'

He looked severely at the Zapmor captain, who rose at once in self-justification: 'The disappearance of the token gave us no advantage. Can it be that the Rabnon goal-keeper, unable to force it into our godling's mouth, so far forgot the code of war that he used magic to make it disappear?'

All eyes turned to Open-please, who said defiantly: 'I fought according to the code. When I tossed the token away I invoked the Goddess and begged her to take it into her keeping. I have never tampered with magic. I'm a commoner and keep to my estate.'

The Zapmor captain broke in: 'The token was not found in the field where he threw it. If anyone had entered it we should have seen his head above the hedge.'

'That is so,' the Rabnon captain answered. 'Since Zapmor must have found the token there—no Rabnon fighter having found it first—and since no neutrals were allowed to pass through the district because of the war, and since all children and elders were kept indoors; yet since, if they found it, they cannot have dishonourably concealed it or destroyed it—' He paused, glanced around him at the sea of blank faces, then back at Starfish; and sat down.

Starfish thought deeply for a moment, putting his little finger into his mouth for inspiration; but apparently without success. He asked: 'Is anyone present inspired to conclude the captain's sentence?'

I found it embarrassing to make the obvious suggestion; what these guileless people needed was a course in twentieth-century detective fiction. But somehow the spell had to be broken. I stood up, beckoned to the Interpreter, and made a short speech in English, which he relayed while I sat down again. What I said was: 'My opinion of the Rabnon and Zapmor fighters is so high that I cannot believe any of them capable of acting against either custom or honour. Therefore, the captain's sentence must necessarily conclude with . . . . "Rabnon has won the war." '

A few girls giggled and some elders chuckled, but everyone else stared impassively, waiting for me to continue.

'Explain yourself!' said the Zapmor captain, a little vexed.

I rose and said: 'Logically, there are only two places where the war-token can be lodged: the belly of the Zapmor godling and the belly of the Rabnon godling. In any other place it would have been found long ago. However, since it was last seen within throwing distance of this green the chances are that Rabnon has won the war, rather than Zapmor.'

The Zapmor priest made as if to go towards the totem-pole, but checked himself and sat down again.

'Do you too accuse Open-please of making a magical throw?' asked the Rabnon barber.

'Certainly not; though I cannot deny that he acted under inspiration. As you will all agree, he was drunk with the Goddess.'

'Then how do you think that the token was conveyed to the godling's belly?'

'Since no stranger passed, and since no Rabnon men were within a mile of the scene when it vanished, and since sheep are not intelligent animals, and since the apple-tree in the paddock is not hollow, and since all the elders were kept in-doors, the only possible conclusion is that a child was in the paddock when the token fell close by him, and that he carried it off under cover of the hedge and managed to drop it into the godling's mouth without being seen. But it cannot have been an ordinary child, or he would have remained dutifully

at home at an upper window. It must have been a child of
intelligence; and there can be no more than one child in
Zapmor capable of such daring and defiance.'

I paused. The Zapmor boy who had been the ringleader in
the damson-jam rebellion stood up, and I sat down again,
glad to find that I had not made a fool of myself.

He was about seven years old, and because no discrimination between commons and captains was made until the age
of puberty he wore only three bands, not one, on the cuffs of
his black overall; but anybody could see that he was a born
captain.

Speaking with perfect composure, he said: 'The poet from
the past is very clever. He is aware that the people of Zapmor
are honourable, even the children. On my behalf a war was
fought against our village, and when from my bedroom
window I saw Open-please leaping heroically across the
hedges, quarter-staff in hand, and felling four of our best men,
my heart went out to him. I opened the window and let
myself down on to the garden wall and ran along it and slid
down a shed, and hurried across our paddock. There I peeped
through the hedge and watched his struggle against odds. The
token came flying over the hedge. I caught it, and ran with it
towards the green. The totem-pole was deserted, not even
our goal-keeper or his assistant was there: they had both gone
to help the others in overpowering Open-please. I bowed to
the godling, and said: "Godling, with your consent, I am
forced to eat damson jam seven evenings of the week. Now
you eat these for me, I pray, and may your gorge not rise,
as mine has done! Amen!" I dropped the token into his
mouth and ran home. Because the Goddess was with me
nobody noticed either my coming or my going.'

'Why did you not confess your intemperate deed?' asked
the priest gently, as he went to the back of the totem-pole,
unlocked a door and produced the wooden damsons.

'It was a private quarrel between me and the godling. For

this one day honour had made me his enemy, and the Goddess was on my side.' He sat down in dead silence.

Starfish summed up. 'The war-token has now been found in the belly of Zapmor's godling, Rabnon has therefore fairly won the war. The golden verse of the poet Vives applies in this case:

> A friend's hand is as my hand,
> A friend's foot as mine.

Let no one dispute my judgement. It is this: because Rabnon have the glory of winning the war that they declared, they must eat damson jam every evening for one whole month to release the children of Zapmor from the obligation of ever having to eat it again. Zapmor, for their part, will re-name the lane where Open-please was disarmed "Damson Alley", and the paddock into which he threw the token "War-token Field", in memory of these events. As for the boy who made his own godling eat damsons: he has declared war on his kinsmen and must not stay another night in Zapmor.'

The Rabnon captain rose and looked from face to face. After a while he announced: 'The boy will be welcomed by our village. One day he will succeed me as captain.'

The woman in the partridge-feather hat chimed in: 'He may live with me, if he likes, until he changes his estate. He already loves my cheese-straws.'

The boy's mother said quietly: 'Take him, with my blessing! You are welcome to him. My house could never hold the boy.'

So all was settled to everyone's satisfaction, and singing and dancing followed. The festivities lasted far into the night.

The Chief Recorder of Zapmor planted himself near me and bombarded me with questions about wild animals of my epoch, now extinct.

I tried to answer him as well as I could, but my mind was

distracted. All the while I was wondering: 'When will the news come of Fig-bread's death?' For on the night before our Monte Cassino attack while 'Legs' was holding forth on the virtues of the Large Black pig, our regimental doctor, Mac-Whirter, had taken me aside and said: 'Venn-Thomas, laddie, mark my words, ye'll be left in command o' the company by this time tomorrow. *Yon puir fule's fey!*'

CHAPTER XIV

The Pattern

THE dancing was not of the easy ballroom sort in which I should have been pleased to join. It was distressingly profess-ional folk-dancing, in which teams from the two villages gave alternate performances under the blaze of bright arc-lights fed with turpentine. I was told that children began to learn the steps and convolutions at the age of four or five but did not become adepts for another twelve years or more. The style varied with the local marriage customs; monogamous Zapmor went in for all-male quarter-staff dances to the accompaniment of pipes with high leaps and quick gyrations, and decorous all-female flower-dances with a great deal of finger work in the Indian style and complex interlacing of the dancers' orbits. Polyandrous Rabnon specialized in orgiastic dances: I recall particularly *The Queen Bee*, a very wild performance to bagpipe music in which a woman was courted by thirteen men in succession yet satisfied them all, and *The Nine Ladies*, in which nine women, dancing in a ring, pursued and assaulted a drunken trespasser. These were all religious dances and therefore no more to be applauded than the complicated ritual of High Mass in a Catholic cathedral.

Inaction and a full stomach made me feel sleepy. I was wondering whether I should be allowed to go home soon, when an elder strolled up and touched my elbow. He was an ex-commoner dressed in a blue linen smock with a broad-rimmed hat and cherry-coloured stockings; evidently a Rabnon man. He wandered off again without a word. I had the curiosity to rise from my hassock—the tables had been removed before the dancing began—and follow him into the darkness.

'I have a message for you,' he said, after a time, with a yawn and hiccup.

'From whom?'

'From a woman who wants you to go to her at once.'

'Thank you, but as you are an elder and also pretty well soaked, am I to take your message seriously?'

'You're under no obligation.'

'That'll be Erica,' I said to myself. 'She's got friends among the elders. Now, shall I go, or shan't I? I might as well. I've promised not to break her neck, but there can't be any harm in trying to persuade her to undo some of the mischief she's caused.' I asked the elder: 'Where is she waiting?'

'I'm under no obligation to answer,' he said, yawning again and strolling back to the green.

'That's very true,' I agreed. 'Good night.'

'Well, I asked for that,' I thought, standing there irresolutely. As my eyes grew accustomed to the darkness I found that I was standing on a path between hedges of some highly-scented bush. I might as well go on and get away from the revels for a while; the path would always lead me back. After about five minutes' walk I paused. The sound of flutes came very faintly down the breeze; that must be the Zapmor women again. I sat down on a tree-stump.

Here was my opportunity for a little serious heart-searching. What sort of a man was I by emotional instinct? All else being equal, if I had to make the choice, would I live in Zapmor or would I choose Rabnon? I wished that I knew myself better. I had never had the opportunity, because in my own age the choice had not been clear cut: it was complicated by the stupidity, hypocrisy and dullness of the general run of monogamists and the silliness and drunken bravado of the usual polyandrous set. To be precise: had I ever loved Antonia, who was a one-man woman, as much as I had loved Erica, a queen-bee if ever there was one? Not as intensely perhaps, not as insanely certainly, and how else can one measure love, except by its intensity and insanity? But then I had never hated Antonia even for a moment, as I had hated Erica quite half the time that we were together. It seemed years since I had seen Antonia (and, of course, it literally was years—hundred of years, perhaps even thousands) whereas I had seen Erica only the day before yesterday, looking younger and more mischievous than ever. Antonia had my heart; but it was only fair to admit that Erica had not recently displayed what I used to call her glow-worm light—an almost phosphorescent aura of sexuality that etherealized her not at all faultless features. In the old days she could switch it on and off at pleasure, and when it was in full glow, I was at her mercy. I greatly hoped that she had lost the knack; I loathe retracing my steps in love, as I loathe returning to a house of which I have once taken final leave. There was peace in my love for Antonia, peace and confidence which I wanted never to be disturbed. Antonia was good, in the simplest sense of the word, and with a quiet, constructive humour; Erica was evil, with a beautifully destructive wit that matched the intense dislike I felt for my age.

Now Sapphire confused the issue; and Sally. I felt safe with Sapphire, however equivocal my relations with her might be, and she and I were paired here, by general agreement. Yet, I must have been jolted into my summary declaration of love by a self-protective intuition which warned me that if I did not take refuge with her, Sally was bound to get me. Sally was a witch, and I knew that she too had a glow-worm button under her thumb if ever she cared to press it for my benefit; but first she would have to eliminate Sapphire, and I was not going to stand for that.

I reconsidered the problem of Erica. She was real enough; in a sense she was the only real person I had met since my evocation, yet it occurred to me that she was a little over life size and indeed the Hag had hinted to me that she was not the Erica I had known, but the Queen of Elphame in disguise. I knew that at the end of the sixteenth century the Queen of Elphame had made one Andro Man her lover, 'suffering him to do that which Christian ears ought not to hear of'—by the way, wasn't Andrew Mann the name of the writer with whom Erica now claimed to have had an affair in Scotland?—and that 'Thomas the Rimer' had also claimed intimacy with her a century earlier. 'She can be old and young whenas she pleases.' But who or what was this death-less and preposterous character?

There was a slight movement in the grassy ditch only a couple of yards away, and a whispered sigh of endearment. It was Peaches and the Rabnon captain, both naked and locked in each other's arms. I jumped up in embarrassment and made off, but Peaches called me back. 'Give us a poet's blessing!' she pleaded.

I was just drunk enough to rise to the occasion. Raising my hand, I declaimed magisterially in English:

> 'Blest payre of Swans, Oh may you interbring
>   Daily new joyes, and never sing;
>   Live, till all grounds of wishes faile,
> Till honor, yea till wisedome grow so stale
>   That, new great heights to trie
> It must serve your ambition to die . . . .
> May never age, or error overthwart
> With any West, these radiant eyes, with any North, this heart.

In the names of Nimuë, Mari and Ana,' I piously concluded in New Cretan.

'That sounds very beautiful,' said Peaches.

'Please don't move on our account!' said the polite captain.

'I'm sorry that I can't stay: I have an appointment up the lane,' I said hastily and went off, speeded by their grateful adieu. And with an oddly contrasting memory of Crosby Links near Liverpool where one fine summer evening I had sat down on the edge of a bunker to smoke a cigarette: oh, the obscenely expressed bursts of outraged modesty from a sailor and his girl already curled up there!

The woman was waiting for me under an oak. I heard the rushing sound of a waterfall. She came forward to meet me. I could not see her face, which was shadowed by a hood, but she was too tall to be Erica, and too young to be the Hag. She was sobbing quietly. It was the stock romantic situation: an unknown young woman—beautiful, of course—weeping under an oak in the forest. Like Coleridge's Geraldine, or the enchantress from one of the mediaeval romances of chivalry. When the knight approaches with courteous sympathy, she displays her dress all in disarray, beats her bosom, and complains of an outlandish knight. . . .

As soon as she spoke I realized that she was Sally. 'Come quickly,' she said. 'I need your help.'

'More trouble?'

'Yes, it's Fig-bread.'

'Oh, yes? How did he die?'

'You know, then? I thought that I was the first to find him. Who told you?'

'My little finger, as they used to say in France; in fact, simple intuition, a quality with which both See-a-Bird and Starfish seem to be strangely ungifted. They should have realized early this morning that Fig-bread was a doomed man. But tell me what happened.'

'His horse must have gone crazy, thrown him and savaged him on the ground; the beast came home, guilty and dejected, about two hours ago, with blood all over his muzzle and hooves. When I mounted him and gave him his head, he brought me here and I found the body behind that tree. Then he lolled his head and waited for me to kill him, poor creature. And I did.'

'What did Fig-bread mean to you?'

'He was in love with me—you must have known that—and of course a woman can't help having tender feelings for anyone who falls in love with her and behaves irreproachably.'

'But you weren't in love with him, I gather?'

'How could I be?' she asked accusingly.

She was trembling from head to foot. I knew the reason, of course—'by the pricking of my thumbs', as one of the witches in *Macbeth* put it—and felt acutely uncomfortable.

'One thing at a time,' I said hastily. 'We can discuss our emotions all day tomorrow, if you like. Meanwhile, what do you propose to do with the body?'

'You and I must bury it.'

'Very well. It's a shame that you had to destroy the horse, but I'll go back to Zapmor at once and fetch mine. I'll borrow some sort of shroud and tie the body across his back. We'll be home before dawn if we waste no time. Is there a cemetery in our village?'

'There are no cemeteries in New Crete. We must bury him here. In the hut that you passed on your way up the lane you'll find a pick and a spade.'

'What about getting hold of a priest to say the burial service over him?'

'That isn't our custom. Whatever dies is laid underground and turfed over without religious ceremonies or spectators.'

'Oh, as you please. It seems a bit hasty and heartless, but if it's the custom. . . .'

I went back down the lane, found the hut, groped about inside until I found the tools and was back again soon afterwards.

Sally stood by the waterfall, letting the water splash over her hands. Fig-bread's body was lying not far off; it was in a dreadful state: the face smashed in, one of the hands bitten completely off. His dead horse lay beside him; there was no evidence of violence. But I gathered from what she had said about its lolling head that she had given him the *descabello*, the neck prick with which bullfighters finish off weary bulls; she probably used the lancet that she always carried.

'Do we have to bury the horse, too?'

'Yes.'

'Look here, Sally. I'm not much good with a spade. The job will take me hours. I don't mind burying poor Fig-bread, but surely the disposal of the horse can be left to local labour?'

'No, that's impossible. Both bodies must be buried before dawn and we can't call anyone away from the feast to help us. The Goddess will give you strength. First remove the turf and lay it carefully aside.'

Sally unbraided her hair and began to comb it, singing softly. I set to work with some reluctance; but under the turf the soil was quite soft and I did not need the pick. While she combed her hair she sang a ballad of adventures in the Bad Lands. I missed the first two verses, but the next ones went something like this:

> We sailed through the channel
> Across the Atlantic,
> The lordly great channel
> With ramparts of stone,
> Six weeks we were sailing
> From island to island,
> Our cargo was dana
> And butifaron.

When we came to New York
Where the sea-lion bellows
And gulls scream aloud
On the desolate sands,
We said our farewells
To the crew and the captain
And marched up the river
With bows in our hands.

There was Sealskin and Teazle,
Red Gauntlet, Plum-porridge,
Old Rock, Never-see-me
And Happy Reply,
Kissing Mouth, Little Bedstraw,
Snail, Cloud, and Forked Lightning;
The Captain was Holloa,
The poet was I.

The tree-bears were tumbling
Among the blueberries;
We camped the first night
Where a tulip-tree stood,
But a sudden tornado
Swept by from the westward
And tore a wide swathe
Through the heart of the wood. . . .

We warred with the wild men,
We hunted the bison.
Plum-porridge fell wounded
While crossing Hyde Park.
Though we clapped on a plaster
And prayed to the Goddess
He spoke his last wish
And was dead before dark.

In cool Saratoga
We met with a portent:

An eagle devouring
A fawn with two heads;
So we halted five days
And I danced out a penance,
Head shorn, body painted
With yellows and reds.

When we came to Lake Champlain
And saw the twin statues
We spat on the ground
To avert the ill-luck,
There we met with a wild man
Tattooed like a serpent
Who offered us raisins
And breasts of wild duck.

I can remember only a few more lines of this part of the ballad—the adventurers had unexpected trouble with man-eating bears near Niagara Falls—but no complete verses, because though I continued to dig steadily I was soon conscious of little except the rhythm: the words and even the notes fell away until I was fast asleep and Sally's voice sounded like the dancing tick of a cheap alarm-clock. I could have sworn that I was home and in bed with Antonia. Rain pattered on the window and presently I heard the purring of a motor-cycle along the road to the station, followed by a sleepy whimper from the nursery next door and Antonia's voice saying: 'It's nothing, darling, go to sleep again!' and then: 'Damn that young doctor and his motor-bike!' But the ticking grew louder and more musical and I woke to hear Sally concluding her song:

With joy in our hearts,
Though with knots in our girdles,
We pushed out the gang-plank
And hastened ashore.

> A weary long time
> We had passed in the Bad Lands,
> Which, Ana be praised,
> We need visit no more.

'Who wrote that?' I asked, to show I was listening.

'Fig-bread.'

'Will it be recorded on gold, do you think?'

'Of course not. It's what we call a barber-shop ballad. I sang it to pacify his ghost. He left no real poems. He was too conscientious to commit his work even to clay—not a line of verse, not a bar of music.'

'Well, well. . . . I seem to have put Fig-bread underground already. I didn't realize I was a natural sexton. Now what about that unfortunate horse? Where do I dig his pit?'

'You've already dug it and turfed it over. Look at the blisters on your hands.'

'Good God! The things I do in my sleep! And a neat job, too. I shouldn't have believed myself capable of it, though when I was a boy I once got out of bed, put on my roller-skates and went careering down the long passages of the Rectory in the dark. What comes next?'

'Presently we'll ride home; you can sit behind me on your horse.'

'What? No tears, no prayers, no headstone, no last words, no nothing?'

'He's dead. Ana has his body, and the murderer has made amends. I'll report the death at Sanjon tomorrow; then his real name will be published and everyone will be free to use it and say what they please of him.'

'And his soul? Does that go to the Other World?'

'There is no Other World. There's only New Crete, where his name will live on for a few generations perhaps—in the barber-shops.'

'Well, I like to think that, when I come to die, my liberated soul . . . .'

'You like to think! That's not the same as knowing. Children like to think that there's an island across the water where all their hopelessly broken toys go to be mended.'

'You mean that your religion offers no consolation of immortality?'

'Only the Goddess is immortal.'

'That's what we liked to think about God.'

'You liked to think! All gods must die in the end. They grow senile and dribble at the mouth; their priests steal the offerings and tell lies about them. Then their temples fall in ruins and they close their eyes. Only the Goddess lives for ever, blessed be her name!'

'What on earth are you doing now, Sally?'

She had thrown off her cloak and spread it over Fig-bread's grave, unclasped her belt, and kicked off her shoes. Now she was peeling off her dress and chemise. She did not answer, but lay down on the cloak, naked as Eve, and held out her arms for me commandingly.

The unexpectedness of her action shocked and paralysed me.

'Come here!' she said. 'Come and share my cloak; it's a religious obligation! When a man dies violently his ghost has the right to a chance of rebirth. We'd be impious to deny him that.'

I stared at her incredulously. 'So that's it, is it?' I said at last. 'You're actually making me an offer of what you call the rights of fatherhood?'

Her face was drawn with passion; her stretched-out hands shook wildly. 'Come to me, darling barbarian,' she said. 'I love you, I love you more than all the world.'

I spoke as calmly and brutally as I could: 'No, my dear Sally! I'll admit that the Goddess has blessed you with shapely legs, slender arms, ripe lips and a seductive bosom.

I'll also admit that I'm as hot-blooded as the next man. But I've never yet committed adultery on a murdered man's grave at the invitation of his murderess, and what's more, I refuse to do so now. Naturally, I don't want to baulk Fig-bread's chances of rebirth; he was a fine fellow, though a little heavy-handed. But I can't accept your invitation. That sort of thing isn't done where I come from, barbarians though we may be. Get someone else to share your cloak—get Starfish, if you like. Perhaps he'll be less squeamish. Sapphire says that he's one of your admirers, too. Then if Fig-bread gets reborn he's got at least a chance of bearing a family resemblance to himself.'

She had never before been spoken to like this. It startled and momentarily sobered her. Turning half over on her elbow she said in a small, uneven voice: 'But I made quite sure that you wanted me. You told the servant to put your fearful love-gift under my pillow, and you didn't return to Sapphire at noon, when she expected you. And please don't worry about Fig-bread. You see, he often told me that he was ready to die for my sake. And he meant it literally.'

'Good God! So you bewitched the horse and deliberately sent Fig-bread to his death to provide a religious pretext for spreading your cloak for me?'

She nodded, rolled over, and buried her face in her arms. Then something began happening to me: I found myself relenting. This was not my age, I argued, and Sally did not show any guilt for what she had done. If she really felt as strongly for me as all that, and I had a religious obligation to humour her, perhaps . . . .

'Sally,' I said.

She looked up and the glow-worm light shone about her, so brightly, so evilly, that I felt a sharp physical pain at the pit of my stomach.

'Hell! No, not that again!' I thought. 'I finished with

that for ever on the day Antonia said she'd marry me. I'd rather be savaged by a mad horse like Fig-bread, poor devil, than get burned up in that green fire.' I said aloud: 'I'm going home, Sally. Your deliberate murder of Fig-bread and your transferring of the guilt to his horse may be your own concern; but there's still Sapphire to consider, and she's my concern. You've treated her hatefully, and I hope that the Goddess plagues you as she should.'

'How can she plague me more than she is doing now!' she wailed. 'Me, a witch of New Crete, fallen obscenely in love with a barbarous demon of the past.'

'Would you like me to find Starfish and send him to you?' I asked coldly.

That went straight home. She leaped up and began to bewitch me, running around the clearing, widdershins, at top speed and stark naked, with her long black hair flying and madness blazing from her cat-like eyes. It was a hideous experience. My skin crawled. I knew what it felt like to be a bird fascinated by a snake: try as I would I could not stir from the spot. But my brain was still working normally and I found that I could control my hands and voice.

I tried taunts: 'The other evening, Erica Turner told me that your patterns were well worth watching; though she didn't think much of them as magic. She's quite right. I've paid money to see far worse performances in low dives at Cairo and Alexandria.'

But she circled all the more rapidly, making queer, click-ing noises with her tongue and fingers, slapping her breasts at each complete turn, and gradually closing in on me.

I grew desperate. In another minute she'd either tear me to pieces or make a sexual assault on me, or both. Who would be a male spider when the murderous female begins her rhythmic courtship?

I searched feverishly in my mind for a counter-charm. The furtive, intimate charm against the evil eye that the peasants of St. Jean used to make whenever the Vicomte de Martinbault passed?

I tried it, but without result.

The sign of the Cross? *In hoc signo vinces?*

I tried that, too; with no better success. Either it had lost its efficacy since the close of the Christian Era, or else I did not use it with sufficient faith. I am a Christian only by virtue of infant baptism.

She was almost upon me, when I suddenly remembered that interview with the Hag. My hands dived into my pockets and felt for the locket. It was still there. I raised it above my head and said solemnly: 'In the Mother's Name! Set me free and give me safe conduct to the house where I live!'

She made two more complete circuits, fanning me with the wind of her career, and then another half-circle, before my words sank in and she slowed down to a stumbling halt. Quietly and soberly she turned about and unwound the pattern, coil by coil, moodily braiding her hair as she went, her eyes on the ground.

'Thank you, Sally,' I said, when she had finished and I found that I could move again. 'Now get some clothes on like a good girl.'

She obeyed meekly and modestly, retrieved her shoes, resumed her cloak and stood waiting for further orders.

'Now let's find See-a-Bird and Starfish and ride home.'

She gave me her arm and we walked calmly off down the lane towards Zapmor.

Peaches and the captain were still in the ditch as we went by.

'Excuse me, my dears,' I said. 'You'll be doing me a great favour if you finish your love-making by the waterfall at the end of the lane. You'll find two mounds there, newly turfed. Spread your cloaks on the smaller one, and give loving hospitality to an injured ghost. He was a good man, and my friend.'

CHAPTER XV

The Break

FROM a small crowded knoll where the horses were tethered Sally and I silently watched the dancing until the first signs of dawn appeared; then formal goodbyes were said between the representatives of the two villages and the party broke up. Presently Starfish and See-a-Bird came along for their horses. They stared in surprise as they greeted us, evidently expecting Sally to explain her presence, but all she said was: 'I'm very tired, let's go straight home.'

The four of us rode off together, Starfish and I taking turns to sit behind Sally. Apparently in New Crete it was the woman who always rode in front when magicians of opposite sexes shared a horse. As soon as we were clear of the crowd I heard Starfish ask Sally, who was riding with him for the first stage, whether Fig-bread had come home. She answered with a simple 'no'.

After a pause, Starfish asked whether she had walked all the way to Zapmor. Again she said 'no', in a voice that warned him to refrain from further questions.

Since Sally had calmed down and made at least a show of decent behaviour I had decided to say nothing either to antagonize or charm her. Though anxious to know what had happened to Sapphire in my absence, for the sake of peace I had not so much as mentioned her after we had left the clearing. I wondered whether she had already been bewitched, or encouraged to break her promise and go off. Sally had been capable of any mischief that day. I blamed myself for following the Hag's advice about not going home at noon.

See-a-Bird asked the question for me. 'How's Sapphire?'

Sally shrugged. 'I can't answer for her any longer. She's gone away. This evening she rode off, just before I started out myself.'

'Where did she go?'

'Probably to Dunrena, to consult the Goddess Ana at the royal shrine.'

'Why Ana, not Mari? I don't like that. She must be in a bad way.'

'Not through any fault of mine.'

No more was said. We clattered through Rabnon, which was illuminated by victory bonfires, and turned down the lane for home; I was now riding behind Sally. As the light increased we began to exchange greetings with peasants from Horned Lamb, already working in the dewy fields, and smell the wood-smoke that drifted from cottage chimneys. I recognized it as chestnut-wood smoke; abstention from tobacco had made my sense of smell abnormally keen, as it had also sharpened my sense of taste.

'Normally, you mean, not abnormally,' Sally said over her shoulder.

'I beg your pardon?'

'That's the reason why we smoke only one cigarette a day. Constant smoking would dull our appreciation of the Goddess's gifts. It's normal to distinguish one sort of wood-smoke from another.'

'But I didn't say a word, did I?'

'Only to yourself. But I overheard you.'

'How on earth did you do that?'

'I'm a witch, aren't I?'

'And you've been listening to my thoughts ever since you evoked me?'

'Oh, no. Only since you've been riding behind me.'

'You might at least have warned me that you were listening.'

'I forgot that you didn't know why the women always ride in front. If the man did, he'd overhear the woman's thoughts, which would be indecent. I wondered why you were being so open with me. Well, if you have any thoughts that you don't want me to share you'd better dismount; but we're all friends here, and it's most unfriendly for a man to close his mind to a woman. I was listening to Starfish on the road between Zapmor and Rabnon; he had very generous thoughts about me.'

We had nearly reached home, so I refrained from making a scene by dismounting. As we passed the Nonsense House I decided to cover my mental nakedness by silently repeating the more abstruse of Lear's Nonsense Rhymes. But the impudence of the woman! It was difficult to keep my mind on the verses.

I went straight up to the bedroom. Looking around carefully, I was reassured to find that Sapphire had not taken any of her toilet things, except a toothbrush: evidently she had not gone off for good. Now that I'd got the locket, I felt much happier about the whole situation; it would give me the whip-hand of Sally. What a fool I had been, though, to miss the perfect chance of using it! If it was an all-purpose pass, why hadn't I produced it just now and made Sally yield me the front seat? Then I might have been able to listen to her thoughts. I resented the theory that it was decent for a woman to eavesdrop, but indecent for a man.

I undressed, got into bed, and was soon asleep. I had taken the precaution of tying the locket around my ankle with a piece of ribbon from Sapphire's dressing-table. Sally was quite capable of trying to steal it.

A gentle knock at the door woke me soon afterwards, and Antonia came in.

'Hullo, Tonia,' I said sleepily.

'Oh, hullo, Ned.'

'How did you come here?'

'A woman with blue legs and a tall fancy-dress hat evoked me.'

'That was very nice of her. I've missed you a lot, these last five days.'

'How do you mean: five days? We were together all yesterday. . . .'

'Five of their days. And because of the tobacco shortage they seem twice as long as ours. How are you?'

'A bit puzzled, but a good deal happier now I've found you. I thought I was dreaming.'

'Well, you're not. This place is real enough. Who's looking after Mun?'

'Nobody, but Mlle. Blue-legs promised me that I'd be away only between one heart-beat and the next; and even Mun can't manage to fall out of his cot in that time. I rather like the look of this place. I wish we had servants like the ones here. Just look at the polish on that chest-of-drawers!'

'I can't see it without sitting up and I don't feel like moving at the moment.'

'Shall I come to bed with you? It's still very early.'

'There's nothing I'd enjoy more. In this brave new world we poets are expected to twine and float platonically in the air with our disembodied loved ones.'

'But how charming! Like Levitated Lottie and her boy friend?'

'That's right. Or else we have to defend our virtue against assaults by stark naked maenads.'

'But how alarming! I hope you've managed to defend yours, my sweet?' She slipped into bed as she spoke.

'So far, Mari be praised!'

'*What* did you say?'

'Mari be praised!'

'Do you mean to say that they've succeeded where even

Ronnie Knox failed, and made a *Cat*holic of you? Oh, Ned, I never thought I'd see the day!'

'Here, don't shrink from me, you black Protestant! Everyone in New Crete says "Mari be praised!" It doesn't mean a thing.'

'Promise me you're telling the truth. I'd never forgive myself if I found myself in bed with a ruddy Papist. It's my oldest superstition.'

'I promise faithfully. I'll even sing "Clitter, clatter, Holy Watter" for you, if you insist. But, really, Tonia, you ought to know me better by now. I've still got C. of E. stamped on my identity disc.'

'Oh, is *that* what you're wearing round your ankle?'

'I was speaking figuratively. The thing round my ankle is a sort of New Cretan passport. When we get up we'll go places with it.'

'I say, those are lovely brushes on the dressing-table! I wish you'd buy me a new ivory brush; I've never felt quite a lady since mine was blown to hell by that Good Friday bomb. Whose bedroom is this, by the bye?'

'A nice girl called Sapphire lives here. She's away at the moment. You'll like her. Something almost Lady Margaret Hall about her.'

'Are you in love with her?'

'What an untimely question!'

'Oh, Ned, isn't this fun? Let's have a look at that passport for a moment. Is there any mention of me, and does the photograph make you look any less criminal than usual?'

'It isn't that sort of a passport. And I'm not untying it from my ankle. No, leave go of it or I'll tickle you till you scream! It stays where it is. I don't trust anyone with it, not even you. We live precarious lives in this somewhere-nowhere place and I'm not taking any risks. One slip, and we might topple off into nothingness.'

'You make me feel like Mrs. Discobbolus on the wall with Mr. Discobbolus.'

'I didn't realize you knew your Lear. You've always said you had a rhymeless and storyless childhood. Anyway, stop chattering now and lie still. I'm going to start serious proceedings by kissing you on the tip of your unluminous nose.'

'Why unluminous?'

'Hush, darling!'

I slept till nearly dinner time. When I awoke, Antonia had already dressed and left the bedroom. She must have had breakfast by now. This was Wednesday, the day when the recorders took their holiday, so there would be no Interpreter to help her. But she could always make signs to supplement her French—French was, after all, closely related to Catalan, the basis of New Cretan—or draw pictures on a scrap of paper. 'No, not on paper,' I reminded myself, 'but she always made herself understood perfectly, even to our dumb Sudanese cook at Heliopolis.'

As I dressed, I wondered why Sally had evoked Antonia. Was spite the motive? Since I had refused to share her cloak, had she made up her mind that I should at least not share Sapphire's? No, that wasn't right; obviously she could not act on her own. I had the Hag to thank for my present happiness. All orders for evocation came from her; Sally could only have been the agent. But what I did not understand was how Sally had managed it so quickly. She had been away all night, and when we came back I could hardly have been asleep for more than half an hour before Antonia knocked. Yet my own evocation, according to the Interpreter, had lasted from dawn to midday, and then I had not woken up until fairly late in the afternoon. Evidently Sally had improved on her technique and cut down the time to a few minutes. Or were women perhaps more easily evoked than men?

I went out to look for Antonia. She was not in the dining-room, nor in the sitting-room, nor on the veranda, nor in the study behind the sitting-room where I had first found myself. Through a window I saw See-a-Bird pacing up and down the garden and called to him: 'Have you seen my wife?'

'No, I haven't. She hasn't returned from Court yet.'

I had used the word *dona*, which in New Cretan means 'lady' or 'sweetheart' as well as wife, so See-a-Bird had misunderstood my question.

'I don't mean Sapphire, I mean Antonia,' I said.

'Oh, Edward, has she died?'

'What are you talking about?'

'I thought you said that Sapphire was no longer called Sapphire, but Antonia.'

'If she were dead I shouldn't ask you whether you'd seen her. No, you've got the wires hopelessly crossed. I am asking you whether you've seen a young woman wandering about—not Sapphire, nor anything to do with her—long-legged and rather purposeful with dark, wavy hair, wearing a striped yellow-and-black skirt, a white blouse with short sleeves, and high-heeled black shoes. She's called Antonia.'

'Nobody like that has been downstairs since breakfast time.'

'Then she must have missed breakfast.'

At that moment Starfish came up and See-a-Bird passed my question on to him.

'No, I've seen nobody,' he answered. 'Nor can anyone have gone out by either of the gates before breakfast. They have the "keep-away" symbol marked on both sides.'

'Then she can only be in Sally's bedroom. Antonia's my wife, you know—from my own age. Is Sally up yet?'

'No.' Now See-a-Bird was looking scared.

I went to Sally's door and knocked. Presently she opened the door, tousled and cheerful. She was wearing a red, Chinese-looking dressing-gown and her legs showed no sign of woad. 'Hello, how are things this morning?' she asked.

'Fine, thanks.'

'Good. Is there anything you want?'

'Yes, I want Antonia. Is she in there with you?'

'What's your hurry?'

'She doesn't seem to have had breakfast.'

Sally eyed me inscrutably. 'No, not a bite. I'll be along in a moment. It must be nearly time for lunch.'

'But where is Antonia? I want to see her.'

'I said I'd be along in a moment.'

'Don't tease me, Sally. She's in there with you, isn't she?'

'In a manner of speaking—yes!' She shut the door, laughing softly to herself. Then she half-opened it again and asked me: 'Why unluminous?'

Then, of course, I understood. It had not been Antonia: it had been Sally, hypnotizing me into building up a false Antonia from my scattered memories of her—like the false Helen, the *idolon*, that had precipitated the Trojan War—and then giving it physical reality with her own body. She had started that game on the first night I spent with Sapphire. The conversation had been an invention of my own, of the unilateral sort that people often carry on in their minds with absent friends or lovers—this was proved by the reference to Lear's Mr. and Mrs. Discobbolus: as soon as I put it into the idolon's mouth I had recognized that it was not the sort of remark the real Antonia would have made, and immediately corrected it.

I glared at Sally. 'You faggot!' I said between my teeth.

'I'm sorry you didn't manage to defend your virtue any longer, my sweet!'

She shut the door in my face and bolted it after her. If See-a-Bird had not happened to come by at that moment, I think I should have run at it with my shoulder, broken in and scragged her. But there he stood beckoning, his gentle, sheep-like face turned appealingly to me, his whole body sagging.

'What's wrong now, old chap?' I asked, following him into the sitting-room.

'News has just come from the barber-shop: about two fresh graves by the waterfall at Zapmor. It's thought . . . .'

His voice failed him and he slumped down on the sofa.

'I'm too old to face these trials much longer,' he whispered. 'We were such a happy family until three or four days ago—'

'I hope you don't mean to imply that I've disturbed the peace? I didn't ask to be evoked. . . .'

He smiled sorrowfully. 'No, Edward, it's not you, but what you have brought with you.'

'You mean the brutch of Erica Turner?'

'I do, indeed. Sally has told me about the obscene metal case found in Sapphire's cupboard.'

'Then allow me to correct you. I did not bring Erica with me. She's been living here for years. She told me so herself.'

'That cannot be true: we should have known of her presence long before this. She must have come with you, clinging to your hair. And now, it seems, a second brutch from your epoch is wandering about, the woman in the yellow-and-black skirt, who you say is your wife.'

'Sally can explain that apparition, if you ask her. She created it herself, for reasons best known to herself.'

'But Sally's job is to lay brutches, not to create them.'

'I entirely agree, and because I see that you still trust Sally, I refrain from comment.'

'Why, of course I trust Sally. This is our age, not yours. We all trust one another and expect to be trusted in return.'

'I hope the day keeps fine for you.'

'Eh?'

'My dear See-a-Bird, may I give you a piece of friendly advice?'

'Please do.'

'It's this: I advise you to go to your room, collect your bits and pieces, and then report at once to whoever officiates on occasions of this sort, and announce your intention of becoming an elder. You're old enough to qualify, surely? Good. Things in this house are bound to grow more and more confusing from now on, I suppose until I'm returned to my epoch, and then for a long time afterwards. Wriggle out from under the trouble while you still can. You'll be perfectly happy in a nonsense house, where you need take nothing seriously, and where nobody outside will take you seriously.'

'Oh, but, Edward, my dear friend. . . .'

'You mean that you don't want to enter the local institution for fear of running up against Erica? No, See-a-Bird, you needn't be afraid. Erica is both everywhere and nowhere. You'll be as safe from her there as at the other end of the world; or as unsafe.'

'Who is she then?'

'Someone whom you know very well.' For as I spoke I realized that Erica had not been an *idolon* of the same sort as the false Antonia, not, in fact, Sally at her tricks again. The cigarette case, which Sapphire had found in her cupboard while I was away in Sanjon, was concrete proof of that. No: behind Erica loomed a more powerful magic than any Sally could command—the magic of the incarnate Goddess herself, in whom, absurd though it may sound, I was bound to believe by the logic of my recent experiences.

See-a-Bird hesitated. Then he returned to the subject of the graves. He asked me timorously: 'Is it true about the grave . . . . that Fig-bread won't be returning to this house?'

'Such queer things have been happening here lately that I wouldn't like to make a prophecy about his return. If I could be evoked from the remote past, I don't see why Fig-bread can't be evoked from the recent past.'

'He is dead, then? And you buried him?' He looked ghastly.

'Yes, Sally asked me to dig both graves. The larger one

contains his horse. The horse had turned on him and savaged him. Afterwards it felt conscience-stricken and brought Sally to the scene of the murder. She destroyed it. Then various other things happened. In the end two lovers spread their cloaks over Fig-bread's grave.'

He cheered up a little. 'Ah, then the horse was the murderer, after all. Mari be praised! A rumour was going around that Fig-bread had been struck a blow by a Zapmor man whom he was trying to separate from an opponent and that he died of his injuries. Now I understand everything. When you tried to take the short cut home across the water-meadows he must have ridden to head you off from the sacred grove, and accidentally disturbed the crane in her meditations. Involuntary trespass is always punished by a violent death and the Goddess has before now made a horse the instrument of her vengeance. Yet his death was an honourable one; love between man and man has not been broken, and Fig-bread's name may still shine in the records. He sinned with good intention.'

I did not care to undeceive him. 'You should have warned me about the crane,' I said.

He was going into the garden to break the news to Starfish when he stopped with his hand on the door knob. 'But, Edward, I implore you to trust Sally. Your lack of love towards her has caused us all great pain.'

'Lack of love!' I exclaimed. 'That's rich! It may interest you to know that last night Sally honoured me by offering me the rights of fatherhood, and that our love has now been consummated.'

'So it was you?'

'What do you mean by "So it was you"?'

'But I thought that you and Sapphire had a lovers' understanding?'

'That's right. If Sapphire had been about, things would have taken a different turn.'

He came back miserably to the sofa. 'I think that, after all, I shall take your advice and apply for elderhood,' he muttered.

'What's wrong now?' I asked.

'Starfish is deeply in love with Sally, and I know, as truly as I know anything, that this further blow will wound him to the heart.'

'You mean that he'll be jealous of me?'

'No, it isn't that. He wasn't jealous of Fig-bread when Sally invited him to her bed last Friday. Poets are never jealous. But he'll be deeply mortified, feeling that he, not you, should have been invited to share her cloak on his brother's grave.'

I could not correct this slight misapprehension without saying more than I intended. 'That's exactly what I tried to make Sally see,' I growled as I put on my hat.

'Where are you going now?' he asked.

'I'm going to ride to Dunrena and find Sapphire. The situation here is becoming impossibly complicated.'

'And when you've found her?'

'Then I'll warn her never to come back, not even to collect her belongings. The servants can see to all that. I'm not coming back either. I'm sticking to Sapphire.'

'But that sounds as though you didn't love Sally after all— as though you . . . . I fail to understand.'

'Don't try to understand. You're completely out of your depth. Don't even try to explain things to Starfish—Sally will do that. Get your things together and clear out as soon as possible. Leave these two alone here to work things out as best they can.'

I went to the stables and called a groom. 'Saddle me a horse and get someone to fill my saddle-bags with food and drink for two days.'

When the groom came back from the kitchen, he asked: 'Do you think, Sir, the Witch will be exercising the Nymph's mare this morning?'

'What? Has Sapphire gone off on foot?'

'I suppose so, Sir; I was not about when she left. She didn't take the mare out yesterday either; the beast is getting fretful.'

'But the Witch told me distinctly that she had ridden off to Court.'

'You must have misheard her, Sir.'

This was bad. It looked as if Sapphire meant, after all, to turn commoner, or kill herself: as if Sally had persuaded her to break that promise to me. I told the groom: 'I'll take the mare with me. I can manage the two of them.'

'Will a headstall be enough?'

'No, put a saddle on her.'

A window opened above us. I could feel Sally's eyes piercing my back, but I did not look up.

CHAPTER XVI

Quant

A MILE down the road I saw the Interpreter sitting on a stile, and stopped to pass the time of day. Near him stood a little old man with a face like a wizened apple, who eyed me shrewdly.

'This is your learned colleague Quant, I presume?' I asked in English. (His name, by the way, meant 'How Much?' but I shall always think of him as Quant.)

He spoke for himself. 'Yes, that's who I am, Mr. Venn-Thomas, and I'm delighted to meet you. Mallet-head here has been sending in detailed reports on your English vocabulary and syntax, which have cleared up many of our outstanding *cruces*. We're most grateful to you for your help. Have you a moment to spare, by the way?'

'Not for a discussion of anomalous past participles, I fear. I'm going off to Dunrena to find my friend Sapphire.'

'Yes, I recognize her mare. Do you know anyone at Court?'

'Not a soul.'

'Is it even certain that she has gone there?'

'No, not altogether. Can you give me any news of her since she left home?'

'I can. She came straight to me for advice.'

A New Cretan woman magician going to a man-recorder for advice! But the Interpreter interposed, beaming with admiration: 'Sacred parentage exists between him and her, i.e. he is her mother's brother. But, *ceteris paribus*, everyone comes to my colleague Quant for advice, because he is the most practical of men, and also he is the most sympathetic.'

Quant winked at me, almost imperceptibly; but as the first wink I had been given in New Crete it startled me. It implied a secret from which his colleague was excluded, and I recognized this as something thoroughly un-Cretan: since my arrival everyone had been impressing on me that the cornerstone of society was perfect frankness between man and man.

'Hullo!' I said to myself, 'here's a fellow-human at last!'

'Well,' I told Quant, 'if I can't be sure of finding Sapphire at Dunrena, it would be stupid to take her horse there. I'll tell you what: shall we sit down somewhere and settle the Late Christian inflexions of irregular and defective Old English verbs?'

'Capital! By all means.' Quant turned to the Interpreter: 'Cut along now, or you'll be late.'

'Are you sure that I can be of no further service, my dear?' the Interpreter pleaded.

'Your duty lies in the concert room,' said Quant with decision. 'I should never forgive myself if I thought that you had held up the performance for my sake.' Turning to me again, he explained: 'My colleague Mallet-head plays the oboe. He plays it correctly and dispassionately. However, he's a superb croquet-player, and in croquet those are the qualities that win matches.'

The Interpreter took his leave, smiling happily: it was clear that he had missed the critical force of Quant's 'however'.

'Sapphire's not gone to Dunrena,' said Quant, when we were alone. 'She's not even left the village—I was to tell you so privately. You'll not be needing either of those horses. Why not take them up the side of that wood and through the gate into the paddock beyond, unsaddle them, and then come back here?'

I did as he suggested. The paddock contained a set of

hurdles for jumping-practice and I left the horses going fault-lessly round the course together, whinnying for pleasure at the turns. Then Quant and I crossed the road by the stile and struck across country until we came to a small weather-boarded hut in a quince-orchard.

'We can talk here undisturbed,' he said, pushing open the door, 'and I don't mean about past participles.'

The hut was furnished with a table, two chairs, a charcoal stove and a bunk.

'Make yourself at home,' he added, sitting down.

'Whose place is this?' I asked.

'It's a painters' hut; that's why it's in a quince-orchard.'

'I don't see the connexion.'

'Quinces are sacred to Mari, who inspires our painters of magical pictures. As you may know, we have two kinds of painting, the magical and the popular. The commons paint their house-signs and decorate their fire-boards and chests with flowers, fruit and animals, or with lively illustrations of barber-shop ballads; but that's about all. No, they aren't allowed to paint portraits of living people; not even magicians may do that, for fear of bringing ill-luck. The magical paint-ing is done in quince-huts. Colours, brushes and boards are on the shelf above your head, if you feel inspired.'

'I won't; but tell me about magical painting.'

'It's a way of consulting the Goddess. The magician paints a picture on a mythical subject, and when it's done the answer to the problem, whatever it was, is found on the board.'

'What sort of a problem?'

'Every sort. It may be diagnostic: for example the cause and cure of an epidemic. Or it may be about love. Or about some question of public morality. I'll give you a simple instance. A few years ago, a body was found in a peat-marsh, well-preserved and wearing a waistcoat with gold buttons, one of which was missing. There was a bottle in his pocket, also a snuff-box. The buttons were made from coins, but the finder asked permission to wear them. He claimed that they had long been converted from money into buttons and that, since they were struck by hand, they were not against custom. The problem was referred to a council of magicians and one entire morning its fifteen members sat staring at the buttons, but not one of them felt inspired to say a word. At last Bee-flight—who is the mother of See-a-Bird's children and an elder now—stood up. "Perhaps the quince-trees have a message for us," she said. The others then went out into the garden and played cambeluk; it was a Thursday.'

'What's cambeluk?'

'A game not unlike chess or draughts for two players, played with nine pieces a side—eight commoners and a captain: you'll have to learn it. Bee-flight went off at once to this very hut, said a prayer to Mari, and got down to work. She painted the legend of Nimuë, Dobeis and the golden wheels and when she had come out of her trance, she tied the board behind her and rode home. She waited until the cambeluk tourney was finished, because we never interrupt a game unless in an emergency, and the council reassembled to look at the picture. There stood Nimuë, her hand poised in the act of killing Dobeis, and in the background was a liquor shop. The man in the waistcoat, his face bloated with drink, had cut off one of the buttons and was handing it over the counter with his left hand, while with the other he reached for a bottle. From the shop a path wound across a marsh, and a raven hovered in the sky. That, of course, was decisive. Clearly, the buttons had served as money and one of them had caused the man's death—he had got drunk on his way home and the marsh had swallowed him up.'

'What happened to the buttons in the end?'

'They were sent to the Queen of the Witches for purification, and afterwards beaten out into a gold sheet for the archives. However, the finder was allowed to keep the snuff-box, which was judged to be a work of love.'

'And why have you brought me to this hut? I can't paint, and you're no magician.'

'I'm hoping that Sapphire will come here.'

'Very well, tell me about her.'

'But first, if you'll excuse me, a little about myself. Or do you want to ask me something before I begin?'

'Yes; I'd like you to put your hand on this locket and swear that you're the Interpreter's colleague Quant, and not just another of those annoying illusions that have fooled me these last few days. Your English is so correct and idiomatic that I'm a little suspicious of you.'

He smiled and took the oath in New Cretan.

'Did *She* give you that?' he asked, greatly impressed by the locket.

I nodded. 'In the alder-grove,' I said.

'Did she seem pleased with you?'

'She was good enough to tell me that I was doing very well.'

'You're a lucky man. Now, listen and interrupt me whenever you like. First about myself. I'm what they call a *margoton* here: so far as I know there's no English equivalent. It means someone who, though a reputable member of one estate, has the capacity of belonging to another. We margotons are extremely rare, but the poet Vives was one of us, and that provides the necessary precedent. He was born in the magicians' estate, but at the time of the Cyprian Flood, when all the captains of his district lost their lives, he assumed command and carried on the rescue work to everyone's admiration. "Thereafter Vives rode a skewbald," the *Brief History* says. I was born in the magicians' estate but had all the earmarks of a recorder, except a temperamental incapacity for croquet, which I have never been able to overcome; then when I had already been initiated as a recorder, at the same time as my sister, I suddenly discovered that I was also a poet. I debated with myself whether I ought to ask for a transfer to my original estate; but decided that I was as much recorder as I was poet, so that there could be no advantage in changing. Besides, when I came to specialize in English—a language, I find, which can't be read without poetic intuition—I realized that the time had passed when it was possible to write true poetry in my own language. . . . I think Mallet-head mentioned our recent find—the Liverpool hoard of Christmas-cards?'

'He did; it was about the first thing I was told after my evocation.'

'Adventurers found the box in a cave. I gave him the task of transcribing the texts before they were destroyed—all paper has to be destroyed when the year ends. In the same collection was a manuscript book of poetry which I intended to transcribe myself. When I deciphered the poems—the ink was badly faded in places—I found that they had far greater bite and poignancy than any of those included in our English Canon; but I realized at the same time that their inclusion would have had a disruptive effect on New Cretan thought. The book had two names on the fly-leaf—your own and Erica Turner's.'

'It had a speckled cover, hadn't it?'

'No, the cover was missing.'

'Well, anyhow, I remember it well.' (How the hell did it get to Liverpool?—that must have been long after my time. I bought it in Algiers when I was there with Erica in 1932. I had brought my books with me and one day, after we'd had an argument about poetic integrity, she challenged me to copy out all the English poems I knew in which the poet had really come clean about himself without holding anything back. There weren't very many, I found. But even so, Erica was scathing about my choice. She said: 'There's not a man among them who'd have died twice running for the same woman.' I asked her: 'Why twice?' 'Once is no proof of integrity,' she said. Erica was a queer girl.)

'I didn't show them to Mallet-head or anyone else, but I began to write English poetry myself. Since English is a dead language and my poems were not intended for anyone's eye, I could see no harm in this. At any rate, it solved my personal problem as a margoton, and I was pleased that I hadn't changed my estate again: as a magician I would have been obliged to write in New Cretan and hand my poems around. Then one day the Goddess came to talk to me about you.'

'Look here, Quant! You're now in the position of being able to think and talk in terms of my age as well as of your own: no other man in New Crete can do that. So you owe me a commonsense explanation of what you mean, when you say: "The Goddess came to talk to me."'

'But you've had the same experience yourself. She gave you that locket in the alder-grove.'

'Experience isn't the same as explanation. I took the Hag for a representative of the Goddess, not the Goddess herself.'

'That's a distinction without a difference. She always assumes the form of a living creature. Do you happen to know the *Iliad*, one of the myths of the ancient world?'

'I do, as a matter of fact: I read it in Greek at school.'

'Then perhaps you'll remember that the Goddess—there's really only one Goddess, not several—sometimes appeared in human disguise during the Trojan War, and even on one occasion as a man: as the Trojan Prince Deiphobus, just before Hector's fight with the Greek champion?'

'With all respect to Homer, it never occurred to me to take the story literally.'

'You would have done if you'd served in the Trojan War.'

'That's possible. Go on.'

'Well, you'll admit that it isn't natural for you to worship a Father-god?'

'Wait a moment, that's a rather sweeping statement. It came naturally enough to my father, for instance.'

'Indeed, and was he a happy man?'

'When he wasn't worrying about his soul or his accounts.'

'Yes, what I mean is that the Father-god isn't in the blood like the Goddess; he's an artificial concept which your ancestors have done their best to naturalize, but you should have abandoned him long ago in the interests of sanity. Your chief trouble in the Late Christian epoch is unlimited scientific war which nobody likes but everybody accepts as inevitable; that's a typical by-product of God-worship. In the archaic days, whenever tribal life grew too monotonous the Goddess used, of course, to allow her peoples to go to war; but she kept it within decent bounds, though not perhaps as strictly as now. When your ancestors rebelled against her they invented a Father-god whose sole business was war—Sunday, Monday, Tuesday, Wednesday and all—a ferocious demon who stole her battle axe and set out to conquer mankind. He ousted the Goddess from sovereignty, made her his bond-woman, and eventually announced that she no longer existed.'

'If she's as powerful as you New Cretans believe, I wonder she submitted to that.'

'She not only submitted to it, she arranged it. You see, a few millennia of chaos can mean very little to an immortal, and she had two objects clearly in mind. The first was that she loved man and didn't want him to feel fettered and repressed: she would emancipate him and allow him to fulfil his destiny (as she ironically expressed it) by letting him find out the absurdity of creating a supreme deity in his own phallic likeness. In the end he would voluntarily return to her rule. Her second object was to demonstrate the existence in him of certain intellectual capacities hitherto unsuspected by woman: woman was taking her sexual superiority too much for granted and treating him as a plaything.'

'In theory it seems to me as natural to worship a male God as a Goddess.'

'Exactly: she had to grant man the power to theorize and

that was one of his theories. But in practice a male deity is a contradiction in terms. Presently your ancestors lost all faith in the Father-god's wisdom and justice, and even began to doubt his existence; a few secretly returned to Goddess worship. But others turned rationalist and created a God of Reason and Learning as a substitute for the Goddess of Love and Wisdom.'

'To what point in history does that bring the story?'

'To the time of Socrates and Aristotle. You may already know the lines:

> Socrates and his demon
> Made insurrection. . . .

I'll give you them later, if you don't. The War-god still maintained his sovereignty and since love had ended between man and man—except in the secret fraternities still sponsored by the Goddess—he also became the God of Robbers. The third place in the Rogue Trinity was taken by the God of Money, whom we call Dobeis.'

'You seem to be by-passing Christianity.'

'It's not important, except as a symptom of man's spiritual fever: it brought diversion, rather than change. Christianity grew out of the foredoomed attempt of a few Jewish sages to regularize and purify the worship of the Father-god by a complete suppression of Goddess-worship; they anathematized the God of Money and identified the Father-god with supreme Love, Wisdom and Justice. But the sages were soon shouldered aside by Gentile converts to Christianity, which came to comprise all sorts of contradictory beliefs—everything, from a perverse philosophical theory of not-being, and a half-hearted cult of the Goddess as a chaste Virgin, to pure War-god worship. By your epoch, the Rogue Trinity was supreme in every practical sense. There's a famous verse passage in our *Myths of New Crete*:

"The sword decides," rumbled the God of Robbers;
"Science is Truth," the God of Reason piped;
"And each man has his price," chanted Dobeis;
"All else is superstition," roared the Rogues.
Nimuë heard their chorus. . . .

It seems to me that a Late Christian poet was committed in
the name of integrity to resist, doubt, scoff, destroy and play
the fool; it was only when he met with a like-minded fellow-
poet, or with a woman on whom the spirit of the Goddess
had secretly descended, that he felt all was not yet lost. Is
that right?'

'More or less.'

'Mallet-head has told you of the origins of New Crete.
When the Sophocrats came to power at a time of almost
universal despair, they were persuaded by ben-Yeshu's argu-
ments to plant the colonies from which our present social
system has developed. The Anthropological Council accepted
the contention with which ben-Yeshu's famous, though
heavy-handed, book opened: "Civilization has suffered a
global *crise des nerfs* resultant on an attempt to eradicate a vital
religious element from the psychological inheritance of the
dominant Alpine blood-group."   In other words, they
agreed that, if mankind were to survive at all, the Goddess
must be re-instated in power, and they had collected sufficient
archæological data to be able to restore her worship in convincing detail.'

He paused and drew three stars in the air with his finger, to
show that he had finished his historical introduction.

'So now you're back again in pre-Trojan War times,' I said,
'but with the advantage that man has learned the danger of
rebelling against the Goddess; and that in the course of his
rebellion he's made a number of useful inventions from which
you still benefit.'

'That's the credit side of the balance sheet:

For here five-fingered custom rules us well,

as Solero put it; but there's also the debit side, which I was able to assess only after reading your manuscript book. I realized then that ever since the last three abortive attempts to overthrow the New Cretan system from outside—there's never been an internal revolt—we have lived what your age, in idealistic prospect, called "the good life", and that is a very easy life indeed. I don't mean that we haven't worked hard and played hard, kept in good physical and spiritual health, fought our one-day wars with enthusiasm, and gone for occasional adventures in the Bad Lands. But somehow that's not enough.'

'Did you ever come across Bernard de Mandeville's *Grumbling Hive*? Ben-Yeshu seems to have overlooked that in his list of Utopias.'

'No, it hasn't survived.'

'Well, it's pretty much to the point. He held that virtue— which he defined as every performance by which man, contrary to the impulse of nature, tries to benefit his fellowman out of a rational desire for goodness—is in the long run detrimental to mankind. He describes a society possessed of all the virtues which falls into apathy and paralysis, and insists that private vices are public benefits.'

'That, of course, was an over-statement of the case, an invitation to chaos. But it's true at least that the thrilling intensity of the love that your poets felt for the Goddess in the Late Christian epoch can have no equivalent as things are now. When Cleopatra wrote her poems the issue here was still in doubt; the old civilization still existed side by side with the new, and our traders were still sailing to Corinth and bringing back doubtful merchandise. Cleopatra's poems are a passionate plea not to relapse into humanity's former madness. But ever since the days of Solero and Vives and our other legislative poets, what have we to show? There's Robnet, who lived a good deal later, but he was brought here as a child from the American Bad Lands and kept something of his natural wildness until his death; and he died young. Who else is there?'

'The other night at the Santrepod, Erica Turner came into the room—well, you know about Erica.'

He nodded. 'But I haven't yet heard this part of the story.'

'Sapphire had played something by Alysin; I found it insincere and told Erica so. She took the same line as you do: that since the days of Cleopatra music and poetry have gone into a decline.'

'And what did Sapphire and Sally say to that?'

'Nothing. They were asleep. Everyone but myself was asleep when Erica defied the spell they had laid against her and walked in.'

'She was the Goddess,' Quant said.

'I had suspected that. "She will be old and young whenas she pleases." But it's difficult for me, brought up in the theory of a God who is a supernatural being of dazzling brightness, portentous size and thunderous voice, to be awed by a Goddess who can appear in the likeness of Erica Turner.'

'She wasn't trying to awe you,' said Quant, 'any more than Athene was trying to awe Hector. And would you really be awed by a celestial giant with a voice like thunder? I can't believe you're that sort of man, Mr. Venn-Thomas.'

I laughed. '*Touché!*' I said. 'But now let me hear about Sapphire. You say she came to you for advice: what did she tell you?'

'About Erica at the Nonsense House, and about finding an obscene metal case in her cupboard, and about your suspicions of Sally. She kept nothing back.'

'And what did you tell her?'

'I said that she mustn't be afraid: that she was safest with you in the very vortex of the whirlwind. I used that expression deliberately: and I'll tell you why. It was because one evening, when I was transcribing the last of the poems from your book, the Goddess entered my study wearing a white-striped coat and green shoes. I knew who she was and abased myself. She stood over me and wrote on the clay directly under your name: "Before the year is out, I will whistle up this seed of wind to blow the rotten boughs from my trees." So when I read Sally's report of your evocation, I felt little surprise. But I kept in the background and watched the mare's tails in the sky and listened to the sound of the wind in the acacias, until yesterday, when the Goddess sent Sapphire to consult me.'

'I'm sorry for Sapphire,' I said, 'but sorrier still for Sally. The Goddess has given her the most difficult part to play.'

Quant sighed deeply. 'I must go home now for the evening-smoke,' he said after a pause. 'Mallet-head will be waiting to fill my pipe. He's a good fellow and an industrious colleague. Good afternoon, Mr. Venn-Thomas. Thank you for a pleasant chat.'

I detained him. 'Quant, may I see your English poems?'

His hand went to his breast pocket. 'I have taken the liberty of bringing one with me. I wrote it some time ago when Sapphire's mind was obsessed by premonitions of her present grief; the ties of sacred parentage are very strong and I express my sympathy in the poem. As you see, it's already engraved on silver, with the New Cretan translation opposite.'

'But surely, you have no sheets allowed you? You're not officially a poet?'

'Being the curator of Late Christian texts, I transcribe on clay any poems that come to light, and the magicians judge them. A council ordered this one to be engraved on silver: they attributed it to the poet Marvell.'

'Well, well, what it is to be a margoton!'

He chuckled. 'I can't expect that your opinion of the poem will be as favourable as theirs,' he said. 'You may not think that it stands as a poem at all, but the Council believe that it's destined for inclusion in the *English Canon*.'

Then he hurried off with an authorial embarrassment that touched me. When he had closed the door, I read the poem, which was in characteristic seventeenth-century style, though nothing like Marvell's; but then, the editors of the *Canon* had credited Marvell with poems by various other hands, not all so competent as Quant's.

A sunbeam on the well-waxed oak,
   In shape resembling not at all
The ragged chink by which it broke
   Into this darkened hall,
Swims round and golden over me,
   The sun's plenipotentiary.

So may my round love a chink find:
   With such address to break
Into your grief-occluded mind
   As you shall not mistake
But, rising, open to me for truth's sake.

I shouted after him: 'Hey, Quant!'

'Yes?' he answered from the end of the field.

'Thank you. The poem stands.'

He came back, pressed my hand gratefully, replaced the silver sheet in his breast pocket and went off again, humming softly to himself.

What a nice chap he was!

CHAPTER XVII

Who is Edward?

WHILE Quant was talking, I made up my mind to live in the present and think as little as possible about my own epoch. I might be in New Crete for years; I might perhaps never get back, and while I was here it would be ungrateful not to make the best of things. Now, at any rate, I was free of the grosser aspects of our down-at-heel pluto-democracy; the food was wholesome; the people were courteous; the countryside was magnificent. I had a thoroughbred at my disposal and so much to amuse or interest me that, frankly, it was absurd to hanker sentimentally after St. Jean-des-Porcs as it had been, or for the mad, anonymous whirl of Piccadilly Tube-station in the rush-hour, or for a deck-chair, a packet of Old Golds, a glass of Tio Pepe and Simenon's latest novel in my own rather scruffy back-garden in Sainte Véronique. Especially, I must put out of my mind all emotional ties that linked me with Antonia; Antonia had no part in this life and my sentimental thinking about her had enabled Sally to outwit me. It had been stupid of me to equate Sapphire with Antonia; they were entirely different people. And in bad taste: I had behaved rather like a widower who forces his new wife to keep the loved one's memory green by wearing her frocks and underclothes and using the same scent.

'Tell me the latest news,' Sapphire said, coming quietly in and settling down in the chair Quant had vacated.

'I'm here and you're here, and that's all that matters,' I said rising and placing my hands on her shoulders.

'Really all?'

'You heard what I said.'

She gave a sigh of relief. 'Something's changed you, Edward. I can feel it in your touch. It isn't so nervous and prickly as it was.'

'I've not been treating you properly,' I said. 'I'll do better from now on.'

'That's nice to hear. I didn't expect you to become a New Cretan in a day, and the hauntings made things very difficult for us.'

'I don't think there'll be any more.'

'If you say so, there won't be. How are they all at home? How did they take my going away?'

'I've only heard See-a-Bird's view. He's rather down in the mouth and talks of becoming an elder.'

'On my account? How very wrong of him, even if Bee-flight's just done the same. We must stop him at once. He's still too young and vigorous to play billiards in the Nonsense House every evening and spend his mornings just pottering around.'

'Well, I think it's a wise move. He's living up to his name; he can see the vultures hovering above the clouds. Anyhow, it's rather on Starfish's account than on yours.'

'But what happened to Starfish?'

'To break the news as gently as possible: Starfish thinks that he should have been asked to share Sally's cloak on a newly turfed grave.'

Sapphire gasped, clutching at her throat. 'Whose grave?'

'Fig-bread's, I'm sorry to say.'

'Oh, poor, poor Fig-bread! Did he get killed in the war?'

'No, his horse mauled him.'

'Ana have mercy on us all! But he was so proud of its manners, and it was such a gentle creature.'

'Before it was bewitched.'

'Bewitched? You don't mean that! By whom?'

'Can't you guess?' I looked hard at her.

'I don't want to try,' she faltered.

'By Sally, of course.'

'I don't believe it, darling. I won't believe it. It's utterly impossible. Don't tell me such dreadful things—it's like those nightmarish stories from the ancient world. Fig-bread loved Sally; and she loved him.'

'I'm sorry, my dear, but that's what happened.'

'But why? What reason could she have had?'

'She wanted a religious excuse to spread her cloak for another man.'

'For another man?' she asked in a strangled voice. 'For whom?'

'For me, of course.'

'And did she? And did you. . . ? Oh, this is a waking nightmare! Say you didn't!' Sapphire wailed.

'Of course I didn't. Not on the grave, at any rate. But early this morning while I was asleep she tricked me by disguising herself as Antonia again and coming to bed with me. I gave her all she asked.'

'But really you love only me?' she whispered. 'You are sure of that?'

'Only you,' I said. 'I did love Antonia, as you know. But, as one of our poets has callously put it, "that was in another country and, besides, the wench is dead." It's you now. And I'll try not to forget your warning—what you told me that first night we spent together. Only don't cry! I can't bear to see you cry.'

'I don't think I'll ever shed another tear after this,' she said faintly.

We ate supper in silence; both of us were thinking hard. But first we chalked the keep-away symbol on the door—

three cranes with their wings raised menacingly—and lighted the stove because the evening was chilly and rain was pattering on the quince-leaves. Now that I had decided, for Sapphire's sake, to shed my old habits of thought and become a New Cretan I was reminded of the day when I had swallowed my insular pride and tried to talk French as the French did with all their habitual gesticulations and vocal tricks. 'Am I being dishonest?' I asked myself. 'Am I just putting on a theatrical turn? Or is this really myself?' I didn't know.

In my previous life—I had to refer to that again, but with the emphasis on 'previous'—there had been three distinct Edwards, each developed in relation to a different woman with whom he had been in love. The first of any importance was Virgilia, a district-attorney's daughter from South Carolina: she was blue-eyed and ringleted, with a fascinating Southern drawl, devoted to horses, dancing and success. For her sake I had cultivated these first two interests until I outdid my rivals and so achieved a limited degree of the third. For her sake, too, I deliberately played at being an American, even to the extent of drinking quarts of bourbon —I don't really like the stuff—playing practical jokes in and out of season and following the doings of the Katzenjammer Kids in Virgilia's favourite comic-strip with obsessional fervour. She called me 'Ward' and thought me very interesting and worthwhile for an Englishman, until, deciding one day to marry me, she gave me a heart-to-heart talk about the future and found to her consternation that I baulked at her definition of success. Success to her meant the rapid acquisition of a great deal of money by selling at a high price things that someone else produced at low cost, and then adopting standardized high-income-level habits as dictated by the higher-toned shiny-paper weeklies. I couldn't change her views, even when I tried to high-hat her as a cultured European of ancient lineage; nor could she convert me to hers, even when she threatened to give me the air. I told her that my education at Oxford—she had heard of Oxford —had made me incapable of selling even a sack of corn in a famine year, but she said 'nuts'—in that case her Uncle Henry would put me in the soft-drink business and help me to meet up with influential and worthwhile people. So I said: 'Oh, b—— your Uncle Henry!', forgetting for the moment that there are some words one can't use to nice young American girls and hope to get away with. That tore it.

I left the next day, and within a fortnight was back in Europe, at my father's, where I met Erica—Erica with her knife-like wit, her utter contempt for the world's opinion, her strange mixture of fastidiousness and filth, of deceit and singlemindedness, her easy and contemptuous command of every social accomplishment to which she gave her mind— from ski-jumping to hat-designing. She had been in ballet and the first time I tried a rumba with her she made me feel like a hick, though I fancied myself as a dancer; and the first time I played poker with her, she stripped me to the skin, though I fancied myself as a poker player. I fell for her hope- lessly and tried to adapt myself to her style by playing the déclassé rough-neck and translating her outrageous caprices into action, and by acquiring a taste for Pernod, which was not my drink either. I became Teddy then; Ward was forgotten. But the Catalan adaptability and enthusiasm that I had inherited from my mother was tempered by the stub- born Yorkshireness that I inherited from my father; and, after all, I had been educated at Rugby and Oxford. In the end Erica found me intractable—I wouldn't take part in her grisly scheme for murdering the Vicomte de Martinbault, or even in a profitable dope-smuggling racket—and broke with me in as ugly and humiliating a way as she knew how. I should perhaps explain that the Vicomte had fallen for Erica in a big way and was making a thorough nuisance of himself in our small circle. When he died violently soon afterwards the police pinned the crime on one of his valets, a Corsican, who confessed to having mutilated the body in a fit of revenge, but insisted that the throat had already been cut when he found it. Neither Erica nor I was called to give evidence; the valet obligingly closed the case by committing suicide in his cell on the evening of his arrest. But she must have known something, because she had skipped across to Switzerland by plane two hours before the murder was reported.

Then came Antonia. Her family was Anglo-Irish, but they were burned out of their Co. Sligo castle by the Sinn Feiners while she was still a child, and emigrated to a village near Oxford. She had gone to the University a year after I was sent down, and read History. What I liked about her was that she had no special talents. Though she played a fair game of tennis, swam and danced creditably, could manage a horse, sewed and cooked quite well, she neither wrote, painted, acted, sang, nor played a musical instrument, and cards bored her. She drank an occasional Dubonnet or dry sherry—for her sake I stopped mixing my drinks and reverted to my English conventions—and had neither illusions nor ambitions. Her prejudices, such as her refusal to wear a fur coat or smuggle the least thing through the Customs or make close friends with Catholics, were all half-humorous. But though she had no special talents I recognized that she had genius: the subtle and peculiar genius of being herself, knowing herself and always rising superior to the situation. If she said something witty, as she did quite often, her words came out so simply and casually that one didn't realize until too late that they deserved applause. Antonia was, in fact, a lady. Genius makes the lady; talents, the gentlewoman. She called me Ned, and I was consistently happy with her. Erica had ruled me by fear, Antonia by love; Virgilia had never ruled me—we had played together like overgrown children.

One night Antonia told me, *apropos* of nothing, and in so conversational a voice that it made no impression on me until the next morning: 'But in the end, of course, we have to understand that we're separate people: it's not enough just to love each other.' She had not meant that one of us would probably outlive the other and either have to live alone or find another partner; she had meant just what she said. That was all very well for her: she always kept a clear sense of herself, as I think both Virgilia and Erica did in their entirely different ways. But I had been successively Ward, Teddy and Ned, and though those characters were not historically irreconcilable it was a difficult task to disentangle my true self from among them. Perhaps New Crete was my opportunity; or could it be that the Edward who was slowly emerging from my friendship with Sapphire was merely another historical variation on the well-known theme?

After supper was cleared away Sapphire and I sat by the fire, looking at each other. At last she stirred in her chair and smiled, and I felt that I ought to speak. I talked about myself. I asked: 'But who *is* Edward? We must clear up that question first.'

She seemed to have been expecting this and the answer had already formed in her mind.

'Being a poet,' she said, 'you turn towards the Goddess as flowers turn towards the sun. Cleopatra, speaking in her name, put it differently in her *Song of Light:*

> No poet but is twisted by my hands, twirlers of light,
> From countless coloured strands that merge at last in white.

The Goddess, she is saying, is capable of a myriad manifestations: ond the poet adapts himself successively to each of them until, at last, the rainbow colours are integrated in the pure light of heaven—which we call white.'

'And what about black, the black of the eclipse?'

'Why do you ask that?'

'Because though the Goddess blesses, she also reserves the power to blast.'

'But she blasts only what is bad.'

'Don't you distinguish what is merely bad from what is evil?'

'She banished evil from our world when she set foot in New Crete. Evil was the illusion of good raised by the Rogue Trinity. Evil has vanished without trace; the good only remains—that's always been our faith here.'

'And is it still your faith?'

'Yes.'

'Would you call Sally bad?' I asked, coming to the point.

'From what you said, she must be very bad.'

'That's where you're wrong. Sally is not bad; if she were, she wouldn't be a witch. Isn't it the function of witches to destroy what's bad?'

'Then I say that she's a bad witch. How else could you account for her cruelty and lack of love?'

'The other night she defined bad as a freak or error, a failure in natural function, a falling short of the normal. But she knows that the good isn't merely the normal. There's another sort of good which is as much above normality as the bad is below it; and that sort of good can be known only in relation to another concept, which is evil. The Goddess banished evil from New Crete in the name of this supreme good—and the occasion was marked by man's voluntary return to her worship. For many centuries now you have had peace in New Crete, peace and love, and whenever the bad has appeared, your witches have destroyed it; but as your memories of the evil old days faded, your notion of good was gradually reduced from supreme good to normality. Your poets and musicians ceased to honour the Goddess as she deserves; her decision to sow a wind in order to reap a whirlwind shows clearly that the normal isn't enough to satisfy her.'

'But you haven't yet defined evil. If it isn't a failure in natural function, and if it isn't normality, what is it?'

'It's the means by which supreme good is contrasted with the merely normal.'

'Then you mean that Sally is the Goddess's instrument of evil?'

'Yes. I do.'

She was silent for awhile and then said: 'Well, I suppose that's what Cleopatra meant by the verse:

> When water stinks I break the dam,
> In love I break it.

Ordinary goodness grows stagnant and customary and the Goddess proves her love by destroying custom—by re-introducing evil.'

'I'm afraid so.'

'But what then? Will the sequel be a return to the same loveless horrors that have lined your face and hands? Will the Three Rogues return?'

'I'm certain they won't. The Goddess never repeats herself. This will be something quite new.'

'What sort of thing?'

'I haven't the least idea. But what were you saying about the lines on my hands?'

'They're hatched and cross-hatched all over with creases of pain and sorrow; ours are marked with only the four main lines. I fell in love with your hands and face as soon as I saw them; somehow they reminded me of my grandfather's coat. When he was young, he went adventuring in the Bad Lands of Africa, was separated from his comrades by a dust storm and was lost for months; when he returned, his coat had been torn by a thousand thorns but each rent had been neatly sewn up again. He hung it up in Nimuë's shrine at Sanjon, and there it remained until his death.'

'Your face attracted me for the opposite reason. You can't imagine how startling it was to see a grown woman's face as unlined and unclouded as a child's.'

'But now, if it becomes lined and clouded, will you still love me?'

I laughed: 'Do you want me, after all, to go on seeing you as I first saw you?'

'If it keeps your love for me fresh, I shan't mind.'

'Are we staying here tonight?'

'I must stay. I have some painting to do.'

'Then you'll want to be alone. In any case, it's stopped raining now and I shall have to take the horses back; they're in the paddock on the other side of the road. Is there a message for the servants about your things?'

'No, Edward, don't go to the house: I'm afraid of what might happen. Take the horses down the road and tell them to trot home. They'll understand.'

'Will you have finished your painting by midnight?'

'I hope so. I need sleep.'

'Shall I come back then?'

'No, please, you mustn't. There's only one bunk, but in the morning we'll ride to Dunrena together. The King's last day begins tomorrow at curfew, and since I've decided to remain what I am for your sake, I shall have to attend. Good night, and don't be too late to bed. Any house will welcome you. Come back early. You will, won't you?'

Her lips were trembling.

'But I don't understand. Why can't we share the bunk? I don't want to be parted from you at a time like this.' I tried to embrace her.

'No,' she panted, 'no, you mustn't touch me! Not yet. You're tied to Sally now.'

'To Sally? What nonsense. I don't intend ever to see her again.'

'She gave you the right of fatherhood, and you accepted it, so you and I can never again sleep in the same bed, until—'

'Until what?'

She continued in a voice so cold and low that it scared me.

'—Until I spread my cloak for you on Sally's grave.'

CHAPTER XVIII

The Nonsense House

I RODE down to the bridge, with Sapphire's mare trotting behind, then dismounted and shoo'd both horses home. As I strolled around the deserted streets of Horned Lamb I felt rather at a loss; unhappy too. Sapphire's parting words re-echoed menacingly in my head, yet the threat of murder disturbed me far less than the insistence that our love was to be consummated. I knew now more clearly than ever that I did not want this; it would have spoilt everything. A few more drops of rain fell. Was there a village inn? I did not remember having seen one either here or in any of the villages I had visited. A cottage door stood open and I peeped in. The interior reminded me irresistibly of the frontispiece to an early Victorian novel, *The Weaver's Cottage*, which I had read as a child; a placid domestic scene caught just before the neighbour runs in, all dishevelled, with news that the Bristol press-gang is in the village. The woman of the house spinning, a young man working a hand-loom, a rosy-cheeked girl mending a shirt, another embroidering a waistcoat, an oldish man in the chimney-corner telling them a story with dramatically raised forefinger; kettle simmering on the hob, cat asleep on mat. For a little while I stood listening to the story:

'It happened one day about noon, going towards my boat, I was exceedingly surprised with the print of a man's naked foot on the shore, which was very plain to be seen in the sand. I stood like one thunderstruck, or as if I had seen an apparition. I listened, I looked round me, I could hear nothing, nor see anything. I went up to a rising ground to look farther. I went up the shore and down the shore, but it was all one, I could see no other impression but that one. . . .'

Not wishing to interrupt at that perpetually thrilling point, I walked quietly on. 'These villagers work all day and all night,' I said to myself, 'and not because they're exploited by a tyrannous squire or mill-owner but, I suppose, because their backward economy doesn't allow them to let up for a moment. Or perhaps because they really enjoy work, poor blighters! But no evening paper with the list of tomorrow's runners, no football-pool coupons to fill in, no Odeon round the corner, no variety programme on the radio, no nine o'clock news, not even any nine o'clock. Nothing but work and custom, and more custom, and custom again and, for a treat, Uncle reciting his bed-time story of the footprint on the sand. Terrible!' But here I was breaking my resolution to leave the past alone; besides, I wasn't even sure whether I was being sarcastic about my own age or about New Crete. 'The best place for you tonight is a nonsense house,' I reproved myself. 'The Hag's pass will let you in.'

At the Nonsense House I dawdled for a moment on the porch and listened. A great deal of noise was going on inside, shouting and arguing punctuated by occasional high screams of laughter. I knocked, but as nobody came to let me in, I pushed the door open and went into a large entrance hall, furnished with five hat-stands each with a different type of hat on it, a table with refreshments including anchovy-paste sandwiches—one of which I sampled—a barrel of draught beer, a pier glass, several high stools, and about a hundred capacious lockers each painted with a symbol that represented the owner's nickname. I gently pushed open one of three silk-curtained glass doors and looked into a big room full of elderly women. Nine of them were squatting in a ring with their hands spread out level with their faces. In the centre, about four feet above the floor, a bloody human head was revolving slowly on what seemed to be an upward current of air. I withdrew at once but one of the spectators rushed after me. 'Hey!' she cried, catching me by the collar. 'What are you doing here, young man?'

'Paying a visit,' I said mildly.

'Back with me to the women's room!' she ordered, and dragged me along.

'Look, my dears, what we have here!' she shouted. 'We're in luck to-night!' There was a cackling of joy, the ring broke up, the head dropped to the floor and rolled under a chair, and about forty women thronged round me. They started by kissing and petting me and went on to offer me even more embarrassing caresses.

'I don't want to infringe custom, ladies,' I said in a loud voice, 'but I'd be much obliged if you'd let me alone until I've had a chance to introduce myself. Your attentions overwhelm me.'

They screamed with laughter and began to unbutton my coat and trousers and pull off my shoes.

'Butterfly has first whack!' someone shouted. 'She spotted him first, and then it's Two Cows, Head-in-Air and Grip-tight.'

'No, you're wrong, dearest: Grip-tight's at the head of to-night's roster.'

'Ladies, ladies!' I pleaded, struggling to rebutton myself. 'Give me a chance, I say!'

By this time Butterfly and two others had dragged off my coat and an old woman with a mahogany-coloured face and silver ear-rings had unfastened my belt and was busily debagging me. I socked her hard on the jaw and dislodged her. She squealed with rage but before she had time to return to the charge I slipped my hand into my trouser pocket, pulled out the crystal locket and waved it above my head.

'Stop!' I shouted against the hubbub. 'In the Name of the Goddess! Stop!'

They broke away at once. Two of them who had taken down cats-o'-nine-tails from a wall-bracket and were swishing them menacingly round their heads, hung the nasty-looking things up again in contrition. They all turned their backs politely, giving me an opportunity to adjust my dress.

I gasped with relief. 'In the nick of time!' So the Soldier in the Hans Andersen story must have felt when he produced the tinder-box on the scaffold.

'You must forgive us,' said Butterfly. 'Naturally, we mistook you for a trespasser and were going to deal with you as is customary. We had no notion that you were under protection.'

'No, forgive me,' I said, 'for intruding without first showing my credentials. And you, madam, whom I struck, I hope I have done you no injury?'

The mahogany-faced woman stroked her jaw and grinned. 'That's nothing, youngster, don't speak of it. You should see the hooks and hay-makers that fly about here on Tuesday Eve when the whisky's been round for the third time. But it's lucky for you I didn't land you a packet before you got your hand into your trousers; I'd have laid you out stiff.'

'Aren't you the fellow from the past?' asked the woman they called Grip-tight. 'I thought so. We've been hearing quite a lot about you recently. I bet you know a thing or two to amuse us. A new bad little story, or a bad little game —something really contraband. Don't you think you ought to pay us for the disappointment you've caused by not being a trespasser?'

'Oh, shut up, you couple of old bitches!' said a distin guished-looking woman who turned out to be Bee-flight. 'Is this the way to talk to a man under the Crane's protection?'

'Thanks for your support, Elder,' I said. 'At the moment I can't say that I feel in the right vein for entertaining your friends. And, in any case, it doesn't look as though I could teach them anything. What were they doing with that head under the chair?'

'Oh, that's Claud's.'

'And who was Claud?'

'You knew him well: he was Fig-bread. When his death was registered we borrowed his head from the grave at Zapmor—the witch Sally dug it up for us—and made him answer a few questions. He was just telling us about the set-up at the Magic House. What an amusing story! But he's dreadfully cross with you for having refused him the chance to be reborn as Sally's child. Would you like to apologize to him?'

She retrieved the head from under the chair and offered it to me. Fig-bread's earnest brown eyes stared dully into mine.

I declined the gift and the suggestion with a shudder, and though I felt that some intelligent comment was expected of me, all I could say was: 'Nobody ever warned me what to expect here!'

'Nobody ever is warned,' said Bee-flight, 'not even people who elect to become elders and look forward to a mild continuance here of their former life. It's known, of course, that within the walls of this house we're not bound by custom and that strange sounds sometimes float out through the shuttered windows, to which it's bad luck to pay attention. But it always comes as a shock to newcomers to find that what goes on here is as different from what goes on outside as Ana is from Nimuë. We're free to do more or less as we please among ourselves from noon to midnight. Then we return, like good children, to the dormitory house across the road for bed and breakfast. That's subject to outside custom, so we always get a good night's rest. In the mornings we pay visits, unless it's raining, of course.'

'Did I understand Grip-tight to say that you had rough-houses here once a week?'

'Ana bless me, yes! Often two or three times a week. There's a lot of women who enjoy a good free-for-all scrap, but we always get them to the dormitory sober and with their black eyes and swollen lips doctored. You see, as children we're kept under perpetual restraint and when we grow up we keep to custom voluntarily, but Ana doesn't like us to die without a taste of liberty.'

'I should have thought that the licence came rather too late. What happens, for example, if one of you falls desperately in love with a young man from outside? How is she to satisfy her passion? Or doesn't the case ever arise?'

'If this were Friday Eve,' said Butterfly, 'you'd never have asked that question. I can assure you we're not starved in any way. Bee-flight conjures up ass-imps for us and transforms them into the young men of our choice; and she turns us into young girls sometimes, just for the fun of it.'

'What about the old men?'

'They have their fun, too, but since they're nearly all impotent they mostly resort to what we call little piggeries with their imps. Ana is generous: she looks on and laughs.'

Grip-tight was still hanging about expectantly. I couldn't think of any new bad little games for her but I remembered two or three old bad little stories from my Erica period which went down very well. She and Two Cows slapped me on the back enthusiastically and called for more. 'Another day, ladies, another day!' I pleaded.

Bee-flight took me to the men's room, where I showed my pass once more and was hospitably received. 'If you have time,' she said, as she rejoined her friends, 'come and see us again before you go home.'

I looked around me. Except for some revoltingly erotic frescoes on the walls and the absence of newspapers and magazines, the place reminded me of the smoking room at

8

the Athenæum, not only in shape and size but in its leather and oak furnishings. The frescoes, which would have made the House of the Two Brothers at Pompeii look as respectable as the parlour of a Bournemouth lodging-house, were delicately executed in yellow, violet and a particularly poisonous sweet-pea shade of pink. Little piggeries indeed! And I had fondly believed that old age dulled the sexual appetite!

'Have a cigarette, my boy,' said a tall emaciated ex-captain, offering me his case. 'We smoke at all hours here.'

'Thanks, I'll know where to come in future,' I said, lighting one. 'What's all the excitement over there?' I nodded towards a table at the end of the room around which a crowd of elders was gathering.

'Oh, nothing much. Tiger-Tiger, one of our ex-recorders, has just invented a naughty little toy, thoroughly against custom, and the boys are having fun with it.'

'What sort of a toy?'

'He calls it a model steam-engine. It's a reconstruction in gold of a machine of the Late Christian epoch that turned up in a quarry some years ago. Tiger-Tiger's not entirely satisfied with it yet, but it works. Most ingenious. You pour ordinary water into a tank at the back and heat it up with a little fire of brandy, and it whistles, and the steam jets out and the wheels turn round. He's a very clever fellow. The other day he discovered how to make paper, at least he swears it's paper; but something seems to be wrong because he's made ink too, and the ink soaks the paper when he writes on it.'

'What's your particular interest, if I may ask?'

The ex-captain smiled and shrugged his shoulders. 'I lived an energetic life before I retired. Here I like to stand by the fire warming my backside and doing a bit of reading: I've learned to read since I came here. Mostly I read contraband books written by elders. There's quite a library of those in the billiard-room, apart from the usual Hundred Volumes. At the moment I'm interested in astronomy; a great many rediscoveries have been made lately about the distances and weights of the stars. Just imagine, the stars can actually be weighed—isn't that a surprising fact? And, of course, quite at variance with our mythology. We're hoping one day to be able to reconstruct a small telescope; so far we've only managed to get hold of a single well-preserved lens, but we need two. Optical glass is quite beyond our power to manufacture. You don't happen to know anything about the process, do you?'

I shook my head. 'And if I did,' I said, 'I don't think I'd tell you. Isn't it more fun to find things out than to be told them?'

He assented, though with some disappointment.

'Have you made any re-inventions of a later age than my own?' I asked. 'I'm from the Late Christian.'

At this point an appalling hubbub broke out next door: a hoarse male bellow of agony soon drowned by hysterical female screams. The ex-captain smiled at me, drily: 'That'll be young See-a-Bird being initiated into the ways of the house. If I know Bee-flight, she'll put him through his paces pretty savagely: he'll think his last hour has come.'

I was shocked. 'But they were lovers, weren't they?— from what he told me, the most idyllically devoted couple in New Crete?'

'The lover must be shown the other blade of the labra, as we say, and Bee-flight isn't going to kill him. We all have to go through this sort of thing when we first come here. But you were asking about reinventions. . . . Let me see. No, nothing of any great interest. We have some information about such machines as the Apporteur and the Cic-Fax, but they're quite beyond our scope: they need rare metals and a complicated nebular fissive system. Here we limit ourselves to toys: we're not ambitious.'

'What is, or was, the Apporteur?'

'That was an apparatus for creating a temporal dis-continuum and photographing scenes of the past within a limited range of time and space; it belonged to the Pantiso-cratic epoch. And the Cic-Fax was a complicated device, invented a few hundred years later, for the artificial insemina-tion of one species by another, by what they called chromo-somic inflexion: several extraordinary new animals were produced that way by the Logicalists, including the bear-rabbits which were still roaming about the Indian Bad Lands a century or two ago.'

An ear-splitting crash from the women's room; then a temporary silence and a good deal of laughter. Then again See-a-Bird's frightful bellow.

'I think they're extinct now,' the ex-captain went on calmly, 'along with the vulture-nightingale and the negro-mandril. Perhaps it's as well—they did a deal of damage to crops on the frontier farms. Oh, one moment, please—meet Horn-foot, our boring expert in Late Christian psycho-philosophy.'

Horn-foot, a bushy-haired ex-recorder with a staccato voice, fired a number of questions at me, about monoidism, nullibrism and trauma-tropical illusion, none of which I could answer although he spoke quite good English. My ignorance vexed him and he said that I ought to be ashamed of myself for knowing so little about the one field in which my age had shone.

I told him not to talk nonsense even if he did live in a nonsense house, unless he wanted to get hurt. That sobered him, but did not stop the flow of questions.

'You must know something, at least, about the humani-tarian concept of progress?'

'Yes,' I said, 'I do. I was brought up on it. I should define it as a bumpy journey to nowhere in particular considered as somehow better than the putative point of origin only because it has not yet been reached and because God alone knows either what's doing there or whether—'

'Did you ever meet God?' he interrupted. He seemed displeased that I'd attempted to answer his question.

'Never,' I said, 'though I've met two people who claimed to have done so. One was an old Frenchman who was on his way to fish in the river Alys, as they used to call the stream that flows through Sanjon, when he met God, together with St. John the Baptist and St. Ursula, if you know who they are. The saints told him to give up strong drink and eat only bread and vegetables, and said that if he obeyed, he'd live to the age of one hundred and one and go straight to Paradise. God said nothing but looked wise. My other informant was an English woman scientist who met God in a wood—'

'What sort of a scientist? Be more precise!'

'She was an authority on coal—and God told her to write a message to the Bishops of England on his behalf: they were to advocate the use of contraceptives by married people.'

'What had that to do with coal?'

'Nothing. I wouldn't have mentioned coal if you hadn't made me. She couldn't give any clear description of God's appearance but said that he treated her very kindly.'

Horn-foot gave a hoarse laugh.

'It's no laughing matter,' I said. 'The old Frenchman did live to one hundred and one, though whether he went straight to Paradise I can't say; and the Bishops did eventually issue a guarded approval of contraceptives.'

'You're the ignorantest man I've ever met,' said Horn-foot.

'I'd rather be ignorant than stupid,' I said. 'And I'll trouble you not to ask me any more questions. Run off now and take a dose; you've got a foul breath.'

'That's the way to talk, youngster,' said the ex-captain. 'Let's make the old gobbler swallow a cake of soap in the wash-room, shall we?'

Fortunately at this point I was whisked away to the billiard-room by a jovial group of elders who wanted me to teach them the rules of snooker. I was only too glad to do so. Under my direction they stained a set of balls with the appropriate colours, and then I showed them how to play and gave a demonstration of trick shots.

They kept me in the billiard-room for several hours, plying me with whisky and cigarettes, and I had great fun in a quiet way until someone beat a gong and the party at once broke up. Men and women crowded together into the entrance hall, where they sang a short hymn to Ana and then, since the rain had stopped and the stars were out, strolled across the road to their beds, leaving their hats on the hat-stands. See-a-Bird was in the crowd, looking like a new boy after a junior common-room rag; I did not venture to catch his eye.

Not feeling in the least sleepy, I stayed behind and spent some time in the library, where I studied the *English Poetic Canon*, which was the only book in English that I could find there. In its Supplement I came across my own *Recantation*, an early poem that I had long discarded as being artificial and insincere, and another more recent one, in the main body of the *Canon*, but clumsily re-written and attributed to 'the poet Tseliot'. Tseliot was a composite early twentieth-century figure who had swallowed up most of his near-contemporaries, including W. B. Yeats, Vachel Lindsay, W. H. Davies and Rupert Brooke, and was reported to have died of sunstroke at an early age while preaching the gospel of beauty in the streets of Dublin.

When a clock in the hall struck two I went back to the men's room and fell asleep on the sofa. Yes, a clock, by God! and I hadn't even noticed it. 'Clever fellow, that Tiger-Tiger!' I murmured to the deaf white Nonsense House cat which was purring loudly in my ear. 'He'll be re-inventing income-tax next, if Ana doesn't look out.'

CHAPTER XIX

The Rising Wind

I GOT up, washed, breakfasted on various left-overs, smoked a cigarette and heard the clock strike in the hall. Nine o'clock already and I had promised Sapphire to come early to the quince-hut! I must have overslept; why couldn't I have gone to bed at midnight? I left in a hurry. A servant with an ox-cart was passing as I ran out into the lane, and he was terrified: nobody was supposed to be in a nonsense house at that hour, not even an elder. He put out his tongue at me, growled, rolled his eyes and spread out his hands to represent horns, with the thumbs planted at his temples: the correct procedure to be followed by anyone confronted with a strange or un-lucky sight. I smiled cheerfully, greeted him in Mari's name, and waved my passport at him; but he showed no signs of reassurance and walked away backwards, still grimacing and making menacing noises, until he was out of sight.

After cutting across the park towards the Magic House, I hurried round to the stables. 'I want my horse,' I told the groom, 'also the Nymph Sapphire's mare.'

He saddled my horse and led it out, not saying a word.

'Thanks. Now the Nymph's.'

'I'm sorry, Sir. She no longer exists. Another lady is expected presently, and two more poets to restore our estab-lishment.'

'Sapphire no longer exists? Who told you so?'

'The Witch Sally, Sir. She convened a dawn council of

neighbouring magicians to which the Nymph was summoned; and as a result, I understand, she has ceased to be a member of the estate.'

'Is she still in the village?'

'She died, Sir, and is to be reborn at Dunrena, or so I'm informed.'

I made no comment, fumbled in my pocket for a tip, but finding nothing but my handkerchief and the locket gave him my apologetic thanks instead, and rode off. The impudence of Sally! And why had Sapphire submitted to the sentence? Had she said nothing in her own defence? Surely, if she had told the council all she knew they could never have convicted her. Perhaps I was to blame for this: my suggestion that Sally was the Goddess's chosen instrument of evil. Evidently Sapphire had decided to accept her fate. I felt outraged.

Near the gate See-a-Bird and Starfish called to me from the shrubbery. I pulled up. 'Hullo, See-a-Bird,' I said, 'how are you this morning?'

He smiled ruefully. 'Nobody,' he said, 'need take notice now of anything I say; that's a comfort, at least. As you know, I've left this house. I came here only to pick up a few things.'

'And how do you like the other blade of the axe?'

'I'll get used to it before long. The first stroke, they say, is the worst. It seems to shear the top of one's head clean off, just above the eyes. But once it's struck, pleasant or unpleasant events affect one only indirectly. When Bee-flight was made an elder I felt our separation keenly; now I don't feel it at all. Last night I was glad that the bed in my cubicle was a narrow one. In her strange way Ana's very generous.'

'And you, Starfish, how are things with you?'

He stared at me dumbly, moistening his lips with his tongue and said: 'My loving congratulations!'

'Thanks very much, Starfish—but what have I done to earn them?'

'Isn't it true then, about you and Sally?'

'I don't know what See-a-Bird has told you. All that you need to know is this: that I didn't share Sally's cloak on the grave, and that I've no intention of ever seeing her again, even if it means changing my estate. You needn't give up hope on my account. I'm no rival for her affections. But if you want my advice, it's this: sheer off, or you'll get burned like your brother! That woman has wildfire in her hair.'

Starfish never quite understood my broken New Cretan, and I had to repeat myself. This time I spoke more plainly: 'Tell Sally that I'm off, that I've finished with this house for good and all, and that I'm now going to Dunrena to change my estate and live with Sapphire. Do you understand that?'

This made him even sadder than before. 'But she loves you; she can't live without you!' he groaned. 'She'll never invite me to her bed, never!'

See-a-Bird grinned broadly. 'As an egg without a top,' he said, 'I fully appreciate the hopelessness of the situation. Well, I expect I'll be seeing you tonight at Dunrena; I'm supposed to be there.'

He gave my horse a friendly whack on the rump and sent him bounding down the road. At the stile where I had met Quant, I turned and cantered up to the quince-hut to make sure that Sally hadn't lied to the groom. The door stood open. 'Sapphire!' I called, but there was no answer. It occurred to me that she might have finished her picture and left it behind; so I dismounted and went in to look around. I found nothing until, as I was going out again, I happened to knock against the table, and a thin elm-board about a foot and a half square was dislodged from a rest underneath the table-top and clattered to the floor.

I picked it up. It was Sapphire's painting and the subject was Nimuë's removal of the Rogue Trinity. I recognized Machna, the sharp-nosed god of Science, clasping a handful of

8*

broken machinery; Pill, the shifty-eyed god of Thieves, with crumpled sheets of paper strewn behind him; Dobeis, the plump god of Money, with golden coins dropping from a hole in his trouser pocket. On the left of the picture the young Goddess, mounted on a white horse, was dragging the three corpses towards a river by a rope hitched around their necks. A covey of cranes flew overhead. On that side of the river all was desolation—burned houses, sparse crops, skeleton animals and birds, bloated corpses; but on the far side the crops were tall and abundant, the animals sleek, the people active and radiant, the houses undamaged.

I held the picture to the light and studied its background; then I saw that the prosperity had its limits. The fertile scene was bounded by another river half-hidden by alders, and beyond these I caught a glimpse of mackerel sky, and of a hill with two naked figures on it running hand in hand—a man and a woman with averted faces, pursued by a snake that brandished a club in a loop of its tail. I disliked the look of that sky. 'It's going to blow hell's bells over there within an hour,' I said to myself. 'And who are those people? Sapphire and I? Or any man and any woman? They seem to be running for shelter to that cave under the hawthorn. Let's hope they get there before the snake strikes. Poor Sapphire: she must have known when she came out of her trance and looked at her painting that there's a snagged and slimy river to cross, with trouble in plenty on the far bank.'

I returned the picture to the rack, went out and closed the door behind me. As I turned round, I nearly collided with Nervo. 'Hullo!' I said. 'Greetings in Mari's name. What are you doing here, if I may ask?'

'On my way to Dunrena,' he said briskly. 'The village contingent has marched ahead, I was about to overtake them. Then I saw you and cut across the fields. I came to thank you. Just so.'

'Thank me? Whatever for?'

'You have been very kind to me. You've given me a new nickname—Nervo the Fearless. For that I'm most grateful. If a new nickname is bestowed on a man, he accepts it without question. I do so now. It's as if I woke in the morning and accidentally put on my shirt inside out. It would be unwise and ungrateful to change it.'

'I don't see the connexion.'

'It's quite simple. Ill luck threatens me under my old nickname. You change it; ill-luck is baulked. Or ill-luck threatens me in my working shirt, but I happen to put it on inside out. Ill-luck strikes my chest, finds the button turned inwards, cannot undo it. Ill-luck retires. Just so.'

'I wonder you don't always wear your working shirt inside out and change your nickname daily.'

'That would be cowardly,' he said.

I did not pursue the subject. 'I'm going to Dunrena too,' I said. 'May I have the pleasure of your company?'

'By all means.'

We turned back to the road and jogged along towards Rabnon.

'Wonderful clover fields,' I said. 'What's the secret?'

'No secret. We return to the soil what we take from the soil. Just so. Seeds planted on a lucky day and rolled in well. Prayers morning and night, and pests kept under control. No secret. No! The clover's looking fine, Mari be praised! So, for the matter of that, is the dana. . . . And yet.'

'And yet,' he repeated a minute or two later.

'Something on your mind, Nervo?' I prompted him.

'Yes,' he answered. 'I wish I knew what it was. That's the trouble. What can it be? The commons work hard and pray hard. My private affairs are in order. That little matter of the brutch has been settled. The Goddess has sent rain—not too much, not too little. Yet something's wrong: very wrong, I fear. A feeling only. Nothing I can lay my finger on.'

'Are you too polite to suggest that it is connected with my

arrival in your village? If you think it's that, please say so. I won't be offended.'

Nervo looked away as he said: 'Just now a carter came to me in great terror. He thought he'd seen you coming out of the Nonsense House.'

'I spent the night there.'

'Never!'

'And why not?'

'It's certain death to be in a nonsense house between midnight and noon.'

'Maybe, but mine's a special case. I'm protected. I admit that it was stupid of me to frighten the carter; I suppose I should have drawn a look-away symbol on my forehead.'

He made no further comment until we had clattered through the cobbled streets of Rabnon. Then he said in a worried voice: 'Tell me something. What's going on at the Magic House? The health of Horned Lamb depends on the magicians. Just so. And extraordinary rumours are flying about.'

'What are people saying?'

'I hardly like to tell you.'

'Go on!'

'That you brought a brutch with you; that it's bewitched all five of your companions; that it's already removed three of them; that it won't rest until the house is emptied. And you know what *that* means.'

'I'm afraid I don't.'

'There's a popular rhyme:

> When in a house of five
> Not one is left alive,
> Look to the skies,
> Watch the North wind rise.
> But until that event
> Work, be content.

Just so. It's reassuring. All's well while our magicians are in their house. And so it will remain while we all work, and work hard. Then a vacancy occurs in the Magic House; and what happens? They fill it on the following Monday, and the warning loses its force. But today is Thursday, and count! Apart from yourself, how many magicians are left? Two only! A disaster! What if something should happen to those?'

'Thank you, Nervo. Already yesterday I had a feeling that the village was getting nervous about my presence. So I've decided to leave, though I disclaim all responsibility for what's happened. I'm going to Dunrena now, and none of you will need to see me again. It's embarrassing to be one of Mother Carey's chickens and portend storms. However, if you care to know exactly what's been happening—'

I broke off. Nervo had turned deathly pale, slipped from his chestnut and thrown himself on the grass by the roadside, where he lay as if dead. Red Thunder nuzzled him sympathetically for half a minute, and meeting with no response wandered off down the road. I caught him, hitched him to a tree and stood looking down on Nervo in complete bewilderment. 'Come on, old chap, do get up! I'm sorry if I accidentally said the wrong thing. I'm a stranger here, you know.'

He remained there, prone and motionless, and when I had satisfied myself that he was breathing and not in pain, I mounted and rode on. What could I have said to cause him so much distress? Could it have been my mention of Mother Carey? Ridiculous!

The road was crowded with people walking or riding to Dunrena, thirty ass-carts full of elders, and crowds of children trooping behind a priest. Every village and town had sent a contingent of twenty-two men and women, consisting of a captain, a magician, twelve commoners, six servants and two recorders. The men carried heavy packs, tent poles, rolls of white canvas, cooking pots and umbrellas; the women only umbrellas and satchels. I overtook Rabnon first, then Zapmor, exchanging friendly greetings with them as I passed; then our own village. I was glad to find Quant marching along at the head and walked my horse beside him.

'Aren't you short of a captain and a magician?' I asked him.

'At the moment. But Sally's gone ahead and Nervo's had some business to finish and promised to catch us up soon.'

'That's awkward; because I left him lying on his face by the roadside, about a mile back.'

'Did you indeed? I hope he's not ill.'

'I don't think so. But I believe I said something I shouldn't have said. He threw himself suddenly on the grass and refused to move.'

'What did you say to him? Perhaps you'd better spell it, though, or you may send us all down on our faces.'

'I mentioned a legendary character called Mother C.A.R.E.Y. I spoke in New Cretan, using *Mam* for mother.'

'How very unfortunate; that happens to be a dreadfully sacred name. It's lucky for you that you're under protection. She's the Goddess of Wind and when initiates hear her name spoken in the Mysteries, they fling themselves down at once and wait until they hear the counter-charm. Otherwise she'd blow them over the moon.'

'Heavens! I'd better ride back and say the counter-charm. What is it?'

'Excuse me, but I'm under oath neither to say, spell or even hint at it.'

'That's terrible. Do we leave him there until the grass grows over him?'

'A little grass won't hurt him,' said Quant drily. 'Unfortunately, there's only one person capable of undoing the charm, and that's the High Priestess, and she's not allowed to say either the name or the charm except at the winnowing-feast once a year; but the corn's still quite green. Anyhow, don't haul him to his feet, or the Goddess will blow him over the moon.'

'Do you believe that, Quant?'

'About being blown over the moon? Well, it's our way of speaking. I don't know how literally to take it, because nobody has ever dared to transgress the order. All I can say is that people who transgress in other ways, die in other ways.'

'How did Sapphire die?'

'Oh, she was given a dose of the drug we call lethea. Her transgression was an involuntary one, so she's to be reborn as a commoner. If she had deliberately secreted that metal affair because she admired it, that would have been an obvious lapse in taste and she'd be reborn as a servant. Of course, the servants' estate is as honourable as the commons, but since they have, by definition, no taste of their own they're permitted to furnish their living quarters with any glittering rubbish they please. However, in either case the fault is venial, not mortal. For a mortal transgressor there's no rebirth. Being bad, and knowing himself bad, he's hypnotized by a witch and made to leap head first from a cliff.'

'Then is there a statutory penalty for every form of transgression? I'd like to see your code.'

'No, we have no code, no lawyers, no judges. Each case is heard by the transgressor's estate as if it were the first and only one, and judgement is left to himself to pronounce after he's heard his own evidence.'

'I don't quite follow.'

'A person may have persuaded himself that he was within his rights in doing this or that; it's only when he describes it to his neighbours that he can make up his mind.'

'Are there never any miscarriages of justice?'

'I don't think that I can answer that question; there are no penalties, you see.'

'But isn't death a penalty?'

'Not with us. It's a gift.'

'I see,' I said doubtfully. 'Well, where am I likely to find Sapphire?'

'You mustn't call her that any longer, but she's to be reborn as the daughter of my late sister, who's a commoner at Dunrena now. My sister sentenced herself to death for a similarly venial transgression. But that was long ago.'

'What did she do?'

'She lost her temper at croquet and threw her mallet into a tulip bed. She complained that Mallet-head was giving her advice and putting her off her game. Everyone was relieved when she went; she hadn't the makings of a recorder.'

'Well, Quant, don't you think I'd better go back to Nervo?'

'Why? What good can you hope to do?'

'I might try saying that name backwards.'

'There can be no harm in trying,' Quant said non-committally. 'But probably we'll have to build a little hut over him and wait for the autumn equinox.'

Ten minutes later I was back on the outskirts of Rabnon. Nervo was still lying palefaced in the same position, and ants were crawling all over him. The silly chump! A captain, too! For a moment I was tempted to lug him to his feet. Then I remembered that he had gone out of his way to thank me for his new nickname, and decided that it would be unkind in the circumstances to get him blown over the moon—whatever that meant. Besides, I might feel the draught myself.

'Come back the word I spoke just now!' I said; but nothing happened. Then I tried: 'YERAC MAM', in not very convincing tones.

Nervo stirred uneasily, and I repeated the word with more confidence. It worked. He sprang up, bowed nine times to the North like a monkey on a stick, and ran to mount his horse.

He did not seem in the least scared or put out, and we resumed our conversation at the sentence before the last. So far as I could make out, he was quite unaware of what had happened. 'A very odd thing, Sir,' he said. 'Ants are crawling up and down my neck. Decidedly odd. They must have worked their way up from the horse's hooves. I wonder what they portend. Do you happen to know?'

'You'd better consult Sally or Starfish,' I said. 'I'm no authority on omens. But, at a guess, I should say that ants on the neck portend a rising wind.'

Would I ever get accustomed to the fairy-tale ways of New Crete? Such fantastic ingenuousness of faith! Yet, without such ingenuousness what strength had religion? And without a strong religion, what restraints could be imposed on individual knavery? Nothing effective in the long run, as history showed. Then, in order to lead what philosophers call 'the good life' without crime or poverty, must people be practically half-witted? Apparently: indeed, I told myself, it was only an epoch like the Late Christian that demanded a full and constant exercise of one's wits. Money was the best whetstone for the individual intelligence, and in the American Century to which I was committed on my return—unless I cared to renounce my intelligence altogether and emigrate to Russia—it was likely to be the only whetstone. The freedom of religious belief promised us was, of course, a contradiction in terms. Where a central secular authority, squarely based on the command of money, was imposed on all members of a nation, with the reassurance that their religious beliefs were their own private concern so long as no breach of the peace was committed, true religious values went. There could be no true religion except in a theocratic community. And when—as in America—even a constitutional monarchy, the last tattered vestige of primitive theocracy, had been repudiated, no values remained but money values. The richer the man, the sharper his wits; the sharper his wits, the blunter his religious sense. On the other hand, the richer the man, the greater the need to consolidate his social position, and that could be achieved only by a mock restoration of the super-seded values. Thus, the sharper the wits, the statelier the church-going, which was a phenomenon to which Americans pointed with pride. Cry woe on the rich men of Capernaum! But they had their reward on earth, and though Jesus declared that no man could serve God and Mammon, but all must submit wholeheartedly to the Mosaic Law, the Law itself jingled with gold and silver shekels. Well, I was only a poor European, an incorrigible recusant, for whom none of the higher seats in the synagogue was reserved. Nor did Russia appeal to me in the least: the régime was anti-poetic. However, if I had to choose between New Cretan half-wittedness and American whole-wittedness, I was simpleton enough to choose the former and avoid stomach ulcers, ticker-tape and Sunday best. But come! The wind was rising: things were at last beginning to happen even in New Crete.

We overtook our contingent not far from Dunrena. I recognized the place as Martinbault-les-Dames, in my day a mediaeval walled town from which the Vicomte had derived his title. The walls were now gone and the greater part of the town was built around the lip of a huge crater, about a quarter of a mile across, close to the original site. Quant could not tell me when or how the crater had been formed—to me it suggested the explosion of a vast ammunition dump—but I heard the servants talking with awe about the prophetic fish that rose in answer to prayer from the unplumbed depths of its waters.

A smooth white marble palace with tapering spires and formal gardens dominated the town. We marched towards its crenellated gates, Nervo at the head, myself unwillingly bringing up the rear. I had intended to go at once into the town to find Sapphire—Quant had given me the name of his changeling sister—but Nervo protested that it would be a disgrace if we entered the palace grounds without a magician.

'Stay with us, until the Witch turns up,' he pleaded with tears in his eyes.

'I'm no trained magician,' I said, 'and I won't know what's expected of me.'

'No matter. You ride a white horse. That will be enough to preserve our honour. Remember, it's in jeopardy. The strange things that have been happening at the Magic House, you know. There's already talk at Zapmor of a war against us. This might well bring them out with their conches. And what will the Queen say to our lack of the fifth estate?'

Then he produced a silk flag with the village emblem—a horned lamb—attached it to a stick that telescoped out to six feet, and signed for the band to strike up. We swung down a flagged colonnade between red and white roses to the tune of Brian Boru's March until, wheeling around a huge amethyst-coloured mimosa, we came in sight of the Royal Box.

The King, more than a little drunk, with a small golden crown perched unsteadily on his bright red hair, was cheering the march-past and pelting each contingent with sweetmeats. He wore a white silk shirt with purple cuffs, white knee-breeches and a purple sash. Around him sat twelve beautiful girls, nymphs of the months, all dressed in different colours with emblematic head-dresses; and the Queen, wearing a much grander crown and a robe of scarlet and gold, sat enthroned and motionless above him.

As we passed, Nervo gave an 'eyes right', and three royal lumps of nougat flew from the Box. The first struck Quant on the shoulder, the second missed, the third grazed my knee. Quant at once fell out and joined a group in a railed enclosure to the right of the Box. At a sign from him I dismounted, handed my horse to a servant, and followed suit.

'We're in luck,' whispered Quant. 'We get reserved seats at the Royal Performance tonight.'

As we entered the enclosure a servant offered us drinks in small medicine glasses.

'What's this?' I asked him, sniffing suspiciously.

'To dull your senses, Sir.'

'Why should I want to dull my senses?'

'Against the fatigue of seeing so many new faces pass by.'

'I've seen them all before,' I answered, handing the glass back.

CHAPTER XX

The Sights of Dunrena

THE contingents marched past the Royal Box all morning: some of them had come from the other end of the kingdom, which covered most of what used to be the South of France. We watched for an hour or so, until the King's aim began to grow wild. Then one of the nymphs handed him a toy arquebus that released a volley of sweetmeats when he pressed the trigger, and kept it continually loaded. Gradually the enclosure filled with his bag.

Quant told me that we were free to go when we pleased and offered to take me to see his former sister. I was glad to leave; I was getting rather bored. As we left the enclosure by the back gate an attendant gave us each a goosefeather with a red tip to wear on our hats as tickets of re-admission.

'Have you got any grease-paint?' I asked Quant.

'Of course. For a look-away symbol?'

'Yes, in case we run into Sally. I wonder why she hasn't turned up yet.'

'I'm wondering too. It's unheard-of for a magician to be absent from a parade.'

There must have been some thirty thousand people in Dunrena that day, more than ten times its normal population, and a canvas city was being erected in the Great Park. The tents were pitched not in straight lines but in a spiral, which was constantly being enlarged by new arrivals. Each tent flew its village flag. As we went past, the quiet surprised me:

there was no shouting, no singing, no music; everyone talked in a low voice, and even the tent-pegs were painstakingly screwed into the turf, not hammered. Quant remarked:

> 'When ants swarm,
> Not the least sound is heard
> And each knows his own task.'

His sister lived in the Old Town. 'It's a monogamous quarter,' he said, 'though the wives there have a habit of exchanging husbands once in a while, which makes the atmosphere less severe than at Zapmor. Her name's now Broad Thumb, I don't know why. I've never seen her since the incident with the mallet, but I've been told that she lives somewhere up this street.'

We soon saw her house sign, and went into the kitchen without knocking; nobody knocked in New Crete, except on bedroom doors. I should have recognized Broad Thumb at once by her close resemblance to Quant: the same apple-red cheeks, sharp nose and humorous mouth. After the formal greeting she took her brother by the hand: 'What is your nickname and your village?' she asked.

'I'm Quant, a recorder from Horned Lamb, down the railway line. And this is my friend Venn-Thomas, a poet from the past.'

'I'm happy to make your acquaintance,' she said. 'They tell me that before I died, I too spent some years at Horned Lamb, among the tulips and croquet hoops. But where's the friend you mention?'

When I wiped off the look-away symbol, she acknowledged my existence with a curtsy. I bowed in return.

'Come into the spinning-room, if you please!' she said.

'I hear that you've been blessed with a lovely daughter,' Quant remarked as we followed her.

'Yes, Mari be praised!' said Broad Thumb, sitting down at her spinning-wheel and working away at a tangle of black wool. 'She's a beautiful girl, born after breakfast this morning and calls me "Mother" already. By the evening she'll be quite grown up: but as yet the little creature finds life strange enough.'

'What's her nickname?'

'I'm waiting for one, but so far without success.'

'Why not call her Stormbird?' I asked.

She pretended not to hear.

I repeated the question in a louder voice.

'A poet has the right to bestow a nickname,' she said, 'but haven't you one of better omen?'

'The Goddess put it into my mind,' I explained. 'And, after all, stormbirds ride out the worst gales that blow.'

'I accept it,' she said resignedly.

'Can we see her?'

'The poor creature's not very presentable, but if you insist. . . .'

She led us into the next room where Sapphire sat in a play-pen, pulling a doll to pieces. She was dressed in a loose white nightgown with her hair down and a daisy chain round her neck. 'Nice men,' she murmured, giving us a vague Ophelia-like smile. Then she held out her hand. 'Got a blister—two blisters!' she said proudly.

Quant cooed at her, produced a straw-box full of aniseed balls from his coat pocket, and exchanged it with her for the broken doll. She opened it awkwardly and then began to roll the sweets round and round in the lid.

'Eat them, they're very good!' Quant said, and presently she tried one with the tip of her tongue.

'Yes, good, very good!' she echoed, and crammed a handful into her mouth. 'Nice men,' she said again, dribbling sugar down her chin.

When she threatened to paw me with her sticky hands, I

turned away in disgust. She lisped, smiling coyly: 'Would you like to see my frilly drawers?'

'I think you'd better leave her now,' said Broad Thumb. 'She's growing up rather faster than I expected, and she's so large and well-formed that she might easily get into mischief if I don't keep her quiet. Yes, I think she'll be ready for her initiation by noon.'

We returned to the spinning-room and had a glass of lager with our hostess, but Sapphire raised such a hubbub that Broad Thumb had to excuse herself almost at once. 'She's getting so artful now: pretends she wants attention, and I know she doesn't really.'

So we said goodbye. As we went out, I asked Quant: 'This is only a game, isn't it? Sapphire—I mean Stormbird —does really recognize me, doesn't she?'

'Heavens, no! She doesn't know in the least who you are, any more than Broad Thumb knows who I am. Dead's dead, and reborn is reborn. That's the whole point of the Robnet story. He died as a poet and became Fand's servant, but he had no idea that he had once loved her. That he became her servant was a tragic coincidence—no more. If you're thinking of changing your estate and becoming Stormbird's lover, you'd better think twice; it's most unlikely that you'll pair up again.'

'Then Sally's got the better of me, after all?' I exclaimed weakly.

'It's useless to oppose a witch.'

With Sapphire snatched from me in this absurd and horrible way, I felt completely stranded; what was worse, it looked as if Sally had taken possession of me and would never leave go now. I tried not to let Quant see how hard I had been hit. He felt Sapphire's loss keenly enough himself, I knew, but he had the solace of his religion: he could invoke the Goddess and attain a peace of mind that was quite beyond my power. Where could I turn for solace? The Goddess was strange to me; though I gave her *de facto* recognition, I did not carry her in my heart wherever I went, as the New Cretans did. I had not even been initiated into my estate—though enjoying its privileges—and I was not at all sure that I wanted to be; my status was as honorary as that of a minor royal personage who has been awarded a Doctorate of Civil Law at a foreign university. My sense of frustration gave way momentarily to blinding anger. I would win Sapphire back, by fair means or foul, even if I had to pull the whole place to pieces in the attempt.

'Where are we going now?' I asked Quant, as cheerfully as I could. 'Not back to the enclosure?'

'Wherever you say.'

'I'd like to know where Sally is.'

'But I thought you didn't want to meet her?'

'I don't, but I'll be uneasy until I know. When did she start out this morning?'

'When my niece's fate had been decided. The two of them rode off together before breakfast.'

'Are you sure of that? Then where did Sapphire die?'

'Here, at Court. She had to kiss the Queen's hand, and transfer her insignia to another nymph of the month. That's why they made such an early start. Sally came with her, to hear her last wish and to take charge of the mare after her death.'

'I say: Quant!'

'Yes?'

'Where are the royal stables?' I asked in great excitement.

'I'll take you to them. Why?'

'Because I think I know how she blistered her hands, but I want to be sure. If I'm right, then I'm saved.'

He looked at me solemnly, and nodded. 'Yes, digging,' he agreed. 'Ana have mercy on us all! This is serious.'

When we reached the stables he clapped his hands for the Groom of the Day, who came running up at once. 'Take us to the place where you keep strayed or masterless horses,' he said. The groom showed us a row of loose-boxes. 'Those three came this morning, Sir,' he said. 'One chestnut and two milk-whites.'

'What about the chestnut?'

'It's the horse that the Lord Chamberlain disowned early this morning. Brutched, no doubt. It laid back its ears and showed its teeth when they put on the saddle. The other two were brought in a little later.'

'Yes, thank you, we recognize them.'

They recognized us too and whinnied a greeting. Quant dismissed the groom and I went up to Sapphire's mare. 'Steady, old girl,' I said. 'No, sorry, no apples today! I just want to see that saddle-bag of yours. Here, Quant, have a look at this!' I handed him a flat wooden box.

He opened it. It contained a clay-board covered with New Cretan writing. 'Shall I translate it for you?' he asked.

'Please, do,' I said.

He cleared his throat and read in an unsteady voice:

'My own dear love:

'I can call you that now because you're free once more. Why didn't you come early to the quince-hut, as you had promised? But your answer will never reach me now: I shall have died when you read this. Sally acted quickly; she called a council, and I had to sentence myself to death. She fetched my mare to the hut and we rode off at once. I felt very miserable; I had not said goodbye to you. Before we came to the road that branches back to Zapmor, she taunted me cruelly: "If you loved him, why didn't you give him everything? Wasn't I right to eat what you left on the side of your platter?" There was evil in her voice, and greater evil rose in me. I remembered Cleopatra's *aer*, "The Greedy Child", and resolved to blotch her face with it. I crooked my little finger at her and began: "Listen to me! Cleopatra. . . ." Then, all at once, I noticed a tit-mouse on a branch and stopped short.'

'Why did she do that?'

'We have a proverb: "See a titmouse, think twice, then think again." The titmouse brings a warning from the Goddess.'

'I see. Go on.'

He continued:

'Sally had not seen the titmouse. She turned to me and said obediently: "I'm listening." Having thought twice, I thought again, and thanked the Goddess in my heart for putting Sally into my power by revealing to me that her secret name was Cleopatra. "Cleopatra!" I said, "I'm riding to Zapmor. Come with me! And don't speak again until I give you leave." She obeyed meekly. We rode fast, and when we came to the clearing where she had tried to bewitch you, I said: "Cleopatra, fetch a spade!" She went away and fetched one. "Cleopatra, remove the turf from Claud's grave, and dig!" She obeyed. When she uncovered the body, its head was gone. "Where's the head, Cleopatra?" I asked. "They have it at the Nonsense House," she answered sullenly. "You're cheating Ana of her due," I said. "Make amends, Cleopatra!" She handed me her lancet, knelt down and bent her head submissively. "What's your last wish, Cleopatra?" I asked. "Not to be reborn," she answered. "You shall spread no cloak over my grave!" I stabbed her in the nape of her neck, laid her beside Claud's mutilated corpse, shovelled the earth back and spread the turf over the grave again. Then I rode to Dunrena, and registered her death. I write this in the Royal Stables. Goodbye, my love! These are unhappy times.

SAPPHIRE.'

Quant's only comment was: 'Starfish will have his hands full until the relief comes on Monday.'

'If he lasts until then,' I said, as we walked slowly away.

'Where next?' he asked.

'Frankly, I don't care,' I said miserably. 'A church.' Perhaps I'd find some consolation there. Above all, I wanted to free my mind of the picture of Sapphire murderously despatching Sally with a *descabello*.

'Very well,' Quant agreed.

'Is that a church over there?'

'Do you mean that house with the new moons painted on the windows?'

'I'd have called them old moons.'

'You see them reversed; but they look brand new from inside. No, that's not exactly a church: it's the Moon House, where the holy madmen live. They worship the Moon in whatever way they please, making the Goddess laugh with their solemn antics; and they laugh themselves, of course, just as loudly. They're the happiest people in New Crete and despise the outer world because it's not so holy as the Moon House. A priest and priestess look after them. Madmen are no trouble, not even in thundery weather. They never dream of going out, for fear of dissipating their holiness.'

'Don't they ever break the windows?'

'That would be to destroy the symbol they love best. They're mad, not bad.'

We stopped outside the Church of the Hare, where a service was in progress. I showed my pass at the porch and entered. There was a shrill sound of pipes. Eight horned men, in green, were leaping round a square altar, surmounted by a winnowing basket, and the congregation squatted on the floor clapping their hands in time to the pipes. As the rhythm quickened, the green men leaped higher and higher: a charm to make the corn grow, I supposed. The priestess stood apart, fondling a leveret, her lips moving soundlessly in prayer. I leaned against a buttress and looked around me. Except for seven recesses in the walls, each holding a garlanded replica of one of the idols in the district, and a rack full of flails, the church was as bare and square as a tithe-barn: not even stained-glass windows or frescoes. Without change of tune, the dance went on and on and the green men showed no sign of weariness. One of them leaped nearly his own height and a yellow froth showed on his lips. The priestess paid little attention; she uncovered one of her breasts and pretended to suckle the leveret.

I had soon had enough and went out again. 'Where's the nearest bagnio?' I asked Quant.

'Why that?'

'I must have some distraction—anything. No bagnio could be duller than that church.'

'Up the street—the house with the catkins painted on the stucco. They've just put the lamp in the window to show that it's open.'

'What goes on there?'

'The usual thing, you know. It's a sort of first-aid post where one goes when one isn't in love with anyone in particular but feels unhappily lecherous. That's called the catkin stroke, and it's no disgrace. The place is run by a priestess and staffed with good-looking servants. She keeps them in a continuous condition of heat, ready for anyone who comes in. There's a male and a female ward.'

'Anyone at all? I thought smokes didn't mix?'

'They don't. But anyone visiting a bagnio becomes a member of the servants' estate for the time being; because to go there implies a failure in discrimination. Magicians aren't admitted, though.'

'My pass is good, I've been told. Coming with me?'

'No, thanks. I'm not ill.'

I showed my pass to the tall porter who, after scrutinizing it carefully, tied a brassard with four chevrons on my right arm. 'The catkin makes servants of us all,' he quoted sententiously. 'Step this way, mate! We'll soon put you right.'

He took me past an enormous, realistically tinted china phallus that dominated the hideously papered entrance-hall, down a long flesh-coloured passage, to an open swimming-pool. The broad walk around it was paved with shiny blue, black and yellow tiles, and flanked by a row of cabins roofed and bal-conied like Swiss chalets with flower-embroidered lace cur-tains at their doors. A strong smell of musk arose from the tepid water. As I entered, several naked girls slipped into the pool and swam languidly around like a Hollywood aquacade, while others posed on the edge, like Paramount starlets, cast-ing sultry glances in my direction. I stood irresolute. 'Shapely girls, but how dumb they look,' I thought.

'You're a stranger here, I see, and a bit shy,' said the porter. 'You may play with two or three girls at a time, if you like.' He led me along the scented pool to a pseudo-Moorish café up some steps at the far end, but paused to pull aside one of the cabin curtains, revealing a vast brass bed with a heavy black silk coverlet and bright yellow bolsters and pillows. 'In fact,' he continued, 'they don't think much of a man who's satisfied with only one. Ah, here comes the Priestess!'

He retired, and the Priestess, an enormous pigeon-chested prima-donna of a woman in a gaudy kimono, waddled up and greeted me with a glance of commiseration, clutching a large coffee tray inlaid with mother-of-pearl. She sat the tray down on a sandalwood table in a pierced alcove and poured me out a cup of strong Turkish coffee, into which she slipped a little black pill. 'To enhance your pleasure,' she said, pulling forward a chair with twisted gilt legs and red plush upholstery, and motioning me to sit down. 'Would you like a swim first, or are you seriously ill?'

'To tell you the truth, Madam,' I said, eyeing the squat be-dragoned coffee pot and the enamelled brass cup with fas-cinated horror, 'to tell you the truth, I came here out of pure curiosity.'

'Oh, but that's altogether against custom. I'm quite sure

you're ill; you look terrible, and anyhow you can't leave now without honouring Our Lady of the Catkins.'

'But I'm a magician when I'm not wearing this,' I said, fingering the brassard, 'and really . . . .'

'How delightful for the staff! This is an unheard-of honour, blessed be the Goddess who sent you! I'll instruct the porter not to admit anyone until you're quite finished. But now I'll leave you; you'll feel more at home when I'm gone.' She curtsied herself off.

I closed my eyes, drank the sickly-sweet coffee at one gulp, and rose to go. Almost at once a sort of ethereal mist spread across my vision: all the colours of a soap-bubble, dotted with starry glints of gold. My knees went weak. I slumped back into my chair. The starlets, seeing that the drug had done its insidious work, tripped silently up the steps in single file. Then a fiddle began to play, a black velvet curtain dropped behind them and one by one they paraded in front of me with pink ostrich-feather fans, revolving slowly and sinuously under a spotlight to gipsyish music. To pretend that I was left unmoved by this crudely libidinous display would be dishonest. The mad rainbow of stars and colours swirled before my eyes, heightening the emotional effect. Yet I could not help feeling vaguely ashamed—'at this time of day, too,' I reminded myself—and for a moment wondered what on earth I should say to Antonia on my return. But even with Antonia by my side I had often dreamed my recurrent Arabian Nights dream, a relic of adolescence, in which I was a sultan among his complaisant harem, in a setting not unlike this—always to wake in acute disappointment before I had made my choice between the slender, haughty, high-breasted blonde, the plump little seventeen-year-old with the brindled curly hair and the friendly smile, and the exquisitely fragile, honey-skinned Indian princess with jewelled wrists and ankles and the solitaire pearl folded in her navel.

This time it seemed ordained that I should have my dream

out, once and for all, never to be dreamed again. Our Lady of the Catkins was handing it to me on an enormous mother-of-pearl tray, and it would have been discourteous to decline her well-meant gift merely because my taste in interior decoration differed from hers, or because of a treasured legend of my poetic fastidiousness in sex. A scene from the late war flashed across my mind: godly Sergeant-major Clegg with a scandalized red face, reporting irregularities at a company billet, when we were stationed in Nottingham. 'I'm an old soldier, Captain Venn-Thomas, Sir, and I don't like to ride the men too hard; but begging your pardon, Sir, that billet's no more and no less than a bloody knocking-shop. I've put Corporal Stukes under arrest. Will you see him now, Sir?'

Poor catkin-struck Stukes! And what had he told me? 'You can't stop nature, Sir.'

'But my good Stukes . . . .'

I wondered vaguely what the pill had contained. A compound of hashish and hippomanes?

There was no need for me to indicate my choice: the starlets knew intuitively which of them I desired, and presently my favourites came tripping forward and half-led, half-carried me off to our Great Bed of Ware, with its squabby gilt cupids and brass-knobs as big as urns, drew the poppy-and-passion-flower curtains behind them and undressed me with expert fingers.

Quant was waiting patiently on a bench outside when I emerged an hour later. I was surprised to see no customers waiting for admission. 'I thought the whole town would be queueing up four deep,' I said.

'No, the illness is not at all common; it usually starts with a sudden depression. Someone meets a brutch, or has a nightmare, or a wife or husband dies suddenly, or a lover is lost. Nobody likes to change estate, even for an hour, but a visit to a bagnio puts people on their feet again. It's a salutary experience. . . . On a gay holiday morning like this the girls don't expect visitors, so the Priestess usually gives them access to their fellow-workers in the women's ward. How disappointed they must have been when you told them you weren't ill. And what luck did you have with your game?'

I blushed. 'I can't grumble,' I said.

'I've spent many a pleasant half-hour with the Priestess. However, like all servants she tends to be too much on the defensive. A good player defends and attacks simultaneously. Shall we have a game now? Or have you had enough?'

At this point, fortunately, he produced his cambeluk board, which saved me from further embarrassment.

'You must have misunderstood me,' I said. 'I haven't been playing cambeluk with the Priestess. I only talked to her over a cup of coffee.'

'Then come and learn how to play it at once.'

As Quant had told me once before, everyone in New Crete played cambeluk. It looked as simple as draughts, had as few rules, and a much smaller board; but it was deceptively complex and after the opening moves no two games were in the least alike. I played several rubbers with Quant, but never won a game, though I'm usually good at that sort of thing. One of my first acts on returning to our epoch was to visit a patent lawyer and have him register the rules; so I may yet die rich.

CHAPTER XXI

The Wild Women

THE Royal Playhouse was closely packed, and I was aware of a tense expectation in the audience, more overpowering than at any First Night I had ever attended. Nobody laughed or fidgeted, or came in late, or exchanged greetings with friends across the auditorium. Though there was no sign yet that the performance was about to begin, all sat silent and pallid, hands on knees, heads jutted a little forward, stirring only occasionally to finger a tight collar or scratch an itching ear. They looked like so many prisoners in the dock at a mass-murder trial. White-robed priests walked solemnly up and down the gangways swinging censers that gave off aromatic fumes of rosemary and myrtle. The playhouse was domed, but otherwise built more or less on the model of a Greek theatre. It had no boxes or galleries and no orchestra pit, and seated about a thousand men and women on its tiers of curved wooden benches. Quant and I sat next to each other about half-way up.

'Have the King and Queen arrived yet?' I asked in a minute whisper out of the corner of my mouth. 'I don't see them anywhere.'

'Behind the curtain,' he whispered back. 'Hush!'

It had not occurred to me that this was to be a Royal performance in a literal sense, though Quant had given me a brief outline of the ballet as we returned to the enclosure late in the afternoon from a pleasant walk round the mere. 'It's about the succession to the Throne,' he had explained. 'As you know, the King's seven months' reign ends tonight, and he's due to die unless the Goddess grants him the favour of rebirth as his other self. Now, he can't be reborn as his own successor, so there must be an interregnum, however short, and during this a boy victim succeeds to his throne and marriage bed. In the first act you'll witness the Adoration of the Sphinx, the Dance of the Holy Perverts, the King's Last Day, his Warning and (if the Goddess is merciful) the Reprieve. The second act contains the Seduction of the Victim, Laughing Murder, the Food of the Dead, the King's Despoilment, and the Victim's Investiture. The third begins with his Warning, next he goes rapidly through the Transformations, and in the end the Wild Women tear him in pieces. Then there's the Epilogue: the King is reborn as his other self and reigns serenely for the rest of the year.'

'Who are these Wild Women?' I had asked. 'The nymphs of the months?'

'No, they're incarnations of the nine-fold Goddess: Three Maidens, Three Graces and Three Fates. They appear after the holy perverts—'

'But I was told that your perverts are always killed?'

'So they are, but they're reborn as hand-maids of Mari, and live without benefit of estate in a convent at the back of this playhouse. Other men mustn't come near them, or even see them, except during the ballet; in fact, they're so holy that it's death for any man to be touched by them. However, they have many friends among the women elders and make court dresses and embroideries for the Queen and her nymphs. The Goddess has a tender regard for perverts—not the un-natural perverts of your epoch who despised women and preferred boys, but natural ones, who love her so extrava-gantly that they want to be one with her, as women. She brings them on the stage as a terrifying demonstration of her power; it's known that men who fail to love her as she deserves are liable to die and be reborn as perverts. Bite your thumb when they appear, don't forget!'

I was prepared for a spectacle in which I had no immediate concern. 'I'm a loyal subject of George VI, by the Grace of God King of Great Britain and his Dominions Overseas, Defender of the Faith,' I reminded myself. 'That red-haired drunk with the lollipop gun is nothing to me.' But I had under-estimated the power of the ballet I was about to witness.

The light faded, and nine expressionless servants in royal livery marched in, each carrying a lighted candle which he fixed into one of the glass lamps that served as footlights. Then the curfew rang; Friday Eve had begun.

The Lord Chamberlain, a gaunt figure in crimson, appeared from behind the curtain. Lifting his hand in a propitiatory gesture, he bent forward and hissed sharply three times. The house froze into absolute immobility, and a broken, haunting melody on a single reed-pipe floated in from nowhere in particular—perhaps from the roof. The curtains parted soundlessly, and a sigh of awe went up from the audience, like a chance gust of wind on a stifling day.

The Adoration of the Sphinx

The Queen was standing motionless between the spread wings of a marble Sphinx that crouched, facing us, on a tall pedestal at the back of the stage. She was dressed in a copper-coloured short-sleeved bodice with green buttons, a heavily jewelled girdle, and a flounced skirt, striped in white, primrose and scarlet, with a broad hem of embroidered fruit and flowers. Her breasts were bare; her dark yellow hair fell in glossy ringlets; around her neck she wore a chain of tiny skulls, and on her head a towering crown of silver horns curving around a pale gold mirror. In her right hand she

held a five-pointed star. A spotted snake, about three feet
long, coiled round her left arm.

For some little time nothing happened, then came a soft
cooing, a beating of wings, and a flock of doves flew in,
fluttered around her head, and out again. A gilt screen that
extended right across the stage divided, and the halves slid
back slowly in opposite directions, revealing three groups of
worshippers facing the Queen. On the right seven boys in
blue tunics crouched on all fours; in the centre stood five
young men, naked from the waist up, with red kilts and ivory-
handled axes; on the left seven white-robed elders leaned on
their wands of office. They bowed before the Queen in
adoration, which she acknowledged with a gentle lifting of
the star high above her head; the diamonds with which it was
studded caught a ray of light and twinkled splendidly. She
raised and lowered the star three times, between pauses, then
moved her head to smile graciously at the boys, axe-men and
elders in turn. The screen slid back again, concealing them.

I had fallen under the spell of the ballet as deeply as any
New Cretan and ceased to notice the details of stage
machinery; my critical faculties deserted me, and my body
grew so rigid that I could not have turned my head to look
at Quant, even if I had wished.

The Dance of the Holy Perverts

The Queen's manner suddenly changed. With stealthy
wriggling motions she hid the star in her bodice, drew out an
evil-looking mask, half pink, half green, with a cruel, lop-
sided smile and blue-rimmed eye holes, and clapped it over her
face. At this the perverts, in a grotesque mixture of male and
female dress, entered to mad discordant music, tumbling and
prancing either pathetically alone, or obscenely in pairs. Im-
mediately every man in the audience, myself included, raised
his right thumb to his mouth and bit it; but the women
remained motionless. The Queen descended, vaulted lightly

over the screen and stepped among the perverts, encouraging them in their gambols, which grew wilder and wilder until it was agony to look at them. They tore off their upper garments and began slashing themselves with knives and flogging one another with knotted whips. Blood spurted from their plump bodies, and they danced in ever-increasing ecstasy, spinning round and round like humming-tops. The Queen stood swaying in the middle, her head tilted on her left shoulder, while the snake coiled restlessly round her arms and body. Just so, but for the snake, Erica had stood one evening in a café on Montparnasse, delightedly watching a bottle fight which she had herself provoked between two Bock-soused German painters.

A trumpet flourish rose sweetly above the din, which died away in a nasty whimper. The perverts slowed to a dead stop, grimaced and scuttled off. The Queen removed her mask, and set the snake wriggling after them. From the right advanced a pair of heralds in uniforms magnificent with gold embroidery, and repeated the flourish. The screen had parted to allow passage to the Queen and now, once more her gracious and beautiful self, she sat down on a marble throne at the base of the Sphinx.

The King's Last Day

The heralds sounded a third flourish and the King, my King, strutted in, sober and confident, in full regalia; six nymphs of the months walked ahead of him and six wood-men, dressed in oak-leaves, brought up the rear. He wore a coat of seven colours, buckskin breeches, a broad tasselled belt and high-heeled scarlet half-boots. A pair of antlers, each of seven tines, sprouted from his curly red hair.

The nymphs led him to the throne, where he abased himself before the Queen, submissively kissed her foot, then rose and took his place on her left. For a while they sat in state, motionless, until the Queen signed to the woodmen, who

danced forward making soft, jingly sounds with handbells.
One handed the King a bow, and each of the others a long
gold-headed, purple-heeled arrow; they lay down crouching
and panting like dogs at the foot of the throne. The King
stood up, drew the bow and, the Queen directing his aim,
shot one arrow towards each of the four points of the com-
pass, and the fifth straight up in the air: this expressed the
dominion he enjoyed through his marriage with her. The
Queen placed a double axe between his knees.

   The handbells jingled softly again, accompanied by a small
unseen drum and a dulcimer-like stringed instrument. The
King and Queen advanced, hand in hand, to perform a ceremonious pas-de-deux, the King marking the beat by rhythmic
stamping of his half-boots. The pace gradually quickened,
until the Queen was whirling wildly and the King, slowed
down by his stamping, was left far behind. He flung out his
hands in a helpless gesture, then dropped on one knee, and at
this the Queen divided into two: her gracious self, and her
masked wicked self. The music slowed down again, and the
two Queens danced in stately circles round the King, their
arms upraised. He remained awed and motionless, gazing at
them until the wicked Queen disappeared into the gracious
Queen.

The Warning

   The dulcimer twittered a slight, sleepy melody, and a couch
of sedge and grasses rose up. The Queen led the King to it,
removed his antlers, unbuckled his belt, and pillowed his
red head on her lap. The music died away and all grew dark,
except for the dim glow of the footlights.

   'Hoo-hoo-hoo!' A white owl sailed noiselessly in, sailed
back again and made a series of short, quick rushes, every
now and then brushing the couch with her wings. The King
was half asleep. The nymphs stole away, and the Queen
slowly and gently transferred his head from her lap to a grass

pillow; then tiptoed into the shadows and beckoned to nine dark crouching figures, in conical hats. They advanced in three groups of three, laggingly, almost imperceptibly, and the owl circled round them with doleful hoots, and flew off. A blue half-light spread over the scene, and the King awoke in terror at a burst of blood-curdling, wheezy music. The nine figures threw off their dark cloaks and danced menacingly in a wide ring round the couch. The first three were adolescent girls in tight greenish calf-length frocks; the second three were full-breasted women in copper-coloured bodices and short bright skirts; then came two elderly dames in long bedraggled mourning; and the last was a horrifying crone in shapeless rags who danced nimbly by herself, counter-clockwise, on the outer fringe. The music swelled more hideously even than before and a shudder went through the audience.

The Reprieve

The King sat bolt upright, resumed his antlers, buckled on his belt and, finding himself deserted by the Queen and nymphs, looked around in frantic terror. He tried to banish his visitants by grimaces and gesticulations, but this only added to their fury. Gradually they closed in, mouthing at him and cracking their fingers, and were almost at his throat when, in despair, he snatched a hunting horn from his belt and blew a loud rallying call. The blessed relief of that silver-tongued tantarara!

To skirling pipes and rolling drums in leaped the five axe-men, disguised in tall sugar-loaf head-dresses that covered their faces, with the eye-holes ringed in bright blue spirals and with round buttons painted like grinning mannikins' heads at the peaks. They wore garters jingling with small silver bells. Dancing a dactylic Highland Fling, and whirling their axes round their heads, they fell upon the Wild Women. The two dance movements intermingled, but bagpipes and drums finally prevailed, and the blue gloom changed to white light. The Wild Women retreated, and the axe-men marched reassuringly up and down, and round the couch, finishing in a well-dressed line at its foot.

This ended the first act, but there was no interval.

The Seduction of the Victim

The Queen stood, as at the beginning, between the wings of the Sphinx, and the single plaintive reed-pipe took up the thread of the story. The King had settled contentedly on the couch, guarded by three nymphs at the foot and three at the head; the axe-men, posted between the boys and elders as in the opening scene, worshipped the Queen. She received their devotions with gentle wavings of the star, then pointed commandingly to the right and all filed out slowly, elders first, then axe-men, lastly boys; but before they were well on their way, the light dimmed, the blue gloom returned and from the left the Wild Women came prowling in. The youngest trio made a sudden rush at the hindmost boy, who was taller and more robust than the others, and caught at his tunic. He struggled desperately to rejoin his disappearing companions, and made an appealing gesture to the Queen; but he saw to his terror that she had resumed her wicked mask, and the central trio skipped forward, barring his way. The six of them pirouetted round him to the seductive sound of flutes, and while the light changed from white to green, from green to gold and back again, each advanced in turn, curtsied before him and made him a present—an apple, a scallop-shell, a bell, a ball, a mirror, and a silver cup. These he accepted with delighted wonder, and no longer tried to escape.

Laughing Murder

The drums rolled majestically, and the Queen pointed to the vacant throne, promising the boy with stylized gestures that he was to be the King's successor and her lover. He shrank away, he protested, he pleaded, he wept, but to no

9*

avail: he was the chosen Victim, the King's surrogate, and finally he bowed in mute acceptance of his fate. The Queen descended and stood surrounded by the Wild Women, who went through an orgiastic dance called Laughing Murder—so horrible and obscene that I will not attempt to describe it. I tried to close my eyes, but the lids would not obey me, and I was forced to watch the dance to the end.

Food of the Dead

There followed a long eerie pause; low lugubrious bass voices chanted a spondaic dirge and women sobbed softly. Their voices sounded gradually nearer, but the expected funeral procession did not come into view. All that could be seen was a slight flurry on the couch where the King lay, as something black and furry detached itself from his corpse—a thing that seemed a cross between a monkey and a tadpole: his ghost. It flapped about despairingly under the strong red light shining on it from above, and I saw to my disgust that it was still connected to the King by a long red navel-string issuing from his throat. The frightful third trio swooped in and made a grab at the ghost. It fought like a pike in the gaff, but Clotho and Lachesis held him tight, while Atropos severed the navel-cord with a pair of shears. Then all raised an ear-splitting shriek of lamentation. I believe that every woman in the audience must have shrieked too, as one screams in a nightmare; the piercing ululation went through me like a knife. The ghost turned limp in their hands and while Atropos sat it on her bony lap, her bedraggled sisters fed it with the red foods of the dead—crayfish, mullet and cranberries and, forcing its mouth wide open, a trickle of blood from the severed head of a black pig. Then they cuffed it, beat it, and rushed it out of sight. It broke away and returned gibbering to the couch, where it made impossible attempts to re-enter the King's body, by burrowing first into the mouth, then into the navel, lastly into the groin; baffled and frustrated, it hopped about in an angry monkey dance, shaking its small furry fists.

The King's Despoilment

The red light still blazed, and presently the reluctant Victim entered, pushed forward by the three Graces. They urged him to strip the dead King of his regalia; but he was still modest and abashed, and even when he screwed up his courage the gibbering menaces of the ghost scared him away at every attempt. At last he gripped the ghost by both wrists and flung it off the couch, unbuckled the King's belt, pulled off the boots, removed the antlers, and triumphantly displayed his booty. Then, at leisure, he despoiled the corpse of its coat and breeches and tried them on, well pleased with their fit. A hoarse groan echoed through the house, and the couch, on which the ghost had once more climbed, sank slowly out of sight.

The Victim's Investiture

The light whitened and strengthened. The axe-men marched in, no longer disguised, to wish the Victim joy and pay him homage with a noisy hornpipe, brandishing their axes above their heads, then laying them like the spokes of a wheel at his feet and leaping vigorously over them. Next his six boy companions made much of him, crowning him with garlands and carried him around on their shoulders. Then the elders, tapping the ground with their wands, danced a stiff little jig of allegiance. But wild, discordant music announced the arrival of the perverts—our thumbs jerked automatically to our mouths—and in they rushed, slobbering over the Victim, embracing and petting him. He shrank from their deathly touch with loathing, striking and kicking them, but they kept glancing at the Queen, who had entered quietly, in her wicked mask, and now stood swaying behind the Victim, slyly encouraging them and shaken by silent laughter.

At last the axe-men intervened: they formed up in line, retrieved their axes from the ground and drove off the perverts.

In came the heralds again, blowing their trumpets, and the Victim was solemnly invested as King to majestic music. Having prostrated himself before the Queen, now seated graciously on her throne, he slowly mounted the three steps, pausing on each, while the music grew louder and more majestic still. It was a coronation anthem in which all the players joined, but I could not distinguish the words; they did not sound New Cretan. The exultant Victim sat down on the throne, and the Maidens advanced to buckle his belt, draw on his boots and crown him with the antlers. The anthem came to an end, handbells rang and the woodmen entered to hand him his bow and five arrows. These he discharged as his predecessor had done, and the Queen set the double axe between his knees.

Then woodmen, axe-men, boys, elders, Maidens and Graces joined in a complicated dance to the sound of a great variety of instruments; making spirals, wedges, stars, figures of eight and other patterns of religious significance. Afterwards the Queen and the New King descended from their throne and performed a nuptial dance, cold and ceremonious at first, but gradually quickening to a passionate climax, the light growing more feeble all the time. This ended the second act.

The Victim's Warning

Another long, breathless pause, and when the lights went up again the Victim reclined luxuriously on the royal couch in full regalia, the Queen at his side. They were idly watching the boys turning cartwheels to the brisk accompaniment of pipes, and then the elders fighting a sham-battle with wands for quarter-staffs. The Victim clapped his hands in childish delight. But after this short interlude the light grew blue once more and a warning 'Hoo-hoo-hoo!' rang out, followed by bursts of discordant music and a wild stampede of perverts. The light flickered and dimmed. Scattering the shrieking perverts in all directions, in flew the owl. She blundered aimlessly about with dismal hoots; the Queen resumed her wicked mask. The dazed Victim turned to her for reassurance, but recoiled in horror as he caught her beckoning the Wild Women from the shadows. They prowled in slowly, and the Queen rose from the couch, abandoning the Victim to his fate. At once they began to bewitch him, as they had bewitched his predecessor. In terror he blew his horn for the axe-men and they entered with nodding head-dresses and jingling garters. The bagpipes skirled again, warring with the strident witch music; but this time the Wild Women were not to be baulked of their prey. They disarmed the axe-men with ease and drove them off in disorder.

The Wild Women edged closer in a shrieking, yelling dance. The couch swayed and began to sink, but the agonized Victim leaped off. Again they mercilessly hemmed him in and one of the Maidens darted forward and snatched off his belt, then another dragged off his coat, until he was stripped of everything but a pair of plaited garters and a shining star that covered his genitals. He stood panting and disconsolate.

The Transformations

The discordant witch music ceased abruptly and the Wild Women stood frozen, feet spread apart, arms akimbo, while an unearthly greenish-yellow light blazed from above. The Queen was standing between the Sphinx's wings, quite naked except for her moon-mirror crown. The stripped Victim sank low in adoration before her and, as I watched, my last defences crumbled: I too adored her unreservedly as the visible incarnation of the Goddess who is our universal Mother, Bride and Layer-out. A weird hallucination overcame me: I saw two giant replicas of myself standing on either side of the stage, like heraldic supporters to a coat of arms. One was light-skinned and red-haired like myself, the other black-haired and dark. They gazed at each other with intense hatred, each grasping a dagger in his belt. 'I am my worst enemy,' I thought schizophrenically. 'I've always known that. But why? Because he and I are both in love with the same different woman?' My heart thumped against my ribs: the Queen was going through a series of bodily changes, becoming in turn all the women whom I had ever loved, each caught at the moment of her greatest beauty, but all calm and smiling. The last to appear was Sapphire, as she had looked when she had said goodbye to me at the door of the quince-hut. 'I love only her now,' I thought, 'and I've no rival but my dark self.'

Heartened by the Queen's gracious smile, the Victim danced the ballet of the Thirteen Months, the light and the music changing with each transformation. He danced the Kid, the Oarsman, the Wind, the Fire, the Hawk, the Flower-gatherer, the Thunderstorm. My private hallucination persisted vividly and at the crisis of the seventh transformation, when a blinding flash of lightning had made me jump, the ghostly twins unsheathed their daggers, dived sideways simultaneously and seemed to merge with the Victim's body. At once he split into two: his pale Star-self was joined by a dark Serpent-self with a jewelled snake coiled at his groin. Star and Serpent squared up to each other, fighting with daggers amid flashes of lightning, crashes of thunder and a roar of rain, until the Star fell stabbed; I felt the dagger pierce my throat and my life-blood seemed to gush away.

The storm abated and the Serpent triumphantly resumed the ballet. He danced the Spear, the Salmon, the Vine-harvest, the Boar, the Breaker, the Drowning Man; and then stood still, trembling and expectant. Up leaped the Star again, avenging his own murder on the Serpent—and on me.

I died a second time, the dagger plunged in my heart. All the lights went out.

The Victim's Death and Pursuit

The Wild Women were dancing round the Victim, clockwise and then counter-clockwise, but gradually the counter movement grew longer, until at last they whirled round and round, widdershins, without a check and he toppled first to his knees, then to his knees and hands, and finally lay crouched in a dying huddle. Presently his ghost broke from the ring in the guise of a fish, but Atropos went after it, like a crane, and pursued it here and there until it returned to the whirling circle and merged with the Victim again. It broke out a second time, buzzing like a blue fly, but Atropos pursued it, like a swallow, and fetched it back again. It broke out a third time as a hare, and she pursued it like a greyhound. Lastly it broke out as a fawn and Atropos, seizing a three-pronged spear, led the whole troop of Wild Women in pursuit. All was again plunged into darkness, and above the laughing shrieks of his pursuers rose the Victim's long, melancholy death wail. I felt myself sinking, plunging down faster and faster into nothingness, and Erica's scornful voice rang in my ears: 'It's not even enough to die twice for the same woman: a poet must die three times!'

The Epilogue—The King's Rebirth

My spirit slowly floated back, and I found myself in the Playhouse again. The *Epilogue* had begun. Lugubrious bass voices were chanting a funereal dirge, while women sobbed softly, but I only heard the last few bars. Presently a fiddle played a little whimpering tune with frequent breaks, and the couch rose again with the King's furry ghost asleep on it. It awoke, rubbed its eyes and bounded aimlessly about until, as the light strengthened, it saw the Queen in a white cloak seated on a birth-stool, with six nymphs of the months grouped attentively around her. It scurried under her skirts, and disappeared.

The Queen underwent her rhythmic birthpangs to the anguished music of fiddles and pipes. At last she joyfully hauled out the ghost from under her skirts as a new-born baby, and put him to her breast. The nymphs sang a shrill pæan of welcome to the new-born King, and three of them cradled him in a winnowing fan, and carried him away to lullaby music.

The light grew stronger, the axe-men reappeared and leaped ecstatically round the cradle beside which the three nymphs were bent; and so well they leaped that at last the old King emerged, smiling and vigorous, to be dressed by the nymphs in his coloured coat and buckskin breeches. But though his features were unchanged, he was now dark and black-haired: his other self, his twin. The heralds trumpeted with all their might, and the nymphs led him to his seat at the Queen's side. Re-invested in his regalia, he sent the five arrows flying in token of his dominion, and the curtain fell on axe-men, woodmen, boys, elders and nymphs dancing a saraband of celebration.

The nine expressionless servants filed in and extinguished the footlights. The Lord Chamberlain reappeared and indicated with a wave of his hand that the silence was at an end.

I stretched, sneezed, and came out of my trance, to find Quant bending anxiously over me, his fingers on my pulse.

'Are you all right?' he asked. 'I thought you'd gone.'

'It's nothing, nothing at all,' I gabbled. Then I recovered my self-possession. 'But oh, Quant, how terrifyingly the Victim danced! It's hard to believe that it was only a mock death.'

'It wasn't,' said Quant. 'The Wild Women are still feasting on his flesh.'

CHAPTER XXII

The Whirlwind

Outside the Playhouse, Quant said goodbye. 'You'll not be returning to Horned Lamb?' he asked.

'No, I promised Nervo that I wouldn't. I've been told that I'm not at all popular there.'

'Then what are you going to do?'

'I'm going to Broad Thumb's house, to see whether Sapphire—whether Stormbird's grown up yet.'

'And then?'

'This is Friday, isn't it?'

He sighed. 'Yes, it is Friday; but if you're thinking of a Friday union, you'll find the going very hard.'

'The Goddess is merciful,' I suggested.

'When it pleases her. Goodbye, old fellow, and good luck! Since you're taking that road, it's unlikely that we'll meet again. And I had so much to ask you, and to show you!'

We embraced in French style, and he went off disconsolately. I watched him go, feeling pretty miserable myself. Yet I had not seen quite the last of him. He came back shyly, to ask: 'Edward, I wonder whether you'll do me a favour?'

'Why, Quant, of course—anything in my power.'

'That poem of mine, about the light shining through the chink: do you happen to remember it?'

'Yes, word for word. I've a good verbal memory for poems that mean something to me.'

'Then I'm very happy, because this is what I was going to

ask you: when you return to your age—as I suppose you must, sooner or later—will you publish it somewhere under your name? You see, I feel a little uncertain about the propriety of what I've done. If I could think that it's been published in the Late Christian epoch, my conscience would be clear.'

'I'll be only too pleased—and, if I'm lucky, I may get a couple of guineas out of it, to buy my wife a new cigarette lighter. Even Dobeis has his uses at times.'

'My affectionate regards to your wife,' he said, and sauntered off, grinning like a schoolboy. This time he did not return, and after taking my bearings I forced my way through a dense crowd towards the Old Town.

As I walked, I was thinking how utterly different a picture of New Crete I should have carried back with me if I had been returned to my age on the night of my evocation. My visit to the Nonsense House had been unsettling enough; but, after all, I argued, it was only right that people should be freed from the bonds of custom at some stage in their lives, and better late than early. In my time it had been the young people who kicked over the traces and made lasting trouble for themselves, and the old people who were expected to behave with unnatural devoutness at a time when it mattered little how they behaved so long as they kept their follies decently to themselves. What stuck in my throat, though, was the public display of ritual murder and cannibalism I had just witnessed. To think that such beautiful, peaceful, sensitive, good-humoured people were brought up to regard that horrifying performance as normal and right! It shocked me to realize that the Goddess to whom I had just made a loving, voluntary submission was still, as in pre-historic times, the Old Sow who ate her farrow. . . .

I paused for a moment at the entrance to a courtyard, and tried to think things out. A girl of about fifteen in a dark cloak came up to me. 'You're thinking hard and bitterly,' she said. 'I felt it as I passed.'

'Yes,' I answered. 'I was thinking about the Victim and the Wild Women.'

Her green eyes and white teeth glinted in the light of a street lamp. 'I was one of them myself,' she said. 'What's troubling you?'

'I'm from the past,' I said. 'You may have heard of me. At the Playhouse I made my peace with the Goddess —I'd never before surrendered my heart to any deity—but now I know that the Victim was murdered and eaten, I feel a shuddering revulsion; I want to recant. In my epoch we did many disgusting things, but we did draw the line at cannibalism.'

'Would you have us eat mock-sacrifices of bread and wine?'

'Well, why not?'

'Because the midsummer sacrifice must offer itself voluntarily, and no loaf of bread and no bottle of wine can do that. Tonight the people take bread and wine in ritual imitation of our feast; but if we had not celebrated it in fact, there'd be no virtue in the imitation. The Victim met his fate of his own free will; he was my dear brother. If no victim died on behalf of the people, the fields would grow barren.'

'How am I to believe that?'

'Before we tore him in pieces, we cut his throat and caught his life blood in a bladder. This will be mixed with water from the royal cistern, and a jar of it carried to every town and village in the kingdom, for sprinkling on the fields before the autumn sowing, to sanctify them. My brother died for his love of the Goddess and of us all, and when the labourers weep for him at the sprinkling rite, their tears will draw down the winter rains from the Moon, the source of all life-giving waters. And they'll work strenuously for the remainder of the double year, grateful for the love he showed them.'

'I see: "It is expedient that a man should die for the people." But why was it necessary to eat his flesh?'

'As a mark of reverence; ordinary corpses are buried in the

earth. But his is the greatest prize that a man can win: to be made one with the living flesh of the nine-fold Mother.'

'And the King? When will he die?'

'The King dies when his term ends. That year's Victim will be spared, and reign not merely for an hour; and the Old King will dance the Transformations himself, and sanctify the fields with his own blood. It's because of the awful holiness of this sacrifice that New Cretan custom forbids the violent taking of life on any other occasion, even in war. If the sacrifice were annulled, murder would be committed on the least excuse, and where should we be then?'

I thought of the strewn corpses on Monte Cassino, where I had been almost the only unwounded survivor of my company; and of the flying-bomb raid on London, when I had held a sack open for an air-raid warden to shovel the bloody fragments of a child into it; and finally of Paschendaele where, in the late summer of 1917, my elder brother had been killed in the bloodiest, foulest and most useless battle in history—as a boy I had visited his grave soon after that war ended, and the terror of the ghastly, waterlogged countryside with its enormous over-lapping shell-craters had haunted me for years. 'The Goddess knows best,' I said to the girl eventually, and she nodded in grave assent.

'You're looking for Stormbird,' she announced.

'I am; how did you know?'

'I know everything, as I told you in the alder-grove. You'll find her by the mere, consulting my fish.' She skipped off, before I had time to prostrate myself. But I was taking no chances: I performed my solemn puja as if she were still visible, in compliment to her omnipresence.

As I turned into the street again, I collided with the Interpreter.

'Ah, what a fortunate coincidence in the extreme,' he said, 'viz: I feared that you would prove to be the needle in the haystack. I have run here post-haste in search of you.'

'More trouble?' I asked. 'Anything happened to Starfish?'

'Alas, you have divined my news. Starfish is no more. This afternoon the servants found him lifeless beside the waterfall on Poets' Hill, not far from our house.'

'I'm grieved, but not surprised. Did he kill himself?'

'Oh, Sir, what a foolish suggestion! A New Cretan to take his own life!'

'Well, how did he die?'

'Of a broken heart, and with no desire for rebirth. He left a clay-board of verses behind him. I'm no judge of poetry; I'm a recorder, but a specialist in the English language. To me they read ill, and far-fetched. I have them in my head. Listen!'

Waving his fingers to mark the rhythm, he recited:

> 'O runnels of this holy hill
>   Beneath the stars that shine
> Attentive to your Muse's will,
>   Who sister is to mine,
>
> And on the heath-flower-scented air
>   Fantastically raise
> Your praises of a cold white glare
>   That none but madmen praise;
>
> With burning throat I bow to taste
>   Peace at your waterfall,
> Where my proud Muse must come in haste,
>   If she would come at all.'

He grimaced, and said: 'Are these not incoherences and quite bad? Thus, there you are: a pretty kettle of fish. And worse: as I entered the town, intending to implore the Witch Sally to come back, I met my colleague Quant, making his exit with the news that the Witch is no more, either! Now there remains only yourself to step into the breach, and by keeping guard at the Magic House stave off calamity. But my colleague Quant assures me. . . .'

'Quant's right again,' I said testily, 'i.e., e.g., *nem. con.*, and *verb. sap.*, I'm not going back to Horned Lamb on any condition.'

'But, Sir, it's the custom . . . .' the Interpreter quavered virtuously.

'Tell that to someone else.'

'Assuredly I will, Sir!' He darted off with a nasty look, and I went on to Broad Thumb's house.

Quite often, when I am half-asleep, I find myself reading a book. It is always in short dialogue, very interesting, very witty, and the author and his characters continue to surprise each other all down one page and halfway down the next. When I wake up, I remember tempting snatches of it, such as:

. . . . and then, horror! in marched Mrs. Blackstone with the little corpse held out accusingly between the pincers of the kitchen fire-tongs.

'So he shanghaied her,' said someone in knowing tones.

'Shanghaied whom? Not Mrs. B.? Ha, ha! No, not Mrs. B.! Nobody has ever shanghaied Mrs. B.!'

Now I felt as though I were reading that book again, but with the critical reservation that when I came out of my dream it probably wouldn't make sense—not even Starfish's poem which (though my translation is faintly Housmanesque) sounded magnificent in the original, nor the Goddess Nimuë's defence of ritual murder.

I was soon at Broad Thumb's house, and Broad Thumb was in. She greeted me as an old friend, and gave me the run of her larder. I was hungry, and ate a great deal of bread and cheese and nearly a whole gooseberry-pie. When I explained to her that I had to restore my nervous energy after visits to the bagnio and the Playhouse, she fried me a couple of eggs as well.

'How's Stormbird?' I asked finally, wiping my mouth.

'Oh, quite grown up. You'd hardly recognize her. Some cousins of my husband's from Rabnon have taken her out to see the fun; one of them's the goal-keeper who's the talk of every barber-shop in the whole kingdom—the berserk fighter, Open-please. He greatly admires Stormbird, and I think she's flattered. Not that I want anything to come of it, because I'm hoping that she'll prove monogamous like ourselves—I should hate to lose her now, she's such an affectionate girl—and settle down here in the Old City with a good husband. I wish now that I'd gone with them to keep her out of mischief, but I wanted to get on with my spinning. She's still so young, initiated only this afternoon; she hasn't even got her gold scarf-pin yet.'

'Would you like me to keep an eye on her for you?'

'I would indeed; besides, it's your privilege, since you named her. Do whatever you think best for the dear child. She'll probably be down at the mere, feeding the fish.'

'Well, goodbye, Broad Thumb.'

'Goodbye, poet. Leave a blessing on this house.'

'May this be the last roof of Dunrena to fly off when the wind blows!'

A tremendous noise of singing and shouting floated down the night breeze: it was as if the fourth and fourteenth of July had accidentally coincided, but I found the mere-side almost deserted. I recognized Open-please at once by his height and his red and white Rabnon costume. He was standing by a honeysuckle arbour—how strong honeysuckle smells at night!—and bragging about his feats to the three admiring relatives. Modesty was not a New Cretan vice, and the account was evidently meant to impress Sapphire. She wore peasant's dress, with a full, river-grey skirt and a close-fitting blue jacket with gold buttons at the cuffs, and was crumbling bread for the fish. I saw with relief that she seemed already bored with Open-please's eloquence.

I went up and greeted them. 'I'm Venn-Thomas, a poet from the past,' I said, 'and Stormbird's mother has asked me to keep an eye on her tonight; she's young and inexperienced and may easily offend against custom. That's my commission, and also my privilege because it was I who named her.'

Everyone looked uncomfortable; Open-please seemed positively angry.

'Would you break up our party?' he protested.

'Mari forbid!'

'But you're not one of us. Smokes don't mix. How can we celebrate with you about?'

I frowned at him. 'At any rate not by boasting of your feats, when the credit's due to the Goddess who, for reasons best known to herself, inspired you to berserk fury. So don't try to crow, Chicken Cluck, or your Mother might peck you; and her beak's as sharp as a thorn.'

'What do you know of custom, or of the Goddess, you barbarian from the past? It's common talk in the barber-shop at Rabnon that you caused the death of our magician Claud, that you spent a night alone in the Nonsense House, and that you brought a brutch in your hair to do us harm!'

'Stormbird,' I said, turning away from him with a gesture of impatience, 'your mother has given you into my charge. If you've finished feeding the fish, come with me and leave this man to ask Ana's pardon for his intemperate words.'

Open-please scowled. 'Stormbird,' he said, 'you must choose between this monster and myself.'

'Stormbird,' I said, 'you must choose between your mother's orders and this man's arrogance.'

'Have you brought anything to show that she gave you those orders?' she asked cautiously.

Open-please and his three cousins at once took up the point. 'Yes, where's your token?' they shouted in unison. 'You're a barbarian, and all barbarians used to tell nothing but lies and practise nothing but cruelties.'

If I had been back in my own year of grace, I'd have run at the bastard and pitched him to the fishes, but I couldn't do that here. There was no need, either; I realized that though he had a good hand to play, I held the joker. 'If the Goddess felt no confidence in me,' I said haughtily, 'do you think she would have caused me to be evoked from the past? You talk like a three-year-old. She is immortal; there was never a time when she was not omnipotent. I am her poet, and by insulting me, her guest, you also insult her. Now join hands in a ring around me: you, Open-please, and you three there. In Mari's Name, obey!' They obeyed, though with bad grace. If one used the right formula, the commons could be hypnotized into doing any ridiculous thing.

I spread out my hand and piously intoned: 'Divine Mari, conjoined in trinity with the holy Child Nimuë, and the holy Mother Ana; omnipotent guardian of sky and earth and sea, mistress of the Five Estates, patroness also of moon-men, half-men and elders; Victory is in your divine Name. You are the sole strength of your magicians: for without you nothing can be ordered, conjured or contrived. Goddess, I adore you as divine, I invoke your Name. Lovingly grant the plea that I make to your godhead: that your child Stormbird shall be free to come with me, alone, to eat from my plate, to drink from my cup, and that these four fools who doubt your power, shall remain here, hand in hand, unable to break this circle until the first rays of the sun gild the white towers of your city of Dunrena!'

I ducked out of the ring. 'Stormbird!' I called.

She ran to me, smiling, and we walked off, leaving her companions under the honeysuckle as if glued together, and looking as stupid as hens with their beaks on a chalk line.

'Wait a moment, my child, and let me look at you!'

It was extraordinary how different she was from Sapphire, though her features were unchanged: no heavy weight of learning on her mind, no pensive, considered gestures, her eyes bright with humour. Beautiful as ever, and not dull by any means—the breadth of her forehead showed that—but completely artless. As I looked at her, my feelings settled: the factitious passion disappeared, and a deep, wistful love remained, the love that I had felt for her at first sight; I recognized it now as the love that a father feels for his only daughter. I had always tried hard to conceal my sentimentality: in fact, I had buried it under so many cartloads of stony cynicism to keep it from sprouting, that I rarely remembered its existence. Not even Antonia realized how passionately I always longed for a daughter. We had three sons, and that was fine, of course, and I would not have been without a single one of them, but at each birth I had prayed that it would be a girl. The arrival of our third son almost estranged us, because she said happily: 'Three sons; I do feel proud! Now we can stop, can't we, Ned?' At last I knew what had drawn me so strongly to Sapphire: she looked like Antonia, but also like the faded photographs of my mother as a girl—she was, in fact, exactly what a daughter of mine might have been.

I lifted Stormbird off her feet and kissed her gently. She laughed for pleasure. 'Why did you do that?' she asked. 'But I liked it,' she added. 'It makes me feel so safe.'

'Where do we go from here?'

'Anywhere.'

'Did you see any fish?'

'I should think I did. When I scattered my bread, they all bobbed up, even the big white grandmother—for the first time for months and months, my cousins told me; they thought she was dead—and they opened their mouths like this, all round, as though they were saying O, O, O! It's wonderfully lucky; and today's my birthday!'

'Let's go towards the noise, shall we?'

'I don't like noise, but you'll look after me, won't you?'

She slipped her arm into mine, and we went off over the

lip of the crater and through the Palace grounds, but when we reached the big spiral of tents, we did not venture into the roaring bedlam there, but stood under a tree near a bed of hollyhocks. Everyone carried an oak-branch and was three parts drunk with the red wine from the kegs that had been broached outside every tent, and I had never seen such unrestrained horse-play, even at the Bar-XL Ranch in Arizona on Christmas Eve, where the girls at least kept their heads and struggled nobly to preserve the decencies of the festival.

For a little while we stood watching, amused and incredulous, until Stormbird pulled at my sleeve, and cried: 'Quick, let's run away; something's going to happen, something new and terrible!'

'No, my sweet,' I said. 'Honourable people never do that.'

'Let's walk then. Only let's start at once.' I caught the terror that was beginning to shake her.

'On an occasion like this, one place is as good as another,' I said. 'We're staying here.'

But I knew that her instinct was right. Soon after she had spoken, a mass of merrymakers crowded together on the fringe of the tents, like bees when they swarm. By the look of them, they were all commoners or captains, and around them darted and sang an excited cloud of recorders and servants; but the magicians had withdrawn and were trooping off to a shrine on a knoll behind the royal stables. Presently the swarm moved unsteadily towards us.

'There he is!' yelled the Interpreter in New Cretan. 'There stands the barbarian, making magic under that tree!'

'After him, lads and lasses!' shouted Nervo. 'He's poisoned our land. Fall on him, crush the life out of him but, for the love of Ana, don't spill his blood!'

I picked up an oak-branch which someone had discarded. Slowly and deliberately, so as not to reveal my alarm, I scratched a wide circle in the soft turf around Stormbird and myself. Drawing her closer, I shouted at the top of my voice: 'Enter this circle at your peril! A brutch will fly into your ear-holes and eat your brains!'

'What does he say? What does the barbarian say? We can't understand him!' they buzzed angrily.

I held up my hand. 'In Ana's Name,' I ordered, 'be silent while I prophesy!'

They kept their distance and the shouting gradually ceased. I hissed sharply three times, as I had seen the Lord Chamberlain do, and they became deathly still.

'Cretans of the Five Estates!' I cried. 'I am a barbarian, a poet from the past, but I did not break into your fertile country like a negro-mandril from the Bad Lands. I was evoked by the magicians of Horned Lamb at the order of the Blessed Goddess herself; and I am now about to perform the task she has entrusted to me.'

I felt my chest swell with a divine afflatus, and my voice rang unnaturally loud, no longer my own. I spoke in the purest New Cretan—some words of which I did not understand myself.

'I have a message to impart to you; listen well! The Goddess is omnipotent, the Goddess is all-wise, the Goddess is utterly good; yet there are times when she wears her mask of evil and deception. Too long, New Cretans, has she beamed on you with her gracious and naked face; custom and prosperity have blinded you to its beauty. In my barbarian epoch, a time of great darkness, she wore a perpetual mask of cruelty towards the countless renegades from her service, and lifted it, seldom and secretly, only for madmen, poets and lovers.

'We knew her for wise, we knew her for good, we turned to her in our despair of the times with a deeper and livelier love than you, fortunate children of the light, can ever know, for all your daily prayers to her and your easy obedience to the divine order that she has restored from chaos. Yet her mercies are infinite, and she is now resolved no longer to withhold from you the knowledge that we enjoyed because of the welter of evil through which we swam. She summoned me from the past, a seed of trouble, to endow you with a harvest of trouble, since true love and wisdom spring only from calamity; and the first fruits of her sowing are the disasters that have emptied the Magic House at Horned Lamb. And this is the sign prophesied for her whirlwind, and its vortex will be the circle in which this storm-child and I now stand. You will be caught in that baleful gust, you will gasp and sicken, and carry the infection to every town and village in this kingdom; migrant birds and insects will carry it farther, to all the kingdoms of New Crete; and the symptoms of the infection will be an itching palm, narrowed eyes and a forked tongue.

'Blow, North wind, blow! Blow away security; lift the ancient roofs from their beams; tear the rotten boughs from the alders, oaks and quinces; break down the gates of the Moon House and set the madmen free; send the King flying into the mere; lay the godlings prostrate on their greens! Look! The Goddess Mari claps the baleful mask over her face, and her holy perverts prance in ecstasy. Blow, North wind, blow, at Mother Carey's will!'

My voice had risen to a bull-like bellow, and at the sound of Mother Carey's name, they all fell flat on their faces. There was a slight stir in the grass on the fringe of the circle, and a yellow wind sprang up and began racing round us with in-creased violence in a widening spiral.

'I must go now,' I said. 'My task is done.'

'Don't leave me,' cried Stormbird, 'don't turn me out into the wind! Where are you going?'

'Back to my past.'

'Then take me with you. You named me, and I'm in your charge.'

The wind was raging monstrously now; it blotted out the

moonlit landscape in a sulphurous swirl. I heard the crash of rotten boughs in the parkland, and the wrenching-off of roofs in the Old City. A frantic figure in white and purple hurtled through the air over my head towards the mere: the King! Yet, strangely, not a single tent was torn from its guy-ropes and the sacred hollyhocks hardly stirred, though the grinding roar of the gale seemed to tear the sky apart.

I grasped the locket in my hand, and when I turned to Stormbird, I knew I could not and must not leave her behind. 'Cling to my hair,' I ordered, 'cling tight with both your hands and hold on through thick and thin!' She gripped my hair where it curls above my ears, and said: 'Go, I'm ready.'

Then I spoke, stretching my hands in supplication: 'Ana, Mother, take me home! Return me to my own door-step!'

The roaring died in the distance, I lost consciousness, and the next thing I knew was that the locket in my hand had somehow got fixed to something else and I could not put it back into my pocket. I turned it round, and found that it was not a locket at all, but a door-knob; and that I had no pockets.

I was standing completely naked on my own door-step, shivering in the night wind. As I opened the door, I heard the motor-cycle—the young doctor's motor-cycle—still rounding the bend near the station. After listening for a moment, I went softly up the stairs in the moonlight, and into my dressing-room. I found a pair of clean pyjamas, put them on, and was on the point of going into the bedroom when, with a start, I remembered something. Very carefully I passed a comb through my hair and laid it back on the dressing-table from which I had taken it.

'Wait here, Stormbird,' I whispered, 'only a little while.'

Antonia stirred sleepily as I got into bed beside her. 'How cold you are, my sweet! Where have you been? Bathroom?'

'A place called New Crete,' I said.

'Please forward to present address,' she muttered vaguely, then, raising herself on one elbow: 'I say, Ned.'

'Tonia?'

'If you were a real friend, you'd buy me a new ivory brush. I've never felt quite a lady since that Good Friday bomb carried mine to Hell.'

'I am a real friend, and I'll buy you your brush, even if it costs the earth.'

'Then kiss me, Ned!' she said, sinking back on her pillow.

Three faint knocks sounded on the door.

'What on earth's that? It sounded like knocking.'

'Your cue,' I told her. 'You say: "Welcome, Stormbird!"'

'Why?'

'Because I'm going to give you that ivory brush.'

'Welcome, Stormbird,' she repeated obediently, hugging me close.

'Welcome, dear child,' I added in a whisper.

THE END